INTO THE UNREAL

CARLY STEVENS

For Jamie

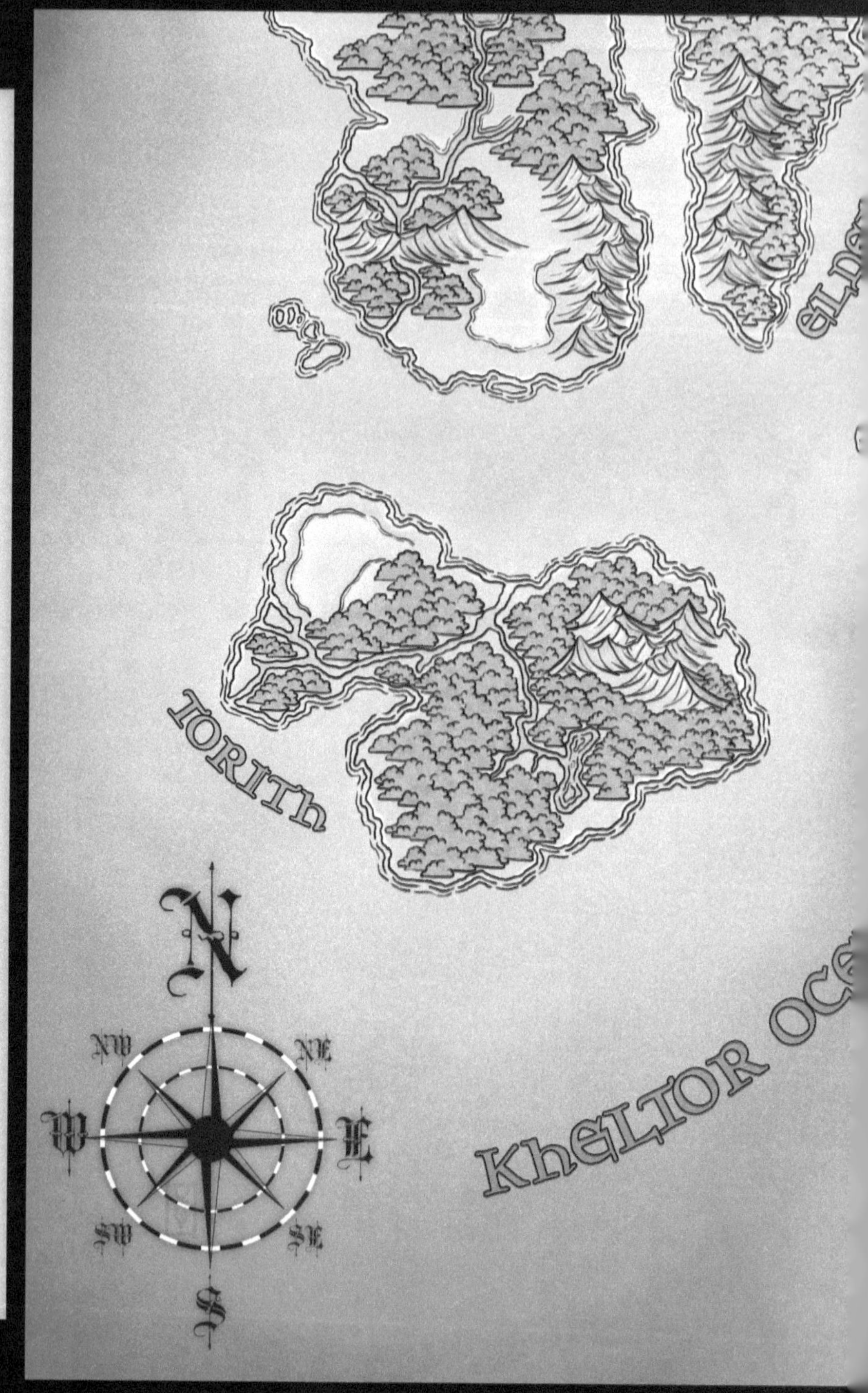
ELD
NORITH
N
NW
NE
W
E
SW
SE
S
KHELTOR OCE

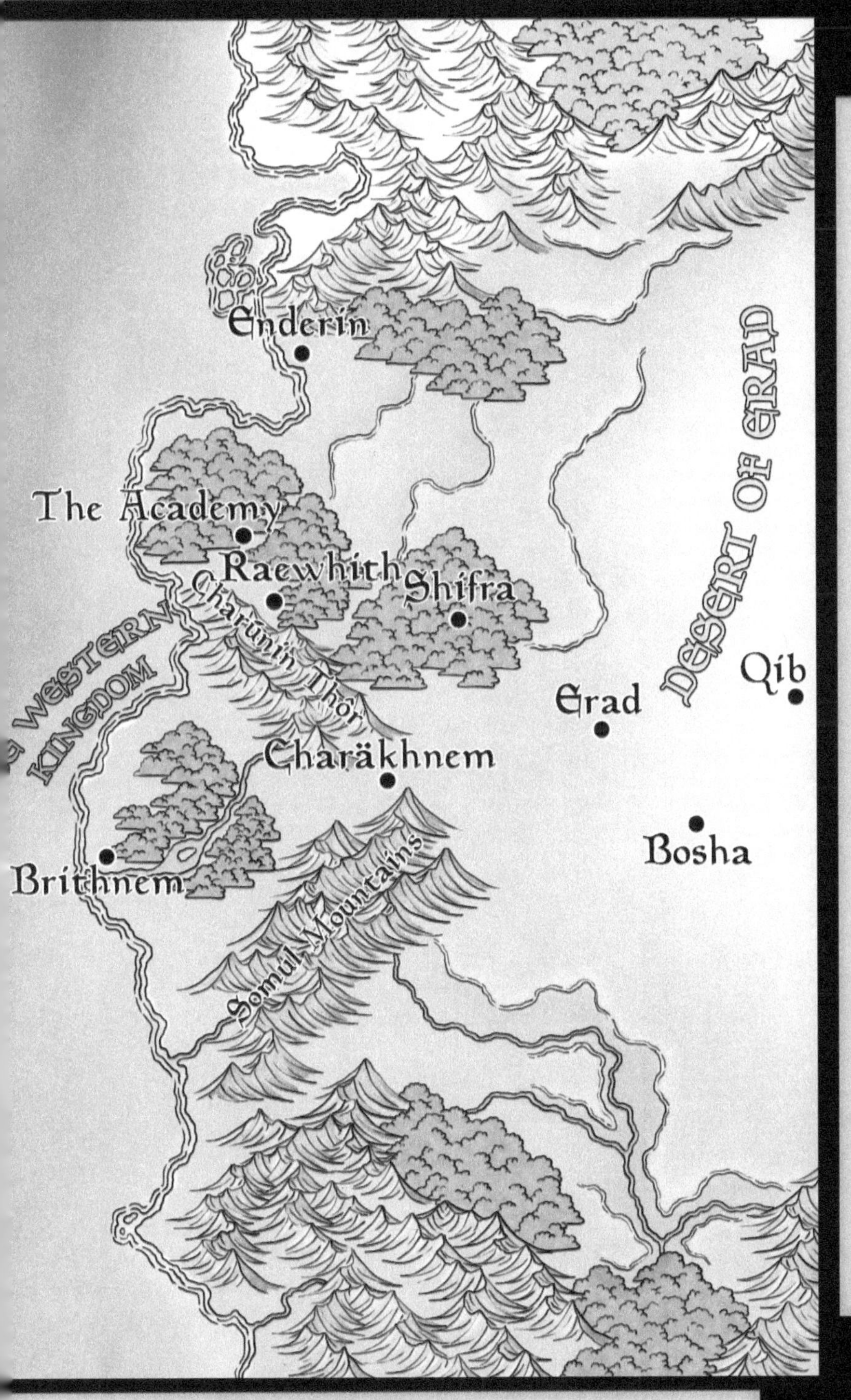

Enderin
The Academy
Raewhith
Charunin Thor
Shifra
a WESTERN KINGDOM
Charäkhnem
Erad
Qib
Bosha
Brithnem
Somul Mountains
DESERT OF ERAD

1

———

FIRIAN

To Yanon and Lithia Kess,

I am the new Head of the Tanyuin Academy. Come with the bearer of this letter.

Firian Kess

THAT WAS ALL the message needed to say. Firian set down the pen, took a deep breath, and looked down at the curve of the letters. When Sias Jairon's invitation arrived in his parents' hands years ago, each lilt of the strong letters had spoken of promise, magic.

Did the last Head's message look so short?

Firian sat back in his chair, running his thumb against the armrests. The Tanyuin Head's office in the Academy was small and stark, but powerful. The blank stone walls, gray like every other room in the Academy, suited him. Scarcity, simplicity, cold —these all made Firian feel more alive. They called attention back to the hot blood coursing through his veins, his own strength, his own stamina. The superiority of the Unreal.

The Unreal. Its colors put reality to shame. And the possibilities... He was a god in that imaginary space. And now he was in charge of its best warriors, those who could take out generals and tacticians through mind warfare, spread fear through dreams, communicate with the farthest reaches of the world in an instant.

His eyes strayed over the page one more time. Stamped red at the top of the paper, the Tanyuin seal confirmed who he was. It left no room to doubt the position he now held, one of the greatest and most feared in the world.

This note would prove his father wrong. Firian had amounted to something.

Brett should come too. The realization flooded his mind like the forgotten answer to a question. His sister, at least, would be proud of him.

Recent memories crowded in and his stomach clenched uncomfortably. *Will she be proud of me?*

The last Head had steered the Academy into darkness, into war and confusion, clinging to fearful traditions, using its warriors like they were property. He had deserved to die.

Firian's heart thumped as the image of the man's face returned. The wide eyes, the ashy skin, the struggling legs kicking for breath, the one word uttered in disbelief— "Firian?" The memory moved as he blinked like the negative image of bright light, bright darkness.

Firian flexed his clammy hands and stood. He leaned over just to add *Bring Brett.*

Taking the letter to the door of the office, he fought the urge to look at it one more time. He couldn't help feeling that the little piece of paper didn't properly convey its own importance. A little note couldn't express how hard he had worked every day to earn his skills, or the sacrifices he'd made on behalf of the Academy to get to this point.

Well, maybe his family had already heard about when he

took Kiria hostage. It was news across the continent. Only his promise to work with her instead of against her, now that they were both in power, had created a tenuous truce.

Master Belik sat just outside in the stone hallway. He must have dragged a chair from a nearby room so his leg wouldn't bother him.

I need to appoint a new guard. Firian didn't want to think about what had happened to the last one.

Belik turned when he opened the door, his bull neck craning. Light from the hall torches reflected off his glasses, hiding his eyes. "Wrote a letter, did you?"

Firian handed it to him. "See that it gets to my family in Raewhith."

The Master moved his head just enough that Firian could see Belik's eyes rove around his face, evaluating where they both stood in this new relationship. Belik wouldn't suffer himself to become an errand boy. But this was important to Firian.

The Master hummed deep in his throat, almost a growl. Then one side of his mouth lifted. "Telling them the good news?"

"Yes."

After all they'd done, they couldn't afford to mistrust each other now. If prodded, Firian still felt rage like a deep bruise from the lies Belik had told. But the Master was also one of the only people who had believed Firian could end up here, in this office.

After Firian moved out of their shared room to stay in the very place where he'd suffocated Sais Jairon in his bed, Bard had hardly spoken to him—as though Firian had done something wrong, when he had only taken drastic action for the good of the Academy. Bard's cautions still echoed regularly in his mind, but the two of them spent no time together anymore. Strangely, he wished Bard would understand. Firian wouldn't admit it, but he missed him.

Still seated, Belik stretched his jaw. "So, do you want me to send this"—he held up the letter, the bottom of it scrunched in his hand—"or wait for the scouts?"

"Send that. Right away. I'll wait for the scouts."

Belik had told Firian what to do thousands of times. Now it was Firian's turn.

Clearly grumpy, Belik rose from the chair, cursing the stiffness in his leg as he walked away toward the inner courtyard.

His uneven footsteps overlapped with the patter of new ones getting louder down the hall. A border patroller marched three people bound in front of him. Bold of him to conduct all three scouts himself. Firian found himself liking the patroller.

The scouts from Brithnem wore brown and green and tan clothing. Firian scrutinized them from their heads to their dirty boots. No weapons.

Unlike scouts from other countries, people from Brithnem almost never matched. Too much Khelê blood. In fact, one of the scouts, the only woman, was definitely Khelê. She was stout but attractive, a few years older than Firian, with a milky white eye and tattoos on the side of her head that didn't have a wave of blonde hair. The two men varied as well. One, the tallest of the group, had a beard and was muscled like a seasoned fighter, while the other reminded Firian of a deer, thin and graceful.

Firian waved them all into his office. The door clicked closed behind them.

"So these are the Kingdom scouts." He strolled once again behind his desk, the one where all the leaders had sat since the Tanyu split from the Amir so long ago.

None of the scouts showed fear. Didn't they know what he could do to them? What any other Tanyuin Head *would* do to them? But he had promised Kiria to send them back unharmed.

She'd be waiting for them, for the end of the Tanyuin War, for proof that she could trust him. Firian took a deep breath.

The border patroller forced the three of them to their knees.

Firian's face flushed. "You've come on secret land," he said. "No one has come from outside and lived."

The thin man leaned, almost imperceptibly, toward the woman in the center as though for protection or comfort. The woman's white eye grew wider, but she bared her teeth, almost animal-like in defiance. Their sweaty stink began to fill the office.

Firian had to watch his words. The border patroller carried a large sword, unsheathed. Firian couldn't let him misunderstand and stain the floor black-red.

"But today," he continued, "we have the same goal. I am the new Tanyuin Head, and my plans are different from my predecessor." His lip curled with the word *different*. "I want to end the war between us." Already tired of the desk between them, Firian came back around it to stand directly over the scouts. His body cast a torchlight shadow across them. "As proof, I will let you live."

The woman's chest rose and fell, the only sign of her relief. The patroller's hand didn't relax its grip on the sword.

"Tomorrow, you'll return to Brithnem with my terms, and the Academy's location will no longer be secret."

He felt the force of the patroller's surprise. His mouth slackened and his knuckles burned white on the hilt. The hum of unsaid questions whirred through the air.

Firian stood taller, sure in his decision. The Academy would be exposed, but this decision would provide undeniable proof that Kiria could trust him. He could recruit soldiers from neighboring towns, fend off bands of curious mercenaries, or even whole armies with the Kingdom on his side. Open trade would bring more wealth and power to the Tanyu. Though he hated giving up a long-held secret, he would just hold tightly to the ones that remained about his famed warriors. "Bring my terms to the Second Keeper. When she accepts them, the war will end." Kiria. He wouldn't let the other Keepers make such a crucial decision. What did they matter? He ended this war for her. Together, they could use their power to do whatever they wanted. She probably still had that notebook of ideas of how to lead the Kingdom with justice, peace, order... Warmth, almost a caress, snuck up the back of his neck into his hairline.

He jerked his head. "Get them up."

The patroller kicked the woman's heels and the three of them trundled to their feet.

"You'll stay with the border patrollers tonight. In the morning, I'll give you the terms." He caught the man's eye as he turned the three of them away. *Don't hurt them.* The patroller nodded, disappointment in his eyes.

2

KIRIA

Kiria adjusted her crown and swung around to check it in the glass. It seemed to be centered. She couldn't help wanting every minute detail to be perfect. Today was her first official session as Keeper. Though she had been coronated, today she would take her throne.

"It looks perfect," her mother crooned, touching one of its silver points with a finger. Kiria could see her and her Amiran advisor Chetana standing in the middle of the bedroom floor behind her.

The only one missing was her father, killed by Torithians a few months before. He would have been so proud of her. She fought back the memory of getting that news, when Firian had tried to comfort her, holding her as she wept, but nothing was enough. Her mother had been even more devastated by his death than she was.

After clearing her throat, Kiria turned to look at her mother. Not long ago, she had worn this crown. Kiria didn't have any regrets about taking over the throne, but seeing only pride in her mother's face made her smile.

"This is a big day for you," her mother said, squeezing Kiria's hand. "Why haven't you changed?"

"I will in a second." Kiria bit the inside of her cheek. While she got ready, putting on the trappings of a Keeper for the first time since the coronation, she didn't want her Beauty yet. She wanted a moment for the title to seep into every part of her, to let its glow be beautiful enough. In the Main, she would appear with her official face, the one blessed by God with painfully complete Beauty, but for a second she was just Kiria. This part of her wore the crown too.

As though she'd been summoned, Candrae, one of her serving girls, rushed to check the fastening of Kiria's dress. Kiria flinched as Candrae touched the buttons.

"Oh, My Keeper!" Candrae cried, laying a palm gently on Kiria's bare back.

"The tattoo's still a little tender. It's not your fault." Kiria's design covered the upper part of her back and shoulder blades. She'd chosen a design similar to the one Mari Calthwaite had received in Carradoc. Artists kept a record of all the designs, and she'd always admired the beauty and ferocity of the founder's. Delicate swirls ending in claw-like points adorned her upper back like jeweled armor. Kiria had added a subtle laird flower in the center to symbolize the peace of Brithnem. The final flourish, a graceful point, rose up the nape of her neck.

Since she'd had the procedure, she'd worn open-backed dresses. This one, all light blue, made her appear every inch a Keeper.

"I'm sure she won't do it again," said her mother, eyeing Candrae, who dropped her gaze.

Kiria squeezed Candrae's hand gently to reassure her that she'd done nothing wrong, then turned her attention to Chetana. "Do you have a tattoo?" She'd never noticed one on her advisor's dark skin, but her advisor was fiercely proud of being Khelê. Most Khelê had tattoos in recognition of their heritage. It was in solidarity with the mismatched race of Khelê that the tradition of royal tattoos had started all those years ago.

Chetana tapped the side of her head with an elegant finger. "Right there. Not all allegiances are obvious to the eye." She pulled down the high-necked collar of her Amiran robe. Beneath her hairline of dark, rusty curls, the edge of a tattoo unfurled. Although impossible to see the whole design, it had the signature curls, dots, and points of most Khelê tattoos.

"You used to shave your head?"

Chetana smoothed the collar back up and patted the sides of her close-cut hair. "For a very short while."

"I didn't know that, Chetana," her mother said, drawing her brows together.

"It's not always best to give every detail of one's past. The present is more important."

Kiria was about to ask why when a voice cut in.

"You know, compared to Atty's, yours is very nice."

Kiria whirled around at the sound of Jori's voice. True to form, Jori wore the finest clothes in the sloppiest ways. His embroidered vest was undone as though he were just arriving at home. How he could manage to seem at home no matter where he was remained a mystery to Kiria. "Atty's is exactly like your father's, though. That has to mean something."

"And? I think it must be something about the skin," he said thoughtfully. He sauntered up beside her. Blushing, Candrae backed up against the vanity.

Despite herself, Kiria smiled. "You're ridiculous."

"The Keeper is right," Chetana agreed with no hint of levity.

"Of course," he replied. Giving into his penchant for theatrics, he bowed his head.

"I'm surprised they let you in," her mother said, with a little more amusement.

"*I'm* not." Jori flashed a mischievous grin. "Well!" He turned again to Kiria. "I just wanted to wish you good luck. With those two, you're going to need it." *Those two* were Cúron and Jori's brother Atty, the other Keepers.

"Hardly," she said. "I can hold my own."

He winked. "That's my girl."

"We need to finish getting ready for the session," Chetana said pointedly.

Jori flourished a hand. "Point taken. You might start talking politics at any moment." He headed toward the door. "All my best, darling," he cried as it shut behind him.

Candrae returned to fiddle with the ties of Kiria's dress. It felt secure back there. Maybe Candrae just wanted to feel like she had something to do.

"Speaking of politics," her mother said, "have you done your research?"

Kiria fought not to roll her eyes. "Yes, I've done my research." She'd dived into the issues until she could barely see by the candlelight. The past week had been packed with nothing but study punctuated by checking for the scouts Firian had promised to send.

She wouldn't know if she could trust him until all three scouts came back unharmed, with peace terms and news of the Tanyuin Academy's location. She prayed he was as good as his word. If her gut was right, and he was telling the truth, then the war against the Tanyu would be over, and they could potentially end their war with the pirates as well. What a victory that would be—peace on both fronts!

If her calculations were correct, it took about two weeks to travel between Brithnem and the Academy. One more week to wait.

She came back to the present and closed her eyes. A tingling covered her body as she put on her Beauty. When the change completed, her mother gasped softly behind her. No one quite got used to the Ability. Beauty revealed everything Kiria was, but more. She'd seen it over and over again in the glass. Her light brown eyes turned golden, her mousy brown hair rich and full, her skin flawless, her figure immaculate. It was everything she was *meant* to be.

Candrae stopped fussing over the back of her dress.

A satisfied smile curled the edges of Kiria's lips. Despite the dangers of war, of wrong decisions, of future anxiety, she felt ready, eager to begin.

"Is it time?" her mother asked, smiling.

"Let's go."

Guards flanked them as they left for the Main, the enormous meeting room for the three Keepers of Brithnem. Kiria couldn't count how many times she had snuck in there as a child, then sat in on sessions when she was older, but now... now she was a Keeper.

When they arrived, two guards opened the grandly carved double doors. Blood hummed through her veins as she saw a familiar sight, now glowing with possibility. The dais in the center of the room held three thrones: one for Cúron, one for Atty, and the center one for her.

From the ceiling hung the blue and purple flags of Brithnem. Movable walls portioned off part of the room so it didn't look as cavernous as it had during her coronation. A collection of chairs ringed the bottom of the steps, spreading back onto the intricate floor mosaic. Daelon, her tutor, smiled encouragingly at her from the front row.

Her mother and Chetana took their place near him in the front row with the other Amir, nobles, and generals. Kiria climbed the steps to her throne between the other two. Surely this was a dream. Atty, dressed in a fur robe much too warm for the season, pursed his lips in a reassuring smile as she took her seat. Not too long ago, he'd had his first session too.

As soon as Kiria sat, Chetana rose to begin the session with a prayer. She quoted part of the passage from the Sacred Scroll carved along the edge of the ceiling.

With the session open, Kiria spoke. "Keepers, Amir, and dignitaries, I am so pleased to be here today to carry on the long tradition of the Second Keeper." She looked at her mother. "I pray that I can bring honor to the position. I know that I'll do everything in my power to better the Western Kingdom, and to protect it, as I swore at my coronation. I look forward to serving you all the best of my ability."

The small crowd gave polite applause.

"We're sure you will," Cúron replied, smiling at her. "Now onto the matters at hand. Because of the Tanyuin threat to our citizens, I have discussed with our military strategist Petra Madola about allowing people to sleep during the day and work at night, since that is when all the nightmare attacks happen. Our normal economy will be temporarily disrupted, but it is important to keep the people of Brithnem feeling safe."

"There haven't been any attacks since the new Tanyuin Head took over," Kiria pointed out.

"No one has reported an attack," Cúron admitted, "but we assume that he's just getting settled. Firian Kess is young and no doubt took the position by force. Once his crown is secure, he'll turn our way again."

When Kiria turned to Atty, he nodded almost apologetically.

"I don't think he will," she insisted.

"Don't forget what he did, to you, to all of us." Even as Cúron turned dramatically to the little crowd, there was a clear warning in his voice.

How could she forget? *She* was the one taken hostage, not him. She bit back a retort. Diplomacy, even when Cúron was condescending to her, was the best way. He wasn't a bad man, she reminded herself, just ambitious.

"I think it works as a solution for now," Atty said, referring back to the sleeping schedules. He raised an eyebrow at her, a friendly nudge to get her back on track.

"There!" said Cúron. The word was a warm reward to Atty for having said the right thing. Was this how Cúron spoke to Kiria's mother when she was the Keeper? To leave everything to Cúron, the oldest and most experienced leader, must have been tempting, but Kiria had known since she was a child that she wanted to be a different kind of ruler than her mother.

Kiria's brows twitched downward. Dimly, she noticed the attention shift to her. Every gesture she made was magnified with her Beauty.

"So, if no one has anything else to say...?" Cúron let the question hang in the air as he regarded the advisors, the generals, the other Keepers. He ran his hand once over his white beard.

"I have something to say." Kiria's own voice surprised her. She shouldn't be rankled by something so small. But this was her first session. Everyone needed to take her seriously as their leader, not push aside her voice.

"I would like to announce that I have received hopeful news from the new Tanyuin Head that our war may be at an end."

Surprised shuffling. Her mother stared at her with a warning in her eyes. Bold moves, according to her, often led to danger. Maybe that was the reason she never proposed any.

That look made Kiria falter, though she was no less sure of what she wanted to say. Surely her mother had to feel proud of her once she heard the plan.

Cúron turned to her with another admonishing expression. "When did you receive this news?" he demanded.

"The day before my coronation."

"From what source?"

She hesitated, just for a moment. "The Tanyuin Head himself." *I stood here and he stood there.* She glanced at the spot on the dais as though she could still see his shadow.

"And you trust this news?" Cúron began.

"What did he say?" The fact that Atty talked over Cúron proved his surprise.

Kiria turned to Atty. "He said he had our scouts, but that he would send them all back safely with terms to end the Tanyuin War. He also promised to help us in our efforts against the Torithians as well."

Cúron's eyes narrowed.

He was probably thinking that, mere months ago, Firian had double-crossed them. The Academy had ordered him to do it. Now that he was in charge, though, things would be different. Probably. Hopefully.

"What does he want in return?" Cúron asked.

"He doesn't want a vote like the Amir. He just wants Torithian prisoners of war." Anticipating their next question, she added, "The scouts should be here in a week to confirm if he's telling the truth."

"Until then," said Cúron, his voice booming now, to include everyone in the small crowd, "we will refrain from negotiations with Tanyu."

He said it as a parent would to a child. There was something final, non-negotiable, about it. Kiria bit her lip. It would be extraneous to add anything else, wouldn't it?

Gathering her courage, she said, "I hope this will mean the end of both wars for us. If we don't broadcast the alliance, then we'll be able to surprise the Torithians. Though it's unlikely, an alliance with the Tanyu could be the most advantageous move for us right now. A risky one, but if it pays off, well worth it."

Obviously a little irritated that Kiria got the last word, Cúron smiled broadly. She met his gaze. Especially since the death of

Atty's father, Cúron was used to being right, to being the one to run these meetings. It was true that he did have more experience, but Kiria planned to contribute just as much as he did.

Parohim, Cúron's advisor, stood, holding a piece of paper. "Next on our—"

With a huge crash, a window exploded into shards. Kiria's arms shook once against the carved armrests as pieces of glass shattered across the floor.

Parohim ducked. She thought she caught the flash of an arrow and her heart turned to ice. But no. Just glass.

Everyone at the foot of the dais twisted to see the many-paned window. Two guards patrolling the door sprinted outside. Others ran protectively toward the Keepers on the dais.

Kiria's spine stiffened with fear. She let out a shaky breath, fighting the urge to touch the wound on her shoulder. No other crash followed, but threat billowed like smoke through the room.

Shouting came through the empty window. Cúron and one of the generals stood. The distortion and height of the glass didn't offer a good view of what was happening, especially now that the dais was surrounded by guards poised to fight. From her seat, Kiria could only look between them.

"What was that?" Atty asked.

Kiria looked at him but couldn't answer.

After a few more seconds, one of the guards returned.

"What happened?" Cúron demanded.

"There's no danger, My Keepers," said the guard, bowing. "We apprehended two protesters throwing rocks at the window. They are being held outside, bound."

Kiria's brow furrowed. She stood to see around the guards, who parted respectfully and stepped halfway down the steps so she could get a clear view. "Protesters? What were they protesting?"

"Please forgive me, My Keepers. They were protesting your ascension to the throne."

Something like guilt threaded through her. She'd heard a passing comment to that effect before she was coronated. Her mother Merian was well-loved by the people. But this disruption took Kiria completely by surprise.

Her mother stood angrily. "Tell them my daughter has my full support." Her tone was strained, as though the anger wasn't directed only at the protesters, but at her daughter too.

"Of course, My... lady." The guard turned his full attention to Kiria. "What shall we do with them, My Keeper?"

All attention shifted to her. She felt herself pale. *This is it.* So soon, she had to make a hard decision on her own.

Why had these protesters snuck onto the palace grounds? Why couldn't they have stayed home? She couldn't let them go. To solidify her reign, she had to show that this threatening behavior wouldn't be tolerated.

It would be easy to execute them. The thought made her still. What a horrible thought! It would be simpler than a just solution, but she wanted justice more than simplicity. The temptation snagged at her consciousness, but, finally, she stood. "Keep them in a cell for two nights. After that, bring them here to me. If they swear allegiance to me as their Keeper and beg forgiveness, I will show them mercy." *Swear allegiance, beg forgiveness...* The solution sounded self-centered. But this wasn't just about her, it was about the Second Line.

She glanced around quickly for affirmation—her mother, Chetana, Daelon, Cúron... To her relief, they all regarded her with a little pride. She looked at Atty last, who seemed like he wanted to clap her on the shoulder in congratulations. She let out a furtive sigh of relief.

"Of course, My Keeper," said the guard. "Right away."

3

———

FIRIAN

Blood coated Firian's knuckles as he pounded the mattress leaning against a tree. He needed something to beat, some way to release the aggression welling up like oil under his skin. The mattress would do. At least he wouldn't break his hands.

Today, the Unreal wasn't enough.

His family was coming today.

The scouts wouldn't arrive in Brithnem for a few days. Though there was plenty to occupy his time, this visit was the most urgent. Some of the older Masters grated against his authority, but he could deal with them after he confronted the monster lurking in his past. After that, he would rid himself of fear and put them all in their place.

Now, though, memories filled him like a disease. His father storming in, coiled as a wire. The sight of him made Firian taste salt in his mouth and scan the objects in the room so he'd know what he might have to prepare himself to face. The fury in those eyes looking for an outlet for his rage.

His sister Brett always sensed the danger immediately too. She touched Firian's upper arm for him to back up, his little body shadowed behind hers. He stumbled back a step, wincing at the fumbling sound it made.

His mother leaned back, placing one palm on the table as Father approached. She looked empty, fragile, like a doll. Firian's throat constricted until he was fighting to breathe. Mother had no power to fight, either for herself or for them.

Father sneered and violently grabbed her wrist. "Don't act like you're afraid of me, Lithia," he spat, flinging her away. "God, it's no wonder your son is such a coward."

Though Father didn't look at him, Firian tensed at every movement. He burned with shame at how thankful he was to have Brett standing in front of him. Father never hit Brett.

His mother, shaking, didn't respond.

"Did you hear what I said?" Father snarled, bending to stare Mother in the eye. The motion made Mother seem like a little girl. "Or are you stupid?"

Mother dropped her eyes, shuffling her feet, maybe to start doing something else. The whole room began to smell sharp and sour. When Firian was very small, he had thought the smell came from the forge, maybe the coke burning, or the panes of glass before they were cool. He learned better eventually.

"Gore!" Father swore. "Look at me, Lithia! Look at me, you idiotic woman!" He squeezed her chin in his hand so hard it distorted her face.

Something touched Firian's arm. He jumped. Brett again. He pressed her hand lightly enough that Father wouldn't see the movement.

"I have to put up with this after working all day? I don't know why I bother to feed you."

"I'm sorry, Yanon," she whimpered.

He struck her across the face. "You know why? It's because nobody would buy you even if you offered."

"I'm sorry..."

"Oh, are you?" He came at her like a man possessed.

Firian knew this part. He shut his eyes tight, trying not to listen, but every attempt just amplified the sounds. The half-strangled screams ripped through his little body. Every muffled thump bruised him in dark, dark places...

Firian swiped sweat off his forehead with the back of his hand, willing the memory away, but it was like sound. Trying not to notice just pushed it into sharper relief. Growling, he swung and hit, over and over, leaning into the pain, into the anger that fueled him. Anger, not fear. His knuckles ached and stung as they made contact.

The mattress ripped. Straw stuck out of the holes at crazy angles, slicing Firian's hands. He pulled back and grunted with another hard swing. The punch made the mattress wobble and almost fall.

He swung lower, jabbing upward, bobbing up and down on the balls of his feet. A red smear appeared where his fists had touched, as though there had been a murder.

"So that's where it went."

Firian twisted violently around. Bard. He'd stolen the bottom bunk mattress from Bard's room. Only Bard's room, now that he had moved into the bedroom attached to the Head's office. He didn't answer.

"When are they coming?" Bard asked softly.

Firian bit back a curse. Bard always knew. He glanced at the sun, rubbing his hands on his pants. "Now."

Bard turned around, preparing to walk back to the Academy with him. He preserved a wise silence for a moment before asking, "What are you going to do?"

Firian pursed his mouth and ran his sleeve across his face. What a time for Bard to talk to him! They hadn't interacted much at all since Firian had killed Sias Jairon. Maybe even before, when Firian had tracked down some of the Sentries they'd freed together.

He still didn't know what he was going to do with his family. He wanted to make his father pay. It would be the first time Firian saw his father since he'd taken the entrance test when he was eleven. The pit of his stomach tightened again.

Still breathing hard from boxing the mattress, he answered, "I don't know."

"You're not going to...?"

"I don't know."

The breeze blew the shirt-sweat cold.

"You got what you wanted," Bard said. "There's no need to hurt them."

Firian lifted his chin. He'd played versions of this meeting in his head for years, but now that the moment had come, he wasn't sure what he would do.

"Fir?"

He gave Bard a pointed look. He would decide when his family stood in front of him. Should he invite them into his office? It wasn't very grand. That was just Firian's style, but at this moment, he wished it were covered in tapestries and heraldry and trophies from the defeated. At least he would wear his crown. He had brought it with him, tied to one of the straps of his black coat. Reaching back, he unknotted it. The hard metal felt cold against his forehead. Who was worthless now?

"You don't want regrets, yeah? Firian, I'm serious."

"I know you are. You're always serious." Releasing his thoughts even that much started to relax his tense muscles as well. He resettled the crown into a more comfortable position. Maybe he shouldn't hurt him, but only threaten...

Maybe they were already here.

His throat started to close. *Damn it, you're the Tanyuin Head! They'll do anything you say.*

Bard looked up at him solemnly, black hair wild. "I'll be just outside."

Firian started to protest, but stopped. If Bard were outside, he might find the self-control not to order his father's death. Brett and his mother would probably be horrified if he killed his father, even though the scut deserved it. They didn't need to see that side of him.

A warm droplet leaked down his finger, pooled on his fingertip, and dropped into the pine needles.

"Okay."

A black figure strode from the Academy toward them, darker than the fortress's dark walls. As he got closer, his features materialized into Ryker, a Learner, about fourteen. More white than usual ringed his brown eyes as he approached Firian. He softened toward the boy. "Master Kess," he said, "your visitors have arrived. They're just outside your office."

Even though he'd been expecting the message, his insides leapt. He nodded, his face uncomfortably hot. "Tell them I'm coming."

"As you would have it, Master Kess."

Ryker ran back to the Academy to deliver the message, and the two of them hiked back at a greater speed. Firian fought the urge to run the rest of the way.

Within minutes they had breached the enormous wooden doors and swept through the fountain courtyard with its chandelier. Learners made way for them.

Firian's pulse beat in his throat as they turned down the hallway to the Head's office. His office.

And there they were. Belik and the door guard flanked the three of them, who all looked soft by comparison. His father's brown hair had grown peppery gray, his thin frame more like human gristle than muscle. His arms were so narrow. Those eyes, those accusing eyes, were exactly the same. They widened only a fraction to see Firian, grown and strong and crowned, coming toward them.

He remembered his mother from the trip to Raewhith with Kiria. Now, though still washed out, she was dressed in her best. The faded yellow dress hung limply on her body.

And then there was Brett. Her baby hadn't come with her. He had almost forgotten his sister was coming. Despite all the anticipation for his father's arrival, she was the one who caught and held his eye. She stood sturdy and vibrant compared to the others. The long, glossy hair he remembered was tied back in a braid. Her lined eyes regarded him with an unreadable expression. She could have been proud or wary or glad or condemning. He tried to find the words there that he'd tacked to his bedpost and then fastened to the Sacred Scroll. *Now you'll be a warrior—a Tanyu—one of the bravest and smartest people in the world! I love you. I won't forget you.* The memory of them made him swell with pride. Brett had believed in him when no one else did. And now he was the Tanyuin Head. He lifted his mouth in a half smile for her.

Though her ambiguous expression didn't change, her eyes twinkled back.

Feeling bolstered, he turned to his father. "Come in," he said, his tone turning cold as he passed them to enter his office.

His father shifted. "Firian—"

"Shut up!"

His mother jumped at the ferocity of his comeback. Firian almost did too. He was a dam about to break.

He would deal with the others later. His blood coursed hot as his father's eyes strayed to his knuckles. Remembering the time Father had struck him for coming home from school with bloody knuckles, Firian could barely see through his rage. That had been one day—one day!—before he went to the Academy. The last insult he would suffer from that man. He couldn't begin civilly. Now, he needed retribution, payment for all the years of torture he and his mother had endured at the hands of this monster.

"Come in," he repeated more softly, burning with the pain of holding in the fury he felt.

Without a word, his father followed him inside. Both Belik and Bard stayed outside with the rest of his family. With a wave of his hand, Firian ushered in the new armor-clad guard, who closed the door behind them.

Now practically alone, he stepped heavily toward his father. They were the same height now. Snarling, he stopped less than a hand's-span from his face. All of his practiced speeches disappeared. What were words anyway? They couldn't make up for what was done, all the sleepless nights, the noises he heard from his mother in the quiet, his life-long fear that his father might have been right about him...

He paused just long enough for his father's stare to flash up to the open iron square on his forehead. "Get on your knees," he whispered.

"Firi—"

"On your knees!" Firian roared, stepping back. His chest rose and fell as though he had run for hours. He ground his teeth, staring down the man who had made his entire family feel like nothing.

Steadying himself, he took a deep breath. "I am the Head of the Tanyuin Academy. If I tell my people to kill you, they will. Without hesitation. So get on your knees."

Hatred radiated from his father as he lowered himself down slowly, tentatively.

Kneeling before him, he looked so small, and Firian hated him more for it. "Now beg my forgiveness."

"I didn't do anything to you."

Heat burst into Firian's skull and he pulled his hand back

only after he realized what he had done. Father's temple was dark red, and a welt beaded up where Firian's Master ring had struck him.

He blinked in horror. What had he done? For an irrational moment, he thought his father would retaliate, grow large as he was in his dreams, and beat him.

As Firian had just done to him.

Fresh disgust, this time at himself, flowed through his thoughts. He was a warrior getting justice, someone who'd learned violence as a force for power and respect and doing good. But for a sickening moment, he felt like he was looking in a glass at a distorted image of himself.

I didn't do anything to you.

He refused to explain all the times his father had called him worthless, had beaten him and his mother, had talked down to him, had not believed in him. He would not itemize his pain. But he would have his revenge.

Collecting himself again, he remembered his purpose. "Beg."

Silence from the head bent downward.

"Beg or I'll kill you." It was still probably true.

His father cleared his throat. "For whatever you think I did..."

"Start over," he growled.

"I'm sorry." The words wrung out of him, grating, quiet, forced.

Firian waited.

"I'm sorry for... hurting you in some way." Even from this angle, his jaw clearly worked with agitation.

Firian cut a grim look at the guard and nodded once. The guard struck his father on the back of the head. The blow made him lean forward and catch himself on his hands.

Firian's blood beat at the sight. *Yes, beg.*

"I'm sorry." Now his voice had more of the right tone. Maybe he thought he was begging for his life. He was. "I'm sorry."

The picture became disgusting. Repulsed, Firian kicked him lightly on the wrist. "Get up."

His father did, coming back into himself like a second skin. Here he was again, the demon from his past, his hate-filled eyes rimmed unhealthily with red. His sallow cheeks paled like a fever victim's.

Firian nodded again to the guard, who opened the door. Firian's mother stood with her hands to her mouth. Brett glared through the opening, her forehead a mass of tight wrinkles. They must have heard the whole thing. Good. Now they knew this monster could be beaten.

His father didn't spare them a glance, but his skin flushed pink with the knowledge that they were being watched.

"You can't hurt me now," Firian said, "but if I hear that you've hurt *them*, I'll harm you in ways you've never heard of. I'll torture your dreams, I'll send Tanyu to fetch your fingers one by one..." He stopped because he was shaking.

Though his father didn't quail, Firian noticed that he barely breathed as he stared back at his son. Firian would make good on every threat. He felt the complicated looks of all four watchers as he glared at his father: Brett, his mother, Master Belik, Bard.

He willed himself back to calm. His hands stilled. "Get out."

When his father turned around, Firian knew that was the last time he'd ever see him. And he was glad.

The guard widened the door for him.

As his father stalked out, his mother's eyes rounded, huge as a doe's. Fear, not relief or thanks, radiated from her.

A wave of grief, surprising in its strength, assaulted him at the sight of her. As a child, he'd reserved some of his anger for her because she hadn't stood up for him all those nights when his father came home and struck him and called him a scut and screamed that he never should have been born. But she was a victim too, even more than he was. How had he never seen it? Trapped in that cruel marriage, it was all she could do to be kind to them. She had never been strong enough to protect them. Firian's eyes felt hot.

He turned to Brett. She stared back, disbelieving, her eyes full of angry shock. The total effect made her look almost like a Tanyu. Despite the accusation in her expression, the sight made him a little proud of her.

"Bring them in." He wanted to be able to talk to them, reassure them, without Belik and Bard overhearing. The women came in and stood where his father had. When the door closed again, he met Brett's glare. "He deserved worse."

"Firian," Brett began, her blue eyes mirroring his own. A dozen questions died on her lips. "Firian, how could you?" They must have overheard through the door.

"You can stay here if you think he'll hurt you."

"We can't stay here." She took a tentative step forward. "We can't live at the Academy. I have a family."

"Bring them."

She took a small, exasperated breath. "We can't." Her eyes softened, a version of the look he'd been waiting for from her. "I was excited to see you. When we got the letter, it felt like the first one, but this time *you* wrote it." She looked down in a sort of disbelief before continuing. "I knew you could do it. Even when kids made fun of you and you weren't sure, I knew you could do this." Her voice was soft and earnest, dropping now to a whisper. "But you don't want to become like him."

His insides curled as she reflected his own thoughts back to him. "I'm not like him."

"You have power now, Firian. If you hurt people with it, you shouldn't have it." She shook her head.

He forced his twitching fingers not to reach for the crown to readjust it again. "I didn't hurt him. And even if I'd killed him, he would have deserved worse. You grew up with him. You know the kind of man he is! He's scum, trash."

Brett lowered her voice even further. "Firian, he'll hurt Mother."

"He already does!" Anger flushed him. Why was she questioning him? Somebody finally put Father in his place, on his knees, begging forgiveness, where he belonged until his miserable life ended.

"No. We're going back."

"No, you aren't."

"Sabir is there." The baby.

"Bring him too. Live in Tánuil. And if he comes back—"

"Listen to yourself. You can't make everything better by controlling it. I can protect myself. Gaius can protect me." The words made a soothing chant, as though she were putting a child to sleep.

Suddenly Firian was eleven again. "I'll protect you," he said, a low whisper through barely parted teeth. The purity of the words filled his body with light. There was something whole about it. Maybe this is why he had become the Head in the first place.

A tight smile passed over Brett's features. "I know you want to."

The idea struck him suddenly. "I'll protect Raewhith." He turned his attention to Belik and Bard in turn. All of them would approve. "It needs us. There's no city wall."

She didn't protest.

"Brett." Here was something she couldn't argue against. He took her hand gently in his, and something inside him twisted with emotion. "I promise I'll look after you and mother. My

Tanyu will guard the city and check up on you. I meant all those things I said, so I'll figure it out."

She pursed her lips as she listened. "Okay," she said, his sister again.

He dropped her hand, smiling grimly. "Okay."

4

—————

KIRIA

"I can't believe you were communicating with that Tanyu!" Kiria's mother muttered, setting down her coffee. The cup rattled in the dish. "It was entirely unsafe." Light from the ceiling-high windows of her bedroom crowned her.

"But look what we got from it," Kiria replied. Technically she'd gotten very little yet from talking with Firian, but she had a decent idea of the Academy's location as well as his promise to end the wars.

Her mother shook her head, flinging the unpleasant thoughts away like water droplets.

The palace had buzzed with the news of Kiria's first session, both the ill-planned attack and her announcement about an alliance. Sessions in the Main were usually guarded secrets, but people weren't guarding their words as closely as they should. At least if quick silences and pointed glances were any indication.

Taking another drink of lukewarm coffee, Kiria eyed her mother. She had something on her mind, though Kiria couldn't figure out what it was. An eager, abstracted look kept flitting across her mother's face. It made a stark contrast to her usual demeanor of resigned grace.

"Now that you are the Keeper," her mother began, as though she'd practiced.

Kiria took a protective sip.

"You need to think about marrying."

Fighting not to cough, Kiria swallowed. "Now?" she asked. She was still eighteen. In all the excitement of the past year, she'd barely given marriage a passing thought. For a second, she envied Kader, Cúron's son, who was too young to be pestered about such things.

"As soon as possible. It's the best way to secure the Second Line." Her mother folded her hands in her lap. "Is there anyone you have an eye on?"

The way she asked the question suggested she wanted to be in on the secret to make up for Kiria's excluding her before.

A brief image of sitting with Firian on the night-dark wooden walkways of Shifra came back to her. He had leaned in, brushed back her hair, breathed against her mouth… She shook off the unwanted memory as a servant approached to refresh her coffee with some newly boiled. Firian had betrayed her almost immediately afterward. It didn't matter that they'd shared a moment, had almost kissed. "No," she replied.

Her mother's face fell a little. "Well, there are plenty of men interested in getting to know you. You should invite some of them here, or even host a party to meet them."

"I'm sure there are." Kiria wasn't using her Beauty now, but she knew how alluring it was.

"You don't have to decide today or this week," her mother said, "but it would help the Kingdom accept you as their leader if you showed a dedication to continue the family line."

Would it, though? Would marriage prevent unrest like they saw at the session? It seemed unlikely. A small part of her was insulted that her mother would play on her weaknesses like that. But maybe she was right. Marriage was a good idea. Before,

Kiria was too young to consider it seriously, and then she was swept up in the danger of assassination when Firian had to be called in as a bodyguard.

Kiria tipped her mouth. Her mother never meant to hurt her. They were each other's only family left. Kiria couldn't let small things come between them.

"I'll think about it," she promised.

Her mother's smile turned mischievous. "I have a couple young men in mind that you might like."

Curious, Kiria struggled to think of who they might be. "Who?"

"Don't look at me like that, Kiria," her mother said lightly. "I know you've never been very interested in the guards or ambassadors' sons." Her face fell just long enough that Kiria could tell she was remembering her own husband, a general. The pause lasted long enough for memories to clog their throats before passing away again. "In fact," she continued, "part of me is glad. A Beauty like yours can be dangerous if used the wrong way."

Kiria nodded, waiting for the names of her mother's suggested young men.

"Have you met General Madola's son Warrick?"

She struggled to remember. The vague image of a tall, thin boy flitted across her memory. "Once, I think."

"What about him?"

She considered. "I'd have to meet him again." She accidentally allowed a slight grimace on her face as she spoke.

"Or what about Tierney Oscal?"

"I'd rather marry Jori!" Every time Kiria saw Tierney, he ogled her openly and she'd caught him more than once making bawdy comments to his friends.

"Don't joke," her mother said, frowning. "He comes from a noble family that has donated generously to help Brithnem through the years."

"I know who he is," Kiria said pointedly. "Have you met him? Aren't Keepers supposed to stay pure until marriage? Stay true just to one person?"

Her mother blushed. "Yes! Is he...? If he's like that, then of course I wouldn't recommend him. But his family..."

"Not everyone is like their family." A meaningful hush fell between them, and Kiria took a final swig of coffee.

A knock at the door interrupted her thoughts. A guard stepped inside. "Pardon me, my lady," he said, addressing her mother before turning to Kiria. "My Keeper, the scouts have arrived."

The cup clattered in the saucer as Kiria stood. "Where are they?" She could feel her mother's gaze on her, scrutinizing her enthusiasm, but she didn't care.

"They're meeting with Keeper Cúron and one of the military strategists now."

"Take me there." *How is Cúron always the first to know?* She turned to her mother, who still sat. "I need to go."

"Yes," her mother replied, arching her eyebrows. But then she softened. "You're right. You should go. I hope we all hear good news."

With a nod, Kiria swept out the door, donning her Beauty as she went. The scouts were convening in the dining room, which sometimes doubled as a small meeting chamber. She arrived in a rush.

Three scouts, still dirty from travel, sat at the table. Two men and one woman. Cúron and Petra Madola sat opposite them. The scouts stopped talking when they saw Kiria, hastening to their feet.

"Ah, I'm glad you could join us!" Cúron exclaimed. He didn't stand.

A guard emerged from his post by the door to pull out a seat for her. She sat and regarded the scouts who appeared weary but unhurt. The woman pushed a shock of white-blonde hair out of her face, revealing one empty-looking eye. Kiria inspected them for bruises, cuts, anything that would indicate that Firian was less than his word. A tinge of fear colored the smaller man's face, but she was used to that look. It faded with time and exposure to her Beauty. A bearded man sat on the other side of the woman, his positively cheerful demeanor a marked contrast to the others.

Kiria addressed him. "Did you reach the Academy?"

"We did, My Keeper." He reached into his travel-stained coat and pulled out a map, which he laid on the table. He jabbed a calloused finger at the forest just north of Raewhith, where Kiria had gone with Firian when they had been attacked.

Her stomach warmed and the corners of her mouth lifted. Just as she thought.

"We'll have it added to all the official maps," Cúron said, as the man kept jabbing with his finger.

Petra waved to see the paper more closely, and the bearded scout passed it to her.

"Did you see the new Tanyuin Head?" Kiria asked. She didn't glance at Cúron, but knew that he'd have a reaction to her question. Firian's conduct toward the scouts would either support or weaken her announcement of an alliance. Despite everything, she had acted like she trusted him.

For a second, she wondered where Atty was. Had he gotten the same message she had?

"We did," the Khelê woman replied. Her words came out measured and slow, almost like a question.

"What did he say?" Kiria was getting impatient. She didn't want to ask any leading questions, but rather to hear their version of events first, the true version.

"He wants to end the Tanyuin War," said the bearded one with a smile.

Kiria realized how heavily her heart had been beating. Heat flushed her cheeks.

"He said," the woman added, as though to clarify.

"He wrote out terms." The thin man nodded, and another paper appeared from the bearded man's jacket.

Kiria took it before the others, feeling almost greedy. The terms. What had Firian said? He wanted to end their war and help with their conflict against the Torithians, as long as he could keep the prisoners of war. That was it, right?

Her mind whirled. She tried to focus on the paper. It lacked the niceties that usually came with diplomatic documents, but cut straight to the point. As she read, she could practically hear Firian's voice. There were no extra demands. All was exactly as he had promised. It looked as though, for now, it really was a new age for the Tanyu.

She fought to control her excitement. Her mother and the rest of Brithnem would have to respect her decision now. The gambit had paid off. One war was over, and she could engineer the end of the second with Firian's help.

She wanted to laugh. She wanted to see Firian, but she couldn't get ahead of herself. Instead, she beamed a huge smile and handed the paper deliberately to Cúron.

5

FIRIAN

Firian looked himself in the eye, and another, and another. His mind strained to keep all the copies of himself intact in the blank mindfield. It felt like a good stretch or a fall when adrenaline cushions most of the pain.

That copy didn't act naturally. Its chest caved in and its knees bent slightly to the side. *Stand up.* Slowly, the version of him straightened, the broad shoulders brought to attention. Firian looked from face to face. Light skin grazed by the sun, dark eyebrows, dark brown hair just longer than his ears...

He tried to create a sixth. The whole construction wobbled. *Five for now. Not too bad.* Later, he would make them move separately. He had heard of Tanyu employing a decoy in a fight, but never more than one. Dizziness swirled around him as he animated the five Firians.

Gasping, he swam back to the Real. Cool air from his office drifted across his sweat-sheened face. He drummed his fingers once over the armrest of the chair.

The door opened with a tentative stutter that could only mean Bard was coming. He'd walked in on Firian before in compromising positions. "Fir, hey," he said, his hesitancy falling away as he saw Firian was alone. "You okay?"

"Just practicing."

"You're always practicing." His friend scratched his spiky black hair. Something else was on his mind.

Firian leaned back. "Is something wrong?"

"No." The word trailed off into a forest of unsaid things. "I was just thinking. About the war on Torith. You know, the one we're joining now, for Brithnem." He looked up from the floor into Firian's eyes. "I want to help, any way I can."

One side of Firian's mouth lifted. Bard sounded so earnest. "How?"

"So I've practiced *katah* for years now and I've never used those skills. People usually tell generals to watch out for a female presence"—his ears turned red—"and I'm not. I don't... I wouldn't do everything, of course. But that's not what Master Gerand taught me. She knows I'd be terrible."

Firian burst out laughing. "You want to seduce a general?" Calling *katah* on someone usually included seduction to speed up the victim's belief in the Unreal, making them easier to kill.

"No! No, obviously. Fir, I'm serious. Do you think I could? I've practiced on you more than anybody." He writhed a little as his explanation didn't take the smile from Firian's face. "No!" he repeated. "That's not... Okay." He pulled up a chair and sat across from him. His eyes caught the green and brown flag Firian had taken from Raewhith when he went to visit Brett and see the new recruits there. He felt it between his fingers. "You're in charge now," he said thoughtfully. The statement set distance between them, but distance Bard was willing to breach. At least there was a glimmer of hope they could remain friends after all that had happened.

When Firian had murdered the Head, he felt as though he'd fallen into a place so dark that Bard wouldn't be able to see him.

He didn't regret killing him, but he didn't want everything else in his life to die too.

Bard fanned out his fingers on the desk. "So I want to help you end the war."

Firian nodded. "Your family."

"Yeah, they're in Enderin and Jac's on the front line. I think. Haven't gone home in a while." He scratched his head again. "I'm pretty sure they hate me."

Firian scrunched his forehead skeptically. Bard's family couldn't hate him.

"They do," Bard protested. "Or I think... sometimes... they would just because of what I am." He didn't say the word. Tanyu.

Bard's presence at the Academy had always baffled Firian a bit. Not everyone there had extraordinary ability, but Bard's skill set didn't seem to match the Tanyu at all.

"The Academy isn't at war with the Kingdom anymore." *Or its allies.*

"I know. It's just..." Bard looked down at his feet. The faint smell of cinnamon wafted off his clothes. With a deep breath, he drew his splayed hands into fists on the tabletop. "I want to do some good. I want to help you make the Academy great."

You want to make up for what I did to the last Tanyuin Head.

Using a *katah* to gain information was actually a good idea, though. Bard wouldn't attract as much suspicion as a woman or Firian himself. There wasn't enough time to set up a full *katah*, a full death sentence, but Bard could still get somewhere with the general.

"I'll get you the name," Firian said.

Something hard eased in his chest when Bard smiled. "That's great!" Bard jumped up from his seat. "Oh, okay, I can do this. I'll get the information about the Torithian general or strategist or whoever you give me, and then you can finish it."

He flashed another grin, black eyes sparkling. "Wanna get an ale?"

Everything was like before. *Well, not everything.* But Firian had to admit he missed this easiness. These days, Jovan stiffened at his authority, Belik spoke only of strategy, Tiev was broken from his time Lost in the Unreal and rarely spoke to anyone.

Firian nodded. "I'll meet you there. First, I'll get the name."

"All right," Bard agreed, darting out of the room.

He closed his eyes again. *Kiria, Kiria...* She beat against the inside of his eyelids and he sent his mind toward that energy.

Closer now, he heard music. The melody wasn't as sad as the one he had heard her play before—still like silver, but now living instead of mourning. He waited until the last note sounded. "Kiria," he said gently. As Head, he could finally afford to be patient.

Her image grew sharper, but not more beautiful. Still, he liked her like this—her little heart-shaped face turned to him. It felt natural. She was standing in a room of the palace Firian had never seen before. About the same size as her bedroom, this one was full of musical instruments.

When she saw him, gladness, like light, shone on her features, though she didn't smile. She adjusted her long russet skirt, an unnecessary gesture in the Unreal. "Firian. I was going to contact you. The scouts arrived today. They seem safe and they had your terms." She tripped almost playfully over the last few words.

"As I said."

"You said a lot of things." A note of caution shone now in her light brown eyes, like a lens carefully placed there.

His eyes wandered to the silver tiara she wore. "I did." He realized he was tapping his thumb against his leg, and stopped. "I also said I wanted to end the war. Both wars. So you agree to the terms?"

"Yes. We read them and all three of us agreed they were reasonable." She drew herself up. "We are willing to make a conditional alliance."

He frowned. "Conditional?"

"Assuming you follow through on your end of the terms."

"Ah. That's actually what I came to talk about. About Torith." He tripped over the last words, but rallied when Kiria didn't seem to care.

Instead, she stood, coquettishly waiting at attention, eyebrows raised.

"I need the names of the top men on the Torithian side. I have somebody ready to gather better information for you."

She tensed. The royal tattoo peeked black over her shoulder. The idea excited her too. His stomach tightened a little. "Who?" she asked.

Information for information. "Bard."

"Your friend?" The name was like a spell to cast them back to how they used to be—the best time, between the attack and the Academy's ultimatum that involved taking her hostage. Bard was a safe subject, an intimate subject.

Firian smiled. "Yeah. He practices *katah*." He hoped she recognized the trust he had in her to share that much.

"*Katah*?"

Firian considered how much to tell her. "Bard will be able to... read his mind, sort of." That wasn't right, but it was the explanation that would probably make the most sense for now.

She dropped a bit of her royal bearing. "You're serious? He'll relay information to you and—"

"I'll tell you everything."

She gave him a searching look that reminded him of that moment outside Carradoc when they had almost kissed.

"You can't betray us," she said. "We have the exact location of the Academy." She lifted her chin as she said it.

He took a step toward her. He could almost smell the citrusy musk of her hair. "Are you threatening me?" he teased.

"Yes," she replied.

A strand of her hair fell loose across her collarbone. He could sweep it back behind her ear, a move he knew would quicken her pulse.

He smiled again, gazing down at her. "You'll see I'm telling the truth. So"—he lowered his voice to a whisper—"those names."

Little goosebumps rose on the skin of her bare arms. He skimmed his gaze over them, just to show he noticed.

She backed up, raised her chin again. Her eyes grazed him up and down before answering. "Tibor Wat," she said, pronouncing the name clearly. "He's more of a captain than a general. You know, pirates."

"Perfect." He drew out the two syllables. Her lovely face held so much potential. In her eyes he saw all that he could be—not only the Head of the Academy but the lover of a queen. "I'll come back with information."

As though she were coming out of a trance, her shoulders relaxed and her attention refocused. Her lips lifted in a small smile.

Suddenly his demeanor felt like a mask, the one he wore when he was flirting with somebody else. That honest smile seemed to pierce its armor and give her the high ground. It made her more of a friend than a target—a co-conspirator.

He caught his breath and the vulnerability washing over him passed. When she didn't speak, he said, "Look for me soon. Get your soldiers ready." He nodded once and opened his eyes.

Silently, he prayed Bard could make good on his offer. They'd see to it, he assured himself. Bard never lied.

He shivered pleasurably and grabbed his long black coat.

The guard at the door nodded at him as he passed. Everything was fine.

His encounter with Kiria hadn't lasted any longer than five minutes but he didn't see Bard. Must already be outside. With long strides, he hurried into the fountain courtyard. Learners made way; Masters had mixed reactions. Though no one openly defied him, he caught the edge of several dark glances. He would deal with those later. Feeling lighter than he had in a while, he swept out the massive double doors into the cool spring air.

Helping Kiria would set the world right again. Everything from the sky to the sizzling energy under his skin all felt different since he assassinated the previous Head. But all these shops and faces and roads hadn't felt the world shift as he had. They all looked the same, but as though he were peering through a window that distorted certain details and minimized others.

The Old Pub hadn't changed either. Wind moved its hanging sign with the wrong proprietor's name on it. Would Hyrum ever change that?

Firian creaked open the door, his hand brushing against the groove in the wood worn by thousands of visitors. Raucous talk and the smell of ale swept over him as he entered. Dozens of patrons squeezed into the space, almost everyone sporting gaudy colors. Normally, citizens of Tánuil wore gray or brown, easy colors to make and maintain, but here everyone had bright red scarves or green hats or yellow streaks of paint on their faces. The planting festival. He'd forgotten that was today.

More than one person turned when Firian entered. Tanyu rarely participated in parties like this even though many Masters technically lived in town. The Academy stayed insulated. Still, one or two others in black stood out like blotches on a colorful canvas. Rian was the only one Firian recognized. Not surprising.

He was going with Maya now, so she was probably nearby. The idea should have aroused more jealousy than the tiny twist of his stomach, but it was curbed by the possibility that he could soon be with Kiria. Kiria outshone Maya in every way except availability.

Bard waved to catch his attention. Firian held up a hand at him before ordering at the counter. A man in garish red face paint made way for him, colliding into a pale woman with fuzzy-edged tattoos wiping down tables. The smudgy quality of her hair and the listless awareness of her gaze announced she was a former Sentry.

Firian flicked one token onto the counter and Hyrum shoved an ale over to him.

Before going to sit, Firian spun back. Bard wouldn't say that Firian owed him anything for helping with the war. Still, why not? "Another," he said, holding up payment. Raewhith's tribute coins were fresh in his pocket. "And a sticky bun."

Hyrum's glare darkened. "Old Danior's got those. None here."

"Just the extra ale, then." Hyrum obliged and Firian brought both mugs to Bard, who beamed at the sight.

"Thanks, Fir!" he said, taking the brimming flagon. His nose stopped just above the foam as he smelled it. "I forgot all about the planting festival."

Firian slid into the seat opposite, facing the rest of the room. "Me too."

"Why don't you bring the guard with you when you go out now?" Bard's black eyes flitted to the iron crown.

Honestly, it hadn't occurred to him. He'd always taken care of himself. He shrugged off the question just as he used to.

"Maybe you should," Bard continued. "You're... more important now." A shadow fell across his face, almost his whole body, as he said the words.

Firian tipped his chin. It wasn't a terrible idea, but losing his autonomy sounded stifling. Autonomy was one of the reasons he became the Head in the first place. But power had its cost. He couldn't forget what he had done to get here, and that others could do the same. "Maybe," he conceded.

"Did you get the name?"

"Yes, I did." He leaned back luxuriously and took a deep draught while Bard waited.

Bard gestured with his ale, barely moving away from his face as though anxious to keep it close. "There was no need to do this."

"It's fine."

"So, did you ask the Keeper?"

"Right. Who else?"

"So? Who is it?"

"His name is Tibor Wat." He pronounced the odd name carefully.

Bard smacked his lips meditatively, casting his eyes to the ceiling.

Firian felt eyes on him and looked up to see Devanie, the herbalist, her hair done up in braids around her head. She touched her yellow scarf suggestively as she eyed him. He raised an eyebrow. Tánuil's planting festival went until sunrise the next morning, with dancing and coupling and feasting and general abandon. Later, maybe.

He turned his attention back to Bard, who said, after a pause, "I'll start right away. Tonight I'll find him." He gave a quick succession of nods as though agreeing with himself.

Firian grinned, something he'd done a lot lately. "That's great. Let me know." An odd sensation gripped him that here was something easy and good. Two people walking in the same direction.

"I will." Bard brought his voice down. "Do you know *katah*?"

Kiria and their accidental connection didn't count. Most Tanyu saw an unintentional *katah* as weakness. "I never took Gerand's class."

"I know, but can you do it?"

Could he connect to another person so completely that their lives intertwined, that he gained the ability to kill the other or be killed because of all the reality between them? Could he practically read the other's mind and emotions? "Maybe," he answered.

"I bet you could." When Bard sipped again, a little foam got on his lip, sticking to the shadow of facial hair covering his jaw.

"Probably. I'm sure if I tried." The gravity of his order struck him. "Find out if the general has more Talent than they normally do. Be careful."

"I'll just get information. No worries, yeah?" Bard hated war. If his ability to beat Firian at Indisfate was any indication, he could handle strategy or tactics, but he wouldn't kill.

"Okay, good."

"When are the soldiers from Raewhith coming?"

"Three days."

"And then Torith?"

"I'll organize with Kiria. A few weeks, probably." Firian downed the rest of his ale.

"A few weeks," Bard repeated. "Okay. I'll get it done." He reached out, grasping his hand in a promise.

Firian's mouth quirked. This was just what he needed. His best friend was on his side again.

6

FIRIAN

THE NEXT DAY wore away as swiftly as fire burnt paper. Two more days until the volunteer troops from Raewhith arrived and he had to plan the Torithian attack in earnest.

Belik stood before Firian in the Head's office, rubbing one hand over his rough chin. "Bard is going to declare *katah* on the Torithian captain?" He asked the question in a slow, thoughtful way. Digesting, perhaps criticizing. His eyes, narrowed behind his glasses, offered little clue.

"He has the skill to do it," Firian said.

"I know he does."

Firian sat back in his chair. He could still smell Devanie's musky perfume on himself. In the new daylight, the smell bothered him, as though he had done something wrong. But that couldn't be. At least Devanie wouldn't say so.

Belik, despite his bad leg, continued to stand. The old feeling that the Master held power over him because of his secrets, his decades of knowledge, crawled over him. It was time to take some of that power back. "You used to be the lead strategist," he said. It wasn't a question. Belik had dropped enough hints about his past that it was almost certainly true.

Belik didn't deny it, but shifted, waiting for the point.

"I'm going to reinstate you to that position. I need to know what you know." As much as he hated to admit it, Belik had far more experience than he did, and he needed support if this new mission was going to succeed. It had to succeed.

Apparently unsurprised, Belik eased himself into the chair across from Firian. The movement meant agreement. "What do you want to know?"

"How many fighters can we spare for the Torithian War? How many Tanyu do we have, including those on mission?"

Belik raised his eyebrows. "You think I know about everyone on mission?"

"Don't you?" It was a challenge. A man like Belik wouldn't abandon his job of knowing everything, only the title.

Belik pursed his lips with amusement. "Yes. We have about three hundred battle-ready Tanyu here, if you send them all."

"And abroad?"

"Almost two thousand."

Firian leaned forward, his brows lowering. "*Two thousand*?" That wasn't possible. Memories of Belik's lies came back to him like poison and Firian's hand became a fist on the table. The small white scars stood out in relief. "Don't lie to me."

"I wouldn't," Belik replied easily. "The others are on mission or embedded strategically across the Western Kingdom and beyond it. Remember the man in Carradoc?"

The one who had told him to keep Kiria hostage. Yes, he remembered. "Where are these people?"

"Everywhere. Tanyu have infiltrated even closed societies in case we need someone on the inside. The movement started just before my time."

"So they're all older."

"Most of them."

He thought of how young the Tanyu in the Academy tended

to be, apart from the teaching Masters. Had all the rest gone on missions? "Do we have someone with the Torithians?" Since the group was more of a pirate organization than a race or country, it was unlikely.

"Yes, there's one man."

Firian's face flushed hot. "Who? Why didn't you tell me before?"

"You were so smitten with that Kepress and so angry at me that I thought it better to keep it to myself. What good could that information have done you?"

"You don't get to decide—"

"*Now* I don't. Now you're the Tanyuin Head. And never forget who helped you get there. I'm on your side, Firian." Belik held his gaze long enough that Firian felt seen, man to man. The recognition made his stomach crawl—did he want others to see him this intimately?—but he saw Belik's humanity too. Another person sat before him, not an obstacle or a book of answers.

Firian's fist relaxed.

Belik resettled his glasses on his nose, a soothingly familiar gesture.

"So, how many can we spare?" Firian asked.

"I wouldn't send more than half. You announced our location to Brithnem, so they have every opportunity now to attack the Academy if they want to."

With Kiria on his side, he hadn't given the idea a spare thought. Other cities or nations might come to test their strength or steal their stores of tribute, but not Brithnem. "I told you I ended the war."

Belik's voice was carefully steady. "Still, you need a standing army here, as you said before."

To the Tanyuin Head. Those were some of Firian's last words to Sias Jairon before smothering him in his bed.

"Half," Firian repeated. "I'm not going to pull everyone from their stations around the world for this. They need to stay in case I need them. So I only have a hundred and fifty? That's not many."

"Not for an ordinary army." One side Belik's mouth rose in a smile. "But these are Tanyu. You know what we can do. A soldier is a rainstorm. We are hurricanes."

7

KIRIA

Kiria stared at the map, at the pieces on it, and tried to remember every detail, to make everything as realistic as possible. The edge had been folded accidentally when Daelon carried it from the room in the Amiran Academy into the palace. She added a triangular crease. The trees of Á Quihilmar were a tiny bit smudged from the oil in people's fingertips. A couple of the colored pieces representing troops had spider fractures through the wood. She smiled. Even the arena hadn't been this precise. She didn't need to go to the Tanyuin Academy to practice her Talent in the Unreal. She could smell, just faintly, the wooden table on which the map lay.

That's it. That's as close as I can make it. So far.

She traced the route her coronation tour would take through the Kingdom when this conflict was over. As it was, she couldn't afford the luxury. Now was the time for planning and for war.

Firian's dark form, wearing black as ever, materialized beside her. Right on time. Had he meant to appear so close to her? She stepped sideways to make room for him to admire her work.

It still felt odd offering him information, but he had kept his word. The scouts had all returned safely, and there was a new marking on the map for the Tanyuin Academy. If he was willing to risk the location to a former enemy to prove his loyalty, and then offer help in the Torithian War, who was she to doubt him? After a little more convincing, even her mother reluctantly agreed that this was the best way to end the war and bring peace to the Western Kingdom. Kiria longed to be able to say that they had achieved peace, and that she had helped orchestrate it.

Politically, she would work with the Tanyu. Personally, she would stay wary around Firian.

He cast a quick look at her and then gazed at the map. His dark brows shadowed his sharp eyes as he ran them over the cities, rivers, ocean, troops. He briefly scrutinized her work before turning to her, his closed lips pursed in a smile. "This is good work."

"Since we need to talk about precise strategy, I knew it had to be correct," she said, not sure how else to take the compliment.

"No, I mean, you've been practicing, haven't you?" His head fell a little to one side as he looked at her, a cross between an amused puppy and a man conducting an experiment.

"Well, of course," she said, squaring herself toward the map. "I mean, you know it's better to hone your abilities if you have them..." He had said something very much to that effect when they were alone in the wilderness.

He hummed, obviously pleased. Turning to the map as well, he somehow had closed the distance between them again. Their arms nearly touched.

She reached hers out of range as she pointed to the Tanyuin Academy on the map, beyond the northern mountain range of Charúnin Thôr. It would take the Tanyu several days at least to reach a sea port. "How many troops do you have to offer?" she asked, all business.

"One hundred seventy."

She whirled on him. "That's it? That's nothing!" She blinked as she realized he might be insulted by her tone. Regardless, one hundred seventy was a measly number. Her gut sank at the thought of it. Endrians disappeared almost daily, soldiers, trade ships... All were in continued jeopardy if they didn't succeed. The two of them knew firsthand how ruthless the Torithians could be. They bore the scars.

Maybe she never should have trusted Firian. That seemed to be a common theme.

"Nothing?" he asked gently, meeting her gaze. "These aren't ordinary soldiers."

She looked over his face, searching for the truth behind the arrogance. Searching for the lie that she could call him out on. She felt her pulse beating as she stared at him—his dark hair falling over his forehead, his blue eyes, his lips, his jaw... She clenched her teeth. "Our soldiers are excellently trained," she snapped. "How are the Tanyu so much better?"

The lines in his face softened. He was sure of his answer. This was his life, his anthem. His eyes glowed as they did when he first appeared in that iron crown. "We see everything. We see the body"—his eyes flickered over her plain form—"but we also see the mind. We see the whole person... and we see the whole world. There are possibilities all around us. Every window is a door. Every object can be a weapon or a shield. We can do more, endure more. We are the ones that can bring justice and peace. That's why so many people still revere the name, our name. And that's why I'm proud to be a Tanyu."

Her shallow breath matched his. That level of intelligent warfare on behalf of justice and peace—the idea swam like liquor, intoxicating her mind.

An uncomfortable clinging sensation left her feeling that she was being dragged toward him. The heat from his body welcomed her.

She planted her feet in the carpet, felt the fibers rise up

around her embroidered pointed shoes. "We'll see." She cleared her throat. She had no time for these destructive thoughts. Without fully trusting him, she couldn't entertain foolish ideas. "So you only have one hundred seventy troops." She rolled her fingers together and a new piece appeared between them. She placed it on the tiny Academy with a click. "Your friend Bard will gather information from the captain. I suggest that you set off either from here or here." She pointed to two ports along the western coast, Redshore and Enderin. "Ships can transport you from either location. We'll take care of that. Your job will be to locate the top men on the island and eliminate their leadership. You know, they're basically pirates. All men. Just a group that stays together because they can terrorize resources out of others. Without leadership, they'll continue to pillage, but, if they don't have a strategy, we can stop them one by one if we have to. And you can take those who resist as prisoners of war, per our agreement."

"Where are they on the island?" Firian leaned forward as he studied the map. Torith was a large, misshapen island almost directly west of Brithnem over the Kheltor Ocean.

She drew her nail gently over the southeastern area of the island. "Right there. It's a fortress."

He turned to her. "Bard can get us the interior layout if you need it."

"How long will that take?"

Firian paused. "I'll let you know when he has it. Where are your troops now?"

"We have quite a few stationed in Enderin." She touched the top of one of the wooden pieces. "To—"

"—protect the citizens," he finished.

She nodded, glad he saw the necessity of that. "Right."

"What about the others?"

"We have some ready to move on the western side of the

island. The residents have been gracious enough to let us move into their villages. They don't want the Torithians either." Kiria realized it was a shame that everyone called these murderers Torithians as though they belonged on the island, when the real islanders had been terrorized for a decade.

"So why haven't you attacked the east side already?" Firian tapped one finger on the pirates' base.

"We have. Obviously we have. We've been at war for years."

"And?"

"And their base is too heavily fortified. We just end up sacrificing lives. We need a more surgical approach."

Firian lifted his chin in acknowledgement. The Tanyu were the surgeons. He inhaled deeply. "It seems like a simple plan."

"Sometimes simple is best."

"Sometimes it's predictable. How do you know they won't see us coming?"

She was almost glad he didn't agree with everything she said. She had started to get the sense that he would pretend to agree just to draw her in. Now he was acting as any other ally would. "No one outside the palace and the Academy knows that we're working together now. The Tanyu will be a complete surprise."

He smiled and so did she. "Perfect," he said. "Make sure it stays that way. I haven't informed anyone from Raewhith."

"Raewhith?" That was the little town Firian came from. Why would he mention it?

"They're sending soldiers to assist."

"Then how could they not know about this alliance?"

"I offered them a chance to exchange soldiers for safety. It was a general offer. Everyone there wants to be a Tanyu but very few get the chance, so now they can fight on our behalf—whatever battle we see fit."

She peered up at him. The Tanyu had taken over Raewhith,

a small conquest, but something about it felt off. "Will any of them go with you to Torith?"

"A few. The majority will be Tanyuin warriors. Don't worry."

She wanted to defend her soldiers who had risked their lives for years to accomplish peace. They were well trained, maybe not to the obsessive level of the Tanyu, but they deserved respect. Firian's confidence suggested he underestimated them. "Our men are spread too thin. Their priority is protecting the civilians."

"There's no need to explain. They have their job. We have ours."

One hand on the map, she faced him. The colors were more saturated here. The black of his clothing was deeper than in real life, his eyes bluer. Maybe her hair looked less mousy here than it did when she was plain in real life. She had still never intentionally shown him her Ability when they were alone. But maybe, to him, she was beautiful, even when she was herself. Without Original Beauty.

Their business mostly done, they stood in silence for a moment, neither making a move to leave in case the other had something to say. She tried out a couple of lines in her mind: *We'll meet again once you have more news. I'll watch to see what kind of leader you become. How did you become the next Head? Why are you helping us?* None of them made it into the air. Part of her knew that she wouldn't want to hear the answers.

"Do you want to float?" Firian's voice took her back to the present.

"What?"

"You said when we were traveling that you wanted me to show you." His boots left the carpet and he levitated easily, almost insolently, a hand's-breadth above the ground. His long black coat flowed around his legs in a phantom breeze.

She chewed the inside of her lip. Yes, she did want to learn. But she didn't want to get too familiar with Firian again.

He held out a hand. He was already taller than she was by a head. Now, floating, he towered over her. He beckoned with his fingers, flicking them open and closed over his palm. Those little white scars, small details, crisscrossed his rough hand.

Stifling a smile, she lifted her chin, avoiding his hand. "How do you do that?"

He touched down on the carpet again, light as air. The look he gave her, that knowing, teacher look, reminded her strongly of their time in the mountains. She could almost smell the piney air. Almost as though things were normal again. As though her history with the Tanyu weren't as rocky or as heartbreaking.

"Is this real?" he asked.

"No," she said automatically.

"Are you sure?"

"Yes."

"Then you can manipulate what you see. Change the background." He brushed his fingertips over the map. A small compliment.

"Okay." At her thought, the little room melted away—the map, the table, all gone—and a wooded clearing appeared in its place. She had seen something like it in Á Quihilmar outside Brithnem. Sunlight bathed the tips of the yellow-green grass. Seeds or insects floated like dust in the streaming light. Around the meadow stood tall trees, not pines but tulip poplars.

"You've gotten better." Genuine pride edged his voice. "So you can change where we are. You can also change yourself."

She seized up, a rock forming in her stomach.

"You know that," he continued, one side of his mouth lifting. "You can change where you are, what you look like. Even size is no barrier at all. You always envision settings in the correct dimensions." He gestured to the air and glanced up. "Let me."

The meadow fell away so quickly that Kiria got dizzy and almost collapsed. It became the size of a soft rug below her. The trees came only to her knees. She felt the urge to crouch. In the clouds she was too visible, too vulnerable. She softened her knees, but fought the feeling enough to stay upright.

"See?" he said, standing as he would in any other space.

With a crush of gravity, the ground rushed up to meet her again and she found herself in the same clearing as before. Slightly nauseated, she nodded.

"Levitating is a bit easier."

Once again he approached her, hands outstretched. This time she took them. The sudden changes had made her knees watery, and she couldn't risk falling over.

Soft but firm, he closed his fingers over hers. "Just let it happen," he said, rising from the ground.

She stayed resolutely earthbound. She had to raise her arms to keep hold of Firian.

"Let go," he said. "Come with me."

Still nothing.

"Close your eyes and open them again."

She ran her tongue over her teeth, bristling at his commands. But she wanted to learn this aspect of the Unreal, even if it was from him. She shut her eyes barely longer than a blink. When she looked around, she was floating with him.

"That's it, that's it!" he said with a real smile.

She squeezed his hands reflexively, afraid to fall. "How are you doing it?"

"Anything you can picture, you can do. Remember that the same rules don't hold you back in the Unreal."

A place with no rules. What a frightening, intoxicating thought! A thrill ran through her. He seemed to sense her thoughts, that they ran to more than physical laws.

She waved her feet. "So I could become invisible or glow or anything I want?"

"Anything you want."

"Let me try it myself." She untangled her fingers from his and floated backward, the air like a water current waiting for her command. She picked up speed, rushing around the clearing near the tree line. Her dress and hair whipped in front of her. When she stopped in front of Firian, her arms tingled with the rush of wind. He waited for her, standing on the grass. She checked her hands to make sure she hadn't changed. Windblown and happy, she grinned at him. "Thank you."

His eyes softened. She'd seen that look before when they were traveling and he said he could protect her dreams. She'd believed him then. He paused a beat too long before answering. "Any time."

She swallowed, dismissing the invitation in his eyes. She hated to admit it, but being with him validated all she had worked for. Plus, they met in the Unreal with its heady freedom. It (and he) reminded her about what set her apart, what made her uniquely suited to rule. And no one could reach them here. That edge of danger, as long as she went with a purpose, thrilled her.

"I need to talk to you about one more thing," she said.

He raised his eyebrows, cuing her to go on.

"If we're going to be allies, you need to send someone to Brithnem to swear loyalty on your behalf."

He clasped his hands behind his back in a thoughtful posture, digesting her words for a few seconds before replying. "I see."

"Since our troops are scheduled to leave soon, you should send someone immediately."

He looked back up at her. "Anyone you would prefer?"

"No," she said, meeting his gaze defiantly. She paused a

moment too long as well. Gathering herself, she explained, "Obviously someone loyal to you and to our cause, as I assume they all are." She assumed no such thing, but Firian seemed to be able to keep the Tanyu in check, so she wanted to promote the best in them.

"If I came, would you pledge your loyalty to the Tanyu as well?"

The question struck her in the gut.

The Tanyu had to prove themselves to her first. She owed them nothing until the war was won.

For a moment she squirmed, hating that he would probably read her hesitation as indecision. He drummed his fingers against his leg as he waited for her response. He wore a dark ring with a red stone that he hadn't had when they left Brithnem together a few months ago. Maybe it was only for Masters, or just for the Tanyuin Head. A position he had gotten suddenly, too suddenly. Under those circumstances, she couldn't pledge loyalty to the Tanyu, even if Firian came himself. Hopefully that decision wouldn't jeopardize their tenuous alliance.

She shook her head. "No. Not until the war is won."

He stopped tapping his fingers and nodded slowly. "I would do the same thing."

She had never thought of their leadership styles as similar. "Then you understand. Let me know who you plan to send."

Firian would probably not come himself. The journey might put him in danger with people who held a grudge against the Tanyu for the all-too-recent war. Surely, he would rather stay at the Academy where he could rule in safety. The way he talked indicated that he was planning to go to Torith with the troops, though. Who would he put in charge in his absence?

"I'll come, and sail to Torith from your port."

What? She knit her brows. Part of her was relieved that she would know who they were dealing with, but another part seized up with anxious energy. She hadn't seen him in person since she was a hostage. Things between them were just starting to go back to the way they had been at their best. "Are you sure?"

A smile pulled on one side of his mouth. "Yeah."

He wasn't coming to swear loyalty. He was coming to see her.

Well, if that were the case, she would just surround herself with guards and advisors, and not allow them to be alone. He was too unpredictable, and, if she were honest with herself, she was too unpredictable around him. But she still needed his help. The Torithian conflict had worn Kingdom soldiers thin, so it was time they ended this war.

She raised her chin. "Good. I hope you can leave immediately."

8

———

FIRIAN

Firian lost no time. Taking a horse and some provisions, he set out the next day. Only when he got closer did he consider that maybe Bard was right when he said it was stupid for him to go by himself.

But what better person to travel alone from the Academy to the capital? If Firian had brought someone else, they only would have slowed him down. Alone, he could make the journey in almost half the time it took him and Kiria to do it.

On his way, he'd received news from the Tanyu stationed in Raewhith to check on his father. No visible signs of abuse. The report couldn't be true, or maybe it just didn't matter if it were. His father had collected enough sins already in the past without new ones added on. On nights when Firian couldn't sleep, he'd haunt his father's dreams, dropping him from a height or chasing him as a mountain ghost. Once, he transformed into the sea creature that had terrified Shiro during their hall test.

Firian's sweating horse bobbed from a canter to a trot just as the familiar sight of Brithnem shone through the trees. The sun gleamed on the ocean he would cross tomorrow, almost too bright to look at, silver and burning. He gathered the reins in one hand and slowed the mare to a walk. He had pushed her hard that day. Now that he could see the city walls, he felt less anxious to hurry.

Kiria's warm presence lingered there in the palace, like drink or strong perfume. He didn't submerge himself fully in the Unreal, but he touched her mind lightly, reaching out almost as though he were brushing her with his fingertips. Just a few more minutes.

He crossed the fields and farmhouses of the outer edge, getting closer to the wall. At the familiar scenario of the guards about to challenge him, he bristled. Maybe he should have taken Jovan, in case the soldiers gave him any trouble. The Master often bragged about being the Charäkhni king's personal bodyguard before he became a trainer. He resented Firian's leadership, though. He could see it in his eyes every time he looked at him. As though he deserved to be the Head. But Firian, not Jovan, had smothered the life from Sias Jairon, giving up a portion of his humanity to lead the Tanyu toward a better future. No, it was better that he go alone.

He sat tall, kingly, upon his horse as he rode toward the Abrecan Gate. Ten soldiers flanked its towering doors adorned with elaborate metal designs, only a few more than was needed to get the doors open or closed.

A guard with a square face, almost like Belik's, stepped forward, hand on his sword hilt. "State your business with Brithnem." Exactly the same greeting as before.

"My name is Firian Kess. I'm the Tanyuin Head. Your Keepers are expecting me."

A second guard came forward to whisper in the ear of the first, then stepped back to his original position. "You come alone?" said the first guard.

Firian's throat tightened just a little. He was a fool not to bring another Tanyu, after the Academy's dangerous recent history with the Kingdom. "As you see."

Unbidden, the memory of blood running down his hands thrust him back to a month ago. Master Jairon's guard had had no clue that Firian would murder him. And Firian had had no clue that he would murder the guard until seconds before. The idea that he could not know in the morning who he would kill in the evening made him feel dizzy and sick. The power gave him an unhealthy vigor, like metal in his veins, but the thought nauseated him.

More whispering and finally they began to open the ponderous double gate for him. "Very well. You may enter."

Firian swept his black coat back over the horse's flank as he rode through so he would have easier access to his boot. He'd only brought the same two weapons he'd carried on the trip with Kiria—one small knife and one large. He needed to be able to reach both of them. Just in case.

The dusty smell of the city wafted through the air, a clear change from the fresh Gray Forest from which he had come.

As he entered, a stable boy took his mare, leaving him to go the rest of the way on foot. Two grim sentinels flanked Firian on either side and he had the odd sensation of being a prisoner. How could he incapacitate the two of them if he needed to? The guards wore armor, but their heads were exposed. Moisture glinted in their eyes. Yes, if he had to, he could take care of a couple guards.

They followed stone streets leading up to the palace. Banners flowed on its battlements, tiny and dark in the distance against the bright sky.

One woman they passed seemed familiar. She could be no more than thirty, with dark hair tied up in a kerchief. Her lively eyes glared as though she could murder him with the force of her hatred. Then he remembered. The wife of the bearded man he had been ordered to kill in his sleep. He hadn't actually hurt the man, though he could have, choosing instead to defy orders. She didn't know to be grateful for his restraint. Maybe someone else had finished the job.

She wasn't the only one radiating anger. From an upper window, a large man watched him as a hawk would watch a snake.

Something struck his shoulder blade hard. Hot fury rushed through his bones as another object hit the back of his calf. "Tanyu! Tanyu!" cried children's voices. "Get out of here!"

The guards on either side of him didn't react except to wave a languid hand in the children's direction, shooing them away. It hurt to keep walking in measured strides rather than respond. The children must have thought he was a prisoner, or else they wouldn't dare throw stones at him. The guards could treat him like a prisoner now, if they wished. After he helped them win the war, he could parade through the streets and they'd treat him like the king he was.

With the deliberation of a predator, Firian turned his head to look at the children out of the corner of his eye, and left them alone.

Like last time, the sun was setting by the time they reached the enormous castle. His gaze traced the stone walls up to the battlements. How many times he had seen this place in the Unreal? Reality made it simultaneously bigger and smaller—bigger because it was undeniably, unshakably in front of him, and smaller because the colors were muted and it would never be more than what it was right now.

Unlike last time, they led him not to a side door, but up a private stone-paved road up the lawn to the front entrance. Children played and families picnicked on the grass, keeping a respectful distance from the castle. The space seemed meant as a public park. It was strange to see such a grand place open to the entire community. Gardeners tended flowers and hedges that became more elaborate the closer they grew to the palace. The smell of grass and sea filled the air.

Magnificent double doors, three times the height of a man, fluted with statues and script, were flanked by enormous blue flags. Guards opened the doors in unison. Firian stepped ahead of his conductors just for the joy of going in first. His blood hummed in anticipation.

A high-roofed gallery lined with potted trees and finery led down one of the wings. Through his roiling thoughts, he still paid meticulous attention to the layout of the palace as the guards took him around corners to return to his quarters. He knew where Kiria slept and his room was far from it. *No surprise.*

It didn't take long to reach their destination. "You may clean up in time to meet the Keepers at full sundown," said a guard who reached to open the door for him, his metal armor oddly silent. "These are your quarters, Master Kess. I hope they are to your satisfaction."

They weren't. But it didn't matter. There were some good elements. Its size, for instance, fit his importance as the Tanyuin Head. This had to be the largest state room in the palace. A gigantic four-poster bed laid with pillows and dark purple silks dominated one side of the room. Opposite was a fireplace, already lit. Tapestries fell from two walls, depicting scenes from Brithnem's history, including the coronation of Cúron. The image showed a much younger man, brown haired, but with the same distinctive beard and commanding eye. *This must be his wing of the castle.*

Lush rugs covered the floor and a marble step led down to the washroom. A claw-footed tub, almost large enough for two people, was just visible through the arched opening. With the washroom attached, Firian had no reason to leave the room and go roaming through the palace. Probably part of the reason they gave him something so nice. No doubt guards came with this arrangement.

He never would have chosen these furnishings for himself, but he found himself seduced by what they represented. Wealth and power. To one who could offer a guest something so magnificent, the world bowed.

"This will do."

FRESHLY WASHED, Firian resettled his crown on his head. The motion reminded him of Belik and his tic of fixing the glasses on his nose. He had nothing to worry about with Belik in charge in his absence. They had the same vision for the Academy, the same drive to make it better with Firian's leadership.

A suit of fine clothes had been laid out in the mint-scented washroom for him, but he chose to wear his all-black outfit, though it was stained. The clothes made him feel like a Tanyu.

One glance out the window told him the guards would reappear any moment to take him to the Keepers. To Kiria. His head swam with the thought of it.

Before they could summon him, he stepped out of his sumptuous room to join the small group of guards outside. "Are the Keepers ready to see me?"

One of the guards, this one a woman whose skin was matted with freckles, nodded curtly. "Yes, Master Kess. We were just about to fetch you."

Something about the word *fetch* annoyed him, but he didn't respond. Instead, he walked quickly, not waiting for the guards to lead him. He knew where he was going. If the Keepers weren't going to meet him in the Main, then they didn't know the importance of the man they were dealing with.

Sure enough, more guards stood on either side of the

soaring wooden doors leading to the throne room where the Keepers held their audience. Scenes of the Kingdom's history were carved in relief on the huge slabs.

He recognized most of the figures from the Scroll. He had partially memorized the rare copy he had back at the Academy.

"Wait here, Master Kess," said the freckled guard as she went in to announce him. The name "Master Firian Kess, Head of the Tanyuin Academy" reverberated through the room beyond.

He fought the urge to clasp his hands victoriously as he passed through the massive doors and into the Main, with its soaring ceiling that rose even higher than the one in the fountain courtyard. His bootsteps echoed through the room, empty save for the Keepers, their advisors, and a coterie of guards lining the walls.

One guard stood directly in front of a glass pane Firian recognized. He had removed it on his last visit when he had snuck the younger royals into the Main. Lantern light glistened on it now like a secret.

Though the enormous Main dwarfed him, every sound was magnified, every decision enhanced. There was an expansiveness to the power he felt here, and he wanted more of it. Now, he was the Head of the most powerful group of warriors in the world, but he had no kingdom.

All three Keepers of the Western Kingdom sat on their thrones on the raised dais in the middle of the room. At the foot of the steps leading up to the platform stood their Amiran advisors. Firian immediately recognized Parohim, Cúron's advisor, who had led him aimlessly through the streets on his first visit. The dark-skinned woman with short, rusty curls looked familiar as well. He had definitely seen her last time, but couldn't remember her name. She had the eye of a Tanyu, not an Amir—dark, piercing, and unafraid. And the third was a new face, standing below Atael's seat.

Crowns—bronze, silver, and gold—perched on each Keeper's head. Cúron wore flowing light blue robes edged in fur, which gave him an impressively regal aspect, especially since he was so much older than the other two Keepers. Atael wore a dark purple cape clasped around his neck, a bad idea for practical reasons.

He saw it all in a blink.

Once he saw Kiria, his attention for anything else melted away.

A sound as though he were clearing his throat ripped out of him. Very little could make him stop dead in his tracks, but the sight of her Beauty almost did. He willed his legs to move forward, toward the center throne where she sat. His heart hammered in his chest and dry throat. It hurt to look at her.

He wanted to stop time, to linger and memorize her. Every line was perfect, suggesting the Kiria he knew, but elevating her to a goddess. She looked back at him, her piercing gaze showing no apprehension or hint of changing back.

Those lips seemed made for truth and justice. He'd believe anything that came out of them. Any word—any kiss—would be fierce and right.

Golden brown hair twisted up around her crown as though that symbol of authority were rooted to her head. The crown only confirmed she was a queen; it didn't make her one. Light blue gems edged in gold dangled from her ears, matching the blue of her dress. Its wide neckline revealed her collarbone and the tip of her royal tattoo, just visible on her shoulders. The gown gathered around her bust and flowed down over her knees, sexy but not self-consciously so. Anything she wore would have highlighted her body, whether she intended it or not.

There was something primal but pure in her bearing, like a

queen from a story, or how he had imagined the great heroes to be before he met them and found out they were flawed.

Power and Beauty. He fought to keep his breathing even. She was everything he wanted.

When he reached the foot of the dais, he stopped and dipped his head to her. His stomach knotted and re-knotted.

"Thank you for joining us, Master Kess," someone said.

He flicked his gaze to see it was Cúron, whose expression wavered from magnanimity to suspicion.

"I understand that you are here to swear your loyalty to the Western Kingdom."

Coming from him, looking down from his high seat, the words chafed unexpectedly.

"My Keepers," Firian said, "now that the war between us is over, we can benefit each other." The heat from Kiria's gaze made it difficult to focus on anything else. Speaking was difficult, but her attention elevated his words. For a moment he'd been afraid that his words would sound small next to her, but they didn't. "The Tanyu have a long history with the Western Kingdom, and this is just the next step."

"Before you proceed," Cúron again, "Parohim will speak of that history. For without God, our efforts fail."

Kiria and Atael both bowed their heads slightly in agreement. Firian already guessed which part of the Scroll the advisor would recite. The Amir were so predictable. But Kiria's reverence cast a seriousness over the words that made him listen, as though he would find answers there.

From memory, Amir Parohim began. It was a lengthy section, passed among the advisors like a long-practiced chant. They spoke of the Exmorei, of the defense of the Khelê, of the sacred responsibility to God. The words, half-remembered, kept Firian's mind occupied as a game would, with just enough mental stimulation to keep him from becoming agitated.

"Therefore," spoke a musical voice, Kiria's voice, after the passage was complete, "what do you swear?"

He'd waited for that voice, familiar yet transformed by Beauty as her body had been. She gazed down at him from her throne, the delicate points of her crown adorning that head he wanted to take in his hands.

The tall, dark woman stepped in. "You will kneel before the thrones as you pledge your allegiance."

He set his jaw hard. Kiria should have been the one to say those words. He had known this moment was coming, but kneeling before anyone went against his nature. Soon, he would win the war in Torith, win more troops, win Kiria. To do that, he had to kneel. *This is just a step toward more power, not less.* Still, it took him a moment to convince himself to bend. The Tanyuin Head should bow to no one.

He stared at Kiria, at that Beauty that went beyond the bounds of the world. That woman, that ruler, would soon be his. He wouldn't bow to Cúron, and still less to Atael. But he could make himself do it for her. If their positions were reversed, how much this would make him want her...

His long black coat spread out over the floor as he went down on one knee, never taking his eyes off her. She remained impassive, but he suspected she enjoyed the sight.

"Master Kess." It was Atael this time. Atael, who was always out of his depth. "You will repeat the words of the oath."

Parohim spoke again, pronouncing the words of the pledge. Firian repeated, and kept his eyes fixed on the center throne.

"I swear to serve my country, the Western Kingdom... to the best of my ability, regardless of danger... and should I betray her, may the punishment be death."

The brief ceremony over, he rose to his feet. A greater ease filled the room now that he had pledged his oath. Now there was nothing left but business.

Firian spoke first. "I will sail to Torith in the morning with your troops. Tonight I'll inform the Academy that they should leave too. When we return"—Kiria met his gaze—"we will earn your allegiance as well."

Her eyes brightened. Did he imagine it? "Do so," she said, a smile playing on her mouth.

His chest rose and fell with a deep and satisfied breath.

Cúron dipped his head courteously, not agreeing with Firian's words, but rather closing the meeting. "The guards will show you back to your room, Master Kess," he said. "The ships will be made ready for a dawn departure."

Firian cracked his knuckles. This dismissal felt too familiar. His whole life had been about proving himself, and now he had to do it again. At least he knew how.

He allowed himself to be led away. Boots tapping the mosaic floor, he wondered if they all knew where he was about to stay the night. Even now, Kiria's consciousness hovered on the edge of his mind like the buzz of a Sentry, but kinder and more familiar.

Evening light glinted on the polished floors of the Main, the refined atmosphere of the place almost condescending. Well, there was external luxury, and there was internal strength. He knew which he preferred.

The ponderous door swung after him as he left, Kiria's presence still coloring all he thought or saw. He almost shook his head. He wanted her. There was no doubt about that—her beauty, her warmth, the way she saw him and didn't look away —but his feelings couldn't outstrip hers. She had to come to him. They already had an unintentional *katah*, something that Tanyu viewed as weakness. Though she tempted him to trust her, to fall hard, he had to keep the upper hand to maintain control. He had already resolved: if she didn't show that she cared for him, then he hadn't won.

Sometimes he felt as though he were looking down from a height, staring at the view, longing for it, but then he would waver, just the slightest muscle spasm, and he'd realize how close he'd gotten to the edge. The same feeling had overtaken him in Shifra. That same vulnerability, of falling. No. He couldn't let her have so much power over him.

Once inside, he stripped off his jacket and threw it on the bed. Huffing a breath, he dragged his fingers through his hair. Something hard, metal, hit his hand. His crown. He threw it beside the coat.

Needing to flex his own power a bit after dwelling under the authority of somebody else's, he sank into the Unreal—just the First Level, no need to strain himself. He had told Belik to be ready to report at sundown.

In a few moments, his old mentor appeared. Belik's jaw twitched. Maybe he had to remember to change his greeting. "Master Kess."

"How is construction at the Academy?"

With the influx of new soldiers to be trained in the Tanyuin fashion, and the imminent return of more after their battle against the Torithians, Firian had planned to build a barracks and training facility in Tánuil.

"It's coming along." Something odd, distracted, flitted across his face.

"What?"

"Tiev got Lost in the Unreal again."

Firian gritted his teeth. "But there's no war!" Tiev was always a liability. He'd gotten Lost a few months ago too.

"He might have wanted it this time. I went in once to get him. Wouldn't come out."

"How long?"

"Four days. The Head is the one with the final word."

Keep him alive or let him die. Firian felt oddly stoic about the decision. Tiev was always a gory pain, and hurt him even in his lowest moments, but he hadn't made life easy for Tiev either. He worried the inside of his lip. "Do whatever Bard says."

Belik scoffed. The sound made Firian flush hot with anger. "You're leaving the decision to him? He's not even a Master."

"He will be once he gives us information on that captain," Firian bit back. "Just do whatever he thinks."

"You know what he thinks." The reply came almost too quickly.

Keep him alive. Firian drew his fingers into a fist. "Then try again. Don't let him die. We need all the Tanyu we have."

Belik grunted. "We need *more*, with your plan."

That was true, but first Firian needed to see how many Torithians he would be able to take back as prisoners of war. "By the time it would take anyone to mobilize against us, we'll have enough."

"We need more."

The repetition grated on him, as though he were a child again, listening to his teacher.

Belik must have sensed Firian's mood, because he changed the subject. "Have you seen the Keepers yet?" He only meant one, though he said the plural.

"I just came from the Main."

"And?"

"Everything went well."

"You vowed your loyalty? Something about death after betrayal?" He said it almost mockingly.

Firian sneered back, refusing to be mocked. "Yes. You know this alliance helps us. Or would you rather be at war?"

"I'd rather know you weren't following the whims of a certain princess." Something darkened in Belik's face. "Be careful, Firian. Don't let—"

"She doesn't control me."

Belik just tipped his chin. Apparently, Firian's protest had been enough to prove the point. The silence stretched thin. Coming from the quiet, Belik's next question sounded clear and loud, the low, almost raspy tenor of his voice filling the Unreal. "Are you seeing her tonight?"

Firian had thought about it. In fact, he'd started running through plans in his head. He simply hadn't considered those plans until now, like remembering a dream.

He didn't answer.

Belik continued. "Don't trust her. Working together doesn't mean she won't betray you. Just get what you can and get out."

He said it with such finality that looking back at his Master was like looking at a wall. "She won't betray us."

After a beat, he said, "You're young."

That old condescension filled Firian's body with lightning, anger coursing through his veins and muscles. He glared. "She won't betray us." He said each word more slowly this time.

Belik let out a humorless laugh. "Ha, but what about the others?" As though he had won a hand at cards, he removed his glasses and rubbed them with his shirt between his fingers.

Cúron. Atael. Only Cúron might have the balls to betray the Tanyuin Academy, and he seemed like someone who wanted to keep the populace happy. Taking that kind of risk might not be worth it to him. What could he gain?

A knock sounded at the door.

Without another word, Firian left Belik alone in the Unreal to discover a guard standing in his room. "Your pardon, Master Kess. The Second Keeper is here to see you."

9

KIRIA

Kiria watched the guards lead Firian toward the doors.

Hopefully he wasn't able to tell that her chest tightened when she saw him again after all this time. It felt as though they had just spoken—they had!—but seeing him in person was different. More shocking and emotional than she had anticipated. The last time they'd seen each other in person, he'd tied to her to a tree. And now...

She was on the throne and wielded power she didn't have last time. For appearances' sake, she stayed Beautiful. That was, after all, her royal face. To become less beautiful, to shrink to a lesser target for his gaze, would have been cowardly.

Seeing him again reminded her not only of the recent hostage trauma, but also of his greater moments. That pledge was one of them. Now that he ordered the Academy, things might be different. *He* might even be different. Honestly, she missed the better parts of their rocky relationship. He challenged her, in good and bad ways, it was true, but there was almost a game to his kind of challenge compared to the difficulty of ruling a kingdom. A piece of her fancied a taste. Or just an interaction, a question. That would be enough.

How did you get this power, Firian?

His answer would tell her if she could trust him. Or would at least give a better idea. Whether he inherited the position or took it by force, she had to know. If his answer wasn't what she hoped, then she would pray he could help them gain peace in Torith. Afterward, they would have almost no dealings with each other. The Kingdom would not pledge its loyalty to the Tanyu, as he wished. It was a foolish, radical request from an organization so small, no matter how influential or strong.

But it didn't surprise her that he'd asked.

That desire for control, for order, flooded even her own thoughts at times. The protesters at her first session came to mind. If everyone could just do as they should!

The door shut with a reverberating click.

Cúron shook his capacious sleeves up over his wrists. He turned to Kiria with a stormy face. "I'm glad that's over with," he said, rising from his throne. Atty did the same.

Frankly, Kiria was glad too. Her shoulders had felt tense all day and she longed to stretch them now that the meeting with Firian had passed. "He'll be a great asset in the war." She hoped that dispassionate summary would be enough to end this meeting, which had begun hours before Firian even arrived.

Cúron didn't reply to that, but his eyes narrowed enough to show his skepticism.

"Will he?" It was Atty who asked the question. The Amiran advisors stalled and shifted their weight, redirecting themselves from the exit back toward the Keepers, all now standing on the dais. None of them betrayed irritation, but she thought they must be tired of this topic. Amir were no fans of the Tanyu, but they had put up with her idea to have them help in the war. She suspected they all just wanted to go to bed.

Atty gave her a searching look. He, at least, must have noticed that Firian didn't take his eyes off her the whole time, as though he were swearing allegiance to her alone. In fact, anyone who didn't notice didn't belong in the Main. He hadn't tried to hide his infatuation.

"He's been very cooperative so far," she replied.

"He has to be cooperative." Cúron's voice boomed. "The Tanyu were never going to win their skirmish against us. We outnumber them a hundred to one. It's in his best interest to form this alliance."

A few of them nodded out of habit. It was almost impossible to disagree with him. His stature, his voice, his logic—all of it was more regal than Atael and, she suspected, herself.

"We can't take him for granted," she protested.

Chetana set her face in a hard frown. She would put up with Firian, but she wouldn't praise him for making what she would see as the obvious choice.

"Maybe *we* can't." Atty stepped off the platform like an angry child.

Abandoning decorum, she called after him. "Atty!" He had to know the target he painted on her with that remark.

Parohim drew his hands together in a request to speak. "Master Kess did seem more interested in one of you than the rest," he said carefully.

Kiria ground her teeth. *Obviously.* But was it that much of a surprise? They had gone through that ordeal together a few months ago, had gotten to know each other, and now she was his point of strategic contact in Brithnem. Of course he would pay her more attention. Didn't other dignitaries when she was Beautiful? Perhaps it was a silly reason to command the attention of a room, but her royal Beauty did draw the eye and sometimes the hearts of palace visitors. It put Brithnem in a wholesome, shimmering light.

Atty whirled around. His fur-lined cloak, much like Cúron's, flew around him. "I don't trust him. I don't like that he's staying in the palace. I say we put extra guards on him while he's here. Public opinion is against the Tanyu, so we can say it's for his safety." The *s*'s began to slur at the end of his declaration.

Cúron held up a hand. "I second that."

It wasn't a bad idea. She knew Firian's unpredictability well. He was a dangerous young man. Guards would help, but unless there were very many, they couldn't guarantee they could contain him. She raised her hand as well. Chetana and the other advisors followed suit.

"Unanimous!" Cúron said, striding down the steps. "We'll set up an extra guard right away. Then they will conduct him to the ship in the morning. Let him fend off these Torithian barbarians. Or die trying. Either way's our gain."

Strangely, she hadn't considered the possibility that Firian could die. Only that he would succeed. His confidence had made her confident. Her hands grew chilly at the idea. How could Cúron talk about him like that, as though he were just a pawn, or a tool to be used?

Coming abreast of Atty, Cúron turned to face her again, the only one left by the thrones. A different, new idea lived in the lines of his face. "If this works and we win the war, we'll have you to thank for coming up with this"—he laughed, a jovial sound—"this fool alliance!"

She put on what she hoped was a smooth smile. "Yes, you will," she said defiantly. *This will work, this will work...*

Cúron's large frame bustled across the floor, robe flowing. Atty walked beside him. The advisors' attention was still on Kiria, who hadn't moved. Realizing they were waiting on her, she hurried out.

Guards acknowledged her as she paced out of the Main, down the long hallways, toward her bedroom in the Second Keeper's wing. She had chosen to keep the second-best room, while her mother remained in the Keeper's suite. There was no need to move a couple spaces down.

Once alone with her girls, she paused. One look around the room confirmed that she wouldn't be able to rest until she had answers. Firian was here, actually here. This was the time to ask about anything that could get in the way of an alliance. Until now, she had tiptoed around some of the harder questions, reaching only for a peaceful interaction. And even that had made her feel daring.

She stretched and yawned, an excuse to close her eyes. Nothing. That was strange. She assumed he would be waiting in the Unreal. Had she misread him?

It didn't matter. She had to find out about his rise to power. Better to find out late than never.

"Candrae, Vayci." She drew herself up as they came forward. "Come with me."

The girls obeyed silently as she exited the room again and strode back to the First Keeper's wing. No one had told her where Firian was staying, but she had a good idea. Flanked by her girls, she headed quickly in the direction of the Main, trying to ignore the voice inside her that said that this was a bad idea—a dangerous, self-indulgent, irresponsible idea.

Guards. She slowed. There were extra guards posted outside Cúron's main guest suite. Lanterns glinted on their armor. That had to be it. With more confidence than she felt, she approached a man with a dark goatee. She had seen him many times before but couldn't remember his name. He lowered his head respectfully at her approach.

"I need to speak with Master Kess."

"I hope all is well, My Keeper?" the man responded. Stalling, maybe. Though she hadn't given an order that he was to see no visitors, Cúron might have.

"All is well. But I need to discuss something important with him before he leaves with the ships in the morning."

"Very well, My Keeper. Would you like one of us inside?"

It would be wise, but that would mean another ear for Firian's story. *Would that help or hurt?* "I'll be all right," she heard herself say.

"Very well, My Keeper," the guard repeated, and he conducted her past seven other guards to the door.

He knocked. A courtesy. Then he went in to announce her.

In a flash, tingling crept all over her body as her Beauty fell away. Though her plain face wouldn't give her the same leverage, it was the face he knew, and still the only one she felt comfortable showing him one on one. Candrae laid a soothing hand on her arm. Seconds later, she and her girls walked in after the guard.

Firian betrayed no emotion when she walked in, though she captivated his attention. "Thank you," she muttered to the man with the goatee, who didn't respond.

After he exited the room, silence fell.

Firian took in the presence of Candrae and Vayci, who stood a little behind her, and he raised one dark eyebrow to demonstrate his curiosity. He had thrown his black coat on the bed but still had his boots on. The Tanyuin crown lay beside it. Firian's dark hair, shiny and clean, looked a little mussed from wearing it so long, as though he had just woken up. Pieces of hair arched around the invisible iron circle.

She felt oddly embarrassed as he waited for her to speak. "Firian," she began. It didn't feel right for her of all people to refer to him as Master Kess. To her, he was just Firian. "You're only here for a short time, so I wanted to talk to you about something before you leave." A couple chairs lined the walls by the fireplace. She gestured to them. "Please, take a seat."

He pushed up his sleeves to the elbow and grabbed two

chairs, setting them in front of the hearth. His tentative silence kept her on edge. She settled in one chair and he sat angled beside her. Candrae and Vayci stood at attention nearby. The fire popped and crackled.

She drew a breath to speak, but the air didn't seem right.

He stretched out a hand and touched hers, cracking a smile. "It's all right." He suddenly was as easy as he'd been at the best point of their journey together. She saw no bitterness for her escape or dangerous lust or any of those things she was afraid she would find. Instead, here was her friend. Almost as though he invited her to forgive the past too.

The presumptuous gesture was oddly comforting. Something unwound inside her, and she could speak. "Before you leave, I need to know." She glanced at the crown on the bed. "I need to know how you became the Tanyuin Head."

Distraction passed over his face a moment, his blue eyes going hazy. Normally he was so present that the shift was striking. "Is that why you came here?"

She nodded.

His eyes passed again over her serving girls.

"We can trust them," Kiria said. *We?* Brithnem and its citizens and Keepers should be *we.* Firian shouldn't be swept into that pile. Not yet, at least. Not until he proved a worthy ally. Warmth filled her cheeks, but it could have been the fire.

Flickering orange light played over one half of his face as he spoke. "There are only two ways to become the Head. I chose the harder route."

"I don't know what that means." His words felt like a riddle, drawing her in to ask more questions, which annoyed her.

One side of his mouth stretched crookedly. "You can be appointed by the current leader, or you can take power by force."

Force, then. She dropped her voice almost to a whisper. "Did you kill him?"

His chest rose and fell a couple of times before he answered. "Yes."

Her breath caught before she could stop herself. She looked at those hands that had committed such a deed, now spread over his knees. Nothing had changed about them. Thin, white scars still laced his rough knuckles.

"I had to do it. You know what he was doing to your people." He leaned forward as though willing her to understand. A spark of vulnerability showed through his eyes.

"I do, yes." So many people still reeling in pain, still afraid to sleep at night for fear their nightmares would kill them. As they killed Salaar. Firian wasn't innocent. "But is that why you did it?"

He rubbed his fingers over his knees. On the pointer finger of his right hand, he wore his new black ring with the tiny red stone that she'd noticed in the Unreal. "Why else would I do that?"

"Power. Control."

He blinked, not in shock but like a cat at ease. "Is that why you took over for your mother?"

"How could—"

"I can do a lot of good now. You understand that. Power isn't evil."

"No," she agreed. The heat of the fire was starting to make her face sweat a little, but she didn't move her chair back. "The decisions, the people in power..." She left the thought unfinished. "How did you do it?"

He lifted his chin and straightened his back, leaning away from her. "I don't think you want to know."

"That's why I came here."

Sardonically, he raised an eyebrow. She kept her expression at a practiced neutral. The fire cracked and hissed. When the flame flared up this time, she saw it shine on something. A knife in Firian's boot. She'd forgotten about that. He arched his back in a stretch and then relaxed. His face, however, looked more drawn. "I'd rather not talk about it."

"I need to know. I'm the one who brought you here, back in good standing with the Kingdom. So tell me."

"Are you reminding me that you are my Keeper?" he asked, almost purring.

Her insides twisted. Was he being disrespectful, or seductive, even with these others watching? "Just tell me."

He let out a sigh and crossed his arms, sitting back against the chair. "I killed him in his sleep." He said the words quietly, clearly, without remorse or pride.

"How?"

"I suffocated him."

Her lips twitched. *How horrible.* But what had she expected?

"Is that enough?" He set his mouth in a line.

"Yes, that's enough."

"Not everyone can request power and have it given to them."

"I know."

"So I did what I had to." He shifted in his seat. "Do you hate me for it?"

"No," she answered. Too quickly.

He smirked conspiratorially. He'd known exactly how she would answer the question. His ability to read her was simultaneously unnerving and comforting. A game with high stakes. The small jolt of adrenaline that coursed through her at those moments was addicting.

"We'll see," she revised.

"It's good to see you," he said, leaning forward again.

Reality was full of little details that didn't always manifest in the Unreal, at least not with her level of Ability. The fabric of his pants wrinkled under his forearms. He'd sat on the back of his long-sleeved shirt, so, when he leaned, the shirt pulled tight across his chest and the sinews of his neck. A slight sheen of oil shone on his forehead in the firelight, and an eyelash had fallen on his cheek. Hopefully he would rub it off.

She wouldn't be bated. It was *interesting* to see him. *Good* went a little far. "Why did you come alone?"

"You know I don't need anyone else."

She blew a breath out her nose. She recalled a few times when another set of eyes could have helped him, but she let him have his arrogance.

Another silence fell between them. Memories populated the space. As the seconds drew on, it became more and more apparent that she should leave. Her business was done here. But she didn't move.

She drew her hand over the side of her skirt, the side that faced the fire. It had grown hot during their conversation. Perhaps that would damage the silk. Normally, she didn't sit so close to fireplaces.

He scrubbed his cheek—the eyelash came off—and drew his fingers through his hair. "Is there anything else?"

It had long since gotten dark outside, and he was rising before the sun to sail across the Kheltor to Torith, where he would fight on her behalf. She chewed her lip. Part of her was angry at herself for not leaving, but something made her want to stay, to see what he would do next, to see if their horrible past could be put right by greater things.

She rose. "Be careful," she said.

"Will you be there to see me off in the morning?" He gave her a knowing look. The flames flickered in his bright eyes. He laughed a little as he rose to stand beside her. That precarious easiness was back between them. That part of them that knew each other's strengths and weaknesses in a way that others were afraid to point out, like partners. "I'm going to win this war for you. It's the least you can do." Perhaps he was joking, but probably not.

She weighed whether to call out his cockiness or let his confidence soothe her. Despite herself, she smiled. "You know I'll be there."

10
___

FIRIAN

THE MORNING SKY had turned from black to dark blue. Firian scanned the beach for Kiria. She'd promised to be here. Chilly air rose from the sloshing waves beneath the *Talori*. Above the beach on the crest of a hill, Mon Párinath looked down, lights beginning to wink to life through its windows.

The deck pitched unevenly as he secured the final provisions for the trip. The voyage would not be long, they'd assured him—just a matter of a few days—but they couldn't be sure how long they would need to be on the island. He was already glad that their time on the sea would be short. He'd never spent time on the ocean, and he disliked the thought of being at its mercy.

Pulling a knot hard, he looked again toward the beach.

Kiria walked down the steps from the palace gardens, the train of her dress falling behind her. Even in this pre-morning light, the line of her jaw, backlit by the palace lights, told him she wore her Beauty. It was in her silhouette, the way her hair fell, the power he saw in her movements.

He stood up straight so she could see him over the deck rail. With her attention falling fresh on him, he felt like a hero. All the rush of power with none of its consequences.

Together, they had engineered this alliance. Together, they would win this war.

He stood still a moment, torn between wanting all the soldiers to notice them gazing at each other, or turning away so they could keep this secret. This connection between them, this desire she held at bay. There was no mistaking the signs last night. He was almost there.

All that stood between them was a war. A battle, really. What had she said? Tanyu would be the surgeons. The others from the Academy would arrive about a day after the *Talori* with its Kingdom soldiers. Then they would find and kill the Torithian leaders in their fortified base. It sounded simple, a small hurdle on his way back to her. When he thought that way, he knew he was showing his inexperience. But hadn't he proven himself before? One or two battles, with over a hundred Tanyu at his back... It sounded thrilling, not frightening.

He walked to the rail and touched it. A farewell. A promise. Exhaling, he strode to his cabin on the main deck.

A laugh almost escaped him when he opened the door. Across the bed lay a full suit of silver and blue Kingdom armor. For a second he considered trying it on, but only to feel how clumsy it was. The large breastplate and shoulder guards had to restrict movement. The smiths in Brithnem were talented enough to make the armor all but silent, but that was the best thing Firian could say for it. Light blue cloth draped across the top in a flourish that would make him feel as if he were wearing the Western Kingdom's flag.

Firian stacked and folded it as best he could and shoved it under the bed. His long black jacket might not turn a blade, but it sure as hell looked better.

Shouts from the deck and the flap of sails announced they were pulling away from the dock. How long would Kiria watch from the beach? Until they disappeared over the horizon of black water?

As though on cue, he felt the small thrill of her presence. Immediately he dove into the Unreal. Seeing her standing on the beach in the Unreal made him grin. She'd stripped away her Beauty, he saw with a pang of disappointment, but he liked this face too. This was the face he could look at straight on, the one that knew him best. They were alone with the sand and sea. She made the sun peer up behind them, casting light on the empty waves. Apparently she didn't like the dark.

The waves were actually passable. He didn't tell her that creating believable water was one of the first truly difficult tasks of being a Tanyu. Light struck the waves in a too-predictable pattern, and the line between sea and sky was too marked. But, all in all, he was impressed.

"I thought you'd wait until I was gone," he said.

Her face was alight with a smile that didn't show and nerves that didn't break through the surface. The result was fascinating and fixed on him. He fought not to stare.

"You told me to come and say goodbye," she said. "And I wanted to make sure you remembered everything. The Torithians aren't ordinary fighters."

"Neither are we."

She nearly mouthed the words along with him, as though his response was imminently predictable. "I know, but we've tried to take their fortress before. I'm a little worried."

"About what?" He stood his ground, longing to soothe her concerns away with a touch.

"It's almost impossible to get in. And Torithians use human shields..."

"We'll be careful. Bard has the whole layout. You've told me this before." The waves rolled further up the beach at his command. The next surge soaked his bare feet in cool water. Kiria stepped back. "What did you change?" he asked.

She pointed. "Do you see that shell?"

It was small and pink, half buried. "That's a good one. It didn't stand out."

"Isn't that the point?" she said, trying to sound matter-of-fact but only managing to sound pleased.

"Yeah." It really was impressive. She didn't practice obsessively like he did, but she learned quickly, even when he wasn't actively teaching her.

They both turned and watched the artificial sea. She shivered beside him. Since she wasn't wearing her crown, the gesture made her look helpless, a marked difference from a moment before.

"You're not cold, you know," he said.

She pressed her lips, casting him a sardonic glare. "I know. You said I was doing so well a second ago. No, I was just thinking... about what we'll do if you can't stop them."

"We will."

"But what if you can't?" She reached out and touched his arm.

His skin burned with the knowledge that her fingers had been there. She had chosen to touch him. Even though this was the Unreal, it felt as though it had really happened. Why did he react so violently? She wasn't touching him in a romantic way, but somehow this friendly closeness felt even more intimate. He'd had plenty of romantic encounters, but he had few friends. He let his heartbeat return to normal. "What would happen?"

She played with her bracelets before answering, one hand straying up to her shoulder. "A lot would happen," she said quietly. "People would still be taken from their homes in Enderin... all those people... all those livelihoods would still be trapped on that island... and I'm not sure where else we could go for help."

And Brett's husband could be killed. Firian didn't care about the man, but he'd like to spare his sister heartache.

Kiria looked up at him. "Some people aren't happy I asked you."

He nodded. "They will be soon."

She dropped her gaze.

"What about Charäkhnem?" he asked. The waves touched Kiria's shoes now too. "I thought I heard you had an alliance with them."

"We're friendly, but they've never agreed to supply troops for us. For a long time we didn't even have that, so I guess it's better than nothing. At least we can trade now, and our people can get through the pass..."

She looked abstracted again. She really was worried about this war. "It's different being the Keeper, isn't it?" he asked gently. Her title felt intimate to say.

She rallied, looking out at the piercing bright sea against the darker sky. "It is. I'll be glad when this part is over."

"When I end two wars for you?" he teased.

"When *I* end two wars." She whirled on him with an impish expression.

"I'm the one who's going."

"I created the alliance and gave you information."

"I sent the peace terms."

"Would you have sent them to anyone else?" She blushed bright red and stepped back. Somehow they'd come to stand very close to each other. Even though Kiria was the one blushing, Firian found he had to catch his breath. Close to the edge again.

He didn't answer the question. Instead, he looked at the pink shell to ground himself. *This is not real.*

"I really hope this works," she said, digging her now shoeless toes in the sand. "Thank you for going. I probably sounded ungrateful just then. But I'm not. I'm really, really thankful that you're willing to help me."

"Of course."

"Not of course. You make your own decisions." Her careful tone revealed which decisions she was talking about. Siding with the Academy when it told him to take her hostage, killing a strategic Amir during the war... Maybe she even counted the Tanyuin Head.

He tipped his chin in an admission.

"So I'm glad you're with us now," she finished. Something like fear flashed over her expression. It was quick, almost too quick to see.

"And I will be," he said.

He should have been triumphant, but the same fear made his stomach feel light. He hated how much he loved it. He'd been with girls before, but never had they made him feel on the brink of losing control, of falling completely under their spell. The challenge made his blood race.

If he hadn't promised himself he'd let her come to him first, he would have kissed her right there.

She gave a nervous laugh. "If you don't get yourself killed because you're so cocky."

He shoved down the small rise of irritation. "I know what I'm doing."

"It doesn't always seem that way." She gave him a teasing look.

His insides melted. Few people could get away with saying that about him and being right.

He had to back away from the cliff now. He'd let this go on for too long. As long as he just wanted her body and her admiration, he wasn't in danger. But looks like that made him want to let down his walls, to give her everything. It was time to reestablish his position. "Don't let that be the last thing you say to me."

She opened her mouth in angry protest.

He smiled and leveled his gaze. "Don't worry, Kiria. There's a reason you sent me. I'm the best, and I know exactly what I'm doing."

Catching his stare, she colored. He couldn't tell if it was from desire or anger. He almost didn't care. Her eyes and thoughts were locked on him.

She didn't speak for a long time. Maybe it was only minutes. He didn't speak either.

Finally he shifted, preparing to go.

"Come back, Firian," she said.

Heat flushed his face. *Is this it?* The ocean faded away. Just the two of them left suspended.

"That's what I would say," she added quickly, clarifying. "Come back."

A promise echoed in the words. He would definitely come back. He would come back for her.

11

FIRIAN

FIRIAN GRIPPED the guardrail of the *Talori*, pretending to look for Torith on the horizon. When would that cursed island appear?

His stomach roiled. Why had no one told him about seasickness? By the end of the first day aboard, he'd felt horrifically sick. Staying in his cabin hadn't helped. The only thing besides the Unreal that mitigated the bile rising in his throat was being out in the fresh air. It was an improvement, but not much of an improvement. He'd waited until the crew and soldiers were out of sight before he vomited over the side.

Rubbing the back of his hand over his mouth, he wearily straightened. With his skin feeling so clammy, he had to be paler than usual, but since these soldiers didn't know him well, they hopefully wouldn't notice.

Kiria had told him the voyage would take about three days. It was the third day now. Give him a horde of angry Torithians before another day on this ship. It creaked all night and rocked all day. The wind, the food, and the small space didn't bother him. But the everlasting rocking that turned his stomach did.

A crewmember, a boy no more than fifteen, scrambled down the rigging from the crow's nest, landing with a thud. "Land spotted, sir," he said to the captain. The captain shouted directions and the deck came to life.

Finally. Firian pushed back from the rail. He didn't know how to sail, but at least he could get lost in the bustle. He could lose no more time contacting Bard to see what he found. Before they landed, he needed to have a better idea of what he was getting into.

Nausea churned inside him. He pressed it down. His practice with the Unreal had gotten him through the night, but when his attention slipped, seasickness irresistibly surged up again.

He took measured steps to his cabin and shut himself in.

"Bard!" Firian waited in darkness, considering a setting. He could switch it to—

"Fir, hey."

Bard materialized before him. His hair was frazzled and his eyes ringed with gray, as though he had just woken up. *Katah* was serious business, never-ending vigilance.

"What do you have for me?" Firian asked.

"Tibor Wat," he began wearily, almost grimacing. "He's in the compound."

"Where?"

A map appeared in Bard's hands. He rolled it out in the air and pointed to the same area of the island Kiria had shown him. Confirmed, then. "The base is right there. Fir, it's..." He turned his dark eyes to Firian's, almost pleading.

"What?"

"It's terrible."

"Where's Wat?" First things first. The fortified base, including the interior layout, took up the majority of the map when Firian looked back to it. "Is this correct?"

"It's all I know."

Some of the edges of the plan were pale and hazy, but a few particular rooms stood out in sharp relief.

"So where is he?"

"Right now?"

"Right now. We're coming up on Torith."

"Aren't you going to wait for the other Tanyu?"

"Yes." He would need at least a few minutes on dry ground before he'd be at his best.

Bard pointed again. "He's right there. He moves around, but he's usually there." Something haunted passed over Bard's face.

"What?" Firian asked again.

"So I've followed him around. He doesn't have the Talent," he clarified, rubbing his knuckles over the back of his head. "Not a ton, but some, I guess. It's all hazy. I can't get a full *katah*."

"Headache," Firian sympathized.

"You'll have to be careful, Fir. There are a lot of people there."

"Obviously."

"A lot." Apparently Firian didn't react the way Bard wanted, because he went on. "Innocent people."

Firian paused. "Kiria told me there are human shields."

Bard nodded rapidly. "Yeah, and... women."

Firian raised an eyebrow. "Prostitutes?"

"I don't know. It's not..." But whatever it was not, he didn't say.

Firian turned his attention again to the map. "So, what's this?" He pointed to the room Bard said held Tibor Wat.

Bard sighed. "I think it's his bedroom, or office, or something. He talks to his lieutenants and has a lot of the treasure is there. Yeah. And he meets with ladies."

"*Ladies*?" Firian smiled sarcastically at his choice of words.

Bard colored.

"Well, that's good to know," Firian said, feeling seasickness return. "And he's usually there?"

Bard nodded again.

"Have you gotten a layout of the entrances and exits?"

He touched the map at a few points. "These are some of them. They might be all. It's actually pretty secure."

"So I've heard."

"What are you planning to do?"

Honestly, he wasn't sure. He'd been waiting for Bard's intelligence. So instead of answering, he asked, "What about the lieutenants?"

Bard named them and gave descriptions.

Maybe sensing Firian's confidence, Bard gave him a warning look.

"I'll be fine," Firian protested.

"Just be careful. These people aren't like a normal army. They're like..." Bard searched for a word, didn't find it. "They're out for themselves."

"Isn't every army?"

"It's different. They're just..."—he searched for a word—"marauders." That one seemed to satisfy him. "They're not really an army at all. They just want what they want, you know? They want treasure and so they kill or steal or whatever they can to get it. Some of them steal people and just keep them. It's..." He winced.

"That should make them easier to beat."

"They don't have rules. At all. They'll kill their own people, yeah? But they've gotten good at fighting together too."

"If they can get money and women."

Bard nodded, obviously remembering a number of specific incidents.

The troubled look on his face made something squirm in Firian's gut. Was that nerves? He couldn't afford nerves. "So you've had to watch this captain with girls, have you?"

Firian thought he could feel the heat from Bard's deep blush.

"We'll get him," Firian said, stifling a laugh. With Bard's prudishness, this *katah* was truly a sacrifice for him.

Firian's thoughts grew serious again. If Bard continued to give information of this caliber, he would definitely have to promote him to Master when he got back. Even a partial *katah* developed this quickly would be difficult for the best Tanyu to pull off. "When we land, I'll come again to check things over."

"Okay," said Bard, still not looking at him, as though he were ashamed.

"Just keep the information coming." *And then we can win the war.* "It's not so bad, is it?" he needled again, unable to help himself.

Bard hit him on the arm.

Firian laughed. "It's good for you."

Bard puckered his lips in an expression that said it definitely wasn't.

At least Bard's misery would be over soon. Firian had the captain's location. All he needed to do was land, wait for the Academy ships to land, and then the Tanyu could be the expert war surgeons they claimed to be.

12

FIRIAN

FIRIAN CRAWLED on his elbows to see over the ridge. Rocks dug into his arms and the mud coated the front of his black shirt. Huge leaves dripped leftover rain on his face. He wiped off the drops with a grimy hand so he could see.

Most of the compound seemed no taller than a single story, but it stretched back and back into the trees for an undetermined distance. The building was well established, no doubt there before the Torithians arrived to use it as their base. Jungle foliage crawled over the roof until the two blended into one seamless blend of shadowy green.

Firian pictured the plan Bard had shown him. This was the south entrance. Captain Tibor Wat's room lay in the center.

Lowering himself further, he peered at the visible door. Only one man stood guard, partially hidden in the shadows. His head was shaved like every other Torithian. Since they came from different places and had no distinguishing uniform, their shaved heads seemed to mark their allegiance to the gang.

His heart squeezed. The last time he had seen a Torithian was when he and Kiria had been ambushed in Raewhith. Red streaked across his memory. Raewhith, his hometown. He never would have guessed they'd go so far inland, just to get Kiria. They'd been minutes away from Brett. Huge dead bodies must have been big news in the little town. She'd certainly heard about it. Did she realize he left the corpses there?

He forced himself back to the present. The fortress had very little evident security. Firian had expected much more, based on Bard's description. Seeing almost no one was more unnerving than facing a clear army.

"There are hundreds inside," Bard had told him, "and civilians."

It wouldn't be as difficult to rush in like a wildfire, burning the murderous pirates where they stood, but working around innocents was completely different.

He stared for a while longer, envisioning all the ways he and Bard planned their attack. First, they would backtrack to the Torithians' ships and burn their escape route. Then, he would sneak in and kill the captain while more Tanyu blended in among the prisoners. Using the Unreal for communication, Tanyu would direct Endrians and Kingdom soldiers to surround the remaining pirates as the spies revealed themselves and new troops barged in the front.

Now that he was looking at the fortress, though, he could improvise a few more opportunities. They could go in from above, if there were any crack in the stone.

Firian edged backward down the embankment, his elbows sliding in the muck. Tanyu, Brithnem, and Endrian soldiers all stood ready for his command. Many of them were fully twice his age. He stifled a smile.

"The base is below us," he said.

A few Brithnem soldiers all but rolled their eyes. They'd been here before. They'd lost friends. Firian had heard them swapping stories on the *Talori*. Though no one complained, the Brithnem soldiers didn't stand very close to the Tanyu, who had just arrived that morning and had barely disembarked before coming here to the fortress.

He scanned the troops in black and picked five out of the crowd, all girls. "Get to the roof. See if you can find a way in." Bard hadn't mentioned any, but then he wouldn't know if the captain never thought about it. The way the huge stones stood piled on top of one another suggested that there probably would be a crack somewhere. Someone like Tesni, tall but skinny as a candle stand, would be able to wedge herself through even the smallest of openings. The five girls disappeared silently, as though they had never been there.

"You," he said, pointing now to the Endrians, "burn their ships. Give them no place to run." Firian had already left soldiers from Brithnem, as well as a couple Tanyu, guarding their own ships, well hidden in a jungle cove.

"Where do we begin? They always hide their fleets in several places," said one Kingdom soldier. When Firian continued looking at him, he added, "Master Kess."

"We'll find them all. Like we planned, the faster they burn, the better. I'll come with you." He swept his gaze over the remaining forces. "The rest of you, stay here. Create a perimeter around the fortress. Stay out of sight. We'll be back before nightfall."

As the army broke into its tasks, Firian relished the snuff of thick leaves, the mud underfoot, the wetness trailing down his hair. The ships would not be difficult to find. His troops left footprints, but so had the careless Torithians.

The first fleet was in plain sight on a sandy beach not far from the fortress. Tall-masted ships with huge hulls for trans- porting weapons and people and treasure floated serenely on the lapping waves.

Firian crouched down at the edge of the tree line and frowned.

A general from Enderin came up beside him, his leather shoulder guards dark with moisture. "They never guard the ships," he said in Bard's lilting accent.

Firian whirled to face him. "Then why haven't you burned or taken them before?"

"We burned them once, three years ago." He licked his bearded lips and his gaze grew far away. "We didn't realize then, but the brig was full of children tethered to the bars. By the time we heard the screams, we couldn't save them. We tried again last year, but the captives alerted the Torithians and our troops got trapped against the water when they arrived. All killed but two who jumped overboard and swam."

"Prisoners are in the brig?" Firian confirmed.

The man didn't nod, but his stern look conveyed that he thought so.

Simple enough. Couldn't these people think through any problem? If the captives alerted the Torithians, then they had been threatened. Since Firian's soldiers had no way to knock out all the prisoners—no gases or space to do it all at once—they would just have to threaten them with something worse than the Torithians had. Then they'd untie them, burn the ships, and let the people go free, unharmed. Were Kiria's soldiers unwilling to threaten people even to save them?

Firian crooked a finger toward Master Nedi, the tallest Tanyu in their company. He could inspire fear if he wanted to. "You go first," Firian instructed. "Find the brig. Make sure no one down there makes a sound. If they do, stop it." He paused. "But don't kill them."

The Endrian general shot Firian a glance that he ignored. "We go in just behind," he announced in an undertone to everyone else with them.

When Nedi left, Firian counted under his breath. When he reached fifty, he sprinted, staying low, across the beach. His running footsteps were just the crunch and rainy spray of sand.

The ship was anchored just off shore. As Firian charged into the bay, the water got deeper more quickly than he anticipated. In three steps it came up to his waist. He kicked off the sandy bottom and did his best to swim toward the ship. Why did Bard like swimming so much? He always talked about how he missed it at the Academy. It was so much slower than running, or even climbing.

Happily, Nedi or someone else had left a rope dangling from the deck into the water. Firian grabbed hold of the rough, slimy hemp and hauled himself up, walking up the uneven boards of the ship's hull.

It didn't take long to find the brig. Firian jumped down into the hold, skipping the ladder entirely. In the blackness, he heard shifting people, a couple gasps, a child softly crying. The brightness of the sun and water and sand had blinded him. Though he squinted, he could see nothing for a few seconds. A horrible stench of human feces and rotting fish made him gag before he could stop himself. His blindness put him on edge. What if this were a trap? What if he had sent some of his best people right into it?

He started to breathe again when shapes began forming in the gloom. Tiny children, some no more than three years old, sat on the ground, one wrist tethered tightly to metal bars, both inside and outside the square cages that lined most of the space. They were dirty and skinny, without shoes. Their eyes seemed to grow larger in the darkness. Firian fought the urge to shiver with the sense of being haunted. The eyes reminded him of the Sentries, buried underground, listless and hopeless.

There were adults too, all men and boys. Most of them had ratty beards. Nedi stood face to face with the largest man, who looked as though he had lost a significant amount of weight in a short time. Heavy skin hung below the bicep of his raised arm tied to the bars. The hand itself was discolored, too light compared to the rest of his dark skin, like the hand of a corpse.

"Make a sound and you're dead," Nedi whispered.

The boy next to the dark-skinned man trembled, but the man acted as though Nedi hadn't spoken. He began banging his dead hand against the bar, almost as though it were a spasm, an automatic response, and not a conscious choice.

Firian stepped in and grabbed his hand to silence him. His flesh was hard and dry—a thing, not a person. But others started clanging against the bars too. It was odd that they didn't raise their voices.

They don't care if they die, Firian realized. "We're going to get you out," he hissed, hoping that would be enough motivation for them.

The banging continued.

Desperation surged inside him as the prisoners started to wail. Unearthly sounds. Horrifying sounds. The Tanyu and Endrian soldiers who had come in behind him snapped into action, covering mouths, barking quiet directions. One soldier yelped and shook out his hand. The prisoner must have bitten him.

"The kids," Master Nedi said. "We'll kill the kids if you don't shut up."

All sounds ceased.

Firian had said to threaten them. He was glad he hadn't been the one to say it, but even before Nedi spoke the words, he dreaded the inevitability of them. The men might not care about their own lives, but they would care about the children.

Firian sensed the shock of the Endrian soldiers as they turned toward him. He couldn't reassure them yet or else the prisoners would start their din again. "Yes," he said, but he felt like he was going to be sick. *This lie will save them. It'll save them.*

"Now shut up and we'll let you go. You don't want to be on these ships when we burn them." This was war. Sometimes justice and victory required people to do hard things. People killed in war. Surely this was no different.

He nodded to the Tanyuin warriors closest to him, and they began slicing off the leather bonds. Salt and age glued the knots together. Some had been tied so tightly that they couldn't cut them off without harming the arm as well. But freedom was freedom. No one cried out from the pain. Maybe they couldn't feel it. One man—probably the oldest, judging from the white in his beard—nearly collapsed once his arm was free. The prisoner beside him, a man with milk-white eyes, held him up.

"Check the upper deck and take them out," Firian ordered the Endrians. The words tasted like stale fish. He swallowed, his eyes sliding to a boy a few years younger than he was, whose forearm was sliced near his wrist bone. Blood, black in the darkness, flowed over his hand onto the ground.

Again, sickness rose up in Firian's gut, but that could have been the swaying of the ship. He'd had enough of that aboard the *Talori*.

"Get them up," he said again.

Up above, a yell. A clank.

Firian's stomach lurched and he dove toward the ladder, pushing past brown-clad soldiers to see out. Two Torithians, looking as though they had just crested the railing, stood at the edge of the deck, swords drawn against three Endrian fighters.

Potatoes spilled out of a sack and rolled across the planking. The pirates were here to feed the prisoners.

Firian jumped out of the hold and drew his sword with a grating ring. It didn't feel quite balanced, although he'd practiced with it before he came. He preferred knives. If he needed them, he had one at his belt and his small blade tucked in his boot.

When the two men saw Firian and the others crawling out of the hold, they stopped fighting and jumped overboard toward the beach. Without thinking, Firian launched himself over the railing after them. The water went over his head, sucking him down into silence. He kicked and broke the surface again. The pirates were almost to the beach. He thrashed after them, pinwheeling his arms. His pace was maddeningly slow. Bard should have taught him how to swim. Too late now.

One of the men looked back and stopped, while the other continued. Firian realized he still had the sword in his hand. He tightened his grip on the cold handle as he muddled forward. This was ridiculous. His thoughts stilled. This was just like the Unreal. When he was fifteen, he swam in the test against Shiro. He could swim now. He just had to use the elements to his advantage, like anything else. Everything was his ally, if he knew how to use it. He kept himself afloat and took a deep breath through his nose, grateful that it no longer smelled like human waste.

Eyeing the young, bearded Torithian who had stopped, Firian reviewed his options. They weren't good, but he was a Tanyu, and he had come with other Tanyu. Even now, he heard a splash behind him. He blinked and the Torithian was gone. Frowning, he scanned the beach. The second pirate disappeared into the tree line, no doubt to warn the people at the fortress, but there was no sign of the first man.

Another splash. A soldier swam up behind him. Firian pointed to the beach. "Stop them! Go!"

An Endrian soldier, and then another, swam powerfully past him. He almost resented them for their skill, but he was glad someone could go faster than he could. "Get to the—"

Something grabbed his ankle and yanked him under. Water rose over his head, cutting off the air before he could fill his lungs. He kicked, hit something, some*one*, but he didn't move toward the surface. Now someone tugged at his wrist, his neck. Firian arced his sword, but it moved through sap, like a nightmare. He heard the muffled swish of something breaking the surface. Pressure pushed on top of his head, holding him down.

Panic welled up in him. His lungs already burned. The more he kicked, the less energy he reserved for holding his breath just a little longer. He opened his eyes and saw legs treading water in front of him. He grabbed at them, missed, switched his sword to his left hand, grabbed again, was kicked off again. Finally, in desperation, his eyes getting blurry, his nose and mouth aching to take in air, he dropped the sword. It sank gracefully into the murky depths below. Firian lunged with both hands, got a firm hold, and bit as hard as he could. The instinctive thrash that followed was enough for Firian to break the surface.

Sweet air filled his lungs with a loud gasp. Sun beat down. The first sound he heard apart from his own breath was a foreign curse.

Panting, Firian drew his curved knife, lightning quick, and plunged it into the pirate's chest. Again. Again, just to be sure. Red billowed like smoke underwater.

He spat blood and kicked his way to shore. When he reached the soft sand, he turned around to see the first ship on fire and a lifeboat taking the prisoners away.

13
———

FIRIAN

"You all right, mate?" Bard's voice sprang to Firian's mind as he sprinted back along the beach, trying to erase the memory of his incompetence in the water.

Hopefully no one saw him flailing in the water and then gasping for breath on the beach. He had spent a full minute lying on his back before he had enough air in his lungs to run after the man who'd escaped. He would fix the problem. That was all. He would learn to swim, learn to hold his breath, to fight in water. He would fix the problem, as he had fixed all his other weaknesses. It just rankled that he kept finding more.

"Yeah. Get back to the captain," he replied, still running but also dipping into the Unreal.

Bard's spiky black hair looked almost hazy. Could that happen with too much concentration? The *katah* was clearly wearing on him. "You're almost there?" His shoulder twitched restlessly.

"On my way." Firian's clothes were soaked. He'd stripped off his dripping shirt as he ran, but he'd have to stop before he had the chance to wring out the rest of his clothes. Water made his boots feel heavy and sluggish.

Bard hesitated, but didn't leave. "Be careful."

"You've said that before."

Bard hummed, admitting but not apologizing.

"Be ready," Firian said. Bard was instrumental in this plan. He was in the captain's head. He had the layout. If he had created a successful *katah* connection, he could incapacitate Tibor Wat, their leader, from where he was at the Academy.

Bard's Adam's apple bobbed. He nodded grimly and vanished.

Firian focused on the present. It wasn't far back to the compound. He didn't catch up to the two Endrians and the fleeing Torithian. If the man reached the fortress before his troops could enact their plan... He pumped his legs harder. He'd left the rest of the soldiers behind to free the other prisoners and burn the remaining ships. The wind against his bare skin began to dry the seawater.

Through the Unreal, he contacted the nearest Tanyu and ran to her hiding place. It was Xan, a serious girl with a long braid who had fought under Tiev mere months ago. That time felt like a different life. She fixed Firian with a look so fierce it seemed as though she strove to be like Master Gerand when she was older. Now, she stood in a hollow with perhaps a hundred Brithnem soldiers, whose armor sparkled in the sunlight.

Firian wiped his wet hair out of his eyes. "Any word from the roof?"

Xan shook her head.

Firian bit the inside of his lip. No news from the roof, a loose Torithian who knew of their presence... His plan was unraveling at the edges. But Tanyu were adaptable.

His lungs and throat still burned raw from his near drowning. If any others had seen him, their confidence might be shaken. He had to show them what he could do. His whole life, he felt, had been that endless fight.

"I'm going in," he said.

Xan's brows twitched downward.

"We can't wait. One was going to alert the others." The Tanyu were Kiria's last hope of defeating this threat. If he could do this—he, Firian—then he would save them all.

Firian considered the layout of the fortress again. The south-facing door opened into a series of passages full of blind corners and partial walls.

He was the only one who could sneak in through the front door, navigate the maze, and kill the captain. He'd been communicating with Bard, the one whose *katah* would help them succeed. And he wanted to prove he could do it. This was a delicate task, a surgeon's task, and he was born for it.

From Xan's hiding place, he could peek above the long ridge he had climbed earlier and see the pirate's base. Somewhere inside there was supposed to be a Tanyu, secretly implanted years ago. Belik said his name was Moryam Cashel. Though they'd tried to contact him before landing on the island, no one had been successful. Maybe he was already dead.

"You need to distract the guard," Firian whispered. "Don't kill him or alert him that we're here. I just need to get inside."

"As you would have it, Master Kess," Xan replied.

Firian faced the leaf-covered stone building. The door opened left-handed, so he would sneak around the side on his right. He pointed to the spot. Xan nodded.

Firian's black clothing blended with the shadows as he picked his way through the jungle. A bird called. Something dripped on him from above and he ran a hand through his hair. It felt gritty with salt.

When he reached the side of the building, his body tensed, energy bunching in his arms and legs and core. But he saw no more guards. He found a dapple of bright sunlight and pivoted his Master ring until the red stone reflected a dot of light. Xan was sure to see it on a tree near where her company waited.

What felt like a long time later, the lone guard went to investigate something just off to his right, away from Firian. Firian's chest burned, his vision almost blurry with excitement. He edged around the building and slipped through a crack in the door.

Bard had warned him about the two additional guards that stood just inside, but his heart still lurched to see them. Drawing on the inner stillness he had cultivated at the Academy, he bashed the head of one, disorienting him. Then he turned his attention to the second, who was stirring to attack. Firian grabbed the front of the man's clothes and gagged him with it, swinging him by the back of his collar into the first man. One more blow and the two guards lay nonconscious. Firian stood without a scratch. The whole exercise felt nearly graceful, like a stretch or strategy exercise.

Laughter and music greeted him inside. Energized by action, he slid to a dark corner behind a half-wall. This sounded like a party, not an army. *These are the people who almost murdered Kiria.* He remembered the raised scar on her left shoulder and flushed red with anger.

He recalled the map Bard had shown him. Above him was a square wooden door covering a long, continuous storage space that ran most of the length of the first room. From there, he could avoid a few blind corners on his way to the center of the compound.

Shimmying into the tight space, he started to elbow his way along. Bright slivers of light streaked across his face from the other cabinet doors. Edging the tobacco, candle stands, tankards, and pouches of unnamed things out of the way proved to be the most difficult part of navigating the tight tunnel.

Closing one eye, he peered through a small knot in the

wood. The room was full of men of all ages, bristling with weapons, some on their person, some hanging on the wall or leaning in corners. The assortment was staggering: swords and axes and pikes and maces, all cruel and many dirty. They bore the markings of many different cultures, some of which Firian didn't recognize, although he'd met people from all around the continent at the Academy.

And with them were women, all in various states of intoxication or undress. They sat on knees or lay on the floor. Although they moved with little prompting, most of them did so without smiling, obeying automatically. One girl, beautiful, no more than sixteen, wore nothing above the waist but a necklace of enormous rubies. Dark purple burn marks peppered her midriff. The man whose lap she sat on smoked gaily, gesturing to his friends and laughing obscenely. Firian's blood boiled. A couple boys, distinguishable as separate from the Torithians by their long hair, served the gaudier pirates, apparently following some code of rank.

Even if his troops told the slaves to run, many of them probably wouldn't understand or be able to move before their captors grabbed them. Firian looked back toward the entrance he had used. Eight guards, apparently sober, stood with two or three wickedly curved blades at each of their belts. Firian thought of the sword he had lost in the water.

The light was dim. If there had been windows, they were now overgrown or covered up. The only light came from torches bolted into the wall or candles dripping wax onto thick wooden tables. Though it was still midday, fully half the men appeared to be drunk. The better to kill them.

Was Moryam among these disgusting people? The thought made Firian's lip curl. How long would someone have to live a debauched life like this before they didn't acknowledge other loyalties? The Academy might be the only place strong enough to demand instant allegiance from men like these.

Belik had described the Tanyu, but Firian saw no one who matched his description. He was almost glad.

Treasures lay piled in corners too, along with the weapons. An Endrian carving of a tree, partially gilded, hung on the wall as decoration. Bard, if he were here, would have pointed it out. Firian had never given much thought to the fact that the Torithians had been attacking Bard's country for years. No wonder he was so concerned. Now that he thought about it, that group of girls lounging on the carpet had Bard's coloring. Firian had only offered to help with the war because of Kiria, but he could actually help many people before the week was out.

A splash of liquid hit the stone floor and a chair scraped back. A couple girls shrank away, but two nearby Torithians stood, their hands full of weapons. One pirate held a tankard in one hand and a short ax in the other.

The man who'd lost his drink gave a lengthy curse. The man he accused barely spoke the common tongue, but he managed to curse right back. Waving a dagger, he pressed the point of a blade against the first man's chest.

Violently, he shoved the offender's hand away, and the swift movement broke into a full-blown fight. More men stood either to watch or get into the action. One girl was hurled off her captor's lap to the ground. Her mouth moved with feeble protests, but she was clearly not lucid enough to fully comprehend what was happening. She drew her legs in a little, hiding them under her skirt, which had obviously been a grain sack before it was clothing.

Though Firian wanted to see how far the fight would go, he used the distraction to mask the noise as he crept to the end of the storage area.

There was a gap between him and the hall that led to the

rooms beyond. Here, he would have to get out of his hiding place.

The captain's room was in the center of the compound. Bard's map had shown a series of large spaces, all similar to the one he had just left, circling around a cluster of smaller inner rooms. He'd have to cross at least one more repulsive cache of people and weapons to reach his objective.

A scream pitched through the air. Heart in his throat, Firian eased open the cabinet door and grabbed hold of a wooden beam in the ceiling. The shouts became instantly louder in that open space. Scented smoke floated in a haze. Though it strained his muscles to hold on, he would be out of reach of most weapons here. He reached from one beam to the next, hiding as best he could in the gloom.

The ceiling showed no sign of excessive age or wear. He didn't even feel a draft. The possibility of a rooftop entrance seemed slim.

Easing himself down, he slipped through a doorway—and bumped straight into another guard. The man reached for something but Firian had already crooked his elbow and smashed it hard against the man's nose. Disoriented, the pirate stumbled back and yelled, the sound blending with the others in the next room. Firian punched his head against the wall a few more times before the man slumped, unconscious, to the ground.

Firian shook out his hand, as much to wind down his adrenaline as to mitigate the pain from hitting bone on bone. His heart skipped unevenly and he melted into the shadows of an alcove to get his bearings.

"There was an extra guard," he told Bard sourly, keeping his eyes open as he went into the Unreal. He let out a slow breath until he felt all his wits again.

"I told you they're all over."

Despite the danger and Bard's snarky comment, a smirk spread over Firian's face. He felt like himself again. "I'm headed to the center room now."

"Remember the outfit."

He flashed Bard a crude gesture before coming fully back into the Real. Heat pumping through his blood again, he moved forward carefully. There were so many entrances, openings leading to half-walls somewhere else.

More raucous laugher and clinking of tableware sounded from the next large room. This time, Firian knew exactly what to expect. Bard was so sensitive that one half-dressed dancer would have made his skin prickle. But he wasn't joking. This place really did have many people enslaved for the pleasure of these pigs. Everything here was a mockery of luxury. It would be sumptuous if it weren't so tainted.

Smells of roasting meat wafted on the air. Part of him hated his automatic hunger.

Firian returned to the man he had knocked out. Faint breath barely fluttered from his nose. Alive, then. As quietly as he could, he yanked off the man's long tan vest and he put it over his own clothes. The pirate's body odor clung to the fabric, but the stench still wasn't as bad as the ship's brig. Then he unwound the silk scarf around the man's neck. Pausing, he chose to tie it at his waist like a belt. The man's red pants were baggy enough to fit over Firian's slim black ones, so he pulled off the man's heavy shoes and then the pants.

Casting around for an excuse to go in, he found a wooden box full of flints. Good enough.

He pulled the small knife from his boot and hid it under the flints before closing the lid. The borrowed pants had too much fabric that could get in the way of his hands.

He ran his fingers through his dark hair a few times, so it would look more like the servants' did, smoothed back and curled at the ends. His hair was shorter than that of the boys he'd seen, but it would have to do. With what he hoped was a servile attitude, he approached the doorway. He'd have to keep his head down, even seem meek.

Guards would be posted outside this room too. These he would probably have to bring down. He could already feel their hot, sticky blood on his hands.

Would any of them recognize him? Had his description gone out after the encounter at Raewhith?

The air seemed to grow thinner the closer he got to the roasting meat and the cackling men and the bare-legged women. Firian was tall. Would that matter?

Willing himself to perfect calm, he crossed the threshold.

14

FIRIAN

"Wait up!" Someone plucked Firian backward by the neck of his shirt. He bristled, and his lungs felt like rocks in his chest. He turned and found himself face to face with three leering men.

Was he too late? Had the pirate from the beach already come?

"What's this?" asked one with onion on his breath. His head had been unevenly shaved. A few rogue hairs sprouted up at crazy angles, only visible in certain light.

Firian held up the box with both hands. "Someone asked for flint," he said softly.

A different man, skinny, with a scar along the length of his head, threw back a laugh.

Firian's face heated. He could kill this man in the span of a heartbeat.

A guard who'd stood out of sight leaned forward. "Probably Yotar," he said to the rest.

Nods of suggestive acknowledgement.

"He said to bring one to Moryam too," Firian added quietly, shoving down his disgust.

A chorus of laughter met the name. No answers, and no luck

finding the Tanyu so long hidden among their ranks. So Moryam was dead, or at least gone, then. He'd be no help.

"Always had a sense of humor! Yotar's over there," said the one with the scar, pointing, altogether too close to Firian. His finger grazed Firian's chin as he pulled it back.

Choking with rage, Firian nodded, unable to hold back a sneer of contempt, and turned away. He wanted to spit, to curse, to destroy it all.

He wove his way through pirates pawing at their captives, smacking at their meat, asleep in magnificent velvet chairs. The men had pointed to a man with a birthmark covering half his face. Even his lips were two-toned, dark and light. *He's Khelê.* Firian wasn't sure why, but the presence of any Khelê surprised him. The man's outfit hung down in strings. Firian hadn't heard of a culture that dressed that way, but the matching pants and shirt—if it could be called that, since it revealed his whole chest—were clearly made of a single fabric.

Firian realized he had forgotten to keep his eyes down. His boldness had drawn the looks of several Torithians. He lowered his voice to make up for the mistake. Flipping open the box, he said, "You asked for a flint. To... smoke."

The pause that followed made Firian's insides squirm. Had Yotar even heard him over the din?

When Firian glanced up, he was relieved that the man wasn't reaching for a weapon. A smile curled across Yotar's face. His gaze took in Firian and he languidly shuffled through the flints in the box, seeming to touch each one. The knife was buried deep enough that the pirate's wandering fingers wouldn't find it.

Don't kill him. Don't kill him.

Finally, the man chose a stone and flipped the lid of the box down himself. Unsure of what do to, Firian gave a fractional bow and backed away. His arms shuddered with anger. He could hardly see. But he had free reign of the room now. No one noticed he was out of place. They must have brought in new captives all the time.

And there—there!—was the captain's room. Without breaking his step, he called to Bard in the Unreal.

"I'm here."

"In the center room?" Bard's voice echoed through his head.

If he was focused enough, he could hear other Tanyu's voices without picturing them in his mind. Besides, it felt like Bard's voice was always echoing through his head.

"Yes. Is there any way in through the roof?" Firian knew it was a useless question.

"I dunno. Maybe?"

"I have people on the roof. I'm outside the captain's room now. Is he with any guards I should worry about?"

"They rotate in and out. Right now there are six with him. Yeah, six." A pause, and then, "That's a lot. You should have told me when you were going in."

Firian ignored him. "What's the captain doing?"

"He's planning a trip. He's charting... to Enderin."

"Okay." Firian's mind spun with the possibilities. Seven people. With extra weapons and an enclosed space, he didn't like the odds. Difficult, but not impossible. "Explain the guards to me."

Bard didn't answer right away. It was challenging to maintain a *katah*, get information, and communicate with someone else at the same time. Pride washed over Firian at the thought. He and Bard would be the ones to take down these gory pirates. He wouldn't have pegged Bard as such a helpful ally, but he was glad this time that he'd been wrong.

"There are two right next to him, helping him plan... and two by the door. Mm hm. Another one is on the other side of the room, against the wall. Another guy is sitting on the bed. I think he's drunk."

Firian numbered them off in his head. Two with the captain, two by the door, two extra. Six in all. His mind spun with strategies. Seven at a time... Even with Firian's elite training, it would be close.

In the Real, Firian offered his wares to another group, four people reclining together in a tangle on a luxurious rug made of the fur of some exotic animal. A young man who looked little more than seventeen took a flint from the box and invited Firian to join them. He pretended not to hear him.

The encounter made him feel more on edge. While in this compound, he constantly went from confident to nervous to excited to enraged. Now, as he bought a little more time to consider what he would do in the captain's room, he felt an odd fluttering of nerves. If there had been three guards plus Tibor Wat, he would have felt assured of victory. Surprise was on his side. One of the men was drunk. But six?

"Fir?"

"If you take Tibor Wat, I can take the guards. It's a *katah*, right?"

"I don't... I don't know."

"You don't know?" Firian demanded, tension making his words sharp.

"I don't know if it's strong enough."

"Bard, it has to be! You want to be a Master?"

"Yeah."

"This is where you do it. I'll count to thirty."

Weaving aimlessly through the revelers, Firian offered flints to anyone who asked. Mostly they just wanted a closer look at their new slave. A few called him over, glanced at him, waved him away. The girls noticed him with dead or vaguely pitying eyes. Not the responses he was used to. The whole place made his skin crawl.

He had to use the knife under the flints to stop these men.

The Torithian War wasn't something talked about in taverns and debated in the Main anymore. It was something that roiled black rage through his blood. Bard had been right. This *was* different. They weren't an army. They were pleasure-seeking murderers that banded together for power.

Killing one man wouldn't destroy their influence. It would just hamper their unified decisions. But it was a start.

He lay a palm against the captain's door handle. Scenarios played through his mind. One against six. Hopefully not seven.

After a deep, steadying breath, he knocked.

A grim-faced man, bald like the rest, scowled as he opened the door. Firian heard a voice. Maybe the second guard. "Did you ask for someone?"

Keeping his head down, Firian crossed the threshold as though he had been called inside. The guards didn't stop him, but rather shut the door behind him. From the corner of his eye, he tried to take stock of weapons. The space crawled with shadows and smelled like sweat.

The chamber was as eclectic as the rooms outside. Two beds sat pressed together side by side, covered with an assortment of skins and blankets. In the opposite corner, locked wooden chests had been piled in two stacks as high as the ceiling. A painting of four men against a landscape of yellow grasses and lakes dominated one wall. Carvings in the background made Firian think they had been stolen from Enderin. An oddly tooled piece of metal—it might have been tarnished gold— leaned unceremoniously against a tall round table where three men stood. One had a pen in his hand, evidently writing down what the captain said, while another stood closer, pointing at the map in a studied manner. A recorder and a map expert. He recognized the men at the table from Bard's descriptions: Tibor Wat's lieutenants. An elaborate colored lantern hanging from a tall stand provided enough light to see, but the room was still dim, even for Firian.

A drunk ruffian sat on the edge of a bed, clutching the neck of a bottle. Another man propped himself sullenly against the wall, as though he weren't part of the group, or they weren't doing what he suggested.

The talking man at the table looked up sharply when Firian entered. Tibor Wat. It had to be. He was thin and rigid, perhaps in his forties, with discerning eyes. A diamond shone in his ear.

"Did one of you call him here?" Wat asked. His raspy voice was captivating.

They all shook their heads.

"I heard you wanted a flint," Firian said, ushering as much humility as he could into his tone.

"No," said Wat, shooing him away. "We'll call you if we want you."

Firian's stomach tightened. He had counted beyond thirty. It had to be close to seventy by now. Still, the captain stood unharmed. "Now!" he told Bard in the Unreal, not losing his focus on the men in the room.

The captain wavered. It was a small motion, but enough that Firian could see him grow momentarily weak. That was all he needed.

He flipped open the box and grabbed the knife, letting the box and the sharp stones clatter to the floor. Ammunition for later.

He stabbed the scowling door guard in the neck before anyone had a chance to draw a weapon. Warm blood spattered out over his hands.

Ducking down, he let the second guard charge at him, lose balance. He slashed at the tendon in the man's knee. With a scream, he faltered, giving Firian enough time to stand and kick him out of the way.

Others were coming. No time to finish him off.

A fist slammed against his ear and the world spun. The room pitched like a ship's deck on a stormy sea. Firian staggered to the side until he hit the wall. The captain had backed away and was digging through a pile of blankets beside the motionless drunk. What was he looking for?

Pushing off from the wall, Firian slashed at the man in front of him. The recorder. Had he been the one to punch him? No matter. He barreled into the man, using their momentum to crush him against the table.

Behind the table, the map expert backed up a step, slipping on one of the fallen flints.

The crack of splintering wood sounded through the room. The table had split, but the recorder only winced before straightening again with his pen held firmly in his fist. Firian faced him. The captain was still burrowing through the blankets and the drunk only stared, uncomprehending. The map expert struggled to get back to his feet.

Behind Firian, the man who had languished against the wall approached, sword in hand, quick but clumsy.

They had him surrounded, but Firian had practiced this. He stomped hard on the insole of the man behind him, ducking to avoid being stabbed by the recorder. The sullen man grunted in pain. Firian brought his knife up with him when he straightened, drawing an uneven line from crotch to neck. The man screamed and stumbled back, thrashing until he fell to the floor.

When the map expert, now standing again, didn't make a move, Firian spun to face the man with the now broken foot.

A sword. A sword was all he saw.

He dodged to the side. He was fast, but not fast enough. Surprise more than pain sent a shockwave through his body as the sword sliced into his right ear. Was it still on his head? Did he still have his ear?

Firian savagely hacked at the man's sword hand. His little knife didn't go all the way through, but it was enough to disarm him. The sword clattered to the floor. Rather than pick it up, exposing his back, he drove the knife into the man's heart, all the way up to the hilt.

"Hey!"

The slur in this one word told Firian it was the drunk. Almost annoyed at the interruption, he spun and stabbed the man before he'd gone two steps.

The bottle rolled across the floor, chugging out reddish liquid over the floor.

Now with time to grab the sword, he snatched it from among the skittering flints and quickly finished off the injured guard and the frightened map expert.

He was shaking by the time he turned around to find the captain unconscious on the bed. Behind him, a girl shook, holding a blanket up to her face. She stared, terrified, at Firian.

He scanned the bodies, blood still burbling out of the wounds. The captain's chest didn't rise. When Firian stepped forward, the girl squeaked. A flint skittered forward. He hadn't needed them after all.

"Don't worry," he said, reaching out to touch the captain's back with his knife. After poking him a few times, he was content that the man wouldn't get up again. With his other hand, he gripped his shoulder and rolled him onto his back. Wide-eyed surprise was branded on Wat's face.

Firian sighed, almost giddy, though there was more to do. Bard had come through. And so had he. Barely. He raised his hand to his ear, but couldn't bring himself to touch it. He could feel the warm blood oozing down his neck. It was starting to hurt.

He cocked his head to the side, feeling oddly playful. "Is it still there?" he asked the girl.

She didn't answer.

"The ear," he clarified, before realizing that she might not speak the common tongue.

"Yes," she breathed.

He let out a sigh of relief.

A thump in the other room caught his attention. He held out his hand for her to stay where she was—on a bed with two dead bodies—and listened at the door. Another thump followed the first. He smoothed back his hair, wiped some of the blood from his neck onto his red pants, and opened the door.

The sight sent a smile over his face.

Two Torithians lay dead. Several others were already facing the wall with hands on their heads. The knives aimed at their backs kept them in line. Tanyu, disguised as he was, dealt with the remaining pirates as others threw bewildered prisoners to the far side of the room. None of the slaves appeared injured at all.

"Master Kess."

He turned to see Erron, his former hall master, at his side. Unlike many of the others, Erron was still dressed in Academy black. The knife he held in one hand gleamed with blood.

"We're subduing the other areas now."

Grunts and ringing steel echoed through the cavernous rooms. His Tanyu were brutal and quick, using all means to force the pirates to surrender. Firian adjusted his grip on the sword. The hilt felt sticky with blood. From his vantage point, all he had to do was watch as victory became his. It was mesmerizing.

"Can you see any of this?" he asked Bard, whose presence he could still feel as close as he could feel his own tripping heartbeat.

"See what?" The voice was faint.

"You did it. You killed the captain."

When Bard didn't respond, Firian went fully into the Unreal to picture him. Bard stood in a blank space, shoulders hunched, arms trembling. "You did it," Firian repeated.

Bard nodded, then he looked up at Firian. "Did they surrender?"

"It's happening now."

Bard's chest rose with ragged breaths. "And the slaves...?"

"All fine."

Firian could see Bard swallow hard. No wonder. He had just killed someone for the first time. Though he was reeling, he had helped win the war.

Standing up taller, Firian addressed the room. He still felt blood trickling at his neck, but he almost relished it now. He would wear any scar that came from today as proudly as he wore the iron circle. "Captain Tibor Wat is dead," he announced from the doorway.

The news spread rapidly as the Tanyu passed it to the other Talented minds in and around the fortress. He felt it buzzing. After the Torithians' surrender was official, he would tell the Western Kingdom of the victory.

No, not the Western Kingdom.

Kiria.

15

—————

KIRIA

Kiria wrung the moisture from her hair with a towel. Hanging her head sideways, she squeezed until her fingers felt damp. A few candles had been lit around her room, but it was still dark since the setting sun no longer shone through the multi-paned windows. She could barely see her own reflection in the glass. But she didn't care.

She hadn't heard from Firian all day. She had checked the Unreal compulsively, but he was never there. She knew he was on the island, that this was the day he was planning to storm the Torithians' compound. What if he rushed in on his own? It wouldn't surprise her. Firian always wanted to seem the hero. But, if he could manage this—if he could end the war—he really would be.

When would she hear from him?

She realized that she was gripping the towel in frozen fists. Easing it off her head, she waved Candrae over to brush out her tangles. The seat felt hard as she sat on it, wrong somehow. How could she sit, how could she do anything, when the Torithian War hung in the balance?

She squinted at her reflection, trying to see if the raised scar from the arrow wound were visible through her thin night dress. She didn't think so. Not only had the Torithians attacked her, but they had killed her father, and killed or imprisoned hundreds of Endrian and Torithian citizens. It was time for this conflict to end.

She pictured Firian standing in the Unreal throne room just before her coronation, both of them new world leaders. *I said I wanted to show you*, he had said. *So show me, then!* Although she was getting ready for bed, no sleep would come to her that night without news. *Come on, Firian!*

Maybe he didn't come because...

Her gaze shifted back to the darkening window. It wasn't late. He could still come to her. She wouldn't fear that something had happened to him until many more hours had passed.

She gave a small smirk. Firian wouldn't let anything happen to him. He was too cocksure and, frankly, too talented. At least from what she'd seen. She shoved away her fear. *He can do it.*

A small mental tug sent her tumbling into the Unreal, checking for him again. As soon as she closed her eyes, Firian appeared. Intense relief coursed through her. The halls of the palace materialized around him as he walked toward her.

Firian wore dark clothes, stained with brushed-off mud, his hair disheveled from fighting. He hadn't bothered to clean up his appearance for her, and he looked better for it.

She caught her breath enough to ask the question. "So?"

"It's done," he said in a low voice.

Her hand flew to her mouth and tears started in her eyes. "They surrendered?" she whispered, hardly daring to believe it.

The background wavered as he half-smiled at her. "I said I could end the war."

"You did say that," she replied. "And I told you *I* could end it. Remember?" She paused. Face to face, they said nothing more for a while. A thin streak of red leaked down his temple. She craned to look closer and saw that one of his ears was covered in blood. "What happened?" she asked, raising one hand to hover over that ear.

He brought her hand down again. The touch burned. "War. I'm fine."

"You always say you're fine." She barked a laugh to calm her mounting nerves. Why was she nervous? "We did it." When she blinked, tears stung her eyes.

He lifted his mouth in a smile. "Your wars are over."

Both of them. Faces passed before her mind—people who had lost loved ones, those who could now come home, those who never would...

When she came out of her reverie, his face was very close to hers. Maybe too close. He looked unwaveringly into her eyes. Her heart pumped hard in her chest. He had light freckles, this close. She didn't move away. She should go, tell the other Keepers... but she stayed. The moment stretched, warm and tingling, between them.

She closed her eyes and hugged him tight. The hug was a decision, a leap. A sob escaped her as all the tension started to ease away. "The war is over," she murmured, her voice almost breaking. She pressed her face to his chest as she held his strong body in her arms. *Is it okay to do this?* They had been through so much together, for and against each other.

He smelled like sweat and trees, not pine this time but something more tropical, like the smell in the solarium. She backed up to look at him. "Thank you."

He leaned forward until their foreheads touched, his strong arms reaching around her. It was hard to breathe.

Then, slowly, she tilted her face forward. Her nose rocked against his, and then her lips. As she pressed closer, his lips felt soft against hers. Heat flushed through her body.

After a beat, he responded so intensely it made her stumble

backward. She grabbed onto him for support, feeling his back tense under his thin shirt as he pulled her into him.

With a sort of desperation, he raked his fingers through her hair as he kissed her. She felt the heat of his breath against her mouth as he thumbed the shell of her ear from top to bottom.

Her fingers closed around the neck of his black shirt. Tentatively, she felt his chest, his neck, his hair. When she reached his ear, he tensed and squeezed her wrist, bringing her hand down to his chest again.

Firian had bound her wrists another time too.

"Wait, wait," she murmured, stepping back, looking at the ground. *What am I doing?* Her wide eyes found his, mirroring the confusion she felt. "Wait, I..." Her cheeks flamed and she glanced away, feeling small and winded.

A few moments ticked by. "Have you never done this before?" he asked, betraying surprise.

She shook her head solemnly. "No."

"It's just thoughts," he said, mouth twisted in a smirk. The background materialized again. Palace hallway. She glanced at the *sachion* tree, the patterned rugs.

Her face burned.

Just thoughts. He's right. It's just thoughts.

She changed the pattern of a rug from purple to blue and back again. Her gaze traced a few leaves on the tree. Hard to believe this was all Unreal. She had forgotten.

She looked back in his eyes. They were shining with the fight and the victory and the kiss. The kiss. She released a deep-held breath as he held her and closed his mouth over hers again. Her insides ached as she craned into him.

He walked her backward until she hit a hard wall. His body followed and pressed her against it. She gripped him closer, closer. His brow furrowed as he bent his head to hers, sucking the kisses from her lips, dragging his hands through her hair. She arched against him, wanting more.

One of his fingers traced a gentle line over the side of her neck. His hand slid down her neck, her collarbone, her ribs, her hip, and into the open space at the small of her back. His dangerous hands. They knew where to go to make her crave just a little more. More heat, more pressure, more weight of his muscular body against hers.

Breath came hard as she reached for his hair, soft and dirty, and scraped her nails gently across his scalp.

With a moan, he pulled back and drew his shirt over his head in one swift motion from the back of the neck. He was on her again, muscles straining as he touched her in a thousand small ways.

She wrapped her arms around him and felt the muscles slide under the skin, his shoulder blades shifting as he held her and pressed his lips to the hollow of her neck. Raised, calloused scars punctuated his skin like notes, and one long scar she remembered. She traced them with her fingers, playing him like music.

Her core grew hotter with every hungry kiss. He kissed her like he needed her, like he had practiced before. She let herself sink into his expert hands. Yes, no inner voice telling her...

Inner voice.

"Wait," she said breathlessly again. "Wait, Firian." The dry-mouthed huskiness of her voice surprised her and sent a fresh ache to her stomach.

He licked his lip absently as he stood up, barely a finger's width between them. The panes of his strong chest, his disheveled hair, his sultry blue-eyed gaze, the muscles over his arms, his abs, his hips, ripped away her words.

She fixed a flyaway hair as she caught her breath. "We can't."

He sidled closer, his legs against hers. "Why not?" His voice was low, teasing.

Her burning face betrayed her. "We can't go so far." Keepers had to stay pure.

He hummed and she felt the vibration in his chest. An agreement and an invitation. "I've waited a long time for this. You"—he licked her bottom lip—"are so beautiful." A firm kiss on the mouth. "And we"—he drew close, lingered, the point of his upper lip barely grazing hers, drew back again—"ended two wars together."

His breath played on her mouth, waiting. Her heart pounded painfully. He thought she was beautiful, just like this. Her chin tilted up to meet his lips again. He pressed her back with new passion. She gave into the kiss, letting her hands roam over his body, running over the white scars on his torso and adding to the ones near his neck. Relief and pleasure blended together as she stopped thinking of anything but his hands, his mouth, his warrior's body on hers.

Finally they released each other and stepped back, breathing heavily. Neither spoke.

But they'd admitted something to each other that they couldn't hide anymore. More than the war had changed.

***

KIRIA'S STOMACH still felt twisted as she ran out of the room to tell the other Keepers that the war was over. Not about Firian. She'd keep that a secret for now, but hopefully not for very long. The excitement of the kiss was still burning off, but so slowly that she thought she could live on the high for several days.

The look in his eyes, the relief of accepting what she had felt for a long time, longer than she wanted to admit...

She sighed. Firian Kess could be a good man after all—still a dangerous one, but a good one. At least, he'd followed through on his promise to help with the war, and that counted for something.

Okay, she thought, remembering the Tanyuin War and the last Head, maybe Firian wasn't a good man, but he was on his way to becoming one. And their tryst had only been in the Unreal. These were tempting, luxurious thoughts. That was all.

But that wasn't all. Something about that kiss had gone beyond the Unreal. To her, he was darkness and thrill. And very real.

The way he had kissed her... like he'd longed to do it for months.

She could be rational about it later. Today, the Torithian War was over, and she could still feel Firian's lips on hers.

Stopping outside Atty's door, she grinned, sure she was practically glowing with happiness.

16

FIRIAN

Firian smiled to himself as he walked up the moonlit gangplank onto the ship. It creaked and thudded, echoing through the chilled air. The breath of the water lapping below floated over his face and through his hair.

His heart was still thumping fast. *Finally!* He laced his fingers behind his back and leaned back a moment to peer at the star-splashed sky. *Finally.*

"Master Kess?"

He looked down. The source of the accented voice stood at attention. He was a lithe young man, one of the Endrian recruits, dressed not in the silver and blue armor of Brithnem, but a more subdued bronze and brown. The buttons on his uniform shone in the dim light.

"Yes?"

"Shall I bring the prisoners aboard?"

"Yes, bring them up. Put thirty in the hold of each ship."

"Yes, sir. I'll bring them up now."

Firian nodded once to the young man as he sped away. There was something familiar about his black hair.

Moments later, an escort of armed men led a line of

shackled pirates down the darkly pebbled beach to the ship. The men, stripped of their weapons, now looked like marooned sailors, smudged with grime. Some smelled strongly of alcohol and not all of them were dressed. Others were huge and muscular, with thick necks and jutting jaws. Their eyes darted dangerously, but the guards' swords kept them in check.

Firian stayed by the gangplank to meet them. He had been the Tanyuin Head for only a few weeks and his forces had defeated these men, now subject to him. If he told them to kneel, or to wait, or to fight, they would have to do as he said without question. He scrutinized their hard-set, sunburnt faces as they plodded on board. Fresh images of debauchery assaulted him like a disgusting smell.

The slaves would be safe now. Enderin had been placed in charge of sorting them out and getting them off the island safely over the next several weeks. It would take a monumental effort to bring each person back to their home, if they had one, but, from what Firian understood, they were going to try.

If the Academy hadn't needed more soldiers to defend it, he would gladly have left the pirates to fend for themselves, trapped on a tiny island somewhere. But they were proof of his victory—the victory he and Kiria and Bard had engineered together.

Kiria had looked so beautiful as she adored him. A pleasurable chill covered his body. Kissing her had been so much better than he'd imagined that he'd almost forgotten himself. Even as he reminded her that they were in the Unreal, that she could lose herself in him without consequences, he'd flinched when she touched his injured ear. He would be more careful to keep his bearings next time.

Impatience flooded through him. He was already tired of being around these pirates who had prodded and debased him, who had killed Kiria's father and attacked her without a thought. A shudder of hatred replaced his reverie.

As the Torithians came back into focus, a wad of thick spittle flew to the end of his boot.

Heat rushed to Firian's face. "Who was that?" he shouted.

The column of plodding men marched on.

Firian breathed heavily through his nose, knocking his defiled boot against the planks. He turned to one of the nonresponsive guards. "Who was that?"

"Who was that?" they echoed, prodding the closest men.

One man writhed from being jammed in the rib, but no one looked up.

Firian surveyed them as though staring hard enough would reveal the culprit. How dare they spit at him! He was the Tanyuin Head. He had taken his position by force, and—if he had to—he would maintain it the same way. Tanyu would not suffer indignities.

Overcome by the strength of his anger, he stepped back. He had to think. If he didn't calm down, he would hurt someone.

He turned and stormed across the deck to his cabin, a large one right beside the captain's.

Pulling the door hard shut, he glared at the painting on the wall, tempted to rip it down. Who needed luxuries at sea, anyway? It reminded him too much of the pirates and their spoils.

Shaking with rage, he leaned down and rubbed the grime off the toes of his boots. Hot blood still coursed through his face. It shot down, tingling, to his fingers.

With deliberate mindfulness, he took a deep breath and stood up straight. The effort constricted his throat, but he slowly felt himself getting calmer, though not forgiving.

The pirates thought they had a rough life, thick-skinned, not showing respect to anyone but their bull-headed leaders. Idiots.

They were like animals. He would show them how respect worked. They would give it to him one way or the other. An army wasn't built on anarchy. He had won their services fairly.

Something else bothered him about these men. Their expression. He'd seen the same contempt edging glances back at the Academy. The same venom. Firian had the Academy under control, didn't he? He'd considered threats from outside so much that he hadn't looked inward. He crossed his arms. Anyone could harbor the same disrespect, the same desire for him to die...

Many people had seen the man spit. Firian bit the inside of his lip until he tasted coppery blood. If he was going to remain the Tanyuin Head and see Kiria again, he'd have to give into his first impulse to strike back hard at the offender. It was almost calming not to have to hold back.

First, he would have someone would alert him when they were over the deepest water between Torith and Brithnem.

Convinced his face wasn't as flushed as it had been before, he stepped out of his cabin. The young man with black hair—why did he think he was a young man? He might be older than he was—marched past him on the deck.

"You!"

The man stopped. "Yes, Master Kess?"

"What's your name?"

"Jac Tanery."

Firian blinked. "Tanery?"

"Yes, Bard's brother."

Firian furrowed his eyebrows. They had heard about each other for years, but had never met. He felt almost territorial, and Jac had some kind of challenge flash across his face as well. It took a moment before he replied, "Tell me when we sail over the deepest water."

Jac tilted his head down in agreement. "Of course, sir."

"Master."

"What?"

"It's Master Kess, not sir."

HANDS BEHIND HIS BACK, swishing his long black coat, Firian paced in front of the line of men. None of them seemed repentant for the outrage he had suffered earlier. At this point, he didn't care who the culprit was. They would all pay for it.

He slowed to a stop and faced them. All these Torithians looked similar in the blackness—bulk-headed sailors with veins across their temples. A lantern swayed behind him, casting a pale glow over the waiting figures. Where Firian blocked the light, there was deep darkness.

He separated his words carefully. "Prisoners! The Academy and the Kingdom should have ordered your death, but you have the privilege to become soldiers in the world's greatest army."

One man in the line shifted uncomfortably. Another's mouth twitched. *A laugh?*

Firian felt himself flush again. Did these men have no respect at all? No, they didn't respect his authority or even human life.

Ignoring the fear pushing at the edges of his mind, Firian pointed to the second man. The Kingdom soldiers brought him forward.

The man brought his small eyes up to meet Firian's. They glinted defiance beneath the submissive exterior. Firian stared back, feeling heat rising to his cheeks. He brought his hands to his side.

"I am the Tanyuin Head," he said, "and I decide who lives and who dies." Saying those words calmed him a little, despite the pesky feeling that they may have sounded childish.

He swept a meaningful glance across the other men standing on the creaking deck. The Kingdom soldiers looked back at Firian with open suspicion. His comment must have rattled them. A few of them had even laid their hands on their weapons, waiting to see what he would do.

Though their threatening attitudes should have unsettled him further, he didn't fear what the soldiers would do. An open threat sent the blood of battle zinging through his veins with grim pleasure. Hidden threats, unknowns... those were the stuff of nightmares. Sias Jairon hadn't seen Firian coming.

As the highest-ranking person in this fleet, Firian had every right to put these Torithians in their place now. The soldiers would do nothing but watch and obey. They'd been trained for it. Scanning the ranks of shaved heads, Firian calculated how much it would take to send a message strong enough to subdue them all. In a commanding voice, he said, "Three of you will die tonight."

A few of them cried out in mixed languages, blaming the man next to them. Had their arms not been bound, a fight certainly would have broken out on the spot. Several of the men seemed to indicate one person in particular, whose loud protests almost drowned out the others.

Firian held up a hand for silence.

The undisciplined pirates didn't even notice at first. Firian's muscles tightened in frustration. Finally, they simmered into near silence. Firian suddenly couldn't wait to be back at the Academy, among the Tanyu, who knew how to be still.

The prisoners' chests rose and fell heavily. They darted glances across to each another. Even the Endrian soldiers knit their foreheads.

Firian turned his attention back to the man in front of him. The laughing man. Drops of sweat beading on his head betrayed his anxiety.

"That number will increase if anyone else disrespects the Tanyu, your protectors."

The sloshing sea was like a heartbeat.

The memory of the welt-covered girl and the emaciated children hardened his resolve. "Throw him in."

After only a fractional hesitation, the soldiers forced the struggling man to the railing and looked back at Firian.

"Throw him in," he repeated.

He was a large man, writhing against his ties, bending his knees to stay low. Ultimately, it took three soldiers to lift him over. He dropped heavily, as the first sound ripped from his mouth. A scream only started, then cut off in a merciless gurgle.

Firian's stomach flipped at the sound, but hopefully no one could see his discomfort. That Torithian deserved it.

When he turned back to the men, not one of them moved, soldier or prisoner alike. Waves splashed against the hull; sails flapped and strained against the masts.

Covertly, Firian took a deep breath, steadying his voice. "That leaves two."

THAT NIGHT, Firian reached his mind toward the Torithians as they lay asleep in the hold of the ship. Not one of them had the Talent. Too bad. He had almost hoped for a fight.

Whirring anger buzzed red in the Unreal, like a film over his eyes, sinking deep into him. He tried to picture the man who had spit. The First Level, the Second Level... He hadn't gone to the Second Level often since he and Belik had managed to take power from the last Tanyuin Head. A little out of practice, he dove down into the Unreal from where he was.

A brief sensation of choking.

Breathe, breathe! He sucked in a shaky breath. It had

been too long. He should have every meeting with Belik in the Second Level so he never fell behind. Belik was his right-hand man—now managing everything back at the Academy—but he could never give him an excuse to lord over him.

He cast his mind once more toward the sleeping Torithians. Now he saw something, like objects in a murky pond. These men didn't have the Talent, but they did have subconscious minds that could be manipulated even below the level of a dream. Here was the small slice of them that intersected with the Unreal.

Firian's heart started racing, blood pumping frantically through his veins. What could he do to them?

Throwing the man overboard had scared some of them, but if he killed two more in a way that none of them understood, that would be even more frightening. He remembered the prisoners they kept shackled to protect their filthy ships, and the young girls they abused for their amusement. These men deserved to die. None of them deserved the distinction of fighting on the Tanyu's behalf. If he didn't kill more of them, they would turn on him. One day, in the dark, a pillow would smother him in his sleep...

He let those ideas circulate a couple more times before advancing. He was not killing innocent people.

Experimentally, he turned toward the farthest room in the hold, focusing all his energy on the two figures sleeping there. He slowly willed the image to change. Now they were corpses. Not asleep, dead.

His heart jumped in his chest. The pulsing of the figures—their breathing, their heartbeat—skipped. One of them woke and bucked upright.

Firian pushed against the figures again, even harder this time. *Focus. Focus.* It felt like bending a thick branch. Bit by bit, splinter by splinter, their minds gave. A startled cry sounded far away. Firian kept his focus.

Something burst.

Firian jumped. *What was that?*

He swam up through the narrow channel to the Unreal he knew, with its vibrant colors and endless space, and then opened his eyes in the real world.

For some reason, he lay sprawled on the ground. His legs felt too heavy as he tucked them under himself in a crouch. His crown had rolled to the edge of his reach. Shaking, he hooked it on the nearest bedpost.

No one had ever done what he just did. At least, he'd never heard of anyone doing it. He squeezed his eyes shut. What had he even done? Had Belik ever mentioned this before? He flipped through years of memories, of practice, of goals. No, he'd never heard of something like this.

That break had devastated the Torithians, both of them. A familiar sinking in his gut told him they were dead.

He settled back on his heels, chest heaving, bothered that his hands were still trembling. He splayed his fingers against the floor to still them. Uncharacteristic exhaustion settled over him, and a mix of emotions so strong that they resolved into confusion. He had figured out a new deadly ability even Belik didn't know. How far could this power go? Did this mean he could hurt *anyone*, just with a thought? Pride and revulsion warred inside him.

The next morning, two Torithians lay dead in a pool of their own blood.

17

———

KIRIA

KIRIA SHOVED a large bite of soft-boiled egg in her mouth, too preoccupied to realize it was unladylike until afterward.

Amir Parohim gave her an imperious look veiled as concern. She met his glance, daring him to comment, and turned away. Candles lined the center of the grand table, the soft light flickering. Despite the hour, this room was still dark. A freshness in the air and the bags under Jori's eyes spoke of the morning, but here, in this windowless banquet hall, time seemed to stop.

Cúron's familiar, booming laugh sounded a few seats down. Since news of their victory broke, it was as though a bottle had been unstopped. Guards smiled and clapped each other on the shoulder as they went to their posts. Jori kept Kiria updated on all the extra parties in the city. Rejoicing followed her everywhere.

Because of the war, her coronation tour had been put on hold. Now that it was over, she could leave immediately, to meet and rejoice with people all over the Kingdom. Her mother had debated whether to come along. She would have been welcome, but, in the end, they decided Merian might take some of the attention that was meant to establish Kiria as the new Keeper. So she graciously stepped aside.

True to his word, Cúron had also publicly credited her with the victory. Because of her successful treaty with the Tanyuin Academy, she was the face of the alliance.

But this victory was Firian's as much as hers. Her skin tingled with the memory of their kiss. If her mother asked now, she would admit that she was interested in someone. But she wouldn't say who. Not yet, anyway. Despite all Firian had done for them, the people around this table had extremely mixed feelings about him. She could hardly blame them for their doubts. In the past, he had done terrible things.

He hadn't appeared the past couple nights. Probably busy with Torithians. There was no way he regarded their kiss as a mistake. They'd both wanted it. She would try to be patient, but even now, she wanted to check the Unreal for him.

Atty burst out laughing, bringing her attention back to the table. He pressed his hands over his mouth as Jori leaned to whisper something else to him. Jori's face distorted into the mockery of a fancy noble. The brothers both looked furtively at the faces around the table.

She couldn't even tell them about Firian. The knowledge brought a slight sinking to her stomach. It wasn't as though she were doing anything wrong, was she?

Jori saw her watching them and winked. He couldn't let them in on their joke with the table between them, but she already suspected she knew what he was saying.

More than once, he'd whispered in her ear, mimicking the voices of two people at a party. Since they were out of earshot, he could invent any wild story he liked. "Oh, my dear, I must go off to see the nymphs on the Sharb Isles." In a higher voice, "Darling, don't think of falling in love with them!" A lower voice. "I already have. Her name is Mephi...bosheba." A laugh at his own absurdity, soon collected again. "I couldn't help myself. After we both rode the fish around the island, it was all over." "You rode fish?" "Yes, saddles and everything." "Oh! No one could ever be as charming as you. I'll never love anyone again." But the woman's mouth hadn't stopped moving and he had to think of more. "The way you smell like an ocean god," he continued in his high voice. "And... make love like a... dolphin." The man began speaking. "Oh, Penelope, you'll always be in my heart. We'll name our half-nymph child after you." "Even if it's a boy?" "Of course, my dear."

The memory made her chuckle. She kicked him under the table.

He finished what he was saying to Atty and then cast her a furtive glance. Atty caught on immediately and looked at her with a question in his eyes.

"You want to come on the coronation tour next week?" she asked Jori in an undertone. She hadn't spent much time with him in recent months, since she had been so busy learning all the duties of a Keeper while being the main point of contact in planning the war.

Atty turned to his brother. "That's a lot of traveling," he explained, as though it weren't obvious. The realization must have hit Atty hard on his own tour. "Never enough hot water."

Jori straightened and faced him. "Why didn't you invite me on yours?"

"My coronation tour?" Atty's eyebrows scrunched downward in thought. "I wasn't sure I was allowed to invite anybody."

"You can invite anyone you like when you're Keeper," said Jori.

Atty half-shrugged, not exactly apologetic, but a little ashamed of his past naiveté. "Well, I didn't want to bother anyone."

In mock astonishment, Jori put a hand to his chest. "Are you calling me a nuisance?"

"Well, you're not exactly cut out for Kingdom business."

Kiria waited until no one seemed to be looking before shoveling her side of capers onto the plate Atty held out for her. He was the only one who liked them. Jori had already added his to the little green pile.

"We both know that." Jori turned to Kiria again. "So where are you going on this tour?"

She described the route that started south and made its way northeast and finally back again, roughly in a large circle.

Chetana, her serving girls, and a host of guards and servants were the only ones she knew would accompany her. She couldn't relax with any of them. If a friend didn't come, she would be tempted to spend all her time with Firian. Eventually, someone might find out she was seeing him, and that couldn't happen yet. That is, if he ever came back.

"I didn't go south," Atty said, waving for another egg. "I wonder why they're adding King's Heights to your trip. It's nowhere near Charäkhnem." Atty had formally requested the Charäkhni princess's hand in marriage, but he hadn't talked about his plan for a while. The match would strengthen their most important alliance, he claimed, and Kiria thought he was right. That is, if the King of Charäkhnem agreed. As far as she knew, Atty hadn't heard back.

"I wish it were Shifra," she said. "That was beautiful." She stopped short, realizing they could draw the connection to Firian and ask about him. Thankfully, neither did.

"That's too far away," Atty replied. He nodded thanks as a servant placed another egg cup in front of him. He tapped the shell with his spoon. "But King's Heights. I'm sure they haven't been included for generations, maybe at all."

That was partially the reason it had been added to the itinerary. "They're still part of the Kingdom," she said. Honestly, it didn't sound like it would be her favorite stop either. The people of King's Heights were so private, and their reputation (real or not) wasn't flattering. One could spot someone from that city anywhere. They were stronger, meatier versions of Kingdom Dwellers with their dark hair, light skin. Stories had it that they were proud of their ability to survive, their tough blood, and they were mistrustful of visitors, particularly Khelê. But those were old stories. It was time to repair some of those fractured reputations on both sides.

"You still haven't answered the question," she said.

Jori placed both elbows on the table and peaked his fingers together. Atty rolled his eyes at his brother's theatrics, but there was a smile in the corner of his mouth as he took a bite of egg.

"Hm," Jori hummed, resting his chin high on his fingers. "I'm terribly busy."

She kicked him again. "Liar."

He brought his hands down. "Fine. You're right. I'm not sure I would like it, but you know I like adventure."

"And parties and parades. There will be parties between all the meetings and ceremonies."

Jori turned to his brother. "Can you do without me for a while?" His question was joking, but the slightest bit of serious-ness crept into his tone. Sometimes Atty got lonely, especially since their father died.

"I think so," he said stoutly. "Don't make me look like a fool when you go to Charäkhnem!"

"Oh, you can do that all by yourself, I'm sure."

Kiria leaned forward and lowered her voice. "Did you hear back from Shear Ganesha?"

"A few days ago." The announcement gave Atty a glowing smile.

Kiria grinned. "Why didn't you tell me? That's wonderful!"

"The letter talked about 'final negotiations,'" Jori said, "so it's not finalized."

"But I'm expecting another letter before the end of the week," Atty said. "If he agrees, then Princess Haved will travel back with you."

"Oh, Atty, that's... I'm so happy for you!" She reached across the table to pat him on the arm, the one laced with tattoos from his fingers all the way up until they disappeared beneath his sleeve. She knew Atty had been longing to do something positive for the Kingdom, to prove to everyone that he could make his father proud.

"Have you met her yet?" she asked. "Is that something else you're not telling me?"

"No, he has not," Jori said impishly, separating each word. Atty responded with a look that said the two of them had had this conversation before.

"So you don't know what she looks like?" Kiria asked.

"Hag," Jori muttered.

Atty smacked him. "No, but I've seen a painting and met Prince Amrit, her brother."

"Does she speak the common tongue?" The thought hit her with some force. How would Atty communicate if the girl didn't speak the same language? Atty had always been a hopeless romantic—hopeless, in the sense that he almost never knew what to say or do except follow girls with his moony eyes. She had witnessed it dozens of times. His poor heart. Maybe he could communicate through kind gestures. He'd never been very good with words anyway.

"She's been practicing," Atty said. "I heard she's as good as Amrit."

The last time the prince had come with the Charäkhni ambassadors, his speaking skills had much improved. Apart from his thick accent, his knowledge was fluent.

"I'm glad," she said. "Good."

Atty swallowed another caper-peppered bite of egg and waved his spoon in the air in an almost Jori-like gesture. "See?" he said. "I can't have you messing anything up for me."

"What am I going to do?" Jori protested.

"Flirt with anything that moves, probably," Kiria said, laughing.

Atty gave his brother a pointed look.

A smile slowly widened across Jori's face. "I don't see what the problem is."

"Are you sure you want to invite him?" Atty asked her, half-teasing, half-pleading.

She paused, taking stock of the people already scheduled to leave with her. Jori would be more of a help than a liability. Probably. She nodded. "Absolutely."

FIRIAN

Curiosity to see the famed Academy piqued as they got closer. Firian read it in their body language. He was eager to get back too. He had ordered new training barracks to be built, but he'd only seen the plans. The best place for them was the relatively tree-less area behind the bakery, where the festival had been last month, where Old Danior kept his bees.

Firian marched in front now, guiding The Endrians and the prisoners along the path to Tánuil that he knew so well. Although he'd overheard several Kingdom soldiers talking about wanting to see the Academy too, they had all been ordered to sail back home immediately after they docked to let off Firian and the rest.

The Academy rose before them, a sheer face of dark rock in the fading light. A smile played on his lips as he gazed up at it. Finally his. How different this entry was to his last mission. Now it felt more like coming back to a kingdom. Well, almost. The decision to make its location public changed the face of world politics, tilting it a little sideways on its axis. All because he had decided it would be so. Because the trade was worth Kiria's trust and loyalty.

For a moment, all those years of ingrained secrecy recoiled at having so many strangers with him. He forced himself to stand straight and walk like a returning king.

As they all came closer to Tánuil, Firian adjusted the iron circlet on his head so that the open square faced forward. Behind him came some of the best Masters, then Endrians in brown leather and mail jackets, then Torithians in the center (still shackled), then more Endrians, and finally more Tanyuin forces at the rear. If they walked three abreast, the line of troops would stretch practically the entire length of Tánuil.

Pride ran through Firian's entire body as he stepped into town, the Academy rising above him like a huge shadow of himself. The dark stones were soothing, impenetrable. Something that had been tight in his gut since the pirate's defiance on the ship started to loosen.

Whole families came out of their houses to see them. A man stood in his doorway with one arm around his wife's shoulder and the other across the chest of a small boy standing in front of them. As they passed, Hyrum the pub owner considered them thoughtfully, picking the grime from his nails with his apron. All eyes flitted over the Torithians, the Endrian soldiers, and the Tanyuin troops, but they rested on Firian. Something like fear emanated from the crowd. Firian caught a glimpse of Devanie, watching them through the window of the herbalist. Her eyes blazed. He smiled at her.

Tánuil barely had streets, much less military processions. It was no wonder the townspeople were awed. The strange thing was the silence. Word seemed to spread without anyone speaking. With the caution of animals unused to the sight of people, everyone came out of their homes and businesses until the majority of Tánuil stood gaping at them. The people seemed utterly unsure of what to do. Proud but afraid.

Though he didn't like speeches, Firian knew he should tell

the people of Tánuil what had happened in the war, and how to treat these strangers. Some of them had grown up never having seen any, apart from the new recruits at the Academy. Their wide eyes said they would hang on every word. Suddenly, speaking sounded much more palatable.

He turned back to the men following him. "Lead these men to the barracks!" he commanded as they came abreast of Danior's bakery.

At his voice, more people emerged from doorways, swelling the crowd. Men and women in black appeared on the darkening road from the Academy. Even Tanyu wanted to see him.

His breathing quickened with excitement and he hopped on a slope so more people could see clearly. The Endrian troops started to lead the bound Torithians away. Firian turned to a nearby Tanyu. "Get everyone outside."

In a shockingly short time, more Tanyu and the few towns-people who hadn't noticed the parade came out to hear him. Slowly, everyone gathered around the slope where Firian stood.

Firian scanned the crowd, blood beating in his fingertips. "These are the Torithian pirates," he cried. "Now part of our army. Because of us, the Torithian War is over!" He scanned the darkest portion of the listeners and found Belik, whose eyes shone hungrily, full of amazement. He felt lightheaded. "Too long we've stayed in secrecy and fear. The Tanyu are the greatest fighting force in the world, and we shouldn't be afraid to show everyone what we are. Starting now, our location will no longer be hidden. You can trade freely with other nations."

Astonishment rippled across the townspeople, who all looked at each other. Some frowned, outraged; others acted overjoyed.

"Any strong man or woman can join our army, share in our greatness. All we ask is absolute loyalty." He laid special emphasis on the last two words as he watched the brawny backs of the prisoners disappear into the darkness. If the need arose, he would show everyone what he meant by those words.

A current of energy sparked and hummed under his skin, and he almost wished someone would challenge him right there. No one rose up, but his heart kept beating fast, ready for a fight. He took a deep breath. "Tomorrow, we announce ourselves to the world." An idea struck him. "But tonight, a war is over. Tonight, we celebrate!"

Scattered applause built to a roar. Even the Tanyu joined in. If Firian hadn't let the surrounding cities know about the Academy, this deafening noise would announce them just as well. The screaming became frenzied, the sound of shouting long subdued. Someone whistled.

Firian stepped down the slope and waved over the nearest Tanyu, Master Makai. He lowered his voice and told Makai to gather a few Masters to help watch the Torithians. He didn't want the pirates taking advantage of what was bound to turn into a wild night.

"Making a name for yourself, I see."

He turned around and found himself face to face with Belik, his eyes alight with pride.

"We haven't had a reason to celebrate for too long," Belik said.

Firian suddenly remembered the small funeral the Tanyu had held for the Sias Jairon, the last Head. They'd held it almost guiltily, but with an understanding that the Tanyu were great enough that any leader who had served for so long needed to be remembered and not left for the birds. He was buried too deep for wolves to dig him up, near the other Tanyuin Heads in an unmarked grave. A few Masters had attended. Firian had made an appearance, presiding as the current leader. The whole ordeal had been dreamlike.

Master Belik patted him heavily on the shoulder, his gaze

flicking up to the circlet on his head. Firian touched it, almost unconsciously. Something over Firian's shoulder caught Belik's eye. "I'll leave you to it," he said. Not one for celebration, Belik began walking slowly back to the Academy.

Firian looked over his shoulder and saw Devanie. She had come out of the spice shop, skin flushed. She came up to him, breathless. Before she spoke, she paused, maybe considering how to address him. Should she call him Firian or Master Kess, the Tanyuin Head? The idea left him flushed as well. He took in her eager body—thin dress that clung in all the right places, soft brown hair, scent of musk and sage...

Not long ago, he would gladly have taken his cue and spent a torrid night with her. But now his mind wandered back to Kiria. Since that night in the Unreal, it never strayed far. The mere thought of her left Devanie's beauty hollow. Well, not entirely hollow. *Kiria doesn't have control over me.* The thought ran like a chant through his mind. He could spend the night with Devanie if he wanted to. The thing was, he didn't want to.

"I'm glad you're back," Devanie said, her voice husky and unsure. Her gaze searched his face, his eyes, his lips.

He stood before her for a heartbeat as she waited, anticipating his response.

A shorter Tanyu pressed his way through the crowd, his eyes full of happy tears. "Fir!" he cried.

Glad for the excuse to turn away from Devanie, Firian broke into a smile and clapped him on the arm. "Bard!"

Bard pulled him in for a hug. When he let go, Firian said, "Your layout worked. The job you did here..."

Bard's grin waned. In the poor light, his skin looked grayer than usual. "Thanks, mate. You okay?" His dark eyes gleamed, despite the circles under them.

Firian remembered his sliced ear, invisible under his hair. "Yeah. Just a few scratches." He felt invincible.

Apparently realizing Firian wasn't going to pay attention to her, Devanie turned away and acted as though she'd seen someone she knew in the crowd.

If this hadn't been a night for celebrating, he would have returned immediately to the Academy and dived into the Unreal to see Kiria again. He hadn't seen her since the kiss. His mind had been occupied with the Torithians dead because of his new ability, and, honestly, his vulnerability needed to subside before he encountered her again. Everyone knew a *katah* was dangerous if it went too far. Denying himself the right to see her, even for a few days, had been one of the greatest tests of his self-discipline. Maybe he was being overly cautious, but it would pay off when he saw her and the balance of power had returned safely to him.

"You hear about Tiev?"

Firian snapped back to reality. "No. What happened?" But the answer the clear from the moment he asked the question.

Bard swallowed. "He never came out of it. We couldn't do anything."

"Did Master Belik try to help him?"

"He said Tiev didn't want to come back." His bottom lids filled with weary tears. He cleared his throat and scrubbed at his eyes before they could fall.

"It's okay," Firian said, clapping him on the back and guiding him away from the other Tanyu so they wouldn't see Bard cry. Curious stares followed Firian, conspicuous in his crown. "You won a war!"

Bard sucked in a breath and nodded. He had just killed his first man, and Tiev had always been more Bard's friend than Firian's. He shouldn't have been surprised that Bard was in low spirits. But tonight was a night to celebrate.

"Come on. What can I get you? I'll get you an ale or a sticky bun or whatever you want. Five sticky buns!"

Bard's wide smile returned.

"Oh, and I brought your brother," he added.

"Where?" Brightening, he craned his neck to see.

"He's here. I think he's with the Torithians." Catching Bard's eagerness, he said, "Why don't you watch the prisoners tonight? I need a few Tanyu to make sure they stay under control."

"I'll just say hi." Bard didn't need more incentive. He sprinted off into the darkness. Firian followed behind, more slowly, a smile tugging at his mouth.

They'd really done it. Some of the tension of the past weeks started to melt away. Yes, Bard didn't agree with everything he did—especially the way he had come into power—but they'd won the Torithian War together. Enderin and others would be free from the pirates' oppression. Kiria had kissed him. All that work had mattered. Firian Kess, the boy from nowhere, had made all that happen.

By the time he caught up with Bard at the barracks, he felt lighter than he could ever remember feeling in his life, except maybe when he got into the Academy for the first time.

The barracks weren't finished, but they were coming along. They'd constructed them just where Firian had commanded, and they looked just large enough for the influx of Torithians. Dozens of Endrian soldiers stood outside. Others came and went with supplies and information. Commanders gave instructions. Some looked around with the same hungry curiosity Firian had seen earlier when they'd marched into town. Most of the soldiers noticed Firian with rapt attention when he approached.

A brief pang echoed in Firian's chest. Had anyone told Bard about what happened on the ship? He wasn't ready for him to know about his newfound ability.

Firian found Bard talking animatedly with Jac in the deep

shadow along the back wall. Jac stood at attention when Firian came around the corner.

"…So Edom got married?" Bard was saying.

"Yes."

Something about Jac's response made Bard give a puzzled look before turning around and seeing Firian. He waved him forward. "Fir! You've met Jac? Well, yeah, you have." He turned back to his brother. "It's so weird to have you here!"

Jac cast Firian a glance with a hint of apprehension or defiance in it. "Master Kess," he greeted. It was a moment before he continued. "Yes, Edom got married a while ago. You know how he is."

Bard cut him off. "How old's Aline?"

"She's twelve."

Bard rolled his eyes in happy surprise. "Can't believe it! Oh, what's Edom's wife's name?"

"Istia. They're having a baby soon. Or they had it already. I've been away for a few months, so can't be sure."

"Ah, that's wicked! So happy for him." The lilting Endrian accent came out stronger in both of them as they talked together.

"Hey, why weren't you on the island with us?" A small but unmistakably cold note entered Jac's tone. He looked over Bard's black Tanyuin outfit with a falsely lighthearted smile.

Someone in a group of young Endrian soldiers behind him called out, "Jac! You on duty? Come with us! We're going to find a drink, if they have those here." A second boy laughed as though he'd told a joke.

Jac shot them a dazzling smile, a different version of Bard's. "Be there later!"

With dismissive cries, the group disappeared into the darkness, apparently eager to get on with the celebration.

"I thought you would be," Jac continued, "after everything that happened." His eyes flickered to Firian and then back to his brother.

Firian imagined he could see Bard's blush in the dark and his mood darkened. *Everything that happened?* Jac must be talking about the brief war between the Kingdom and the Tanyu. To Firian's knowledge, the Academy had never attacked Enderin, only the capital. And now that he was Tanyuin Head, all of that had stopped.

"I never wanted to be at war, yeah?" Bard replied. "It's over now, anyway." His shoulder twitched as though he were casting off gloomy thoughts of the past. A smile split his face again as he glanced back at Firian. "It's all over. And you're here! It's so good to see you again."

"Well, you never were a fighter." Jac punched Bard lightly on the arm, but his tone had become even more acidic.

Firian stepped forward and asked sharply, "Do you know what the Academy does?" A beat of frozen silence met his question. "Bard was working for me here. Tanyuin business you wouldn't begin to understand. He wasn't on Torith, but he didn't need to be. It was on my orders that he stayed. Without him, we wouldn't have taken the compound and won the war."

"I apologize, Master Kess. I didn't mean—"

"It's okay," Bard said quickly, but he gave Firian a grateful look.

"I'm going for some ale," Firian said. Bard cared enough about Jac to spend more time with him, but Firian didn't. "Come over when you're finished here. Let me know what I can get you." He gave one more pointed glare at Bard's older brother. "You earned it."

A KNOCK POUNDED on the door. Firian's head pounded with it. He opened his sticky eyes. Still dark.

As he sat up in bed, the room swam. This is why he avoided getting drunk—it made his mind fuzzy. Faint nausea churned in his stomach. Celebrating had been good while it lasted, but now all he wanted to do was sleep.

The knock sounded again. He set his jaw in frustration. *This had better be important.*

When he opened the door, Bard was there. He should have known. There were only two people the guard would let through without question: Bard and Belik.

"Firian, we're missing one of the Torithians!" he hissed. Urgency was written in every line of his face.

Firian cursed, unreasonably angry.

"He got out the window. They told me they thought everyone was asleep."

"Tell them all to find him," he said with a hard edge in his voice. His thoughts came piecemeal. "I don't care when it is. Tell me immediately and I'll come. Bring him to the place we were earlier. And wake everybody up if you have to!" He slammed the door.

Instantly, he regretted slamming the door in Bard's face. This wasn't his fault.

Firian pulled on a shirt and shoes. The crown and coat went on last before he left the room.

What gory timing! The first time outsiders see the Academy and one of them defies me. He couldn't let it stand. Ice raced through his veins. He'd have to make an example of the pirate once he was caught.

An hour later, Maz the border patroller found the Torithian in the woods. It took two men to bring him to the spot Firian had specified. The gray light of dawn shone just enough to see by. Trees and houses looked black in the chilly air.

Bard had apparently told the others what Firian said because everyone was up—people of Tánuil, warriors of the Academy, troops both victorious and defeated—and gathered where they had the night before to hear his speech. Colors were sluggish to return. Everyone moved slowly, some clearly fighting off hangovers. Firian wished their celebration hadn't been quite as short lived. Hopefully this display would instill confidence in him, though, and give them a reason to celebrate loyalty in the future. Or at least fear insurrection. They would be on his side after this, unquestioning, because no one could withstand the new Tanyuin Head.

Maz and another border patroller dragged the huge Torithian in front of the slope where Firian stood. The pirate's bald head reflected the dim light. He bared his teeth in defiance as he was forced to his knees.

Firian regarded him in silence for a moment, letting the gravity of the situation sink in. A light breeze waved his coat and made people in the crowd gather their sweaters and shawls closer.

This silence was different than last night's. Now, no one dared to breathe. They all waited to see what he would do. Tanyu had cut off heads of those who opposed them, but not since Firian had come. Now they preferred to work in the shadows. Nothing was more frightening than what people didn't understand or expect.

Firian closed his eyes.

If only he could do this with his eyes open, as he could with almost anything else in the Unreal. He might get there, but for now, he had to do it with his eyes closed. Maybe that added to the drama of the moment. After all, he wanted them all to remember this.

As Firian reached for his subconscious, the man shifted

uncomfortably, apparently aware of pressure building inside him. Firian heard his knees in the dust. Feet began scrabbling against the ground, all in vain because he was held down. Panicked curses escaped his lips. They were in a different language, maybe Eradi, but curses always sounded the same. Firian felt the man's blood run faster, his breathing turn to terrified, angry gasps. *Focus.* He was almost there. The man's panting became screams, and Firian's heart beat harder to hear them. A warrior's scream held infectious fear. *Focus.*

Something released, and the man's screams stopped. A few new, shocked ones from the crowd sprang up in their place. Firian came up and up and opened his eyes into reality.

Mothers had turned away, hands to their faces. Children started crying, and a few Tanyu had their mouths hanging open in surprise. The Torithian lay face upward with his hands balled into fists. Through his eyes and his clenched teeth, blood seeped out. Black blood slowly soaked the ground beneath him.

Firian swallowed, feeling almost manic. He looked at the remaining prisoners and hoped they'd had a good view. This would happen to them too if they disrespected the Tanyu's gift of letting them live. Firian's hands shook and his too-shallow breathing wouldn't allow him to give another good speech. Light-headedness came on quickly.

Without a word, he marched off the slope and headed back to the Academy. From the corner of his eye, he saw Maz bend down to scoop the lifeless body off the ground.

Everyone knew better than to talk to him. He saw the questions in their eyes, but everybody gave him a wide berth. He stalked down the path to the huge double doors and, by the time he reached them, his arms were shaking visibly. At least he hadn't fallen down this time.

Agitated, unable to stay still, he paced the length of the fountain courtyard and back. Almost no one was in the building. They had all come out to see his demonstration.

As the Tanyu began to come back, he retreated to his office. He almost dismissed the guard, but thought better of it, closing the door instead. He needed to feel alone. Leaning on the chair behind his desk, he sucked breath deep into his lungs and exhaled.

The door opened. Firian's head shot up as he prepared to pour curses on anyone who dared interrupt him. It was Belik with a glass of water. Firian's energy wilted and he fell into his chair. Belik wordlessly set the water glass in front of him on the desk. Firian took it and drank. The water tasted sweet on his dry mouth.

"Gory Torithians," Belik growled, settling into the chair across from him.

Firian nodded.

"I have Jovan over there now, heading up the training. He won't be easy on them either." He paused, looking at Firian with subdued eagerness. "I've... never seen anyone do what you did," he said. "If someone was thinking about going against you, they won't do it now."

Firian frowned. "Is anyone?"

"No, no." Belik waved a conciliatory hand. "Not now."

The next pause was pregnant with a question. Firian was too exhausted to ask what it was.

"Did that man have the Talent?" Belik finally asked.

Firian shook his head.

The answer excited his old Master. Pride shone on his face. "Then how did you do that?"

"I figured it out on the ship."

"Do you use the Second Level?"

Firian was too tired to feel the right amount of satisfaction. His knowledge had outstripped Belik, who had taught him everything he knew about being a Tanyu. Right now he just wanted to sleep.

When he didn't answer, Belik's enthusiasm faded back into his regular stoicism. "You'll have to tell me later," he said, rising to leave.

"I will," said Firian, and he fell asleep on his desk.

19

———

FIRIAN

THE ENDRIAN TROOPS left the next day, ready to spread the news about the Academy's location. The thought spread like fire in Firian's chest. Tanyu had kept the secret for over a century, and people all over the world went to great lengths to get it. Men had even lost their lives. The soldiers should count themselves lucky to be among the first to see it.

There could be no turning back now. The scouts, and now the Kingdom's Endrian allies, knew where to find the mysterious Tanyuin Academy, with its heroes and treasure stores of tributes.

In his castle, Firian felt safer than he had on the nausea-inducing ship, but the widespread news of the Academy's location would bring new dangers. Nothing he couldn't handle.

Part of him was glad that everyone had gotten to see his new ability. Now that he felt better and had had a while to think about it, he wasn't sure he wanted to explain it to Belik. This could be his and his alone.

His new power exhilarated him, running like hot metal through his veins, but it made him feel dangerous or even sinful. Unpredictable even to himself.

If Kiria hadn't already heard about it, he decided he wouldn't tell her. Had it been only a week since he'd seen her in the Unreal? It felt longer. Whether or not he felt completely ready, he had to see her again. Any more waiting and he'd go mad, or Kiria's feelings would turn, killing any chance he had to be with her.

Sitting back in the chair at his desk, he closed his eyes, an indulgent gesture when he hadn't needed to do that to reach the First Level in years.

Inhaling a deep breath, he wrapped a setting around himself. This time it was the island. He could show it to her first-hand. Well, second-hand. The space he built was purely fictional, drawing on the elements he had seen on Torith: the fragrant earth, enormous leaves dripping with moisture, refulgent flowers, crash of distant surf. Maybe that part would feel like home to her. Trees and foliage crowded the hollow he created. Smells from the Academy, like a hint of cinnamon and pine, joined the rich leafy odors. He tinkered with a detail here and there, with the blue of the sky and the call of birds.

Something hitched in his gut. How many of his own favorite things had he included? Glancing around, he saw a portrait of one naked corner of his soul. Each sight or scent felt like a key she could use against him, opening doors he wanted closed. With a thought, he smudged the edges of those personal touches.

She didn't respond. Maybe she was busy. It was mid-morning and she couldn't sense the Talent as clearly as he could. Still he waited, absently stroking a leaf that hung beside him.

The soft silence became pointed. Did she not want to come? Impossible.

He saw himself as another would have seen him, waiting for

a girl all alone when there were so many other things to do. If someone needed him to check on the Torithians or talk strategy, they would make themselves known. Even so, restlessness began to irritate him, the aftereffect of his successes leaving him oddly hollow. Kiria was the only goal he had yet to solidify.

"Kiria?"

She appeared, beaming. "I'm about to go to a meeting," she chastised.

Relieved, he grabbed her arm and pulled her toward him for a kiss. She melted into it.

When he pulled away, a smile still played on the corners of her lips. She had a confident air that hadn't been there last time. "I'm practicing my tour speech in a couple minutes. Is this..." Understanding dawned in her eyes as she looked around, seeing the forest for the first time. "Is this Torith?"

"Do you like it?"

She pulled her shoulders upward in a pleased gesture. "It's beautiful. It's too bad so many horrible things happened here."

"Not here," he reminded her, glancing at the bright red flower he had placed in the clearing to ground himself. No subtleties this time.

"Well..." She cocked her head from side to side, disagreeing. Then her expression changed into something more vulnerable. "I'm glad you're here. I didn't see you for a long time..."

"I was busy." The excuse came too easily. "The Torithians arrived last night."

"Oh!" she said with the speed of someone ready to accept whatever reason he gave.

They were both quiet for a moment. For a reason he couldn't pinpoint, he felt awkward. Kiria was here. She had answered his call and gazed at him expectantly. He had won her, or very nearly so. Then why did he feel a twinge of nerves?

He needed to go back to something he knew. "I'm glad you're here now," he said, tipping her chin up. He felt her breath catch as he lowered his head. "All the soldiers toasted to you last night, for what we did."

"There's more justice in the world because of us," she said dreamily, ready for kisses.

The comment took him by surprise, but it shouldn't have. "You're right. There is." Pleasure glowed anew in his chest.

She raised a hand, shyly moving his hair. "How's your ear?"

For a second, he couldn't think clearly enough to answer her question. It hadn't been like this with Maya or Devanie or the others. Their presence had burned, not turned his brain to mashed potatoes. "Fine," he managed, taking her hand and brushing his lips against her palm.

"Firian." The voice came from outside the hollow. Kiria didn't seem to hear it, so he ignored it.

Time pressed in on them both. Her meeting, this gory intruder on his peace...

She wove their fingers together. Another gesture he wasn't used to, as intimate as an embrace. He squeezed her hand and kissed her hungrily, as though he could devour time.

"Firian." Tap, tap.

He swallowed a curse and broke away. "Kiria, I..."

"I have to go too," she said quickly, face flushed. "I just wanted to see you first."

So many unsaid things lingered in the air that Firian felt he could catch them if he reached out. She was hiding something. It was in her start-and-stop way of speaking. And he wasn't saying everything he was thinking either. He never did.

He nodded. Hopefully there would be many more opportunities. He gave her one last kiss on the cheek and disappeared back into the Real.

Belik stood over him, one eyebrow raised and a finger pressed against the desk. Sitting up straight, Firian rolled his shoulders, shaking off the weakness that had settled on him over the night.

Now that Firian was lucid, Belik took his chance to sit down. He dragged his chair closer to the desk.

"Jovan has the Torithians on their feet this morning," he began in a jovial way that didn't match his body language.

"He should." Almost as soon as Firian had risen, his guard had informed him of potential threats to the Academy—just whispers. But a lot of whispers.

"The people of Raewhith are just trying to keep up."

Picturing Caedmon, his childhood friend, doing laps alongside a Torithian pirate was a funny thought.

Belik grunted, getting to his real point. "But we both know these troops won't be enough. Really, we need some that are already trained. We need an existing militia."

Firian waved his hand. "I know." His brief experience of war was enough to solidify his understanding of that.

"Now that you're back, I can tell you," Belik said, he placed one meaty hand on the tabletop, an invitation to strategize with him. To share with him. "I've scouted other locations to find willing soldiers. Imlin seems like a good starting place, and Archer's Point."

For Brett's sake, Firian wouldn't mix Raewhith's soldiers with those from Archer's Point, which had often vandalized and terrorized his little town when he was growing up. He had only struck a deal with Raewhith in order to keep it safe for her. The Tanyu he'd posted there kept him updated on his father as well. Even though Firian hadn't heard any reports of abuse, he still haunted his father's dreams sometimes when he couldn't sleep, sending him nightmares.

No, for his mother and sister, he wouldn't recruit soldiers from Archer's Point. Imlin would have been more promising, except for one thing. "Imlin belongs to the Kingdom."

"So do we," Belik replied quietly.

An odd silence fell. Firian's limbs went cold at the accusation. One of the main reasons he had taken power was to help the Western Kingdom win the war against the Torithians. He had to pledge his allegiance as a sign of good faith, or the Keepers wouldn't have let him near their troops.

"Do you object?" Firian asked slowly, fixing Belik with a steel gaze. Almost unconsciously, he reached for his power beneath the surface. But he would never use it against Belik, no matter how much he aggravated him. They both knew it.

"No, Master Kess." The title grated from him, revealing the only reason he agreed.

"It's worked well so far. There's no harm in having a strong alliance."

"It hasn't started working at all. They used us to win their war. If a militant group comes for the Academy, do you think they'll step in?" Belik shook his head sardonically. "The Amir will make sure they don't. I just hope they don't ask us for any more favors."

Firian opened his mouth.

Belik spoke again, "Do they owe *us* any loyalty?"

At that, Firian drew a measured breath and smiled. One of the Keepers did.

Belik's face, however, fell. He squinted. "Firian," he started carefully, "you know I'm on your side. I want to see the Tanyu with the power and respect they deserve. Glories like in Corso's day, or Naedra's. We've fallen so far from our purpose. And together we can do it." He regarded him and turned his head to one side, deliberating, while keeping his eyes on Firian.

For an uncomfortable moment, he wondered if Belik was reading his thoughts.

The Master's next words were even more deliberate. "What do we really gain from this?" His eyes darted to the scrap of Raewhith's flag on the desk.

Sensing a challenge, Kiria's word rose to his lips. "Justice."

Belik's brow rose in amusement.

Firian clarified what he was really asking. "I've gotten Brithnem on our side, not just the other way around."

"It's the girl, isn't it?" Belik's question cut like a knife.

"Of course it is."

"What did I tell you?"

Firian worked his jaw. "To take what I can and get out."

"And did you?" Hope and disgust alternated in Belik's face. He curled his lip.

Firian hesitated, letting Belik color in the silence as he wished. "I want her as an ally."

Belik scoffed. "An ally! You want her in more ways than that!"

"And if I do?"

"Damn it, Firian!" he cried, but his voice was soft.

Firian didn't reply.

"If you don't think she controls you, you're a fool. What if this is her plan?"

Firian knew what he meant. A *katah*. Did she mean to seduce him in order to get information or kill him? That was the real question.

He sat back, remembering the kiss in the hallway, every sensation rushing back. That was no plan. He shook his head. "Trust me. She didn't plan this."

"Do you forget when she spied on you for the Kingdom?"

The back of his throat tightened. "No."

"And you still think she isn't capable of guile."

"What is it to you?" Firian snapped. When would Belik get to the point?

"If the Academy falls, so do I. I've been screwed by a woman before." Belik held up a hand when he heard his word choice. But in a moment, the tension broke. His shoulders rounded forward, his perfect posture snapped. "You think she won't turn on you. You'd better be right. Tread carefully or she'll rain hell."

Firian would almost like to see the full might of the Keeper Kiria, above and against the other Keepers, without inhibitions or restraint. He forced himself out of his seductive reverie. "Did you just come to criticize me?"

"Firian." He said his name like a curse. "I keep hearing about small groups of mercenaries coming to investigate us. So far, it's not enough to raise alarm, but the idea of the hidden Academy with its tribute stores and fame is enough to whet everyone's curiosity from here to Bosha."

Firian raised his eyebrows. "We'll invite Imlin to join us."

Archer's Point was known to be more belligerent. Their Lord Ruler would never give into a mere threat, and probably wouldn't respond to an invitation either. Maybe later he could try it. Now that he considered it, if he could control Archer's Point, then he could protect Brett on both sides of their little conflict. Their father would have less reason to rage at their mother. But then, his father would just find a new reason to be angry.

Firian shook his head, freeing his thoughts from the sticky hold his father still had on him. "Let's start with Imlin. It'll be easier to keep an eye on them since they're so close to Raewhith. Everything is adjoining. I'll send some people to demand fealty tomorrow, along with a couple Sentries to act as new Watchmen."

Belik tipped his mouth. "Sentries?"

"They have nothing to do, and their time as Sentries has

made them unfit for most jobs." He lowered his voice. "Technically, I helped to free them, so they owe me loyalty, not like the Watchmen there now. I'm sending a Sentry to Raewhith too."

"Well," said Belik, finally pleased. He had been leaning far over the desk but now sat back as though he had finally gotten the answer he wanted. "Let's make it happen."

20

FIRIAN

"THAT'S NOT…" Firian's voice faded as he realized the move had been a fair one.

Bard cocked his head, a grin tugging at his lips as he tried not to gloat. He'd rubbed the back of his head with his knuckles so often when he thought about his next moves that his hair looked particularly impish.

Observing the wooden Indisfate board on the desk, Firian sucked his teeth. He drummed his fingers once against the desk and sighed. "Fine!"

"Another game?" Bard started settling the pieces back in their original places on the board.

Firian narrowed his eyes. Bard had won two in a row. He would hate for Bard to win every single game. This time, he'd been watching closely. If they played another, Firian could best him. "Set it up."

Even without windows, Firian could tell the sun was setting. When would Master Makai get back from Imlin? Hopefully he would arrive soon. Imlin was larger than Raewhith, and could supply good soldiers for his army. More rumors of looters and foreign armies curious about the power of the Academy came almost daily—small rumors, but enough to put Firian on edge.

After one more game of Indisfate, it would be totally dark outside. A good time to see Kiria. Her nearness could charge through him and relax him all at once.

Impatience shuddered through him. Focusing on the game pieces, he breathed deeply through his nose. A Tanyu was patient, could be patient forever, like a creature of the forest, still until propelled to sudden movement.

Kiria had left for her coronation tour today, parading through the Western Kingdom to demand new loyalty. She would couch it in kinder words, no doubt. Words like Bard would use.

To have a kingdom waiting to adore and serve... Firian felt the heat of it by association. Hadn't he seen a glimpse of that fearful awe in Raewhith, in Tánuil? Together, they could—

"You start." Bard knocked him out of his thoughts.

Firian moved the piece that Bard had touched first in the previous game.

A toothy grin split Bard's face.

"Gore," Firian swore, reading his loss in that look. The word came out as an irritated chuckle. It was no wonder Bard liked this game.

Bard's hand flashed across the board with his move.

What pattern was Bard establishing? Firian still couldn't see it, and it annoyed him.

"Hm, we should add a coin for stalling," Bard said, cautiously nettling him. He reached deep in his pocket for a token.

"No, no." Firian moved his piece, starting to sense a strategy that might work.

Bard's next move tore it down, blocking his Viper.

When Firian groaned, so did the door.

Belik limped in, moving quickly considering his bad leg. Firian could see the guard standing on the opposite side of the doorframe as he let the Master in.

Firian sat up. "Is it news from Imlin?"

"They won't come."

Firian's face went bloodless. "What?" Even Bard's mouth opened in surprise.

Belik's expression was set so hard that his mouth looked like a crack in a boulder.

"Why not?"

"They didn't give a reason." He came closer, a confidant. "Firian, you can't let this stand."

"But if they don't want to come…" Bard's word faded under the piercing glare of the two other Masters. Firian realized he still wore the blue-stoned ring of a Defender.

"If they don't want to come, then we'll make them," Belik said. "You know they can't deny you."

Firian drew his brows together. Belik was right. Any command from the Tanyuin Head had to be followed. The Academy needed their standing army. The Tanyu couldn't trust that the Western Kingdom would send troops at every whispered threat. And besides, they were too far away for soldiers to reach the Academy in time if there were a crisis.

"You can't look like a weak ruler." Belik pronounced the biting words almost too clearly.

Firian's gut twisted, feeling the condescension. He should rage, kick him out… But he was right.

He hadn't come this far to be taken lightly. If the Tanyu required loyalty, then it should be given gladly and without hesitation. Like the people going to see Kiria on her coronation tour.

Belik, not one to waste words, seemed to understand Firian

needed a moment to think. "We'll come up with a plan in the morning," he said, turning to go.

"First thing," Firian responded as the Master disappeared.

Bard chewed his lip. "I don't think you're a weak ruler," he said quickly, as though he were trying to stop Firian from taking drastic action.

"I'm not." Firian edged another piece on the board forward, sensing that it wasn't the best strategic decision but wanting to keep the game moving.

"I don't think you need anybody from Imlin. All the people from Raewhith were volunteers, yeah? And we got a lot of those. We don't need more."

Firian shifted in his seat. If it were just about troops, Bard might be right. Without an imminent threat, they had enough of a standing army for the moment. But this was a matter of principle. "They can't say no to the Tanyuin Head," he said.

Bard still hadn't made his move. Instead, he crossed his arms on the desk. "Is it just the two, then? Just Raewhith and Imlin?" The question felt like a move in a new game—strategy in the Real.

When he asked the question, something jumped in Firian's core. It was never just Raewhith and Imlin. "For now, that's all we need."

Bard raised an eyebrow. He could always tell what Firian was thinking. How could he always tell? At least he couldn't go to the Second Level of the Unreal. There was still one place where Firian could be alone with his thoughts.

"But look how much you have," Bard said. "The whole Academy!"

"It's your move."

Bard meant well, but Belik was right. The Academy would not be pushed aside. Imlin would bow to Firian's wishes.

Only the weak were satisfied with what they had. And what kind of message would it send if Imlin could just refuse?

Despite Firian's effort, Bard won another round of Indisfate. Tired, with a roiling mind, Firian declined to play again. Night was falling, and he needed the comfort of a queen.

He didn't call for her in the Unreal. He waited, picking up little details of the setting, adding to them, changing them. This time he wanted to meet in his office. He knew every corner of the place. The two deep scores in the top of the desk, the lighter patch of stone where something had hung on the wall, the design of the rug on the floor, the scrap of Raewhith's flag still draped across his desk. He marked one of the stones on the wall with an extra scratch.

She flickered in easily, like a piece that belonged there. Today she wore a fawn-colored set of breeches and a tight purple vest over light, billowy sleeves. Her hair was tied back in a braid. Those bright eyes found him first, and then roamed around the office. Her mouth quirked as she approached him. "What's all this?"

A small pang of discomfort struck him when he remembered the Main in all its grandeur. This space exhibited a different kind of power—elemental, not heraldic. Hopefully she would see what he saw in it. "This is the Tanyuin Head's office. Mine." A stab of pride lanced him when he said it.

"You have all your meetings in here?" She pivoted on her toes to take in the space. Divine.

"People come to me, yes."

"People." There was a question in the repeated word.

"Yes." He didn't elaborate.

She spun around the desk and sat in his chair. Those breeches were unexpectedly lovely on her, hugging all the right places. "You look very serious," she said.

"I have serious things to think about."

"Even with the war over." The thought that began as a question became agreement. Every trouble didn't evaporate because the Western Kingdom was ostensibly at peace. "I'm on my coronation tour now," she said, changing the subject.

"I know. Happy to be traveling again?" He came close so he could stand over her.

"It's very different this time."

"I'm sure."

She groaned, running a hand over her face. "Our trip... It was such a mess."

"Not all of it."

"Were you there?" she teased, her eyes sparkling. "No one in Brithnem has gotten over it." Though her mouth still crinkled in a smile, her expression darkened.

It shouldn't have surprised him that the Kingdom still didn't trust him, but the confirmation rubbed him a little raw. What more could he have done to prove his loyalty? And he didn't like the idea of voices in Kiria's ear reminding her of his past sins.

He paused, weighing whether to ask the question at his lips. Had she gotten over it? Could she ever forget what had happened, what he had done to her?

He licked his lips and tried a different tactic. "How would the war have ended up if we hadn't met? And you liked Shifra."

"That's true. I did. The first time." She had returned there after escaping from him. When they'd first arrived, though, she was so incandescently happy that he ached to watch her.

He offered his hand to pull her up. As she took it, her short fingernails slid across the skin of his palm and sent goosebumps up his arms. Even without her Beauty, she had the confidence of a Keeper.

She gazed into his eyes with a knowing look. Air stuck in his throat, that short-of-breath vulnerability buzzing inside him.

She commanded too much power in that moment, looking at him, seeing him.

Slowly, though his mouth had gone dry, he drew his thumb over her jawline. Her eyes glazed a little with the action. "You know," he whispered, "I like you like this."

"Like what?"

He just smiled and bent to kiss her.

21

KIRIA

THANK goodness Jori had come along. He didn't ask questions about how she would handle potential dissenters, or whether she was nervous the Kingdom would accept her over her mother, or if she was in a secret relationship with a former enemy.

Instead, he made their stops more interesting, although the guards weren't always happy with his antics. With so much time to think, she was glad for the distraction. Late at night, and sometimes early in the morning, the Unreal provided excellent distraction too.

In all, fourteen people accompanied Kiria on the coronation tour. The luggage alone required three people to look after it. They brought banners, diplomatic gifts, and elaborate outfits. Guards, servants, a guide, a doctor, and a cook all made up the traveling party.

The experience was far different than when she had traveled with Firian. Now she was waited on and fussed over by everybody. The result was a much slower pace. Or perhaps the pace was the same, but it felt slower because they took main roads, rather than cutting through wilderness. The traveling itself felt like a parade with no spectators.

It took a full week to move past the forest of Á Quihilmar to the rockier plains in the south. Strange mountains reared up in the distance, higher than the Charúnin Thôr to the north. Even though it was springtime, white snow still covered the peaks, like the flat stroke of a painter's brush.

No wonder it had been so long since anyone had added King's Heights to the coronation tours. It was so far out of the way. A few years ago, Daelon had taught her the history—that the people of King's Heights had objected to the reestablishment of the Kingdom as a Khelê sanctuary, still thinking that Kingdom Dwellers were superior. They had broken away and formed their own colony, preserving Kingdom blood and traditions, unmixed with the Khelê. They didn't share in any of the Abilities God poured out on the Khelê afterward, Daelon said, because they refused to associate with them. Largely isolated, King's Heights kept its reputation for suspicion toward outsiders, but it was impossible that they could retain the same level of racism that they had started with hundreds of years ago. After all, they officially became part of the Western Kingdom about ninety years before.

People from King's Heights still rarely traveled to the capital, but Kiria was beginning to see why. The road was long and, after the forest ended, rather barren.

During the day, Jori vacillated between jovial fun and irritable boredom. Chetana said very little, unless Kiria asked her a question. She rode her horse like a queen, but as they got closer to King's Heights, something about her perfect posture and long neck became not only regal but stiff, as though she were bracing herself. Something was wrong with her, but she deflected any question about it. Candrae and Vayci never complained, and actually seemed excited to be traveling outside of Brithnem.

Candrae's aunt was also a servant in the palace, and she got to come too. When the girls weren't tending to Kiria, they twittered quietly and happily with her.

Finally, they saw it. King's Heights, nestled at the foothills of the Somul Mountains, so far inland that the sea wasn't even in sight. An immense stone wall encircled the city. The buildings themselves were stone, blending in perfectly with the landscape, with light gray walls, smooth as if they'd been carved out of boulders, and dark gray roofs. The city obviously wasn't as large as Brithnem, but it was larger than Kiria had pictured it.

This also was part of her Kingdom. She had been so focused on a few aspects of her Keepership that she had all but forgotten the rest. Her priorities had been Brithnem, the Tanyu, and the Torithians. That was it. But there was so much more. Rather than making her shrink with the additional responsibility, seeing new parts of the Kingdom filled her with warm pride.

Jori rode up slowly beside her, open vest flapping. It was drier and warmer here than either of them was used to. "Finally!" he said. "I can have a proper shave. Where do you think they'll put us up? Do they have a palace, or a government building?" He pulled a wry face. "A government building—doesn't that sound dreary? Let's hope it's something more festive. Yes, a shave and a glass of wine."

Jori had been shaving along the way, but he did look more bedraggled than usual. She laughed. "First we have a speech."

"A speech?" He brought his horse closer to hers and leaned confidentially toward her. "Darling, you look like you could freshen up yourself." He scanned her Beauty and said, "I know, I know. But they're putting you on stage the instant we arrive? No rest for a Keeper?"

The bottom of her ivory dress was caked with dirt, and her gold threaded shoes covered in dust. Until today she had been allowed to wear more practical riding clothes, but since they approached King's Heights, she had been strongly urged to wear one of her finest dresses and her crown.

She tossed her shiny hair and smiled, though she agreed. Hopefully there would be at least a little time so she could smell fresh and feel good before presenting herself at this first stop. "You know," she said, "not many people would tell me that."

"I'm not many people." His lips twisted in a smile.

The sound of another horse approaching made both of them look back. Chetana eased her bay mare forward, making the space between Kiria's four guards feel a little cramped. Jori made way for the Amir.

"That is King's Heights," she said, gazing forward. The sun glinted off her laced metal septum ring, bright against her dark skin. She set her brow, almost antagonistic. Memory stirred in her eyes as the breeze stirred her short curls. After a moment, she remembered herself. Not often did she get lost in her memories like that. "Our first stop on the tour." Her face resettled into a pleasant neutral, not a smile, but enough to dispel the terrible energy that had begun to emanate from her. "They will be glad to see you, My Keeper."

"They all will," added Jori, unnecessarily.

"Yes." Chetana spared a look for him. "Now, My Keeper, your flagbearer must go in front, and all must demonstrate unwavering support, smiling, gladness..." It was only when she used words like "gladness" that Kiria saw the family resemblance between her and her son Daelon.

Kiria nodded politely. She'd heard this all before.

As they rode closer to the city, it seemed to come alive. Now they could hear bustling in the streets and see smoke coming from chimneys. Figures, small in the distance, moved between buildings and guards walked along the walls.

"We will support you in all things, My Keeper. First we'll

process to meet the mayor, and then you'll give the speech, and then to our quarters for the night."

Jori leaned far forward to see around Chetana. He caught Kiria's eye and bared his teeth with apologetic disgust.

Kiria looked away from him. "No party afterward?" That was going to be the protocol in Charäkhnem.

"Not at this stop, My Keeper. We will not stay long, and I'm sure you are tired."

Kiria popped her eyebrows up at Jori, who leaned back in his saddle with resignation. Jori would have his share of parties later, but for now, Chetana was right. Kiria would hardly be excited for a late-night revel after a long day of traveling. This was almost a practice stop, just to show goodwill. Hopefully it would resolve the apprehension that sometimes settled in her stomach.

When others didn't question her, it was easy to pretend that she was the Kingdom's darling, but the constant reinforcement of "unwavering support" made her wonder. She had to be more careful to hide her visits with Firian. Especially now, she couldn't give anyone a reason to doubt her.

When the guards on the wall saw the flagbearer unfurl the royal banner of Brithnem, they opened the gate at once. Kiria felt grand looking at the blue and purple flag with its symbol of a laird flower flapping in the wind. The sweat and horse smell didn't bother her as much as she thought it might when all the guards of King's Heights stared at her, open-mouthed. Despite the drawbacks of travel, she was still their beautiful Keeper. Now was the time to impress, to embrace her visibility. Holding her head in what she hoped was a dignified manner, she rode slowly into the city. A crowd had gathered just inside the main gates, so thick that people had to move just for the horses to ride forward. It was like swimming through heads.

Her guards were clearly on alert with so many people.

"Make way!" they cried. "Make way for the Second Keeper of the Western Kingdom, Kiria Arioc. Make way!" They rode forward in a practiced formation to shoo the crowds to the side.

The sea of faces was monochromatic. In Brithnem, everyone looked different—at least there was a wide range of body types and skin colors and hair styles—but it had never truly occurred to her that other places might not be. She had heard the rumors about King's Heights, of course, but the sameness struck her differently in the face of such a large crowd with uniformly light skin, grayish brown hair (shoulder-length, for the most part), and wide gray eyes. Seeing so many together was like an odd version of Jori repeated indefinitely. The facial expressions varied, but the most prevalent was an intense, almost hostile curiosity, as though she were an exhibit in a zoo.

Kiria felt off balance, but she smiled. A few people responded in kind and smiled back. Others tried to touch her, but the guards batted them back.

This was hardly a civilized way to welcome a Keeper.

Up ahead, she saw a huge, flat-topped boulder with stairs carved into the side. A canopy had been erected on the top, light blue and dark purple. The stage for her presentation. She kept smiling and giving demure nods to the crowd as they slowly approached the platform. At the stairs, she and her entourage dismounted and she went up with Chetana, Jori, and her guards. The others faded into the crush of bodies.

A man waited for them at the top. He had the same light face and ashy dark hair, but he wore a ponderous necklace of thick golden threads over a dark robe, almost reminiscent of the Keeper robes, but plainer.

The man touched his heart with respect as he approached Kiria. Although the guards wouldn't let him approach too closely, the brief gesture calmed her growing nerves. "What an honor it is for us to meet our esteemed Second Keeper! My name is Brontes Meaburn. I'm the mayor of this city," he said. His voice was a little higher than she had expected. He looked around. "Did our last Second Keeper, your eminent mother, not accompany you?"

"No, she did not," Kiria replied, surprised by the question.

"Would you have me announce you, My Keeper?" There was something almost tentative in the question.

"My Amiran advisor Chetana will announce me." Kiria indicated whom she was talking about, but the mayor of King's Heights didn't follow her gesture.

"As you wish." He scrunched his nose, maybe a nervous or impatient gesture, but it passed quickly, and he stepped aside as though he were opening a door to his city. The flourish reminded her a little of Cúron.

Kiria, Chetana, and her guards stepped forward, just within the shade of the canopy. Jori hung back at the same distance as the mayor.

After the whispered comments died away, a hush fell over the crowd. Faces craned upward. From this height, about two stories above the street, Kiria realized that the crowd wasn't as enormous as she had thought. Hundreds of people packed the streets, overflowing into side streets, but she could see where the crowd ended.

Her heart beat quickly in anticipation. Giving speeches didn't make her afraid anymore, as they did when she was younger, but she still felt a current of adrenaline. *All this, for me.*

Chetana stepped to the rim of the rock and lifted her chin. *"From the gloom of oppression will rise my people, my chosen ones,"* she began. *"From the dust of scorn, my people will look up and their lips will be cleansed with truth. In that day, I will help them, says the mighty one, the God of all. My Khelê will found a great kingdom. They will build upon the ruins of the old, stone upon stone. Wisdom will rise with its walls, and shepherds as its keepers."*

Kiria sensed unease among the people as Chetana recited the passage from the Sacred Scroll. Some in the crowd squinted suspiciously. It could have been from the sun, but Kiria thought she sensed animosity toward Chetana—a Khelê who reminded them of their historical preference for the losing side of the War of the Kingdom Rebels. Chetana quoted the Scroll with particular gusto, as though she had been waiting to say just these words to just this crowd.

"People of King's Heights!" she cried. Kiria had never heard her shout before. Her voice was like a battle cry. "It is my distinct honor and pleasure to introduce to you your new ruler, one deserving of all your allegiance and praise, the Second Keeper of the Western Kingdom, Kiria Arioc!"

Deafening applause followed, an almost violent sound.

Now it was Kiria's turn. When she walked back into the light, many people gave another gasp and the whispering started again. Apparently her dust-stained dress didn't bother them. Her Beauty overwhelmed other thoughts the first time one saw it. She waited until they quieted.

"People of King's Heights, it is my pleasure to come to your city. I see before me a city of industry, of hardworking men and women, of people loyal to the thrones of Brithnem."

She gave her rehearsed speech just as she had practiced it in front of her fourteen travelers days before. She praised the particular strengths of the area, reinforced their loyalty, informed them of her promises as leader and their duty to serve.

She left her favorite part until the end. "Most of all, I am pleased to inform you that, since I ascended to the throne, the Torithian War is won!" She beamed, and light shone in the eyes of a few at the foot of the stone platform. Applause scattered through the crowd. "Through a strategic alliance with the Tanyuin Academy, I was able to help bring our forces to victory. All troops have already begun to come home from Torith,

Enderin, and all the other fronts where we have fought and died to protect innocent people from harm." Her body warmed with pride. "I love this Kingdom and am proud to serve it. I hope, in that way, that we may be united. Thank you." She stepped back, almost stumbling on her dress.

She made it through her first speech. Blood raced through her veins. The thrill of ruling the Kingdom washed over her anew. She had done so much good for these people already. The thought filled her with satisfaction and brought a grin to her face. Jori smiled back when she looked at him, but Chetana's face was grim and wary as they all marched down the stairs to find their quarters for the night.

22

KIRIA

Kɪʀɪᴀ ꜱʟɪᴅ into Firian's lap. He gave a relaxed smile and wrapped his arm around her back. Happily, they had chosen to meet in the evening. If they met during the day, she was bound to get caught eventually. With all the anti-Tanyuin sentiment in the Kingdom even after the success on Torith, she couldn't risk her reputation by revealing her relationship with Firian.

The watery swamp sloshed against the pylons of the wooden walkway. Twilight filtered dark blue light through the mossy trees of Shifra. Bugs skimmed across the water. The humid air clung to the two of them, soft on her damp skin.

Hanks of moss hung unevenly on the closest tree, and a cluster of lily pads floating on the water included two with browning leaves. Even the smell took her right back to Shifra. Firian said she was advancing quickly in the Unreal, but she couldn't have conjured this many little details.

The difference—she always tried to find the intentional change he placed there—seemed to be the extra lanterns, but she liked that, and he knew it.

"How was your speech?" he asked.

"I think it was all right. You don't have to give speeches, do you?"

He shook his head, his face so close to hers that they almost touched. "No."

"Not if you don't want to," she teased, a little jealous.

He pursed his lips together in a smile. His hair smelled like soap and pine sap. "Exactly."

"That would be nice," she mused lightly, turning away. "But a Keeper has to do more than a Tanyu, I suppose."

He let the comment slide, but she felt him pick at the skin around his ring.

"How do you like being a Keeper now?" he finally asked.

She considered. "You know, before I left"—she didn't need to explain that she meant with him—"I looked at being a Keeper and thought about everything at once. I knew there would be violence and pain and unpopular decisions, and I tried to hold it all in my mind at one time. I tried to comprehend it, to steel myself." She drew a finger lazily down his arm. "As though, if I thought hard enough, I could understand it all, and swallow it in one bite." She puffed out her cheeks to mimic a full mouth. "But it isn't like that. Everything comes one by one, a day at a time. And you can't predict it all." She met his gaze and felt warmth crawl up to her temples.

Firian had certainly been a surprise. The idea brought uncomfortable thoughts to the surface. She liked Firian, perhaps even more than she had thought at the beginning, but she still didn't fully trust him. Wouldn't she be willing to show him her Beauty if she did?

His nearness made it easier to silence the voices in her head that warned her against getting too close to him. He was warm and comfortable and made her forget her worries of the day. They both liked being together in the Unreal, so there was no harm.

Something small ran over the boards, maybe a lizard. It was hard to see in the dim light. "What's that?" She reached past him to point at it.

He caught her as she leaned and kissed her on the cheek. "Doesn't matter," he murmured.

"No?"

"No." He traced one finger up her back until he reached the exposed skin of her shoulder blades.

She shivered at his touch, but shook her head, smiling. She gently pushed away a lock of hair from his forehead. His eyes closed with the motion. How did she have this great of an effect on him?

A niggling doubt, like a lingering sore throat, ached in the back of her mind. Something wasn't right. She scanned the area around them. Nothing could hurt them here. Nothing could hurt her.

She looked around the wooden platform that appeared so much like the actual one where they'd sat together before. A lantern had disappeared.

An odd feeling, like she was back in time, came over her. The terrible things that happened a few months ago were just a dream. She and Firian were really together, now.

She snuggled up closer to him and he responded with kisses. Like people drunk, or in a dream, they held each other. Her stomach tightened. Her shoe moved over the soft, splintery boards of the walkway, catching on the rough edges as she tucked her feet in. She felt his heart beat in his chest and his neck. Nothing else seemed to matter but this.

She jolted.

Firian pulled away for a moment, running his eyes over her to make sure she was all right. It must have been a muscle spasm, because she didn't feel that she was about to fall.

Rubbing a comforting hand over her back, he leaned in again and she leaned to meet him.

A buzzing sound, like shouting in the far distance, made her break off again. "What was that?"

"Nothing." He twirled a piece of her hair in his fingers.

"I heard something."

"I didn't hear anything." But his interest was clearly piqued. He stiffened and looked past her, scanning for what, she didn't know.

She sat up, listening more intently. A strange feeling, as though she had forgotten something, came over her again and made her restless. The noise might be the key.

Her face suddenly went cold. Her hands flew to her cheeks, but they felt normal. Was she afraid? Did she realize something before her conscious mind could catch up? Vague fear covered her body, but only because her body was acting of its own accord. Something was wrong. But then, nothing was real.

Real.

Her insides squeezed tight as she realized what she had forgotten. *This isn't real.* She'd let her guard down, blurred the lines. She stood up, sucking in shallow breaths of air. She couldn't let that happen again.

"What's the matter?" asked Firian, jumping lightly to his feet.

"I have to go."

Without waiting for a response, she opened her eyes. For a second, the Real didn't come. Her heart skipped. *No, no.*

Then the light seeped in, blinding though she knew it was dark. She squinted up from a bed. Her hand touched rabbit fur and the ceiling was slate gray with faint designs etched into it. *King's Heights. That's where I am.* Three people peered down at her, horrified concern etched on every one of them. Candrae and Vayci looked the most distressed. Tears edged Vayci's brown eyes but she quickly sponged them away with a damp towel she was holding.

Chetana was the third. When Kiria looked at her, something unmistakable flashed across her expression. Realization.

She knew.

"Oh, My Kepress!" Candrae cried, handing Vayci the candle and actually hugging Kiria across the bed. In her relief, she'd forgotten to call Kiria by her proper title.

"We must move. Now." Chetana offered her heavily-ringed hand. "People are rioting in the streets and they are headed here, if they haven't already arrived."

Kiria sat up groggily, confused.

"Quickly!" Chetana snapped.

Vayci and Candrae clutched their own bags as well as hers, packed and ready. They waited by the bed, bobbing up and down with nervous energy. Candrae's face was white with fear. Kiria took Chetana's hand and allowed her to pull her out of the room.

Most of the lights were out, but patterns like water grew brighter against the stone walls. From the corridor, she could see down into the street. The mayor's manor had been carved into the mountain itself, so the hallway where she ran rose more than four stories above the street. Despite her vantage point, she saw nothing distinctly but the bobbing of tiny torches in the gloom. The simple, elegant carvings in the rock wall looked sinister in the moving shadows.

Glass broke. Wails like wind rose and fell, angry shouts, a few voices at a time speaking in unison, but she couldn't hear their words. They sounded like a storm, like a tidal wave. The noise got louder and louder, even as she and the others broke into a run. The sound brought terror to her throat. She fought to keep her breath steady as she shed her Beauty. The tingling feeling didn't leave her fingertips even after the transformation was complete.

Why were they rioting? Something in the snarled voices echoed back her name. Why were they coming for her? What had she done?

She gripped a stone bannister as she tripped lightly down a long, spiraling staircase. Around and around it went, doubling back on itself so many times that she began to feel claustrophobic. Once at the bottom, she sped after the growing group of guards and servants showing them the way.

She tried to run quietly, but it was almost impossible with so many people. Others joined them as they ran—the guards, the cook, the porter. There was Jori, tugging on his shoes. Even the mayor appeared. This scenario seemed less real than Shifra had felt just a moment ago.

They emptied into a fenced stone courtyard ringed with stables. "I'm so sorry," Mayor Meaburn whispered in a rush, slowing to a halt beside their stamping horses. "If you would just move to my other location, already prepared..."

Vayci shoved a coat into her arms, and Kiria realized she was only in her nightdress. Pulling her arms through the sleeves, she glared at the mayor. "Who are these people? Why are they coming for me?"

He scrunched his nose as though shaking off a fly. His plea came out as oily assurance. "Oh, My Keeper—"

"Tell me!"

He looked down at his leather slippers. "There are many here who disapprove of your reign. I am not among them! I invited you here, and if you would—"

"I am not staying here."

"But my other house..." He caught her glare and twitched again, huffing with frustration. "Small factions don't agree with your decision to forgive the Tanyu after the war... and others... think you killed your mother."

"What?" The word came out louder than she intended. "I never—"

The mayor put his hand over his heart again, a habitual gesture, apparently. "I am so sorry. I think no such thing. Please grant us forgiveness."

Kiria pressed her nails into her palms. His words were devolving into political pleading and there was no time.

"My Keeper." A guard prompted her to mount her horse. Over half of her entourage was already in the saddle.

With no idea what to say and no time to say it, she turned away from the mayor. Moments later, Kiria, Jori, and Chetana, holding her secret, escaped the walls of King's Heights.

23

KIRIA

THE CORONATION TOUR finally made camp about five hours later. On the ride, Kiria's throat had closed and the air had leaked out of her mouth and lungs and she couldn't breathe and her vision narrowed. It was the same panic she'd felt in Raewhith after the attack.

She'd sent a guard back to King's Heights to gather information and their remaining belongings from the mayor's manor—she needed to get to the bottom of those rumors, find out what had triggered the riot. Their Watchman could report back to Brithnem that Kiria was safe.

As Kiria got ready for bed in one of the large, comfortable tents, her heart rate finally began to slow

Now on her bunk, she looked forward to sleep. Deep breaths. Her racing mind didn't slow as her body sank into the soft blankets. Every fiber rubbed against her skin; every wrinkle suggested it would take longer than she wanted to actually become comfortable.

A cool breeze wafted through the tent flap as it opened. Chetana entered, still fully dressed. After she closed the fabric behind her, she fixed Kiria with an implacable gaze. Kiria sat up.

"You're seeing the Tanyu." Chetana said the words with such conviction that Kiria knew she had figured it out, though how she had done it, Kiria didn't know.

"What?" Kiria said stupidly.

"You have a *katah*."

"What's a *katah*?" The word sounded vaguely familiar, but she couldn't remember what it meant. Firian's friend Bard had done something with a *katah* to help them defeat the Torithian captain.

Fear flashed over Chetana's face. Or maybe it was regret. "It's a connection in the Unreal, My Keeper. A dangerous connection."

"It's not a dangerous connection," she protested, knowing that her comment was as good as an admission. But then, was it so bad that she visited Firian in the Unreal? If no one knew about it, it couldn't harm the people's opinion of her as a ruler. And it looked like that was already shot anyway. Why would Chetana accuse her like this, as though she were putting herself and the Kingdom in danger?

Chetana rubbed her full lips together, clearly unconvinced. "A *katah* is a Tanyuin death sentence, a connection that grows between two people in the Unreal. The Tanyu target their enemies that way, manipulating them until they cannot tell the difference between imagination and reality. The Unreal becomes their reality. They believe it. And then you can get hurt."

"That's not what this is."

She gave her a pointed look. "How do you know?"

"I—"

"You can't!" Chetana's vehemence was almost frightening.

Kiria sat straighter. "I can tell the difference between imagination and reality!" The stress of the day made her more irritable than usual. Maybe she should send Chetana away, demand she quit these accusations. Kiria knew what she was doing with Firian... didn't she?

"My Keeper,"—Chetana sat down on the edge of the bunk, less threatening but more unavoidable—"we couldn't wake you." It looked like she wanted to say more, but decided against it, instead setting her mouth in a line and sitting back a little.

Kiria frowned. "How do you know so much about this?" She picked up her pillow and held it in her lap.

"It doesn't matter."

"Do Amir learn this much about the Talent?" Daelon rarely talked about it, except as a feature of history.

"Some do." For just a second, she dropped her eyes. "That mob would be furious if they knew."

Kiria flushed. Now Chetana was being condescending. "Why should we care what they think?" Kiria snapped more harshly than she intended.

The mob was wrong about her anyway. She had to do right by them, but they didn't have to agree with all her choices. That angry group had terrified her, and they were already furious, so why would Chetana bring them up again just as she was beginning to relax?

"That connection could hurt you, hurt the Kingdom..."

"How?" Chetana had no right to dictate her private life. Kiria valued her wisdom, when she asked for it, but being an Amir didn't automatically give her a say in every aspect of her life. Besides, the lies and unrest centering around her were the more important issues. Unless... "Is there something in the Scroll...?" If God had forbidden such a connection, then it would be her duty to stop seeing Firian, but if Chetana's prejudices forbade it, she didn't care.

Firian's affection sometimes felt like temptation, but right now, she wouldn't give it up. Despite whatever darkness he had, she cared for him. He excited her, motivated her, soothed her.

And he'd proven he was on their side when he helped them end both wars.

Chetana hesitated, glassy-eyed as she reviewed the holy words in her mind. Kiria's heart sank. As the Amir gazed into nothingness, Kiria was reminded of a soothsayer. No one could look into the future, but Chetana's wisdom seemed to supersede this moment and understand what was to come.

Chetana seemed to settle back into her own skin again. "No," she finally admitted.

"Then I will do as I please."

Chetana lowered her head, breaking some of the veneer of an untouchable military and spiritual leader. She looked at Kiria woman to woman. Something about her gaze arrested her. "My Keeper," she said in a low voice, "he *will* hurt you."

Kiria's stomach dropped, but she didn't lower her eyes. Chetana made it sound inevitable, indisputable. But was it?

Most of the palace nobles and staff hated Firian—wouldn't trust him to wash their clothes. Everyone had been so angry after the hostage situation that Kiria couldn't talk about him even after he took over the Academy, turning it in a new direction. Knowing that Chetana knew what she was doing simultaneously relieved and concerned her.

Chetana waited patiently for her to speak, but Kiria didn't know what to say. Then the Amir gently took her hand. After a moment, Kiria squeezed her hand back, and something in her broke. "I like him, and I just want to be wanted, for me," she said. "If it's only in the Unreal, why do you care so much?" Shame flooded her cheeks with heat.

"I know." For such a severe person, Chetana showed a touching amount of empathy. "But we both know the Unreal isn't only in your mind. *It's* real also."

Understanding dawned. Kiria's eyes widened. "You have the Talent too."

"Since I was a girl."

Kiria stared. How had she not known? "Then why... why are you an Amir? Your sister is a Tanyu, and you have the Talent..."

A confusing mix of emotions flashed across Chetana's face—pride, anger... "The Amir follow God. They are not selfish. They have not neglected higher things," she said simply. She bent her rusty head in a prayerful posture and stroked Kiria's hand once. "I became your mother's advisor around the time you were born. I already knew the honor of serving your family, but when I saw you, I knew the joy of it. I hadn't felt joy in a long time, but your presence reminded me of the hope to come. *That* is what you offer your kingdom. And that is why I cannot stand by and let you fall prey to a Tanyu who cares for nothing but his own gain."

The words fell like weights on the coverlet. Their hands felt heavy together.

Kiria breathed in the thick silence, unsure of what to say. A breeze blew around the circular fabric tent in low, dense sounds. A tree branch moved outside. The corners of her eyes blew cold with unfallen tears.

She squeezed Chetana's hand once more and let go. "I love this kingdom, and that will never change," she said solemnly, like a vow. "I wouldn't jeopardize it."

Chetana sighed. Straightening, she looked a queen herself. "You know my mind, Lady Kiria. A *katah* is never something to be taken lightly. Even the most careful person can be deceived by it." She stood, her delicate septum ring shining dully in the light. Her lips twitched once as she gazed down at Kiria, as though she were considering a new way to convince her.

Steeling herself, Kiria found that her heart was beating fast.

Maybe her advisor sensed that she wasn't open to any more input on the topic. Tonight, at any rate, Kiria wasn't going to change her mind.

Chetana inclined her head. "May you have peaceful sleep," she said, and left the tent.

When she was gone, Kiria exhaled slowly and spread her fingers over the covers. Chetana's parting words didn't sound threatening, but the implication was clear.

He will hurt you. She spoke the warning as though it were as sure as fate.

Her heart pounding heavily, Kiria felt small against the pillow. She would get no sleep.

24

FIRIAN

BARD HELD up the black ring, inspecting it in the sunlight coming in through the windows. "What do you think, Fir?"

"It's exactly like all the other ones. It's great." Firian tapped a fingertip against his own ring.

Firian had thought Bard would be ecstatic to pick up his Master ring, but he had spent the last few minutes asking the elderly jeweler questions and inspecting it for flaws instead. The tiny shop had a sharp metallic smell that grated on his senses.

He'd been on edge since last night, when he felt a surge of panic coming from Kiria. When he couldn't find her in the Unreal, unease had followed him and made him irritable. Though he would know if something drastic had happened, her fear still unnerved him. She wasn't a Tanyu, but she wasn't often afraid. He would check for her again after meeting with Jovan.

"I don't want it to be too tight."

"There's nothing wrong with it," Firian insisted. Jovan expected him any minute at the barracks to inspect the new troops.

Firian had sent Master Makai and a few others to Imlin to demand their allegiance. They would relent one way or another.

Soon enough, Jovan would have brand new soldiers under his command, even less tested in Tanyuin methods than the Torithians or men from Raewhith. Firian had to make sure preparations were going smoothly. Firian and Bard didn't have time to waste in a jewelry store.

Torvas, the jeweler, took the ring back in his hand, cradling it as though it would break. It bounced off his knobby knuckles as he eased it from one palm to the other. He bent his liver-spotted head over it with an oddly paternal care.

Firian watched him impatiently. The rings never broke. There was no reason to be so careful.

"It won't be too tight," said Torvas, "Master—?"

"Tanery." Bard beamed, as though the new title were just dawning on him.

"Very well. Master Tanery. We'll need more Masters here with the borders open," he said, voicing a common opinion in a soft, shaky tone. People of Tánuil were nervous that foreigners would come to loot and kill, now that everyone knew where to find them. It was like leaving a castle door wide open at night. If a Tanyu with an army stood on the other side, though, no one would get through. "My family has made the Tanyuin rings for generations. They're never too tight."

"You sure?"

"Very sure." Torvas nodded solemnly. That should be enough for Bard, who was now bouncing up and down on the balls of his feet. He took the ring back and put it on his finger. Wiggling his fingers in front of his face, he looked at... what? The ring again? Surely he'd seen enough of that. And he'd see it on his hand his entire life.

"Okay," said Firian, turning to go.

"Wait, Fir."

Something made him glare at Bard. In this shop so focused on rank, it felt wrong not to be addressed by his title. Bard didn't revise the name. He just thanked the jeweler, waved goodbye, and trotted after Firian as he walked quickly toward the barracks.

"This is great!" said Bard, coming up beside him. "I never thought I'd be a Master already." He smiled up at Firian, his dimples widening.

"Well," said Firian, softening a little, "you deserved it."

Bard kept sneaking peeks at the black ring on his finger, with a private look of pride and achievement. Firian laughed to himself. He knew the feeling, and Bard hardly ever had the chance to revel in his own success.

They went behind Old Danior's sweet shop. The barracks had been hastily put together and looked it. The large, low wooden building stood fairly solid, but it wouldn't be difficult to kick through a board and escape. Most of the Torithians Firian had seen were certainly big enough to demolish part of the outer wall. Firian would talk to the carpenter about converting the walls to stone before autumn.

A tent had been erected against the tree line for meals. Once the cold weather returned in a few months, a tent would be insufficient, but it functioned for now. Loud talking and pots clanking filtered through the air. One company of soldiers ate under the tent. Jovan wasn't among them. His huge form would have been easy to find among the bodies.

"Bard," he said, "run inside and tell Jovan I've arrived."

Without hesitation, Bard did as he was told.

Moments later, Bard emerged from the barracks with Jovan and a line of Torithian thugs. Jovan wore his typical black Academy shirt with the thin sleeves pushed up past his elbows. His swelling biceps were as thick as his own neck. The sun had baked Jovan's face tanner and more rugged than the last time Firian had seen him. He glowered at Firian as he approached. Had a few weeks really taken this toll on him?

Bard walked assertively beside him, probably energized by his new title, but his ashy face betrayed his nervousness. Jovan and Bard had never liked each other.

The line of Torithian soldiers behind them all wore some variety of Academy-issued clothing, but they still looked mismatched. Some of the black had faded to gray, and a few of the outfits were torn. Firian scanned the line carefully. These men were as much his project as Jovan's. Several bore purple or yellow bruises. All looked tired. But none looked ready to spit on his boots, so that meant some progress.

Jovan stopped in front of Firian. "Master Kess," he said curtly. Turning back to the men behind him, he barked, "Form lines!"

Jovan's shout made Bard shudder in surprise.

The Torithians shuffled dully into lines, about twenty by three. Could Jovan break these men down and build them up to a fighting force? Right now, they seemed too listless to be much good in a battle.

"Attention!"

Some raised their heads. All put their hands behind their back. Firian caught the eye of one, younger than the rest, whose shaved blond hair had begun to grown back. He had a long, bony face and large, watery, wandering eyes. When he looked back at Firian, his face blanched and he dropped his gaze.

Firian pursed his mouth and walked to the end of the line of men. Bard stayed there as Firian strode deliberately along the line, considering each man. He lingered on some hardened faces, his eyes zigzagging over them until they straightened or looked away.

"Jovan," he said, omitting the title and waving him over with a hand. "How have you been treating these men?"

"They run for two hours every morning, strength training in the afternoon. No weapons training yet. They need to earn the right, and they're still a bunch of gory insurgents." Anger radiated from him as he stood beside him, just a little taller than Firian.

That anger didn't seem directed only at the Torithians, but took in Firian as well. *Why?* Firian took a deep, steadying breath.

Jovan, who had been such a terrifying figure when Firian first arrived, now had to answer to him. The thought sent energy coursing through him. He felt strong, strong enough to beat Jovan in a fight. Well, almost.

"Of course they are," Firian said. "They have to be broken before they're built up." After a pause, he added, "Don't hurt any too badly."

He ushered Master Jovan out of earshot of the troops. "When do you think they'll be ready?"

Jovan scoffed. "It'll be months at least. These idiots are unorganized, undisciplined, wasteful thieves."

The implied criticism hung thickly in the air. It was no wonder they were thieves. They had been pirates mere weeks ago. "Make them my army," Firian said, meeting Jovan's eyes.

Jovan ground his teeth, barely getting out the next words. "As you would have it, Master Kess."

Firian stared for a beat longer before turning away. Jovan felt like a loose animal, like Imlin's defiant leaders. *Small problems,* he insisted to himself. He felt the Master's eyes follow him as he strode back to Bard.

Every attempt to control his world peacefully became harder and harder. At least he could still soothe Kiria's fears, and she could bring balance back to him as well.

25

KIRIA

KIRIA HAD NOT SETTLED DOWN. One day had passed since the attack at King's Heights, and questions still swarmed within her. It was three days to the next stop on the tour and she could already tell that she would have to wrestle with her questions and concerns and insecurities the whole way.

Chetana rode close to her, as she usually did, with Kiria's four guards. The enormous entourage grated on her today. Could she get no moment to herself? She had to think about Chetana's words last night, about the mob's accusations, about her position in the court of Brithnem. She had to think about Firian and her mother.

She had to think.

Alone.

But there was no alone in the center of this tired procession. Eyes regularly shifted to her. Servants tended to her needs. She found herself wanting to be invisible.

The day passed slowly. Irritable, she snapped at Jori more than once for trying to make light of the riot. By the late afternoon, he backed off, though his absence didn't leave her feeling the right kind of alone.

Did people really think she had usurped her mother? Was she really a worse leader than her mother had been?

The rocking of the horse beneath her stirred her thoughts into a rhythm.

They thought she had killed her mother... deserved to die... led the Kingdom into ruin...

No, she remembered. She won the war... allied for peace... helped the Kingdom...

No matter how much she considered what had happened, the angry mob still left her on edge. Unexpected noises made her jump.

By the time night fell, a mix of fear and annoyance and guilt had settled in her gut like undigested dinner. She didn't stay to sit around the fire with everyone else.

From her tent, she heard Jori telling a story. She couldn't hear the words, but occasional laughter punctuated the quiet. If only she felt so lighthearted. But for now, she needed to be alone. Words burned into her skin as though they were part of the tattoo on her back. *They think you killed your mother... This fool alliance... He'll hurt you.*

She ground her palms, still gritty from the horse's reins, against her eyes. Her Beauty fell away from her like a cloak. A warm presence, never far out of reach, pressed against the back of her eyelids.

For just a moment, she froze with indecision. Firian was only a moment away. She could call and he would answer.

Wiping the dust from her face, she opened her eyes again. Her serving girls hadn't come in from the campfire yet, and Chetana probably wouldn't come again. But was she right about what she had said last night?

Kiria exhaled a frustrated breath. She knew Firian much better than Chetana did. He had his faults, but didn't everyone?

She would be careful. And she would see Firian.

She sat on the bed and closed her eyes, letting the Unreal close over her. In the darkness, she whispered his name. That should be enough.

In moments, a pine forest materialized around her. Soft evening light sifted through the trees, making Firian's black clothes look light gray as he walked toward her. The self-assured glint he usually had in his eyes betrayed some concern. When they were face to face, he took her hands. Releasing a breath that tousled the hair on her forehead, he asked, "Kiria, are you all right?"

She tucked herself against him. He wrapped his arms around her and his solid warmth comforted her like nothing else had that day. "I ran into some trouble on the tour."

"I felt something like that," he said. "Were you hurt?" He ran his fingers along her back and arms as though checking for himself.

The Unreal wasn't like reality in all ways. Even if she had been hurt, she could have hidden those wounds here. Yet he felt along her sides, picked up her hand and pressed the palm open. She didn't protest.

Despite what others thought, their alliance had helped both parties. And despite what Chetana thought, Kiria saw little harm in meeting him in the Unreal. *It's just thoughts*, he had said that night when they first kissed. It was only thoughts. Delicious, dangerous thoughts that took her mind away from the relentless troubles of the day.

"No," she murmured against him, watching a dust mote glow across her vision. "I wasn't hurt. There was a riot in King's Heights." She grimaced at the fresh memory. "We got away. We're fine now." Then something he said struck her. She pulled away enough to look up at him. "You said you felt something? You could tell something was wrong?"

His chest heaved up with a deep breath, almost a sigh. This

whole place smelled like him. "Yeah, I could tell you were panicking, but then you didn't come to meet me. I didn't know what was happening." He planted a lingering kiss on her forehead. "If something bad happened... maybe I could fix it."

A smile curled the edges of her lips. "You can't fix everything."

"No?" He tipped her chin up and kissed her until she was breathless.

Afterward, he led her over to a tree, where he sat and pulled her down with him to sit against his chest. Her roiling thoughts had muted, leaving hazy comfort in their wake. But everything with Firian felt fragile. Fears would creep back in soon. She felt them at the door of her mind. Some fears were reserved for him —what he might do back at the Academy, the kind of person he might still choose to be...

She finally said, "I don't think I should call on you every time I'm having a bad day." This hadn't been the first time. Stress had overwhelmed her suddenly about a week before. Angry that her usual resolve had been replaced with a pounding heart and unfocused mind, she'd excused herself to her tent and gone into the Unreal. He'd come right away. It was just like this. In an hour, her anxiety had disappeared.

"Why not?"

"It's just..." How honest could she be with him? Even the strongest person couldn't deal with every trouble on their own— that wasn't it—but she already had friends, family, people who were close and willing to support her. People who sat outside her tent around a fire. She bit her lip. "I'm afraid I'm using you. I still can't forget those things that happened." All the reasons she couldn't trust him.

She felt him tense. He leaned to the side so he could look in her eyes. "Do you like being with me?" he asked, not vulnerably, but as though he knew what she would say.

That insufferable pride. How had she come to like it? She sarcastically stared back the answer.

"Then use me," he said.

She suddenly understood Firian's obsession with power. She clamped her teeth shut as her heart started pounding. A declaration like that wasn't like him. He hated to be used.

This could lead to nothing good. She felt his lust for power leeching into her. But the darkness called, and she cautiously answered, bringing her mouth to his.

THE NEXT COUPLE stops on the tour went much more smoothly. They had proper parades, speeches, parties... Men she didn't trust wanted to talk to her, to dance with her. She tried new foods and heard new music. The air was full of new perfumes from new plants and flowers.

Most of the people she met were polished nobles, the wealthiest and most powerful from the towns and cities they passed. From them she caught the aura of the place, but she wondered about the people who didn't have such privileges. Kiria grew up in Mon Párinath and was used to luxury, but, to rule, shouldn't she know the difficulties faced by common people as well?

A few times, she thought she saw distrust in someone's eyes as they looked at her, so she adjusted her speech to emphasize that her mother had willingly handed her the crown for the good of the Western Kingdom. Part of her wished her mother had come along to corroborate her story. A snide comment here or there implied that her alliance with the Tanyu was ill-advised as well. So she added a bit more about the merits of that decision to her speech too. Chetana kept silent at her side, supportive but not overly so where the Tanyu were concerned.

Chetana's warning about the *katah* still echoed in Kiria's ears, striking her at odd times—breakfast with the Lord of Rantoul, when her serving girls were lacing up a dress for a formal event, the middle of the night... The intrusion annoyed and unsettled her. She would be careful. Her vow to keep the Western Kingdom safe had been sincere. She knew that, but the part that bothered her most was Chetana's certainty. *He* will *hurt you.*

Three weeks on the road had taken its toll on everyone. The initial excitement had worn off, and their travels felt like a job. Kiria missed simple things like having the rest of her clothes and talking to Atty. Even the ability to relax without fuss or scrutiny or adjustment sounded heavenly. Servants and guards surrounded her at the palace too, but here they were forced into tight quarters that made it feel as though she couldn't fully be alone. She hadn't played her lyra in a month.

Under her breath, she hummed a traditional song she often played back home, tapping the horse's leather reins with her thumb in time with the music. They'd ridden on the plains for several days already, and the bright, far horizon strained her eyes. Mountains rose along their right side in an almost unbroken line that swept ahead out of sight. The Somul Mountains to the south were strange. Seeing the Charúnin Thôr, even the unfamiliar end of the mountain range, felt like they were getting closer to home.

Up ahead, the grasses faded away to what looked like a long swath of white water. The air shimmered above it. The group began to twitter amongst themselves.

Still humming, Kiria looked behind her. Jori was riding confidentially between Candrae and Vayci. Her serving girls were both smiling, but Candrae's smile was shy as she pulled a curl of blonde hair over her shoulder.

Kiria rolled her eyes at Jori. *Incorrigible.*

She turned to Chetana, who always rode as close to her as the guards. "Are we getting close?"

"Charäkhnem is two days away," her advisor replied. "We are approaching the Salt Flats."

Kiria sighed, hopefully low enough that no one heard. She remembered the Salt Flats from the one other time she had gone to Charäkhnem as a child. They were unforgiving and boring. They would have to stop soon to gather extra feed for the horses because nothing grew in the Flats at all. Daelon had taught her the origin of the Flats, but she didn't remember much. Something about the rebels salting the earth of those who sided with the oppressors after they won the great war. A reminder of how the two kingdoms hadn't always gotten along.

"Have you ever been to Charäkhnem?" Kiria asked.

"I haven't, My Keeper. There isn't a large Khelê population there."

That seemed an odd reason not to go. Hadn't Chetana lived in a city like that before? "I went once. King Ganesha has a zoo inside the palace."

"That sounds very interesting."

"It is! I hope it's as great as I remember. Sometimes things aren't as grand and magical as they seem before you grow up."

A smile played on Chetana's full mouth as though she were thinking that Kiria was still young. "I'm sure it will be."

The guard at the front of the column held up a hand to halt the travelers. They all slowed. She heard Vayci laugh, a rare sound.

Chetana continued. "Some things are even better when you grow up."

"Like what?" Kiria struggled to think of a good example. The confidence she had gained from the journey with Firian was more of a reclaiming than anything truly new.

Chetana sat still, considering an answer. Her bay mare

tossed her head.

The things Kiria could do now that she was grown—become the Keeper, drink wine, see Firian in the Unreal (which she kept dead secret from everyone except Chetana)—had merit, but also an edge that could quickly turn them from sweet to sour. As a child, she had pictured becoming a Keeper or falling in love as unequivocally good and fun. That wasn't so. With pleasure came pain or uncertainty.

Chetana, in a good mood despite the dark secret she held about Kiria, waved Jori forward. She hardly ever approved of Jori's flippancy, being so serious herself. "Tell our Keeper the benefits of growing up," she said.

He trotted forward, leaving the serving girls behind. "Ah," he said with a grin. "I wouldn't know. I haven't tried it."

A twinge of irritation crossed Chetana's face.

"One thing that's better now than when you were a kid," Kiria clarified.

"Hm." He looked up at the too-bright sky, tipping his chin. "All my powers are greatly improved." He gestured to her. "And yours, of course, as well."

"Your powers?" Kiria said, knowing she was setting him up for a ridiculous comment.

He ticked the items off with his fingers. "I'm faster, taller, hungrier, more eloquent, and better looking." He scrunched his gray eyes as though daring her to disagree.

Kiria laughed. "I don't know about hungrier. You ate everything when you were little."

"That still leaves four solid ways that I'm better now. You can't argue that I'm shorter."

"No, that's true."

Chetana silently peeled away from the conversation, staying close enough not to be rude, but excusing herself from this nonsense.

"And me?" she asked.

"Oh ho!" he exclaimed. "Don't make me give a full list, my dear. We'll be here till supper."

She waited.

He rolled his eyes. Holding up his fingers again, he said, "You're incomprehensively more beautiful—but you knew that —you're more powerful, you're also taller, also more eloquent, and also hungrier—"

"Do you even remember that one time with the tarts?"

"—and you're tougher too." His eyes strayed to her left shoulder, where the misshapen, raised scar from the arrow attack just showed from beneath her clothing. "Is that enough?"

"That will do," she said imperiously.

His eyes glinted in fun.

She pointed ahead. "We're getting close to Charäkhnem."

"Finally."

"Yes, those are the Salt Flats."

"They sound charming."

"Oh, they are."

"Now, if you don't mind"—he heaved himself off the saddle to the ground—"I'm going to stretch my legs a bit." A groom hustled over and took the reins from him. Jori gave a fractional bow from the waist before walking away, back to her serving girls.

She watched him take each one by the hand, helping them dismount. Jori wouldn't disapprove of her meetings in the Unreal. He might even be proud of her. At least he couldn't say she would be ruined by her decision to let Firian ease her sorrows and stresses away.

She wouldn't tell him just yet. There was still a chance—a small chance—that he wouldn't understand, and she preferred to think he would be happy for her. Not everyone thought she was making a mistake.

26

KIRIA

Huge tan domes and turrets of Charäkhnem's royal palace rose ahead of them. It was at least as magnificent as Kiria remembered. Long red banners rimmed with gold embroidery stood on gonfalons on either side of the enormous metal doors. They must have been three stories tall, decorated with round studs arranged in the shape of wings. Four guards, all wearing traditional pointed helmets, flanked the doors.

A pathway with guardrails, like a waterless bridge, led to the entrance. On the railing burned dozens of small candles. Wax coated the metal edges in a look both messy and religious. The guardrails must have been erected to keep those foolish enough to invade from having too many escape routes.

Kiria glanced at the armed escort that had come to lead them to the palace. These guards had conspicuous swords strapped to their belts and red sashes around their waists, looking fearsome in their shining armor. Her own guards' armor still gleamed, despite the trip. She'd spied them polishing the pieces at night and washing spots out of the blue cloth slung around their shoulders.

She was used to being the one who could call or dismiss guards with a word. Four Kingdom soldiers still surrounded her, but Char Visil, Charäkhnem's capital city, was so much grander than any of the other towns or cities they had passed, that she felt small. These days, she didn't often feel small.

Even amid the places where normal citizens seemed to live and work, huge pillars and sky bridges rose like oversized aqueducts to awe and intimidate. Much of the architecture was sandstone. Understandable, since Charäkhnem faced the Desert of Erad on its eastern side. The reddish tan buildings made the sky seem bluer and fresher, despite the dust and heady spices in the air.

It was a good thing they had planned to spend more than one day here. Kiria wanted to explore.

The tall, narrow metal doors creaked open on ropes to let them enter. Inside was a surprisingly small antechamber, again for defense. Kiria wondered if Char Visil had always been so intent on security, or if they made modifications because her ancestors fought them hundreds of years ago.

The Charäkhni guards stood at attention in two perfect rows on either side of them as the group shrugged off their riding cloaks and generally made themselves more presentable.

The metal doors swung shut. Though it was broad daylight, the tiled antechamber was almost completely dark except for golden bowls full of fire standing on stick-thin pedestals. The darkness became quickly claustrophobic.

Happily, one of the Charäkhni guards pushed open a door that let in some natural light. Apparently, there were actual windows in the next room. Kiria moved with her group into the opening, a short hallway, and into a lobby. Staircases led up in a few different directions and hallways disappeared around corners, but at least this area was more spacious. In front of them was another set of golden-plated double doors. This had to be the throne room.

She swallowed, but found that the roof of her mouth had gone dry. In seconds, she would be presented to Shear Ganesha, the king whose approval she needed most. The grandeur of his palace made her nervous that he might not accept her. Prince Amrit's flippant attitude toward her when they were children rushed back. She was a girl and therefore not a natural choice for a leader, but rather someone to forge marriage alliances. But that was years ago. Maybe Amrit and his father didn't think that way now.

Everyone but Kiria, the four Kingdom guards, and Chetana followed servants to their quarters in the palace. Jori pulled a face as he was led away. Obviously, he wanted to see his brother's bride-to-be. Kiria was eager too. There would certainly be another opportunity for Jori later.

Kiria dusted off her dress and lifted her chin. She wore her Beauty like power, like armor. It would help legitimize her in the presence of this established king. Although she shouldn't *have* to have it, it did make a striking first impression.

Someone announced her arrival in Charäkhni. A flourish of instruments and the doors opened once again to admit them into the presence of Shear Ganesha.

The long throne room shone like gold. Guards and musicians stood in columns on either side to usher them in. Some of the instruments had been dyed red, including one that looked almost like her lyra at home. Lampstands lined the enormous hall. Despite all the fire, the cooler air of the open space washed over her as she stepped in.

The vaulted ceiling met at a peak that stretched as high as the Main. At the far end was a platform, raised off the floor by several stairs, where Shear Ganesha sat on his high-backed throne. His expression betrayed none of his initial opinions about her. Most people had a visible reaction to her Beauty, but the king remained impassive. In the shadows behind the throne stood a man all in black. Did the king have a Tanyuin bodyguard? She would have to ask Firian later.

At the foot of the stairs were two seated figures. Amrit was the one on the left. Kiria hadn't seen him in several years, but he had the same reddish hair. He had filled out and was no longer that scrawny boy she remembered. When he saw her, his mouth went slack and he leaned forward, almost unconsciously, before sitting back again. She suppressed a tiny smirk.

The figure on the right was a young woman. Atty's fiancée, Haved. She had the same sandy-colored skin as her brother. She wore her dark reddish hair long, but tied it back to reveal large golden earrings. She had a square jaw and an expression difficult to read.

An alliance with both Charäkhnem and the Tanyu would render the Western Kingdom all but undefeatable.

The six visitors approached the throne. The king had a stony face, a hardened version of the expression she had seen on Haved. Over his shoulders he wore a stole that fell like a golden set of wings, the pinions stretching in front. Each feather glowed in the light with remarkable detail. Clearly, it was something only the kings of Charäkhnem wore.

Chetana and the guards bowed at the waist. Chetana spoke first, her words flawlessly diplomatic. "Your Majesty, King Ganesha, please allow me to introduce the Second Keeper of Brithnem and the Western Kingdom, Kiria Arioc." She stepped aside and Kiria went forward.

The king bowed his head a fraction to acknowledge her, but he did not stand. "Welcome to Char Visil," he said in a deep, gravelly voice, accented like Amrit's but more refined. "My Keeper, I am pleased that you have chosen to visit us."

"The pleasure is mine, Your Majesty," she replied, dimly aware of Amrit staring at her.

"Our countries are fortunate in such an alliance, which soon will be even stronger." He looked down at his daughter. "And news has reached us that you have subdued the marauders?"

It would have been easier if his people had assisted in the war, but she still felt glad when he mentioned the victory. "We have, Your Majesty."

"That is surely something to celebrate." He didn't smile or break the polite but mechanical cadence of his voice. "In two days' time, we will host a celebration in your honor, both for your ascension to the throne and the pending alliance between our two kingdoms. My son and daughter will attend, and you may bring those who traveled with you."

Two guards, as though summoned, left the room in unison, perhaps to tell the others about the celebration.

"I thank you," Kiria said, though the word *pending* still rang in her ears. "God has truly blessed the Western Kingdom with your partnership."

"Have you brought Atael with you?"

Kiria looked over in surprise. It was Haved. She appeared unashamed about the interruption, but not brash. "No, my lady," Kiria said.

The only evidence of the princess's disappointment was a slight dimming of her eyes.

Perhaps Atty should have come. It was a shame that so many would get to meet her before he did. "But his brother is here." Kiria added the words before picturing the two of them meeting. Hopefully Jori would behave himself.

"The Kepron, Jorrim?"

"Yes."

"Then you will bring him to the celebration, My Keeper."

"Of course."

"Will the late Second Keeper join us?" asked the king.

The late? He made it sound like she was dead. "No, my mother elected to stay in Brithnem." *She's in perfect health. She supports my ascension to the throne...* "She gladly supports me there, but wanted me to experience my coronation tour without other Keepers." *Did that sound odd? That sounded odd.* She bit her tongue to keep from saying anything more. Her mind buzzed a little with shame.

The king shifted in response, the golden wings moving with him.

If he was going to move forward in letting his daughter marry Atty, he had to like Kiria, or at least consider her a legitimate ruler.

Chetana stood forth again. "Your Majesty, we have traveled many days and My Keeper would like to rest."

"Then rest shall be granted," said the king. He turned to the guards. "Take them to their quarters." He said the words grandly, not dismissively. But he still gazed down at her from his throne as if unsure what to think of this beautiful new Keeper. She would have to make a better impression at the upcoming celebration, winning over both him and his daughter, for Atty's sake.

"Thank you, Your Majesty," she said, turning with the rest of them and letting the guards shepherd them to their rooms.

KIRIA HAD EXPECTED the party to be held in the throne room, since the Keepers always held their large gatherings in the Main. Little could have prepared her for the larger, grander room, covered in intricate gold leaf. The floors shone. The ceiling soared above them, lost in dimness. Servants in gold and red took capes, offered food, refilled glasses, brought messages. The wealthier guests, both male and female, had lined their eyes in coal black. She didn't know where to look. Several times, she realized that her face was stuck in a dumb, awestruck grin.

Amrit had the same grin on his face when he approached her, dressed more magnificently than any other guest, the king excepted. His golden vest was cinched at the waist. Beneath it, the shirt had maroon silk sleeves. Heavy metal plates formed in the shape of wings hung around his neck. The same design wrapped around his forearms. His lapels and skirts had matching intricate embroidery in black thread.

The Kingdom guard she kept with her moved to the side so she could speak to him. "Lady Kiria," Amrit said, "are you enjoying your party?" His speech still wasn't as smooth as his father's, but his fluency was far more advanced than when they had first met. It helped that he was home and had the ease of a host instead of a guest.

"It's amazing," she said sincerely. "Everything is beautiful. Please thank the king for me."

He spoke above the rising noise of the party. "I suggested the extra fabric. The red." He gestured to long, thin tables gathered on one side of the enormous room. They all had deep red tablecloths that matched the Charäkhni flag.

"That looks good."

When she looked back, he was staring at her. She couldn't think of a way to fill the silence. There had to be something that would promote goodwill between their countries without making it seem that she was interested in him...

"Yes," he finally said. "A beautiful color."

"Couldn't agree more."

Someone grabbed her hand and spun her around.

Jori, of course.

"Look at that dress," he said. He all but winked at her.

Amrit waited for a second more but saw that Jori wasn't going to float onwards quickly enough for him not to be conspicuous. Appearing to see another important dignitary, the prince excused himself and strode away.

"Button your vest," Kiria whispered. "This is a diplomatic event."

Jori raised both eyebrows at her but stiffly and pointedly obeyed. He spread his arms when he was finished. "Is this acceptable?"

"Yes, just... be good."

"I thought this was a party."

"It is." But their alliance with Charäkhnem shouldn't be tested. They had to leave King Ganesha with no doubts about the Western Kingdom or her leadership.

"Why don't we meet Atty's girl?"

She hissed in his ear. "Don't say that! She's not 'Atty's girl.' Especially not here. And not yet, so *be good*."

He gave a crooked smile. Maybe he had meant to rile her up. He whispered back. "You have to relax. Have some fun." On his breath, she could smell a hint of the fermented honey drink the servers kept offering.

She adjusted her off-white dress with gold and purple trim. "I will."

He waited.

She sighed. "I'll try." She brought her voice up to the normal volume. "It is gorgeous here."

"And all for you, darling."

"Well—" Why was she about to protest? It was true. All of this was in her honor: the new Keeper of Brithnem. It felt too grand, as though there had to be an ulterior motive. If stronger alliances were an ulterior motive, though, that wasn't bad at all. She smiled.

He leaned forward again. "You've already impressed them. If

you go too far, they might start feeling bad about themselves."

She stopped herself from smacking him for the joke. "Go on," she said, laughing. "Have a good time. And thank you." She inhaled deeply. Honey and lamb and roasted vegetables mingled in the air. So far, no one had accused her of usurping the throne or fraternizing with Tanyu. Maybe she could actually relax and enjoy the party, follow Jori's advice.

Jori suddenly strode away, walking with purpose. She followed his eyeline and found Haved, dressed all in gold with a deep red sash. Her hair, darker than her brother's, fell almost to her waist with a simple golden ornament twined on one side. Jori all but ran toward her. Kiria followed.

When Jori reached her, he bowed without a hint of irony. A good sign. Haved regarded him stoically. "It's an honor to meet the princess of Charäkhnem," he began. "I am Jorrim Calthwaite, brother of Atael Calthwaite, the Third Keeper of the Western Kingdom."

His title sounded pretty impressive when he put it like that. Why was he always complaining about lacking prestige?

"You can call me Jori."

"Atael's brother?" she asked, suddenly interested. She drew her dark eyes over him, inspecting, as though she expected to find a family resemblance there. He waited without shame for her to finish looking.

"Yes," Kiria said, drawing even with them, "but the brothers are very different."

Haved's eyes widened at the sight of Kiria's Beauty and she dipped her head respectfully. "Lady Kiria."

"Princess Haved."

"How are they different?" Haved seemed fairly stoic but Kiria decided that she liked her. Haved was so self-possessed, so unashamed of who she was. Her boldness could border on rudeness, but her words had no cruel edge.

"Atael has more power." Kiria cast a glance at Jori, who raised his eyebrows at her in a question. "He's more serious-minded, and he's a little taller."

"Not much taller," Jori said.

"He's bigger," she revised, casting him a glance.

Jori shrugged one shoulder.

"Is he kind?" Haved didn't ask the question in a timid or fearful way, but with genuine curiosity.

Kiria smiled. Yes, that was more important. "Yes, he is."

Haved's stoic face thawed into a smile too.

"Unless you mention that one Dedication Day," Jori said.

Haved, a little concerned, glanced at Kiria for confirmation. Kiria shook her head. That incident was years ago, when they were all little. Atty would never cry about fasting now.

"He's a wonderful person," she said.

Haved turned to Jori, though her eyes frequently went back to Kiria. Beauty was hard to ignore. "You are his brother. Tell me about him."

"I was actually hoping to learn more about you," he replied. "We can trade. I'll tell you something and you tell me something." He winked confidentially.

The arrangement seemed to please her. "All right. You begin."

Jori crossed his arms and shifted his weight as he thought. "We don't call him Atael. We call him Atty."

That information didn't seem like enough to warrant something interesting from her, but apparently this was the first time she had heard of it. "Atty?" she asked, emphasizing the *t*.

"Yes," Jori said. "Now your turn."

He didn't hesitate. "I love learning about the heavens, the stars. Do you have any Qib Navigators in Brithnem?"

"What?"

"Qib Navigators," Kiria stepped in. "They're the best ocean

navigators, from the Desert Colony of Qib...?" She hoped this would jog his memory. Apparently, he hadn't paid enough attention to his Amiran tutor as a child. "I haven't heard of many," Kiria said to Haved, "but I did see one once, a long time ago. The army uses them, and I think a couple trade companies do too."

The princess beamed more broadly than Kiria had seen so far. "That's wonderful! I thought there would be more Navigators near the ocean."

"The Amiran Academy is there too," said Kiria. "They could probably teach you more about the stars if you're interested."

"Oh yes. Our own teachers are very good, but if there is any new information I could learn..." The passion shone in her face. "I like to chart the stars. Brithnem is so far away. They might look different." She wrung her hands, not from distress but anticipation.

"That's true," she said. Kiria wished she knew enough about the topic to satisfy her. Her love for the subject transfigured her from a wooden royal figure to someone she could see as a friend. When was the last time she had stopped to look, really look, at the stars?

"Does Atty go on the ocean? Does he know the stars?"

Honestly, Kiria wasn't sure if he knew constellations. He didn't often go out on the ocean, and when he did, it wasn't very far.

A server passed by and all three of them took a honey drink from the platter.

"I'm sure he doesn't know them as well as you do," Jori said.

"What does he do?" she insisted.

"He serves his country," Kiria said, filling the space she knew would be silent too long. Atty wasn't particularly good at many things. He was passable at many things. But that didn't make him sound like an exciting match. "He enjoys being outdoors."

Jori sucked his teeth, clearly holding back the comments welling to the surface.

"He must be thoughtful to like solitude," said Haved.

"Yes," said Kiria, a little too quickly. She loved Atty like her own brother, but this woman, despite her childlike frankness, seemed so grand, and Atty's destiny had always seemed too big for him.

"Well," said Jori, "that's—"

Kiria gasped as pain rushed through her chest. As though she'd heard a shriek, her heart beat so rapidly that it felt unstable. Panic surged through her. Her mind blurred with dread. The danger wasn't just inside her ribcage; there was something out there too, on the dance floor. She knew it as surely as she felt the breath clawing in her throat. Someone watched her, preparing to strike. She was too visible. Her Beauty made her a target. Instinctively, she ducked, searching wildly for the threat.

Someone was here. Someone would kill her.

The space between her and the other guests now seemed like huge gulfs exposing her to all eyes. Everywhere she looked, people were looking back. Heavy dread flowed thick in her veins and covered her mind, immobilizing it. She had to get to cover. Without a word, she ran through the huge room toward the nearest door. Maybe there was a place to hide, to think. Why was no one screaming? Why were there no sounds of death?

She sucked down air but none of it seemed to stay in her lungs. All its healthy qualities were gone. She was drowning.

She reached the door but her strength had left. She couldn't pull the handle. She was trapped. The door wouldn't open. Her heart pounded so hard and fast it hurt. She had to sit down.

As she began to sink to the floor, someone grabbed her arm. Was it her guard? Someone else took her other arm and half-walked, half-dragged her across the floor. The open floor.

Her head began to clear. Looking around, she saw no one

else in a panic. The two men at either side were her guards. Chetana had joined them, following behind.

What had happened? The truth hit her in a wave of nausea. This was someone else's panic.

Firian.

Firian was dead.

27

FIRIAN

WATER CLOSED over Firian's head. It was late enough that no one else was likely to use the washroom, especially this one in the Head's secluded hallway. It was the perfect opportunity to practice a skill he hadn't mastered yet.

Thirty-four, thirty-five, thirty-six... Without water, he was able to hold his breath for two hundred counts. He calmed himself, feeling the warm bathwater lap over the crown of his head. Some of his dark hair must be floating on the surface. This was the closest thing a body of water for him to practice.

His heart slowed. Calm encased his mind. If Bard could do it, so could he. *Seventy, seventy-one, seventy-two...*

All it took was control, above or under the water. The warm, soundless space lent itself to serenity. *Ninety-five, ninety-six...*

Later, he could think about which towns to take and save. Later, he would check on the state of his growing army.

New recruits from Imlin were coming soon, thanks to Makai, so Jovan had to be ready for them. Firian suspected that Makai had to threaten more than one person in order to gain control of Imlin, but he didn't ask any questions. When the Tanyuin Head demanded allegiance, refusal wasn't an option.

This was the way forward. The Academy needed a new direction, a direction toward justice and power. There were bound to be people who resisted. Bard's and Kiria's thoughts were never far from his own, though, and they didn't understand the cost of success.

Firian could think about it later. Now, he could just practice his skills in and out of the Unreal. This was where he thrived.

One hundred twenty, one hundred twenty-one, one hundred twenty-two...

His chest started to feel tight. He redirected his energy to the calm tick of the numbers. He didn't mind a little pain. He swished one hand through the water, feeling the weight of it press back against his hand. *One hundred thirty-two, one hundred thirty-three...*

A faint pulse meant that someone had jumped or moved nearby. Probably out in the hallway. The feeling barely registered.

One hundred fifty, one hundred fifty-one...

A feeling of eyes on him. He dipped into the Unreal. With all the Talent in the building, any distinct individual was unclear. Everything hummed with life. He still had to master that skill as well. Belik always knew he was coming, even when he wasn't using the Talent. "Come in, Firian," he would say, before Firian had touched the door handle. One day, he would be able to do that too.

One hundred sixty-eight, one hundred sixty-nine...

He was just being paranoid. Almost everyone supported his Headship, and those who didn't feared his ability. No one was watching him. He was alone.

One hundred seventy-two, one hundred seventy-three...

He willed himself not to speed through the numbers. Control in all things. Even a bath could sharpen his wits, if he had enough patience.

One hundred seventy-nine...

Patience. Control.

One hundred eighty...

With a sucking, surging sound, something plunging into the water close to his head. He thrashed to the side, sliding just out of reach of the fingers that brushed against his temple. Panic gushed through him. The tub was suddenly the bay where children were left to die and the Torithian pushed his head down so he couldn't breathe. He couldn't breathe.

He kicked against the tub to push himself out into the air again. When he emerged, his gasped breath came too quickly to fill his aching lungs.

Jovan stood huge over him. Weaponless, the Master lunged again, his massive hands reaching for Firian's neck. Jovan didn't need weapons. He could kill him. In a physical fight, Firian stood no chance. *There are many ways to kill a man.* Jovan knew them all.

Firian was naked and weaponless too, but not helpless. Even before drawing another breath, he closed his eyes and dove into the Unreal—one level, two levels—and savagely attacked Jovan's mind, his body, his subconscious.

Vague pressure pressed on Firian's throat, pressure on his eyes and his tongue...

Firian doubled his attack, feeling his own heart beat under the water so loudly that the whole Academy must have heard it. His fear and rage turned red and black. He hurled all the violence he could muster. He could feel Jovan, feel himself, bending like a tree branch. He *would not* give first. He might not have strength or air, but he had power. He pressed with all his mental strength in one last heave.

The branch broke. Firian gasped. Air. Air filled his lungs. He hurtled upward through the levels and opened his eyes.

Jovan lay half in and half out of the bath. Pink water floated out of his ears.

Furious and horrified, Firian shoved Jovan's shoulder and threw him out of the bathwater. His skull cracked against the floor. Blood leaked from his closed eyes and open mouth.

Firian stood, grabbed a towel with a trembling hand, and got out of the tub. He could barely wrap the towel around himself. He kept blinking, impotent adrenaline spiraling through him.

Unable to stand, unable to shake the panic, he sat on the edge of the bath, watching the red blood pool around Master Jovan's head.

When he had finally gathered himself enough to stand, anger took the place of panic. No one would blame him for what he had done. He'd acted in self-defense. Jovan—he cursed loudly—made him do it. He didn't want to kill him. How *dare* he try to murder him? And why?

He could barely see through the black haze of rage as he marched back to his office, not even dressed. "Get me Belik!" he snapped at the guard outside his room. He hated the guard. Why hadn't he protected him? *I told him to stay where he was.* At the memory, he cursed himself, and then Jovan, and then the guard again.

The guard hurried away.

Firian slammed the door behind him. Almost feral, he checked every corner of the suite of rooms, looking behind doors, crawling to see under the desk and the bed. He ripped off the blankets and threw them against the wall. He needed to scream, throw something, kill Jovan again.

His hands shook. He bit his tongue until it bled. The pain helped. Taking a few slow, shaky breaths, he calmed himself enough to put on his Academy-issued black clothes. Something about the sharp edges of the iron crown made him rethink putting it on, so he left it in his bedroom.

The door opened in the office. He practically flew to meet the newcomer. It was Belik.

"Sit!" Firian roared. That posture would make it harder for someone to attack.

With shame, he felt angry warmth pool around his eyes. Hopefully Belik wouldn't see it. But he would. He always noticed.

Belik sat without saying a word.

The strength of Firian's voice had given out. The next words were quiet. "Did you know about this?"

"What happened?" Belik asked evenly.

Firian couldn't bring the words to his mouth.

Understanding dawned in Belik's blunt face. "Who was it?"

"Jovan."

Belik bit out a curse word. "No, I didn't know." He looked down. "I should have suspected. Firian, I should have warned you."

"Yes, you should have! Who else is there?"

"I don't know of anyone else."

"Liar."

"Firian, I swear. I knew that some people didn't approve of you, but I thought they were all too afraid to act against you."

"Get me a list." His power flowed through him like an evil spirit.

"I can do that." Belik said the words slowly enough that Firian doubted his sincerity. He was trying to calm him down and the effort just infuriated him more.

Firian was about to snap at Belik again when he cut him off. "Where is he?"

Suddenly exhausted, Firian deflated. One of his mentors lifeless as a monstrous sack on the floor. Gray hair mussed by a pillow. Stiff legs under blankets. Blood dribbling from a useless mouth. "The washroom," he said.

"I can get people to take care of that for you."

A wave of gratefulness overcame Firian. A hard lump formed in his throat.

Rage was better than this. Rage could eliminate the problem and show no weakness. All he could do was nod.

"It's done," Belik said with the self-assuredness of a god. He was security itself, someone to trust so Firian could rest.

He rallied his roiling feelings. "Thank you. But I still need that list."

28

KIRIA

CHETANA and the guards led Kiria back to her room. Tears flowed down her face against her will. Grief and humiliation filled her so she could barely breathe.

Everyone had seen her panic in the great hall, but no one else could sense the danger. Even without strange actions like that, everybody noticed her because of her Beauty. They must all think she was unhinged.

She definitely felt unhinged. Something was deeply wrong. Maybe Firian wasn't dead. Maybe he was alive. Maybe it was just... She couldn't come up with a good scenario that would have caused her breakdown. Whatever had happened, it was serious. She had to check, had to see him right now.

Chetana, her arm across her shoulders, guided her gently into the diplomat suite. Guards stood at attention outside. Everything happened far too slowly, as though their legs moved through thigh-deep water. Once inside, Kiria gulped down air and pulled Chetana into a fierce hug. "Okay," she said, pushing her away. "Everyone needs to leave. I have to be alone." Her advisor would already know that her episode had to do with Firian. Kiria didn't look at her again, turning instead to the bed.

"My Keeper, may I get you a glass of water?" It was Vayci, eyes full of concern.

"No," she answered automatically, wanting them gone as well. "Yes." Her mouth felt sticky and her throat burned.

Dutiful as always, Vayci slipped silently through the door after Chetana.

"Please leave me alone," she told Candrae, who waited at the ready. Candrae didn't protest. Kiria knew she would stand just outside.

Finally, she was by herself. She rubbed hot tears off her face with the back of her hand as she changed from Beautiful to plain and shut her eyes.

All was darkness. Slowly, she reached her mind in Firian's direction. Her fingers trembled with apprehension. It felt like opening a door with a murder victim behind it. She didn't want to find his dead body, but she had to know.

"Firian?" she whispered. Even that volume sounded loud in the nothingness. Tears started at the corners of her eyes again. "Firian?"

Her heartbeat pulsed around the lump in her throat. He was dead. He had to be. And she wouldn't find out how it happened until they got the news from a Watchman in a few days. She couldn't wait that long.

"Firian!" She risked saying his name more loudly, though the silence was so charged that it felt as though a hundred people were listening.

A figure in black appeared.

She recoiled, heart pounding. Breathing hard, she leaned forward and squinted. The lines of the person's body became more distinct. She knew those shoulders, that hair, that walk...

She ran toward him, feeling as though her feet were floating. They might have been. "Oh my god!" she cried, and hugged Firian hard around the neck. He was solid. He was there.

Wrapping his strong arms around her back, he held her against him.

"Oh my god!" she said again, her breath hot against his shoulder. "I thought…"

His heart beat hard under hers. Something awful had happened. But they didn't want to talk.

He clung to her as though she could save him from whatever horrible thing stalked him. His hands were hot on her waist. She began to melt in his arms.

The kisses came fast. Her face and body flushed at his touch. She wanted him closer as he bent down over her. He drew one finger all the way up her side, over her neck, her cheek, sending shivers over her body. When he reached her hairline, he raked his fingers through her hair.

She hugged him tightly. Maybe she was cutting off his ability to breathe, but she needed him to know she was there. She could barely breathe either.

He moved his lips from her mouth to her hot cheek, greedily kissing up to her ear. "Show me," he said hoarsely.

She could barely respond. "What?"

"Change for me." The humid warmth against her ear distracted her from the words he was saying.

If she showed him her Beauty now, she knew what it would mean. Even in the Unreal—*the Unreal, they were in the Unreal*—she couldn't let him take her body. Neither of them could withstand the temptation if she changed.

She caught her breath, slowed it down. Her arms trembled with the force of what she felt, but she had to be resolved. Fractionally, she released him.

He swept her hair back around the nape of her neck as he attended to her ear. The back of her neck. It was almost too much.

"No."

"I need you. I need you today," he said in an undertone, not looking at her but running his hands back down over her sides. His fingers fiddled at her waist. He brought his face close for a kiss.

She sank into it a moment. Those lips... but no, she couldn't.

"What happened?" she asked.

At the question, the heat in him died down. He took a deep breath that made his shoulders hang lower and his hands stop moving. He was silent for a moment, head bowed, gently holding her.

Then he bit his lip, probably to keep from swearing, and his eyes darkened. After a few more moments of silence, he looked at her. "Someone tried to kill me."

Even though she had expected that answer, the words still made her stomach drop. "I thought so," she whispered.

Curiosity sparked in his unhappy face. "Did you feel something?"

She nodded. "I did. I thought... you had died." It was hard even to say the words. But it was the truth, and she could forgive herself for the embarrassing display at the party more readily since she had thought him dead.

He pursed his mouth. "No," he said simply. He was alive.

She wanted to repeat her question since he hadn't given an explanation.

He sighed and rubbed her sides, preoccupied with thought. His hands against the fabric, almost as though he were wiping them off, brought to mind another time they were together. In the woods outside Raewhith. When he had killed those men.

She fought off a shudder. "Did you kill him?" she asked, her voice tiny.

He just nodded a small, honest nod. It wasn't boastful this time. It might have been afraid. Dark hair fell down over his forehead as his eyes found the floor.

Almost motherly, she pushed his hair out of his eyes and hugged him again. He warmed up in her arms, like an animal waking up. She felt him take her into him.

She let go and pushed back against his chest. "I can't do this," she muttered.

"Why not?" The question came out rough and husky.

She wasn't sure how to answer him.

As the silence lengthened, anger flickered over his features. Then he softened and grabbed her hand to pull her back in.

She stood her ground, feeling cold. "I can't. But I'm so glad you're still alive."

His fingers recoiled from her into a loose fist and back again. His eyebrows lowered, uncomprehending. "Why are you never Beautiful with me?"

The question stung.

Neither of them made any sort of background. Behind him was only darkness, and he blended in as though he were part of it. The pit of her stomach felt sour.

Today, he had survived an assassination attempt. He wasn't himself. He shouldn't demand that she become Beautiful, or that she give herself to him. She still wanted to be with him, but they had different ideas of what that meant.

Based on everything that had happened, she was fragile too. It was a bad time for either of them to make rash decisions, even in the Unreal.

She swallowed. "It's different with you," she started, not sure how she would explain. "If I... changed, with just the two of us, it would feel..." She cast around for a word. *Frightening, vulnerable, wild, like a promise...* A promise. That was it. It would feel like a promise she wasn't ready to make.

He waited for her to finish. His jaw was clenched tight. The longer she stalled, the more he frowned, not understanding.

You still like me this way. She willed him to say something, but he stayed silent.

"I can't," she said again. "Not... right now."

She felt his surprise follow her as she disappeared back to reality.

She sat on the edge of the bed, heavy as though she had just come back from a swim. A glass of water sat nearby. The torches guttered. Mindlessly smoothing the blankets, she hung her head. All her thoughts were disconnected, more like images than words. Impressions. Desires and regrets bubbling up like the ocean. Wave after wave.

Her eyes felt crusty with dried tears. At least Firian wasn't dead. That was something to be thankful for. But the Charäkhni royal family must think she was insane, maybe unfit to lead. And Chetana knew there was a connection between her and Firian. Though her advisor didn't mention it, she knew Kiria's outburst had to do with him. Would she bring it up again?

Firian acted as though he wanted her to put back his broken pieces, but it was too much to expect of her. He would see her actions as a rejection. She read it like a bold sentence in his eyes, the cut of his hard-set jaw. How would he respond?

Glad she was alone, she put her face in her hands. The golden bracelets she had worn to the party tinkled as they slid down her wrists.

"...said she wanted to be alone."

"We all know that doesn't apply to me."

"It applies to everyone."

"Just open the door. I need to see her. Make sure she's all right."

"Sir—"

"Is she all right in there? You can tell me that at least."

Jori was arguing with one of the guards. Wearily, she stood to her feet and went to assuage his worry.

When she opened the door, he bolted inside, followed by a guard. Jori quickly made a pointed face at the guard before turning to her. He reached out and held her shoulders, observing her face. "How are you, darling?" He searched her eyes as though he could unravel the mystery of her behavior that way.

"I don't know," she replied, suddenly helpless. What was she supposed to say to him? Exhausted, she sat on the edge of the bed again.

"Are you all right? You don't seem all right. Gave everybody a scare in there." He sat down beside her, still maintaining comforting contact.

"I gave myself a scare." She could barely look at him.

This was the part when he would normally make a joke about Haved not wanting to marry Atty now. It was a testament to his concern that he didn't say it. "Ah." He gave her shoulders a squeeze. "You're safe now."

She looked at him and grimaced. "What's happening in there now? Do they think I'm crazy?"

Apparently encouraged about her mental state, he winked. "You've always been a little crazy."

She groaned and linked her ankles.

"Shh!" he soothed. "They'll be fine. And besides, who cares? I just need to know you're all right."

"Jori," she said, suddenly resolved, "I need to tell you something."

His gray eyes widened slightly, surprised by her seriousness.

"Actually, I need to ask you something."

They both waited in silence for a moment. Jori scooted away from her in a listening posture. He picked a feather off his sleeve and flicked it away. "What do you want to ask me about?"

Kiria squirmed. It was an uncomfortable confession. Hopefully he'd support her decisions. She couldn't continue without at least one person telling her that she wasn't doing anything wrong. "It's a little tricky…"

A smirk passed over his face. Leaning toward her, he gave her a confidential look. "That's my specialty."

She shoved him. "No, it isn't. You're never serious." Maybe he expected juicy gossip. In a way, now that she thought of it, that was what she was offering.

He set his face in a serious neutral expression. "Oh, I can be serious, darling. Keep secrets. Kill as necessary."

She rolled her eyes. But he did make her feel better. "Okay." She steeled her nerves with a deep breath. It was time for the truth. "You can't tell anyone, even Atty."

Curiosity blazed in his eyes.

"I… have met Firian in the Unreal."

"More than once?"

"Yes."

"Romantic?"

"Yes."

Jori, impressively, kept the neutral expression intact. A wave of relief swept over her when he didn't judge her right away. Not that he'd have any room to do that. Mon Párinath was filled with rumors of his romantic escapades. More than half of them were lies built on all his obvious flirtations.

"Do you love him?" he asked.

She blinked. She hadn't asked herself the question so bluntly. Firian impressed her. She thought about him often. Together, they were electric. But did she love him? She thought of his face before she disappeared. Vulnerable but angry. "I don't know."

"That means no," Jori said. "Always."

She opened her mouth to protest, but he held up a hand to stop her. "No, it always means no. If you loved him, you'd know it."

"I care about him."

"Of course you do," he said quickly, as though it were obvious. "You're a decent person. Much better than I am. I don't care whether he lives or dies. But he *isn't* a decent person. He was willing to turn on you."

"It's not the same now. He's in charge of the Academy. It's different."

Jori threw his head back in an exaggerated laugh. "Do you"—he readjusted his sitting position—"do you remember when he came to the palace the first time?"

"How could I forget?" Jori had practically skipped with excitement to meet him.

"So you know I want to believe you. The Tanyu. Kiria, the Tanyu! I wanted to be one. I wanted them to be perfect. But after I heard..." He dropped his gaze and fiddled with the buttons on his vest. His voice turned into a mutter. "I'm glad you didn't see me. The pubs got to know me very well."

Jori never talked like this. Almost as though he realized the same thing at the same moment, he tossed his head as if to free himself of the dark thoughts. "You, my dear, are light. Sweetness and light."

She scoffed, feeling anything but those things.

"But he has darkness. If you don't love him, don't let him in your soul."

Though he said the words flippantly, they fell between them like a curtain. Firian had made her a better leader. His drive encouraged her to start earlier, try harder. She pictured the way he had looked at her before the Academy made him take her hostage. Even her plain face fascinated him and opened something inside him. She could see it. And the Firian she saw in those moments took her breath away. He was a warrior, strong and capable, with the focus to topple systems and right injustice. She thought of Firian's hands at her sides, his kiss on her mouth.

She wanted more of both. If only it were easier to do the right thing. Or even to know what that meant. "I have some darkness in me too," she confessed.

Jori snorted. "Impossible! My girl?"

"Jori, it's true." She looked into his eyes.

A smile crinkled the edges of his mouth, but he met her gaze.

"I know there are problems with seeing Firian," she said. "I know. Like tonight."

"That was him?" Jori sat a little straighter on the bed, as though he would charge after Firian that minute.

"It was, it was," she said, soothing him back down. "But not what you think. He was almost killed today. I felt it." She laid a fist on her heart, trying to make him understand.

He frowned.

She continued slowly. "I felt his panic. And I thought... Once I understood what was happening, I thought he died." She dropped her gaze.

"Hey, that's not good." The way he said it made it sound like he meant their connection, not Firian's attack. "This isn't good," he repeated. "He's taking you down with him."

"It could just as easily have happened to me," she said in a small voice.

He took her by the shoulders again, forcing her to look at him. His face was serious. "Hey, no. You survive. You live, free and easy. Always. He should keep his problems with him."

"It's not that simple," she said. "I care about him. This connection isn't what we planned, but I think you have to be ready to suffer with another person if you care about them. And I want that closeness. He looks at me like I'm beautiful."

"But—"

She cut him off with a look. She hadn't transformed for Firian in the Unreal.

"None of that means that you have darkness," he said. "Everybody wants to be close to someone."

"You certainly do," she teased, trying to laugh around the lump in her throat.

He pursed his lips ironically as she lapsed into silence. With a theatrical bow of his head, he let go of her. "There you are. What more proof could you need?"

She wrinkled her forehead.

Jori squeezed her hand. "Everyone wants to be wanted."

"So what do I do?" Her voice had dwindled almost to a whisper.

Jori sat up again, away from her. "Trust me, darling, you don't want to take my advice. Just do what you think is right."

"Is it wrong if I keep going? Secretly? Oh!" She threw her hands in the air. "It's not even real. It's just in the Unreal anyway. The whole thing. I'm not even doing anything!"

Jori's eyes narrowed. "What aren't you doing?"

She blushed. "We're just... nothing!"

He held up fingers as he ticked items off. "You meet secretly in the Unreal. It's *romantic*, you said. You're eaten up with guilt. You said you have darkness in you. Are you sleeping with him?" Jori's expression didn't change, except for a slight crinkling around his eyes.

"No! No, not quite." She dropped her eyes.

"I'm glad you haven't given him the satisfaction." Jori stood and took her hands, guiding her to stand. "You should value yourself more highly, even in the Unreal. I hate him, but you have to judge for yourself. He doesn't deserve you. No!" He held up a hand as though she might protest. "No, he doesn't. The world may not care about a Keeper's brother, the black sheep, but you do. A lovely girl like that deserves someone better than a man who would trade you for more power without blinking." He cocked his head. "You know he would."

"I don't know," she said again. Jori couldn't know the way Firian looked at her. But Firian had looked at her like that *before* too…

"Yes, you do."

She put her hands on her hips, teasing. "Who made you so wise?"

He trailed his pointer finger in the air like a flying bird until it landed, briefly, pointed at her. "I know you'll do the right thing. I, on the other hand, will do the wrong thing and you can just live vicariously through me."

She smacked his arm. He leaned forward and laughed in answer.

"You're terrible," she said.

"Incorrigible." It had become his byword. He rolled his eyes in mock surrender.

Something in her chest loosened when he went back to his normal self. She could have some space to think, and he wouldn't shun her in the meantime.

"No telling," she said, feeling eight years old.

One hand on his heart, he repeated her words. "No telling."

29

FIRIAN

THE DOOR BURST OPEN, slamming on its hinges.

Firian jumped to his feet, a knife in his hand. Adrenaline pulsed through his body like a lightning bolt. Who else was after him?

He pulled his hand back just before it was too late.

"Bard!" he said, throwing the knife to the other side of the room. It clattered on the floor near his bedroom door. He couldn't get another word out. All he could do was bring his hands up to his face. Though his hands felt hot, his face was clammy.

Bard, who had cowered before, now stood up tall. "What happened, Fir? Something happened. Are you okay?"

The alarm in Bard's voice annoyed him. His chest rose and fell heavily as the shock of adrenaline wore off, the edges of his vision hazy from the moment of horror. Finally, he cursed. And again, more loudly.

"Firian?" His whole name. The Bard he knew normally would have left him alone. But here he stood, searching his face with his eyes brimming with concern. "What happened, mate?"

What *had* happened? Everything seemed like a dream. Even Kiria, just now. Why had she left? His skin had gone cold when she pushed him away. *Why did she push me away?* She knew he needed her. He felt the heat in her kiss. And then she left. Always, before, girls had given into desire or had stayed away from him altogether. What was this?

The chair scraped back as he slumped into it, his energy completely sapped. He looked up at Bard, who had approached the desk.

"You have to tell me."

"I don't have to do anything," Firian snapped, before realizing how juvenile that sounded. He ran a hand back through his hair. It was still damp. He rubbed two fingers together to get the moisture off. Sighing, he said, "It was Jovan."

Bard's face became a mask of concern, his forehead bunching down from his spiky black hair. He leaned forward and put a hand on the desk near the flag of Raewhith and the new yellow flag of Imlin, which he had requested from Makai when he went to demand allegiance in person.

"He attacked me in the washroom." Hopefully Belik was getting the body out of there now. Even so, Firian wouldn't go in there for a few days at least.

Bard gasped. "How did you...?"

"I took care of it."

"You killed him."

"I took care of it."

The momentary silence was so pronounced that Firian could hear other Tanyu far away down the hall.

"Was he the only one?"

Firian's heart beat faster. That was the question. "Just now, yes."

Bard pursed his lips, his gaze bright and piercing. Those black eyes... they could see right through him most of the time.

It was as though Firian could never keep a secret. "Yeah, but you think there might be others."

Firian looked down. They were both silent for a while, thinking of Jovan, thinking of Master Jairon...

"What are you going to do?" Bard finally asked.

Fire burned in his brain again as he thought about it. *I'm going to stop it. I'm going to find anyone else before they get to me. I'm going to...* But he couldn't tell Bard any of that.

"I'm their leader," he said. "They all have to see me that way." Something about Bard made him confess the truth. At least, something close to the truth.

Bard eyed him warily. Did he know he was leaving something out? The scrutiny suddenly rankled. Bard had no right to judge him.

"What do you want me to do?" Firian shouted, standing.

Bard's hand popped up from the table, shrinking at Firian's sudden movement. "I don't know." His voice was more hard-edged than Firian was used to.

Firian felt sick. "Then let me get on with it!" Maybe he honestly wanted Bard's suggestion. With certainty, he knew he would hunt down every person that wanted him dead, but Bard's world was softer. These kinds of decisions didn't exist in that world. If Bard could make all threats just disappear, he would.

"I only wanted to make sure you were all right," Bard said.

Firian looked down at him. If Jovan really had managed to kill him, Bard would have cared. And Kiria, and Belik. Maybe some others. Many would have cared out of respect for the office. There weren't many when they buried Sais Jairon, but he had been a bad leader, and had died in bad circumstances.

He glanced at the knife on the floor. "I'm all right," he said softly. But he wasn't.

THE BODY WASN'T THERE ANYMORE. Firian didn't know what Belik had done with it, but an unusual number of crows circled overhead, so he had a guess.

Staying close to the stone walls of the Academy, he went through his exercises. Balance, strength, precision, patience. He normally did this sequence inside, but he needed fresh air.

Slowly, he lifted himself into a handstand, facing the forest upside down. He closed his eyes, blocking out the light. *Just breathe. In and out.* Spreading his fingers against the hard-packed ground, he carefully lowered himself until he balanced on his forearms. Jagged pieces of dirt and rock dug into his arms. Through slitted eyes, he saw the birds wheeling above the trees, just in his line of sight. He bit the inside of his lip and closed his eyes again. Darkness could help him focus on the strength in his body. Keeping his core tight, he bent his knees. His back arched, following the movement. He brought his feet forward until they dangled over his head.

Still the crows cawed, calling to each other.

He inhaled through his nose. His shoulders began to ache from the position he was holding. *Good.*

"Firian."

His eyes shot open. Dropping his legs, he jumped to his feet. Belik stood in front of him. The Master had a limp. How had he not heard him coming?

Blood rushed from Firian's head. "Do you have the list?" he muttered.

"You don't need one."

He was in no mood for riddles or games. Usually, Belik wasn't either, and yet here he was without the list he promised.

"You need to solidify your power outside the Academy."

"Gore!" Firian glared, rubbing the back of his neck. He had enough to do to hold onto power over the Tanyu. As it was, trying to hold the Academy, Raewhith, and Imlin in his mind at once made him feel physically stretched and vulnerable.

"Hear me out." Belik's eyes shone with excitement. Maybe this idea was the reason he followed him outside. "You don't need to chase down every threat one by one. Don't be a fool. You need to threaten them all until there's no one to challenge you."

Now Firian was interested.

"You want more soldiers," Belik said.

After he waited for confirmation, Firian nodded.

"Good. We need more. The world knows where we are, so they'll test their strength against us. People don't need a better reason for bloodshed. So you'll make a show of it."

"Of what?"

"Show our strength. We have Tanyu stationed all over the world. We can't expose them all, but it could strike fear into any would-be enemies if you set a few of them loose." Belik leveled a gaze. The intensity of it was almost unnerving. But wasn't this exactly what Firian wanted when he'd taken control—awe of the Academy's power?

"What are you saying?"

"You know what I'm saying. If you show you're the strongest, then no one will rise against you. That's why you need to be involved. You can't just send people. You have to pick a place and subjugate it in full view."

"We don't need to subjugate people." He could just hear Bard's objections.

"Subjugate—maybe you don't like the word." A muscle twitched in Belik's cheek, an almost mocking gesture.

Firian's face flushed.

Belik held up a conciliatory hand, and then brought it up to resettle his glasses. "But Jovan—and you—showed that people will kill to be the next Tanyuin Head. I'm trying to protect you. You're the one who deserves to be in power, and if you don't let people know it, they'll see you as weak."

Firian hated that word, and Belik knew it. He cracked his knuckles and took a shaky breath. Would it be so bad to take over another town if that would protect him from being vulnerable? "What would I need to do?"

"We can wait until another person attacks you if you want." The Master tilted his head down as though he were reading Firian's hesitant thoughts. In the following silence, the bird calls and the gravel crunching beneath their shifting weight echoed loudly.

Frustrated, Firian cocked his jaw. "No. Just tell me."

"Archer's Point is close but far enough to feel immune from us, I'd guess. They're known for their fighting men. We take that."

Something about Belik's voice was almost too confident. Archer's Point wouldn't be as easy to take as some of the other smaller towns. It was its own city-state just outside the Western Kingdom's borders and their leader was known to be strong, even brutal to his enemies. Understanding hit Firian all at once. "You have someone inside."

"We do."

Firian frowned, wiping the grit from his hands and forearms. "So I order that person to kill the Lord Ruler and then I walk in?"

"Something like that. That's the simplest way. String him up as a message. Let everyone see that you commanded his death. Word will spread quickly."

Firian wasn't convinced it would be that easy. Belik must have seen the doubt on his face.

"The harder way would cost more lives," he persisted. "No

one wants more death. War is an ugly thing." Above Belik's head, the crows continued to glide in wide circles.

"If I order the leader to be killed, they'll want to kill me immediately. It won't be that simple."

"Bring the Scroll."

Firian frowned. "You know about that?"

"Of course. When Tiev didn't have it, I knew you had to. The people there are very religious. Practically Amir, all of them. Bring the Scroll and have all the leaders swear on it. Threaten their people for good measure. Be specific about the kind of pain you could wreak on them. You won't actually have to do any of those things, if you're worried." A sardonic glint shone in his eyes. "They'll listen to you the first time if you do it right. They'd rather have you rule them from afar—barely a change from their lives now—than put up a fight. Just flex your strength, that's all, and you won't have trouble."

Firian stood silent. He could threaten if it meant safety, but the plan sounded so drastic. The cities he had conquered so far, even Imlin, hadn't put up a real fight at all. What was one more?

Walking into the city, a conqueror, with almost no shedding of blood, his black coat flowing behind him, as everyone bowed. The image soothed him, like a mountain at sunrise. He gazed at it in his mind for a moment.

"I can't answer now," he said, coming out of his reverie like a trance.

"I'll post more guards, if you'll stay with them," Belik added, grumbling, "but they all need to see you as a leader. You're young. Untested."

"*Untested?* I helped win the Torithian War. I have... my power."

"*You* are tested. Your people's loyalty is not."

Firian regarded him sullenly.

"Everyone needs to see that you command all the Tanyu,"

Belik continued, "no matter where they are. That your word will be obeyed."

That all sounded good. But to take over another city, to kill its leaders... If it was the only way, he would do it. But only if there were no other option. He'd investigate first, ask someone less accepting of violence. "I said I'll think about it."

KIRIA

A DESERT CAT paced back and forth in its cage, working its long, toothy jaw with the last of its meal. The tip of its snout was square and its back legs bent lower to the ground than the front legs. She'd forgotten those details when she showed Firian this place.

With the day full of rebuilding trust with the royal family, she hadn't had time to see Firian since their encounter the day before. Besides, she needed a moment to think about the attempt on his life, about their connection, about his desire for her. Any time she started to think he was safe to love, his intensity made her step back again, check her own feelings.

Kiria glanced at Haved walking beside her. The princess had smudged her eyes with dark charcoal and pinned back her hair in a complicated knot. She looked as dressed up as she had been yesterday at the party. Memories of her behavior filled Kiria with heavy apprehension. Haved had to trust her after tonight, or she and her father might rethink the marriage with Atty. Kiria couldn't bear it if she were the cause of breaking so many hopes.

Together they strode through the palace zoo, now populated with exotic plants as well as animals. This was the first time since Brithnem that the air didn't feel so dry. The whole place ran humid, which felt good on her cracking skin, but also meant a rank smell rising from the animal cages.

Besides the desert cat, which was Kiria's favorite, a massive gray-green lizard lounged on a rock, each claw as long as her pointer finger. Two blue and orange birds with sweeping tails three times the length of their bodies sat side by side on a branch. A furry creature with small, rounded ears and paws shaped almost like hands paced in another cage. She wasn't sure what to call it. The closest association she had were pictures she'd seen of bears.

"Do they ever get to go outside?" Kiria asked.

"Sometimes," Haved replied. "Normally they stay in here."

Kiria tried not to read too much into Haved's clipped reply. A respectful distance away walked four guards—two from Brithnem and two from Charäkhnem. It seemed that there were always more people to overhear her conversations. "It would be nice if they could have more freedom," she continued.

Haved nodded solemnly, twitching the train of her dress with one hand so that it didn't drag. It seemed as if she were thinking of something else. Her eyes were far away, not angry or cold, but wistful.

"Are you all right?" Kiria asked.

Haved turned her serious gaze to her. "Are you?"

Kiria wasn't exactly all right, but she was in her right mind, if that's what Haved wanted to know. "Yes, I'm perfectly all right."

The desert cat's claws scraped along the floor, a dry, rasping sound. The tiny bear creature gave an answering yowl.

Haved tipped her chin with uncertainty but didn't contradict her. "Let's go outside."

The guards followed them, blue and red, out of the zoo area, through a ribbed, vaulted doorway and into the night. A large garden with flowers smelled strong and green, welcoming summer. It was obvious that they were young flowers by the wetness of them. The walled garden held trees as well. Colorful paths cut through the foliage.

The air was cleaner out here. Dust flowed on the warm breeze, perfumed with exotic flowers.

Haved's head tipped back. She didn't say anything, but a private smile grew on her face as she gazed up at the stars. With a confidential look, she invited Kiria to see them as well.

It was darker here than in Brithnem, so the stars shone more brightly. On her tour that consisted largely of the wilderness, Kiria had noticed the stars, but only in a passing way.

"That one is Sito." Haved pointed upward. "The Cat."

Kiria tried to follow the line of Haved's finger, but there were so many tiny stars that she soon despaired of figuring out which constellation she meant. Still, this shift from doubting her to cautiously drawing Kiria into her confidence seemed like a positive step.

"She's rising." Haved said the words reverently.

So she really had meant what she said at the party. Hopefully she would have the chance to talk to many Navigators one day. Brithnem was a good place for that. Usually, there was one at the docks, dark skinned and moon eyed. Their light eyes had frightened Kiria as a child, so she stayed away from them. They didn't scare her anymore, but she had kept the unconscious habit of avoiding them. Perhaps that was unfair to them, she realized.

"Is that your favorite constellation?" Kiria asked.

"Favorite?" Haved seemed confused by the question. A line formed between her eyebrows as she turned her attention back to Kiria. "No, I do not think so."

A thought struck Kiria. "Do you know if the constellations will be the same so far west in Brithnem?"

Haved nodded knowingly. "Most of them will be the same.

And I will get to see Kandormet, the great hero, I think." She looked pensive, as if thinking about the constellations she'd have to leave when she left her kingdom.

Watching Haved with the stars was like going to the upper room in the Amiran Academy. Golden and dark blue. Reverent.

Kiria hummed. She couldn't think of another response for a while, and Haved didn't seem to need any. Finally, she said, "Atty will love to learn about the stars with you."

Haved turned to her, her expression pleased but skeptical in the darkness. "Will he, though?" She said it more like a statement than a question.

"Absolutely." After a pause, Kiria added, "He'll love you."

And he would. Kiria could picture it without even trying. Though not a great sportsman, Atty liked to be outside, and to be with a pretty woman, and to feel strong. He would love watching the sky with her. He would love her.

A complicated emotion filled Kiria's stomach. It wasn't jealousy for Atty's affection—she'd never wanted that, and besides, he was her cousin, very far removed. No, it was something else. Atty would take care of Haved as well as he knew how. He was probably planning ways to please her back at the palace. And he'd be loyal, adoring, all their life long.

Haved took in her statement stoically at first, her head held regally, but then one corner of her mouth flinched with happiness. "You do not seem crazy," she said.

Kiria laughed with relief, and she realized how much she had wanted to earn Haved's trust. Atty's future should never be compromised because of her actions.

Haved laughed too, but quietly. She was an odd person—privileged and naïve, yet wise and queenly all the same.

"I'm glad you think so," Kiria said.

Taking a large purple bloom between her fingers, Haved bent to smell it. "I am too."

31

FIRIAN

It was tempting just to open the door without knocking. The whole town of Tánuil was his. But he scuffed the dirt with the toe of his boot a few times and knocked. At first, no one answered. Rian had told him Bard was here. Firian should have known better than to trust him. He was going with Maya now, and had always had a strained relationship with the truth.

The door opened. Finally. A stranger looked out. Everything about the man was thin—his body, his brown clothes, the hair on his face. Even his lips and fingers were thin. The wavy and distorted skin around one of his ears suggested that he had once been badly burned.

His throat bobbed when he saw Firian, happiness and fear alternating on his face. The end result was confusion.

"Is Bard here?" Firian asked. Something about the man's eyes and forehead seemed familiar, as though he'd seen him before.

"Hey!" Bard's voice called from inside. The thin man opened the door a little wider and Bard's face appeared in the opening. He gave a wide grin. "What are you doing here? Is everything okay?"

"What are *you* doing here?" His eyes flickered over the stranger.

"Oh, have you not met? This is Wells. No, you've seen him. Yeah, he's a... uh..."

A Sentry. "Ah." Heat flushed Firian's face. Firian wasn't searching for them anymore, but he had very recently hunted them down to get back in Sias Jairon's good graces. Bard's hesitation suggested that he'd known where this one was, but didn't tell Firian when it could have helped him to know.

He batted down the small stab of betrayal he felt. Bard had broken a rule. It almost made Firian proud that his friend was so steadfast, even to strangers who deserved none of his loyalty. Though somewhat annoyed, Firian was right to come.

Bard beckoned Firian inside as he turned away. "I just made tea for us."

The thin man scurried ahead. Firian leaned toward Bard. "Isn't this his house?"

"I was showing him how," Bard whispered back.

Who didn't know how to make tea? Firian had never done it and yet he knew. The years in captivity must have made Wells little more than a shell.

Together they walked to the small stone fireplace with a kettle hanging over it.

Bard grabbed a thin stick of firewood from the stack nearby and handed it to Wells. "Just use that and take the kettle off."

The man betrayed no embarrassment at being so ignorant. Despite the fact that he was older than either Firian or Bard, his movements showed subservience, but he went ahead boldly with the kettle.

"Yeah, like that." Bard watched Wells closely before continuing. "This is... uh, this is my friend." A fractional pause as he looked at Firian, eyes drifting to his forehead, now crownless. "This is Firian. He's... he's the Head."

Wells's neck bowed lower at the mention, like a dog fearful of being struck. His shirt hung down, waving as though it were empty.

"It's all right," Bard repeated reassuringly, gesturing to the tea. But he didn't mean the tea. He turned his attention back to Firian. "So, Fir, you didn't say. Why are you here?"

"I just wondered where you were."

Bard gave him one of those scrutinizing looks. It would be fine today if Bard could see into his inner thoughts. How could he ask for advice without asking for advice?

"Have you known each other very long?" Firian asked.

Another grin. "Yeah, ever since we, uh… freed them, you know." Bard gently patted Wells's shoulder as he gingerly moved the stick and placed the kettle on a small table. The *sachion* tree design on the kettle showed it to be Endrian work. The kettle wobbled as though Wells didn't have enough strength to hold it steady.

"You've been busy," Bard said, getting cups out of a knapsack. "And Wells is really funny, once you get to know him."

Firian glanced at the man, who had rarely raised his eyes above the floor. He doubted he was funny.

Bard dug deeper in his bag as though he had forgotten something. "I only brought two cups," he admitted.

Firian waved his hand. "That's fine. It doesn't matter."

Bard set the cups on the table, one for him and one for his new Sentry friend. "In Enderin we drink the leaves, but some people like their tea smooth," he explained, picking up the kettle. "You can just put cheesecloth in front of the spout if you don't like leaves." He poured Wells's first and then his own. "There you go!" he said cheerfully. "I'm going to talk to Firian for a minute."

They silently went to the doorway of the little house, leaving Wells to drink his tea.

"Okay, something's going on," Bard said in a stern undertone.

"Something's always going on." When Bard wouldn't be deflected, Firian continued. "I need to figure out what to do about this problem. I think I can take out all threats at once."

Bard opened his mouth.

"Without killing them all," Firian added.

Bard shut his mouth again and took a sip from his cup. "What is it?" he asked, eyes bright now with interest.

"I need to prove our strength, my strength, all at once."

The lines deepened on Bard's forehead. "What are you going to do? You know we could just put a Sentry on you when you sleep. Protect you, you know?"

Firian's skin crawled at the thought. And no. That wouldn't help. "No. That's stupid," he said. "I need something bigger. I wasn't asleep last time."

Bard dropped his eyes. "That's true, but it's not a bad idea."

Firian ignored him. Wasn't Bard supposed to be good at strategy? His attempt at a solution was halfhearted at best. After a silence Bard didn't fill, Firian went on. "Yeah, so I thought maybe taking over Archer's Point."

Bard barked a humorless laugh.

"We have someone inside," Firian insisted. "We could control it completely within a few days."

Disbelief clouded Bard's eyes. "How?"

"It would be mostly in name, and good for them."

"How would you take over?"

"Just Thraddock." The Lord Ruler.

"Firian!"

"It's just one person," Firian insisted, beginning to wonder why he had come. If Bard didn't like it, why didn't he suggest something else, something that didn't pretend everything would be all right? "The Academy can't be threatened or unstable. We have to show that we're united, that I know what I'm doing."

In the next pause, Bard's look sent shivers down his spine. "Do you?" he asked quietly.

"What would you do, then?" he snapped. "You weren't there when Jovan tried to strangle me. When I had to kill him or drown. And I almost..." *I almost drowned. I almost died.*

Bard nodded. "I just don't want..." He sighed, as though unsure how to continue. "Fir, are you sure you don't just want Archer's Point, you know? What would happen if you left them alone?"

"I need to choose someone strong."

"You could get hurt. They could get hurt."

Firian scoffed. "They need to see me as a strong leader. If the Tanyu follow me in this, the Academy can keep doing all the good it's doing." His words felt too much like a plea for Bard to understand.

But he didn't understand. He would never endorse Firian's decision to kill the leader of Archer's Point to unite the Tanyu and scare off potential threats.

Why had he come here at all? He'd known what Bard would say.

After another minute that Bard didn't fill with a workable suggestion, he stiffened, and his hot temper hardened into bitterness. "Isn't your friend waiting for you?"

Except for Belik, all those close to him were slipping farther away. Didn't they care that he had almost been assassinated? If not for his new-found ability, he would have been. And Kiria and Bard didn't seem to care at all.

"Yeah." Another concerned question formed on Bard's lips, but he let it die away. Then he rallied. "You can't do this, Fir."

Firian's heart thumped hard in his chest. One corner of his mouth rose in a snarl. "I have to, so I will," he said distinctly.

"There has to be another way to get rid of any threat to you—"

"We're great warriors. People like Jovan are not going to back down because I ask them nicely."

"That's not what I—"

"Everyone has to know what'll happen if they *dare* to threaten me." The power of the words robed him like a cloak of darkness. He felt like a king, so he knew he'd made the right decision.

Bard didn't shrink away, but he did fall quiet. Something hardened in his dark eyes. Disappointment. "I'm going to make sure Wells is okay." And he closed the door, shutting Firian out of the stone house.

Distant birds cawed and a pinecone thudded softly to the ground.

Firian gripped his hands into fists. Despite what Bard thought, he had to do something to protect himself. Great power didn't stay there by inertia, but by continual effort. A small breeze of exhaustion blew through him and passed. He had always been relentless. Becoming the Head wasn't a stopping point, but a stepping stone. The momentum had to continue.

The leader of Archer's Point had to be sacrificed.

Bard wouldn't like it, Kiria probably wouldn't like it, but hopefully they both would understand later, when the Academy was united and he still lived to tell them about it.

* * *

THROUGH THE HAZE, Firian watched his nephew Sabir play in the grass. He picked up pine cones and leaves in his chubby fists and brought them to Brett, who sat cross-legged on the ground. When he brought her a tiny purple flower, she smiled, cooing over the gift as though it were worth piles of tribute.

Sometimes Sabir toddled close to danger as he gathered treasures for his mother. A flash of wolves' eyes in the woods, or a steep embankment. A mother's worry.

His sister didn't notice Firian there. She didn't have the Talent, after all.

Normally, Tanyu didn't invade dreams without a reason, usually instilling fear into an enemy, or killing him. They weren't supposed to watch. It was like seeing a person naked and not turning away. But tonight, he had to remind himself of what had gone right during his reign. His conversation with Bard a few days before left a taste like ashes in his mouth. His friend didn't support his decision to take over Archer's Point, but he also didn't offer a different road to victory and safety.

Brett swept Sabir up in a hug, the image surprisingly touching. Did his mother ever dream like this about him? Maybe not. With Brett, he sensed no new fears. Her dreams were good. Gaius, her husband, back from the Torithian War, slept peacefully by her side.

"Firian."

The voice came from elsewhere in the Unreal.

"Why are you up so late?" he asked Kiria, who stood in the palace hallway where they had had their first kiss. Was she here to apologize for pushing him away when he needed her most?

"I couldn't sleep," she said, meeting his eyes. "I know I should be able to, since we're riding all day, but I can't stop thinking."

"Tell me."

Something softened in her look, but they didn't move closer. This dance was a precarious one. One false step and he knew she'd back away.

"People keep telling me you're dangerous. I even heard a rumor the other day..." Her voice trailed into a laugh edged with nerves.

"I am dangerous," he said, "but not to you." He gave a lopsided smile, his stomach suddenly in knots. He should tell her his plan, see if she approved. But he knew – he knew – what she would say. Taking over Archer's Point was worth solidifying his power, even if Kiria didn't see it.

"You can't go around saying things like 'I'm dangerous,'" she laughed.

"Aren't I?"

"That's what they say." She sighed, tugging at the ends of her long sleeves. Even now, in the middle of the night, she dressed in finery, a backless blue gown, a flag of the Kingdom. A reminder that her choices were not always her own. "Did you mean it before?"

"Mean what?"

"You said... you wanted me to change for you. I won't do that until I'm ready."

He searched her heart-shaped face, her light brown eyes, so earnest as they looked back in his. The knots inside him loosened a fraction. She wasn't here to apologize, but she did say *until I'm ready*. Despite his dangerous reputation, she wanted to stay. That would do for now.

"Okay."

"That's all right with you?" Another question lurked behind that one, the true question. Almost a dare.

"Yes." He waved her forward and she came, head held high as though protecting her dignity. It was true that he wanted her Beauty, but this was the face that had captured him, the one he saw most when he thought about her. They were both Kiria.

He settled his hands on her shoulders. "It's definitely all right." Slowly, he peeled down her left sleeve to reveal the raised scar. Kiria held very still but didn't pull away as he rubbed his thumb over the wound and kissed it.

They stood in silence for a moment after that, something

clicking into place between them. She pulled her sleeve back up and trailed her fingers lightly down his arm. He caught her hand when it reached his.

"You are dangerous," she said, little more than a teasing whisper. But she seemed to have found the answer she was looking for and wasn't afraid.

"Mm hm."

That was truer than she knew.

32

FIRIAN

FIRIAN HELD the bound Scroll tightly in one hand as he strode to Archer's Point. The front page stuck out a little beyond the others, propped up by the wax holding the note from his sister. He would live up to its words. He would protect her in Raewhith from those raiders in Archer's Point, he would solidify his legacy, and he would protect himself.

And this is how to do it.

He forced himself to remember the bathtub. Brett would understand why he had to do this.

Belik's suggestion that Firian conquer this town was a good one. Though he was harsh, he had always kept Firian's best interest in mind. Even after he kicked him out of the Academy, Belik had followed to make sure he didn't die in the Unreal. Few Tanyu would do that.

He flexed his fingers slowly, one by one, against the book of the Scroll. One, two, three, four, five. One for each black-clad Tanyuin warrior that flanked him on either side. Ten in all.

Now that he was resolved, he stepped with greater purpose. His black coat floated behind him. Why had he hesitated? This power was heady and pleasurable. Threats were far away. Rebels would be afraid to face his greatness after this.

He felt his heartbeat across his chest and in his throat. Even Kiria was one of three leaders. He was the only Tanyuin Head.

By the time the walls of the town appeared, a thin smirk had crept over his face. He liked this feeling too much. He'd said something to Bard about doing good after this, but right now, all he wanted was this power. Apprehension at his own excitement thrummed beneath his skin. Later, he could give into his better tendencies. At this moment, he had to make Archer's Point bow.

He stuffed away his smile as they marched closer to the main gate. High above, guards shuffled hurriedly along the wall. A flag flapped above the gate—bright green with the black figure of an archer in the center. Only two stood by the entrance to the city, one on either side of the gate. They both wore brown leather armor and a metal chest plate. No helmet. A sword and small round shield for each. This was a poor people's armor, but it would do if circumstances demanded it. Firian wore none at all, so maybe, he thought, he shouldn't judge their choices.

He and his ten followers strode to the main wooden gate. Coming from a slightly different direction, a man pulling a cart of hay stopped awkwardly before the gate as well, paralyzed at the sight of Firian's entourage.

"Halt!" cried the guard on the left, bracing one foot back. His shoulders and face were wider than the other soldier. "You must declare yourself and your business before we allow you inside."

All the Tanyu flanking Firian remained perfectly still.

"I am Firian Kess," he said. "The Tanyuin Head."

The guard's mouth formed a small, unconscious O.

"Why have you come?" It was the guard on the right. His receding hairline and scarred mouth suggested a battle-ridden life. Still, he watched Firian's entourage warily.

Firian squeezed the book a little harder. He flicked a quick glance at the top of the hand that held it, covered with white scars. Scars he had earned fighting in both the Unreal and the Real. He raised his head. "I must speak to the Lord Ruler immediately."

"On what matter?"

"Someone has a knife to his throat." he said calmly.

Both guards gripped their sword hilts now. Broad Shoulders collected himself. "How do you know this?"

"I ordered it. So bring me to him."

With a metallic hiss, the guards drew their swords. They bent their knees, grim and ready to fight.

"You dare to threaten the Lord Ruler?"

Firian didn't move. He was too aware that one of his hands was occupied with a large book. The tendons inside his wrist pressed against the cover. He could use it to fight, but he didn't want to, which made that hand all but useless if they decided to move against him.

More soldiers joined the two at the gate, running down from their positions along the top of the wall.

Firian saw the guards almost passively. He could kill them just by thinking it. Did they know? The fact made swords less frightening. But his skin still felt like thin protection.

He didn't deny their accusation. Instead, he held up his free hand. "We don't want to kill you," he said slowly, truthfully. His hand was starting to sweat around the book. "I have many people loyal to me. In many different places. Hill House, for example."

Slight movements—some forward on the balls of their feet, some slackening of jaws, some rotating of weapons—told him that Belik had been right about the man embedded in Hill House. It looked like they were starting to believe him.

Hill House was the place where the Lord Ruler of Archer's Point sat in state. A Tanyu named Jaddeo had been installed there years ago. Belik said he started as a minor retainer, but had later taken a kitchen job as a way to be closer to Lord Ruler Thraddock.

Broad Shoulders advanced. Firian held his ground. "I've decided to take this city. So I will take it." Every word he said felt as solid and true as the words in the Scroll. He sensed the power of the ten Tanyu behind him. "Let us in and we'll spare you all. Harm me and the Lord Ruler dies." He locked eyes with a stony-looking guard in the middle of the others. If he had to kill anyone, Firian chose him. His hardened expression and central placement would ensure the greatest impact. "I extend the honor of being part of the Academy's territory. I don't want slaughter."

He reached down into the Unreal, like a man fishing in his back pocket for a weapon. One step further and he could level anyone here. He caressed the Second Level in his mind, holding it loosely, making it accessible. Being surrounded by this many clear threats was almost a relief after fearing so many phantom ones. These people he could manage. These people he could kill before they killed him.

"Show me to your leader," he said, extending his arms as though they were harmless. *Bind me. See if that works for you.*

The guards couldn't risk killing Firian and putting their Lord Ruler at risk, but they couldn't let him go after such threats either. Binding him would probably seem like the safest choice.

He shook his hands a little, one still clutching the bound copy of the Sacred Scroll. A few of the guards noticed with curiosity.

Three men approached cautiously, swords unsheathed. Firian didn't flinch as they gripped both of his arms hard enough to bruise, wrenched the book from his grip, and tied his wrists behind him.

He held his head high as they paraded him through the

gates into the city. The rest of his Tanyu followed behind, also bound. Despite appearances, Firian was still the one in charge.

The smell of glue or tar wafted through the streets, alternating with soap. Most of the buildings they passed were made of slatted boards fitted together without seams. Some were painted with plants or creatures or designs. Clothing hung thick from lines strung between buildings, even the larger ones that cropped up every few hundred steps that Firian guessed were communal dining halls. The men and women coming and going seemed defined by their level of hunger, hurrying in, sauntering out.

People came out of their houses and shops to watch the little procession go by. Eleven Tanyu had probably never come here all at once. And never the Tanyuin Head.

A child appeared from behind curtains of hanging clothes. She had a mop of white hair and gripped the nearby fabric oddly. Only three fingers on that hand.

Again, Belik's intelligence was correct. The people of Archer's Point didn't look the same—different body types, skin colors, tattoos. Khelê.

Hill House lived up to its name, springing up on a little hill at the end of a maze of streets. It wasn't as grand as Firian expected, except for the red and green painted patterns on the walls, and the large trees growing around the bottom of the hill in a ring. Layers of history overlapped each other in a chaotic mix. From the trees hung mementos and flags. Even the trunks had been branded with the now distorted faces of past Lord Rulers.

A back-of-the-throat smell like boiling cabbage with tangy notes of sharp peppers floated by. Maybe Jaddeo had been cooking. The cabbage odor took him back home to Raewhith for a moment. How was Brett doing now? It had been over a month since he'd seen her.

"Up the stairs!" said a short guard behind Firian.

Wordlessly, Firian climbed the long, well-cut stone steps through the ring of trees, up the slope to Hill House. Smaller mounds dotted the hillside, adorned with elaborate displays of twigs, rocks, paints, and flowers. Burial sites.

An armored woman at the door stood waiting for them. She threw her shoulders back and stood with the rigidity of someone who had been bent over a moment before. Stiffly, she opened the door for Firian and his conductors. She scowled at Firian's entourage of Tanyuin warriors and whispered something to the guards as they passed. Whatever she said made Firian's guard twist the ropes holding his wrists until his bones popped.

Incense covered and magnified the dusty smell inside. The interior looked like a mansion, brighter and cleaner than Firian thought it would be—entrance with room for cloaks, kitchen to the left, enormous main room with open fire pit in the center. The guards led him toward the fire.

As they muscled him toward the open flame, he felt placid, utterly composed. They wouldn't burn him. Dull metallic surfaces reflected the fire and other small light sources strategically placed around the room. The result was a blazing space, screaming yellow and heavy with heat.

Firian blinked away moisture forming in his eyes from the warmth. When he could see more clearly, he stiffened. Six—no, seven—guards lay dead around Jaddeo, who held the Lord Ruler in place with one enormous arm over his neck.

They resisted. They deserved it.

Firian had known that this would probably have to happen, but any justification still sounded hollow. The guards would have ganged up on Jaddeo, killed him, and the whole plan would have been ruined. He ran his eyes over the slumped bodies and fought back a shudder.

Jaddeo and the Lord Ruler stood on the platform beside a modest throne, barely large enough to look significant. It was a child's version of the thrones at Brithnem. Hanging behind it was another green flag like the one at the gate.

A thin line of red trickled down Jaddeo's forearm from a wound in the Lord Ruler's neck. Blood leaked onto Thraddock's leather clothes—not the robes of a king, but the clothes of a working man or a warrior. Lord Ruler Thraddock was a large man, rough and tan, with a trimmed beard and blazing eyes, the kind that would make anyone quail. Firian fought not to swallow, to show any apprehension in his manner. But the Lord Ruler's heavy-browed stare bored into him. The moment passed, and Firian's calm returned. This fearsome man was entirely under his power.

Despite the bodies, power made Firian feel peaceful again. Was something wrong with him?

With Firian and the Lord Ruler face to face, the heat in the room seemed to double. A long line of sweat trickled down the scars on Firian's back. The people of Archer's Point were wound like a spring, but the Tanyu stood emotionless. Broad Shoulders kicked the back of Firian's knees and forced his head down. His palm, gripping Firian's hair, had a slight tremor. Though the guard was nervous, this was the first time he'd had anything like the upper hand. The situation suddenly reminded Firian of his helplessness when he'd been grabbed, choked, drowned... Blood rushed to his face until it felt puffy in the heat.

He had to do it now.

"Release Lord Thraddock or we will kill Master Kess," demanded a voice above him.

Firian lifted his head. The back of his neck touched something. A blade. The smallest misstep meant death. His mouth felt sticky as he locked eyes with Jaddeo, who stared at him, awaiting a signal. Firian nodded.

Jaddeo's eyes darted to others around the room. As the guard forced Firian's head back down, he heard a swift, struggling gasp and then a heavy thump like a body slumping to the ground.

Feet scuffled. Surprised noises. A clang. A yell.

A nudge.

Firian stood to see all ten other Tanyu on their feet, the guards on the ground. The guard with the scar and receding hairline stood above Broad Shoulders. Jaddeo stepped gracefully over bodies on his way back to the unconscious form of the Lord Ruler.

A knife slid between Firian's wrists, slicing off the bonds. As Firian rubbed life back into his hands, he ran his eyes over each new slumped figure, looking for signs of life. He had ordered the Tanyu not to kill unless it was absolutely necessary. Besides the initial dead guards, all the forms, including Lord Thraddock, seemed to be breathing. A small, terrible, burning part of him wanted to kill them all because he could. But then he'd see their faces, one after the other, in his nightmares.

They didn't deserve to die. But the sacrifice was small in the face of all he could accomplish with the Academy united in their fear of rebellion. Violence was short so peace could be lasting.

The scarred guard offered him back the Sacred Scroll. Firian wiped his hands on his coat and took it. The incense put the scene and his mind in a dreamy haze.

"Get the people," he said. "Anyone left with authority. Bring them here." He tapped his fingers against the cover of the book. "I'll meet them outside." The Tanyu already knew what to do, but it made him feel better to say it. "They'll swear on the Scroll not to oppose me, or the Lord Ruler dies."

33

KIRIA

"I HAVE it the way I want it," Jori said, stepping backward.

Kiria's mother stopped trying to fix the collar of his leather jacket. She smiled placidly and shot a glance at Kiria, who stood just behind her.

Kiria smiled back. "There are scuffs," she said, picking up where her mother had left off. She vaguely indicated her own neckline. "You don't want to look scruffy today."

Jori raised a chin. "How else will they know who I am?" A laugh almost broke through his twitching lips, but Kiria could tell he was nervous. No, not nervous. Antsy. Tightly wound.

Atty was getting married today.

"By your handsome face," her mother replied.

Jori smiled as if he'd just won an argument.

It was good to see her mother looking so... alive. Since General Rhet's death, she had faded and faded until Kiria almost felt that she couldn't talk to her anymore. That she was an orphan. But she wasn't. Her mother was still here, even though Kiria was now the Keeper. They both were happy with the unorthodox arrangement, even if some people in the Kingdom had the wrong idea about it.

Today, her mother wore a long, deep purple dress with a gold belt and gold embroidery. It made a delicate V at her neckline, revealing her collarbone. That outdoor beauty her mother had shone out clearly in her twisted braids. The flyaways didn't look like mistakes but evidence of adventure and life.

When she'd offered to accompany Kiria to see Jori, she hadn't known why her mother wanted to come. Though her mother never said it, it was clear now that she wanted Jori not to feel alone, to feel that he had family. Because he had. Despite all his flippancy, he was surrounded by people who loved him and didn't judge him harshly for his flirtation and bad habits and light manners.

Atty was the only person left in his immediate family, though, and his affections would be pulled toward Haved. Inevitably, Jori would feel a little bereft. He hadn't sunk into one of his moods yet, but the Ariocs knew it was coming.

"Are we all ready?" her mother asked, just as she had when Kiria was a child.

Kiria checked herself. Beauty intact, silver and blue dress flowing like water, unsnagged on shoes or jewelry, silver belt, silver earrings, silver crown.

Ready.

Jori offered her his arm as they walked out of his room. The walk to the Main seemed longer than usual this time. Extra guards had been posted at the doors, some of them Charäkhni.

Kiria and Jori led the way, her mother walking imperially behind them, and behind her, more guards.

It was odd that at a time of peace there should be more guards in the palace than she could ever remember seeing.

She separated from Jori as they approached the carved doors of the Main. Heralds announced their names as they entered one by one.

It was warmer inside the cavernous Main, a byproduct of so

many bodies and candles and torches. It smelled like lamp oil and lilies. The late afternoon sun had burned away, so the large space was left in that hot time between the light fading and the cool of night coming in.

As always, voices rose and fell at her entrance. Some of the guests had never seen her in person. Her Beauty was shocking, moving—even to her, even after all this time. It had taken danger and escape and a trip over the mountains to grow into her body. For fleeting moments, she sometimes still felt like a fraud. But it had not gone back to the pervasive feeling it had been a year ago.

Her long dress whisked across the mosaic on the floor as she processed toward the chairs at the foot of the platform. Where the three thrones normally resided, the three Amiran advisors stood: Parohim, Chetana, and Reynard. To either side of them, two young Amir in training, probably nine or ten years old, held poles. Across the poles was draped a gauzy white and blue fabric embroidered with blue laird flowers.

The symbol of peace.

The symbol of Brithnem.

She'd want to get married with the sun still up, so it could come through the colored panes of glass in the windows.

Get married. She'd always considered getting married inevitable, but now the idea hit her like a weight.

Could she marry Firian? For the Kingdom, he was a risky choice, still volatile. *Then what am I doing?*

Music began, sudden and loud. The first few notes were unfamiliar, even a little clunky. A wry smile tugged at her mouth. Atty must have written the first few bars. *You hopeless romantic.* The song soon turned into a melody that everyone had heard at other celebratory events. Jori knocked into her lightly as he swayed to the tune.

From behind the same closed doors that had opened to

admit her on her eighteenth birthday when she demonstrated her Beauty, and that she and Atty had gone through during their coronations, came Atael and Haved. The double doors flung wide open, glad to reveal their secret.

Atty wore an all-white robe with some kind of fur mantle on the arm not wrapped around Haved's waist. Someone had pressed his curly hair down so that it shone like his bronze crown. His smile shone most brightly of all.

She knew he would like Haved.

The Charäkhni princess came out all in red, her country's color, with yellow-gold shoes. A large red gemstone gleamed on her bosom. As though Atty needed another reason to look there. Haved's dark eyes, though wise and sober, gleamed with happiness too. The edges crinkled up when she looked at him.

They approached the dais where the three Amir waited. When they had topped the steps, Atty and his bride, who looked like she had Beauty herself, knelt under the fabric. Parohim sang the words etched along the walls near the ceiling. Only during joyous occasions would Amir sing the words of the Scroll rather than saying or chanting them.

"...Be wise, therefore, and follow no other words but those of God. If you do not chase after other gods and invent them for yourself, He shall remain present among His people. Then you shall all be as the Khelê, seeing God's goodness in the ways that He chooses you for Himself.

Forever shall you worship God. In whatever you do, worship Him."

Charäkhnem had never believed in the same God that the Western Kingdom did, but those last sentences before the repeated line had some inclusiveness to them. Neither Haved nor the guards seemed bothered by the verses, anyway. Kiria was glad. Those lines had molded her childhood, subconsciously guided her decisions, her whole life. The Amir were here to make sure no one forgot them.

Atty shifted his shoe just a little. He looked confident with Haved beside him, but that shoe shift reminded her it was just Atty all along. Her friend Atty was marrying a princess.

After the recitation was complete, the couple stood. All five people under the draped fabric took hands in a circle, and then the Amir on the ends brought Atty's and Haved's hands together. Complete support, complete family, a complete couple.

The vows to each other were similar to the vows Kiria had made to the Western Kingdom. They were formal, with much talk of loyalty and children and death.

As the Amir took turns speaking, Kiria watched Atty's face. Wonder radiated from him as he stared at Haved, barely reacting to what they said. He looked so happy he could cry. He'd just met this girl, and yet he wanted desperately to bind himself to her, to create a family with her. He held her hands firmly but gently in his tattooed ones. Atty was many things, but disloyal was not one of them. He was simpler than Kiria or Jori, with their complicated temptations. All that simple love and admiration glowed on his face and reflected on Haved's. Naturally more reserved, she appeared perfectly contented. She was fairly tall, so the couple was almost the same height. She had to tip her chin up just a little to look into his eyes.

Kiria breathed shallowly as she watched them, gut twisting a little. Atty deserved to have something good in his life, *someone* good. Though the oldest son, born heir to the throne, Jori had always gotten more attention. Atty tried harder to be good, though, a struggle Kiria knew intimately.

After waving of hands, more reading from the Sacred Scroll, and ceremonial washing, the formal portion of the wedding was finished. Applause erupted from the crowded room. Beside her, Jori clapped without irony. Joy prompted a fresh wave of noise.

The party began immediately. Servants brought out wine. Tables laden with meat and fruit were uncovered. Plates of fish and delicate bits of candied lemon peel seemed to materialize in every corner of the room.

"...yes, I think so!" Cúron's voice boomed from the far side of the platform. With a glass in one hand and lemon peel in the other, Kiria went to join him. He was talking to a woman whose name Kiria didn't know. She had seen her in the Main before. Maybe an Amir.

The woman ran one long-fingered hand against the other in a movement that looked like a ritual or part of a dance. "But the number of Khelê in Charäkhnem is quite small," she replied.

"This marriage will open up roads." He said it with such confidence that Kiria pictured roads currently being built. "Keeper Atael is ecstatic. Charäkhnem is ecstatic. The Amir have never had such easy access to new documents and research."

Kiria had not known Cúron to sound so excited about "documents and research," but when he used his expansive, kingly voice, he could sound interested in anything.

"Ah, Lady Kiria!" He looped an arm around the air as though he were drawing her forward. "Don't you think this alliance will be wonderful for the Amir?"

"Of course it will." It was hard to think of a group that would not benefit from it. And it was all Atty's idea. A swell of pride grew inside her.

Daelon was on the other side of the room. Even he smiled broadly as he spoke with some of the younger Amir. He would certainly appreciate any additional documents that could aid him in interpreting the Scroll. It seemed like he was always reading, always learning.

When she focused again on the conversation, Cúron was saying something about extra defense. "...in case of another conflict. The Charäkhni are excellent soldiers." He scanned the room approvingly.

"With the Tanyu and Charäkhni, we're almost untouchable," Kiria agreed.

At the mention of the Tanyu, a breath of cold air passed over the little group, or maybe it was just a chilling of tempers. *What did I say?* She drew her brows together, surprised that a casual mention of their alliance could cause such an immediate reaction.

"Yes," Cúron continued, the moment passed. "We're in a very strong strategic position."

"No one is ever impervious to attack, My Keepers," the woman said diplomatically.

"No no no," Cúron said quickly. "But let us feel a little optimism." He smiled broadly.

Kiria took a sip of her drink. It was better than the stuff Jori usually had in his cabinets. The wine had been prepared decades in advance for this occasion.

Excusing herself, she turned away. Politics were important from far away, but close up, she had a friend to see.

He was easy to find. Glowing like a candle flame in bright white, standing beside his bride, Atty talked and laughed at the center of the room. He held Haved's hand as though they'd known each other for years.

Kiria rushed up to him. She paused a moment, and then gave him a hug. The wine in her glass sloshed a little as she cast her arms around him. A drip might have gotten on his white fur mantle, but it didn't matter. It also didn't matter that it wasn't proper for Keepers to hug. The blissful tilt of Atty's mouth and the creases around his eyes made the hug unavoidable. She had only seen that look a couple of times in all their years together. Tonight, it was the purest joy she'd ever seen in him. She felt she might burst, she was so proud.

"Haved," she said, and gave her a quick hug too.

"Kiria, I..." But Atty was never good with words. His whole being was speaking for him. He reached out and squeezed her arm.

She just nodded. The joy was so intense that it felt almost like pain. "Congratulations." The word felt too small to house all the meaning she wanted to put inside it. "I'm so happy for you!"

Jori swooped in from behind his brother. Delighted, Atty turned. Nothing could dampen his spirits, even being startled.

For a second, Atty and Jori just laughed. This inclusiveness and joy felt fragile, bound to crack at any minute. Nothing could be this good for long.

"Atty, Atty," Jori said, catching his breath. He bounced on his toes. Drawing himself up, he became theatrical again. He slicked down his leather collar as though it had water on it. That was for Kiria's benefit. The scuffs. "This is a day I never thought I'd see. Atty marrying someone who's actually very passable."

Kiria and Atty huffed. Haved took the words stoically.

"Very passable," he repeated, more loudly. "And even more than that." He looked at his brother's bride, standing there like a goddess in red. "You, my dear, are perfection. I don't know how he pulled it off. Atty"—he clapped his brother on the shoulder —"you can't screw this up. Make this lady's life magical so she can bear to look at you day after day." He said it jovially, and even Atty laughed.

"I will like to look at him," Haved said, peering at Atty sideways. Her voice was quiet but firm, and cut through the chatter around them like the note of an instrument. Atty grinned.

"Ooh!" Jori bobbed again on the balls of his feet. "Kiss him, then," he demanded.

She did. As they kissed, she brought one hand to his lightly bearded cheek. Atty, eyes closed, looked like he was in ecstasy.

Kiria smiled, but her heart clenched. It wasn't the same with

Firian. Theirs was a fiercer, darker connection, but she suddenly wondered where he was. She wanted somebody to hold her hand at this party and not shut down at the mention of Tanyu, or shy away from her because of her power, or grow jealous because of her Beauty, or accuse her of usurping her mother. She wanted to be kissed like that.

"Congratulations," she said again, smiling at them both after the kiss was over.

She hurried over to the side of the room, where the space wasn't so bright. After draining her glass, she passed it to a servant. In the back was a table covered with creatures made of sugar. These had been Atty's favorite when they all were small. Kiria's favorite was fruit tarts, but Atty loved the intricate sugar animals. They tasted strangely bitter, but she had to admit that the shapes were charming. Squid, dogs, fish, birds. The squid had always been Atty's favorite. He liked to pull off the legs one by one. The brothers had tormented her with them when she was little. Squids were creepy.

After Kader, Cúron's nine-year-old son, scampered up to grab a sugar dog, only guards occupied this area of the Main. Not many people wanted to eat bitter sugar squids. She leaned against the wall, debating whether to close her eyes. Even if she did, and Firian was there, this wasn't the time or place to meet just because she suddenly felt lonely. With her Beauty and position, she wouldn't be left alone for long. And there was that time in King's Heights when she hadn't woken up. Haved had already seen her frightened because of her connection with Firian. She didn't want to go limp and require multiple people to wake her up. Unbearably embarrassing.

So she felt the solidity and coolness of the wall and watched the party. The music seemed farther away than it had a moment ago.

"Kiria?" It was her mother. A slight frown spread over her face. "Are you all right?"

"Yes, I'm fine."

"Did you hear?"

The way her mother said it made Kiria push herself off from the wall. "Hear what?"

She dropped her voice not to be heard over the crowd. "Firian Kess took over the town of Archer's Point and killed the Lord Ruler. You didn't know?"

Kiria felt numb. She swallowed and narrowed her eyes, trying to understand. "He did what?" she whispered.

"You didn't know?" Her mother lowered her eyes. "I'm sorry. I thought Cúron would have told you." She stepped closer, almost speaking in Kiria's ear. "I think he just got the news." It came out as an apology. She hummed, an understanding, motherly sound. "I'm sure the Amir are talking about cutting ties with the Tanyu. It was a good idea while it lasted."

Kiria stared blankly at a pot of laird flowers by her mother. Rousing herself, she looked up again. "Are you sure?"

"Sure of what?"

"Sure that he killed the Lord Ruler, that he took over the town? Was it his idea?"

Her mother pursed her lips. "From what I know. Ask Cúron or the Watchman. They can tell you." Her tone suggested she was a little insulted by the question. Kiria was the Keeper now, so she should have been the first one to know about this.

It was a good idea while it lasted. The words echoed in her skull. No wonder being the face of the Tanyuin alliance felt off sometimes.

A weight in her gut told her that her mother was probably right, that Firian had taken over Archer's Point and killed the Lord Ruler. He had given into his darkness.

34

FIRIAN

FIRIAN STOOD with his back against the wall. His paranoia hadn't gotten better after being declared the new ruler of Archer's Point —it had gotten worse.

For a while he had carried around the bound copy of the Scroll, as though it could fight for him. All the ministers and generals and heads of different sectors of the town had knelt, touched the book, and sworn loyalty to him. The scene almost made him angry because he couldn't enjoy it. They'd made him order the death of the Lord Ruler first.

No one would listen until he did it. He screamed at the gathered leaders but they wouldn't budge, glaring at him as the Torithians had with their blunt, defiant faces. They believed in Thraddock. Even after Firian ordered his death, some of the ministers wouldn't pledge their allegiance until they'd seen his body for themselves.

All those people acknowledging him, trembling before him... That was a moment he should have savored. Some of his most self-indulgent dreams come true.

But he hated it. They swore to him, yet he couldn't trust a

single person. They had only lined up by force. Nobody had come until Firian had ordered Thraddock's head strung up in the main square. The image made him queasy. Why hadn't they all just surrendered?

His ribcage felt as though it were tightening around his organs. Breath came in fits, though he didn't show it. Why did he think this was a good idea?

Other places had followed his orders too. Belik had communicated with the Tanyu embedded in three other towns to enact a similar show of power. Threaten the ruler, swear loyalty to the Tanyuin Head... It was enough to make people suspicious of those they had known for years. Firian saw the uneasiness among the remaining guards and servants in Hill House. They barely spoke to each other, and it wasn't just because Firian was there, pressed up against the wall, silent as a black ghost.

He wanted to go home. He needed the Academy. Compared to this place, the Academy sounded safe.

But it wasn't safe. He had opened the borders and upended expectation. Anyone could find him. Kill him. Drown him in a bathtub.

The fire in the center of the room had dwindled to embers. Tanyu had put out some of the blazing candles, so it was finally a comfortable level of semi-darkness that Firian was used to.

He locked eyes with Erron, the former hall master, now promoted, who immediately strode over to him. His questioning look awaited orders.

"Are the new Watchman and regent set in place?" Firian asked.

The Master nodded curtly.

"Then we'll leave at first light."

A warmth unconnected to the hot, incense-filled room eased up the back of Firian's neck. Kiria waited for him.

"Go. Pack," he barked, keeping his eyes partly open as he swam into the Unreal.

As soon as he arrived, it seemed like a mistake to come. Their interaction after Jovan's attack flooded back to him. He had wanted her, *needed* her, and she pushed him away.

He approached her cautiously. She wore a long, flowing dress that looked realer than some of her other clothing. That meant she was actually wearing this one. He took it in. Flowing skirt that moved when she moved, silver stitching around her waist, a neckline that hinted at an open back. Elaborate earrings and a crown implied an important event.

Her heart-shaped face shot him an accusing stare. "Firian," she began, clipped, "where are you?"

"Right here."

"No, where are you now?"

Oh. That was it. "Archer's Point."

He watched her breaths become shallow and labored. "What are you doing there?"

"You look wonderful." She did. After the long day of feeling as inflexible and twisted as a wire, he longed to hold her. He wanted a long moment of timelessness, to lose himself.

"Please answer me."

"Remember what I told you? When you could feel what was happening with me?" He scrubbed his bottom lip with a finger, waiting so she could conjure up the image of Jovan looming over him. "There's more than one."

"More than one person who...?"

He nodded. "I had to send a message to anyone else who might want to kill me."

She was silent for a long time. Her eyes darted for a while as she thought, and her chest rose and fell fitfully. That dream-falling sensation came upon him again. He actually backed up one small step to steady himself. He couldn't rely on her this much, need her this much. Somehow, her silence felt more dangerous than any of the guards had yesterday.

"Did I interrupt something?" he asked, changing the subject. She'd contacted him but, since she was dressed up, it seemed natural to ask.

Her eyelids fluttered a few times before she looked up. "It's Atty's wedding."

That's right. He'd heard that somewhere.

"What do you mean, 'Send a message'?" She raised an eyebrow.

"It's just the one time," he said, hating to have to explain himself. He already felt unsettled enough. "You understand. When the Torithians attacked you, you had to strike back."

"But this town didn't attack the Academy." Standing aloof, she made no move toward him. She might as well have been walking away.

He leveled his gaze. "I have a lot of enemies. This shows them that I have people loyal to me. That they can't take my crown." Watching her face, he tried to make out if she was one of the loyal ones. *Be one of them.* The others could all go to hell as far as he was concerned, as long as she was on his side.

Again, she paused. Then, finally, "But you killed him." She meant the Lord Ruler.

Ordered him killed. But to her that would seem the same thing. Briefly, he wished he had talked to her before making the final decision to come here. Maybe she could have offered something better than Bard's flimsy suggestions—something strong that left the blood off his hands. But he'd feared the scenario playing out in front of him now.

He stood bone-still. "You understand," he repeated. "You're the Keeper of Brithnem." He loved that title. It slid off his tongue like a kiss. He took a cautious step forward. "I didn't do it because I wanted to. If the town had just surrendered—"

"They were not required to surrender," she said clearly, separating the words. "You aren't their king. They weren't even rebelling. You killed to make a statement."

"It was necessary." Molten heat roiled in his chest. He already felt sick in this godforsaken city. For Kiria to accuse him of doing something evil was almost too much.

"Killing innocents is never necessary."

Killing innocents? Is that what she thought of him? A corner of his mouth rose in a defensive snarl.

Her voice intensified as she continued. "I want to believe in you, but you keep choosing the most selfish things!" One of her hands balled into a fist at her side.

Don't do this. "Teach me, then," he said, trying to keep his voice smooth and even. Bitterness and sincerity warred within him as he tried the gambit. Once the words were out of his mouth, he realized he meant them. He took her hand. It lay dry and limp in his.

She shook her head. "I can't. I've already taken this too far."

His stomach dropped. This was like the last time, but worse. There was something final about her words.

She slid her hand out of his grasp. Her voice became small. "I'm sorry."

Confused rage grew in him like a disease. He furrowed his eyebrows. "What do you mean?" he asked dangerously.

"The Tanyu and the Kingdom can still be allies for the time being, but we will not meet like this again." She lifted her chin.

"Like what?" It was a challenge. He would make her say it.

She flushed red, hesitating.

He stepped closer, feeling the heat of her blush radiate against his skin. He drew her into him, one hand on her back. He had been right. Bare skin met his fingers where the dress plunged. She was shaking a little. Every part of him wanted to hold her like that for a long, long time. "Like what?" he asked again, lower this time.

"Like this." She stayed only a moment longer and then twisted out of his arms. "I can't."

"Then who's being selfish?" he snapped, unable to restrain himself.

"Firian, I can't," she repeated, anger and regret in her eyes. Regret that she had been with him, cared about him, kissed him. His heart thudded and ached as she faded away. Her eyes were the last to go. They stayed locked on him.

Months of memories washed over him, drowning him. His whole body hurt, all the blood in his veins. Faces flashed before him—Salaar, Torithians in Raewhith, the Tanyuin Head, the prisoners in the boat, the escaped pirate, the Lord Ruler... Then other faces, all of them judging him—Bard, Brett, his mother, Belik, Kiria... Kiria. She looked at him as no one else could. She saw his power, his past, his weakness, all of him.

And said no.

When he came out of the Unreal, he couldn't breathe. Air came back to him as though it were black rage. His arms tingled with fury, aching to destroy.

He could barely see through the haze of his pain. Lifting the pathetic little throne, he hurled it across the floor. People skittered out of the way like bugs. He hated them. The chair leg hit the fire smoldering in the center of the room and threw up embers. A couple guards bent to take the fiery pieces and move them where they wouldn't burn.

"Leave them," Firian growled. "Leave it! Let the whole place burn." He was burning. Why shouldn't Hill House do the same? It was just a symbol anyway, not power itself.

Hesitantly, the guards stepped back. Small tongues of flame licked at the chair legs. In the dark fire he saw his father's forge, the coke glowing dangerously under containers of sand. Sand that melted and crystalized, mesmerizing as it transformed. His chest felt as molten as new glass.

Firian looked up, caught the eye of another Tanyu. He ripped off part of the flag that had hung behind the chair and stuffed it in his pocket. "Burn it all."

35

FIRIAN

Pensively, Firian ran the green flag of Archer's Point under his fingernail. Although he stopped picking at his bleeding finger the night before, the raw skin around his black ring still looked ragged.

"I noticed you've been experimenting with duplicating yourself," Belik said across the desk.

"Yes. I'm up to six now." Firian felt ragged everywhere. Declaring himself the ruler of Archer's Point hadn't made him feel better and more secure, but worse. He had new faces to fear. A few of the soldiers had backed down like obedient puppies after they witnessed his strength, but he couldn't check them all.

And all of that didn't matter. The new city didn't matter.

"That's impressive. I've only ever gotten up to seven. Even that wasn't very successful, though." Belik cleaned his teeth with this tongue, lightly smacking.

The noise grated against Firian's memories of Kiria moving resolutely away from him, her expression leaving no room for doubt. He'd had his chance, and he had lost.

"Are you here?"

Firian glared murder at Belik. He wasn't in the mood for

condescension today. He could hardly stand his own presence, much less somebody else's.

Belik's face took on a more diplomatic air. Light reflected off the panes of his glasses when he tipped his head up. "Why didn't you use your new ability on Thraddock? I heard you made Jaddeo do it."

His new ability. Firian flushed hot with pride and shame. The room felt small, as though it squeezed the two of them together. He didn't want to kill someone else that way. He was proud of being able to kill, yet sick of killing. He wanted this murder done without his having to see. "It drains my energy," he said, instead of truer things.

Belik ran a hand over the stubble on his chin, flicking one finger up to resettle his glasses. "It drains your energy?" He asked the question carefully, as Firian had tried to be careful with Kiria.

Firian's anger at himself, at Belik, burned so hot that he took a drink of water to calm himself down. The Real felt dusty and colorless, but he tried to imagine that it was the Unreal, where he could be as calm as a tree or a mountain. "It does," he replied blandly.

Belik clearly wanted more information. Ever since Firian had returned from Torith, he had eyed Firian like a squirrel with a nut, puzzling how to get it open.

"Is it like what we did with Master Jairon?"

All Belik's prying was suddenly too much. Firian's awful, amazing ability was his, no one else's. It was the only thing that protected him when Jovan had nearly crushed his windpipe in the bathroom. "If you can't stop asking about it, get out!" Firian shouted, rising to his feet.

Belik looked infuriatingly unperturbed. "No need for that. I understand."

He didn't. He couldn't. Firian had nothing. No safety, no

Kiria—just more responsibility, danger, confusion, and worthlessness. The crown bit into his forehead as though it didn't belong there. What good had he done?

He settled the circlet a little higher on his head. He still had this, he had control of the Academy, he had the ability to kill anyone at will...

He hated all of it.

That list would have made his heart race mere months ago. Now it felt like sand and blood. A guilty, heavy, lonely life.

He shook off the weight. It was stupid to be sad. He controlled—protected—several towns on top of Tánuil and the Academy. Many were on his side. Belik, for all his secretiveness, was on his side.

Belik, he realized like a lightning strike, could have killed him a long time ago. But he hadn't. For all Belik's own ambition, he'd supported Firian's Headship the entire time. The realization gave Firian a modicum of comfort.

The two sat in silence for a minute. Firian began to pick at the flag again. It was silky, like Kiria's clothes.

"I think this will have a positive effect," Belik said.

Firian nodded without looking up.

"Did the girl disapprove?"

Belik asked the question gently, but it still made Firian furious. It was a low, ember fury, though. He didn't answer. He would never admit that Belik had been right, that he'd let down his guard and now that she was gone, he felt a piece of him was gone too.

"The Kingdom should have helped you. After Jovan, they should have helped you. Made a proclamation or some gory thing."

Firian glanced up.

"I knew they wouldn't." Belik stretched his back a little, getting his leg in a more comfortable position. "I don't know your girl, but I know enough people up there—" He ground his teeth and slowly forced out a curse. When he laughed once, there was no joy in the sound. It was harsh and murderous. Echoes of Firian's father when his supplies were stolen. "I knew they'd do nothing."

"Who do you know there?" The obvious question hadn't occurred to Firian until now. He'd been too blinded by Kiria to care. The furrowed brow that cared but not enough, the warm hair across her bare shoulders, the moment they sat in the hollow after Torithians had attacked them, tired, dirty, but together...

Belik seemed to roll the question around his mind as someone else might roll a drink around their mouth.

"Walk," he said, rising.

Intrigued, Firian followed him out of the office.

Belik led him slowly down the hall, past empty classrooms, through the fountain courtyard—Bard caught his eye coming out of their once-shared room—and out the main doors.

Promotions and banishment rose up like old dinner. Memories.

They swept more quickly now, toward the house Belik owned but rarely visited. The grade of the sloped path assisted Belik's limp. They stopped at the door, but Belik made no motion to open it. How could this be more private than his office? Maybe Belik just needed to clear his head.

Unlikely. Everything he did was deliberate.

"Do you remember your first day?" Belik looked up at Firian, his expression unreadable.

"Yes." He bit back a joking "sir."

"The woman?"

She was one of the first things Firian had ever seen in the Unreal. Some details of her face and clothing remained in his mind, though he'd forgotten her name. When he pictured her, his memory jogged, as though he'd seen her face somewhere else too.

Belik waited for Firian to put the pieces together.

"From Brithnem?" Firian asked, trying to picture everyone he had seen on his two trips to the capital.

Finally, his thoughts gained purchase. The dark-skinned, tall woman wearing yellow shoes and a septum ring had been so out of context in Brithnem that he had let the sense of familiarity pass. The Amir.

But why was Belik being so secretive? Belik was secretive about a few things: his injury, his past, and his agenda. What did this militant-looking Amiran advisor have to do with those?

Belik nodded at Firian's dawning understanding. "I was worried when you went to Brithnem that she would kill you in your sleep."

None of this made sense. Firian shifted, and the gravel crunched under his boot.

Belik leaned a little closer. "Chetana hates Tanyu."

36

KIRIA

KIRIA SAT at the session the next day feeling hollow and alone. She looked out at Cúron and Daelon and Chetana, but felt they couldn't see in, as though she sat in a transparent cage.

How had she allowed her thoughts to go so far with Firian? At random times, her memory assaulted her with images and tastes that she didn't want to relive. She had been selfish, and she wanted to be selfish again.

Cúron sat next to her, tall and regal. Atty wasn't there. He had been allowed a few days respite with his new bride.

The Main was back to normal—thrones on the platform, dividers put up so the space didn't feel so overwhelming with only a few dozen people in it.

She never should have gotten involved with Firian. He'd always been violent and self-seeking. She felt the danger hum under his skin. She'd known it from the first moment they met, when he came to be her bodyguard. He'd walked in like a predator—careful, graceful, deadly—and met her eyes. She remembered wishing he were different. He wasn't easy to dismiss as a mere helpful precaution. As he was, Firian demanded a response. She'd given him one.

Cúron's loud, low voice crept into her awareness. "The Amir and the people of Brithnem demand a response."

They were talking about the attack at Archer's Point. She suddenly realized that Chetana was staring at her. Her dark, intense eyes spoke of Firian. Kiria hoped no one else noticed.

"No one expected he would use those soldiers to build his own empire." Cúron's words were grand. "We looked the other way after Raewhith, one of our cities but small."

City was too great a word for it. Kiria had been there. *Hamlet* would have been more accurate. There were many reasons including his family for Firian to trade protection for troops at Raewhith, so Kiria hadn't held that against him. Now, like a fickle god, Firian thought he could do everything, good and bad.

"And when he demanded allegiance from Imlin, we merely began to watch him more closely. But this blatant act of conquest leaves no room to doubt his intention." Cúron shifted importantly on his throne, readjusting one edge of his long robe. His eyes flicked to Kiria. "What say you?"

"He shouldn't have done it," she agreed, "certainly not while connected to us." Saying the words made her feel hollower than before, as though they had filled her and now were gone on the air.

The following pause filled her with apprehension. Was Cúron planning to propose what she thought he was?

She lifted her head. "We need to contact the Academy to understand why they've done this. Answers are what we need. Diplomacy before rash action. It's what we would expect of them."

Cúron waited a moment for her to say more. If he wanted her to apologize for forging the alliance in the first place, he would be waiting a long time. "The Second Keeper is right," he said. "He may not be allowed to continue his conquests while under our protection. Tanyu are violent and volatile, and have hurt many of our own." Now he didn't look at her. "This act of killing Lord Ruler Thraddock of Archer's Point seems to me an imminent threat against the Amir and the people of the Western Kingdom. If negotiations fail, we must cut off this alliance and stop him before he reaches closer lands."

She felt a little sick. "What do you propose?"

He observed the Amir at the foot of the dais. "That we terminate our connection immediately, and replace Firian at the Tanyuin Academy."

Replace Firian. That meant they'd kill him. Over an alliance that she had helped create. *Idiot!* she thought bitterly. The word could have been for Firian or herself.

Had Cúron planned for their alliance to end this way all along? The placidly aggrieved look he cast over the Amir suggested that he would gain favor by this decision. The Amir didn't visibly react to his words, but they all showed alert attention. She gritted her teeth.

"The matter, to me, seems clear," he continued. "These Tanyu have harmed our citizens, targeted the Amir, and now aim to start an empire. It isn't too late to act, if we act quickly. I say we put the matter to a vote."

Everything was moving too fast. Cúron had a good point, but she had to think, to digest, to do... something. "Wait," she said. "We'll vote if we have to. I'll communicate with the Academy myself if no one else will. This is an important vote, to send troops out again, breaking our new peace," she continued, sounding extra formal as she tried to gather her thoughts. "I move that we wait for Keeper Atael to return before making a final decision. I will gather more information and we can all consider until then." If worse came to worst, she could definitely convince Atty to side with her, not to kill Firian right away.

She became aware again of Chetana's dark eyes on her. Had her advisor told anyone else about her secret relationship?

They'd all seen Firian's undivided attention when he came to Brithnem, but only Chetana and Jori knew that she had accepted that burning attention for a while. Despite herself, she blushed.

Daelon glanced at his mother and seemed to notice the message she was sending Kiria, though he couldn't read its contents. He gave Kiria an inquiring look.

Beside him, Hada, one of the session recorders, hunched over a piece of parchment, recording the proceedings. Every word set down where one could read it later. Something about the finality of that bothered her.

"He returns in two days," Cúron said. "We can all consider the merits"—he put extra emphasis on *consider*—"but I think we know what he will say. Keeper Atael highly values the security of this kingdom."

"As do I." Kiria pursed her mouth. She could barely stomach the veiled accusation. "It was for the security of this kingdom that I formed the alliance in the first place. I don't appreciate the suggestion that I am anything less than loyal."

"Of course you are," Cúron conceded, holding up his hands as though he had meant no such thing.

Amir Parohim stood up. The light coming in through the windows made the vertical lines on his face appear deeper. "Then I move that we reconvene later. In two days, we'll cast a vote about what to do with Master Kess."

THE NEXT MORNING, Kiria lit a candle and yawned. Her limp hair, all askew, cast huge frazzled shadows on the wall from where she sat up in bed. She stretched her arms toward the ceiling and let them fall to her sides. Pressure built up vaguely in her head, despite the lack of light.

This time before the sun rose inevitably brought Firian's face back to her mind. She couldn't save him from himself. She might be able to save him from the Kingdom, though.

For all his violence and arrogance, he had helped them win the war against the Torithian pirates. To kill him would betray their gratitude.

She didn't just think this because of their times in the Unreal, did she? She sat, staring blankly into space, taking inventory of her soul. She wasn't just Kiria Arioc. She was the Western Kingdom, and she had to act like it.

Archer's Point was outside their borders. Firian had never threatened her or the Kingdom directly. Even now, she doubted he ever would. She'd heard no complaints about his treatment of the conquered towns, except for his brutal takeover of Archer's Point. But would those cries reach her, if they did exist?

What had he done with the Torithians? Was he doing the same thing to the people he conquered? Did she know him at all?

She leaned forward, face in her hands. She needed more information.

If she failed, Cúron would stick to his vote, apparently hell-bent on ridding the world of Firian, since he hadn't suggested diplomacy himself. If he proposed an idea, he voted for it, even if he knew better. Parohim was guaranteed to vote with Cúron, as every Amir voted with their Keeper. Atty was the swing vote. He almost always went with Cúron, but Atty was her friend— she could get him on her side. He might be feeling more generous now since the wedding.

Steeling herself, she hopped out of bed, swinging her arms to wake them up. Closing her eyes, she let the darkness take her, then the light, then the nothingness...

Firian was there in an instant, before she could even conjure a background. In a black room, he sat on a huge chair that might have been a throne, his expression grim. Coming closer, she saw hints of longing cross the blue of his eyes, though his face was hard set.

Did he know what they had talked about in the session? Firian was almost always guarded, but now he acted like a tower, looking out from impenetrable defenses.

"I'm here in an official capacity," she began, and then realized she hadn't worn her official Beauty. Maybe it was all for the best.

A muscle twitched in his cheek. "Official?"

"Yes." She cleared her throat. "We have some questions about what you've done since the end of the war. You said you took over Archer's Point." He leaned forward like an animal cornered but she went on. "Why?"

"I told you."

"It had to be for more than sending a message."

He was silent.

Her lungs constricted. This wasn't Firian. The Firian she knew was proud and selfish and determined, but not monstrous. At least, she knew he could be better than this, but he kept regressing, giving into his worst tendencies, his greatest vices. She waited defiantly for him to speak.

"Are you dissolving the alliance, then?" he said flatly. "Did your advisor suggest it?"

His manner continued to shock her. "Firian!" she said, breaking her professional guise. "Talk to me. This isn't you—"

"This is me."

She was standing over him now, and she saw that the crown he was wearing had grown into his head as though he were made of metal himself. They stared at each other, the air between them crackling.

"You're wearing a mask," she said. She'd thought it many times when they were together, even during the good times when they had talked and kissed away evenings. Now she couldn't see him through it. Wishing she could rip it off to see the real Firian beneath, she tried a different tactic. "You took over Raewhith to help your sister. That's what you told me. What about Imlin?"

They'd start with something less violent. *Please let him have a good reason.*

He licked his lips thoughtfully, cutting his gaze away from her. "I needed more soldiers. The Academy is open now." He looked back into her eyes almost accusingly.

Her brows lowered. "The Tanyu weren't enough?" She couldn't resist accusing him back.

He went still. She had thought he was still before. Only now did she realize that there had been soft movements. Those were gone. Anger and pain reflected in his unblinking gaze.

His voice was chilly when he finally spoke. "One Tanyu can take on twenty, but not a hundred."

Kiria's throat had gone dry. "All right." It wasn't a great reason, but it made sense. "Is that why you attacked Archer's Point?"

"We didn't attack Archer's Point. We threatened the Lord Ruler in exchange for security for the Academy and everyone else." Something in Firian appeared to deflate. All his rigidity from a moment before dissolved and he stood, face to face with her. "It was a small sacrifice to keep us all safe."

She wanted to believe him, to agree with him so Cúron wouldn't get the vote he so desperately wanted. But Firian wasn't giving her the answers she needed. With each word, she became more and more convinced that he was lashing out in his paranoia. He was dangerous, just not quite in the same way the other Keepers suspected.

For a while, she didn't respond. They both knew she wouldn't take his side on this. Her mouth felt gummy as she remembered her words to him. She'd been so hopeful, so smitten. *There's more justice in the world because of us.* Was that true now?

"How would that keep us safe?" Her voice was smaller now as she searched for cracks of integrity and goodness in Firian's armor.

"No one doubts my strength."

"Only your kindness."

A few painful heartbeats later, he said, "I could have your kindness."

She ached to see the longing in his eyes. Firian Kess didn't beg. He didn't ask for things. Here was that crack of honesty she was looking for, but it wasn't directed the right way. Their time together was over. She wanted to find goodness, respect, justice in the way he made his decisions and dealt with his people. Instead, all she'd found were fear, ambition, and excuses.

"Is there no more you can tell me?" she asked.

He pressed his mouth into a line and sat back in the enormous throne. For an instant, she wanted to comfort him. She was near enough to take his hand or touch his shoulder or lean down and plant a kiss on his forehead. Or his lips.

She scolded herself for the thought and stood straighter. "If not, I'm going back. I was hoping to understand you better."

"Officially." He said the word softly, like a curse.

"Yes, officially."

It struck her that this might be the last time she saw him. All in black, on a black throne in a black room, with fear driving him to give into his worst impulses. A lump lodged in her throat. She couldn't help him. It wasn't for lack of trying.

She tried to study his face without his noticing, to memorize this moment in honor of who he had been to her and who he might have become, had things been different.

She fumbled for parting words. "I wish you... all the best, Firian," she said, sounding too hesitant and formal.

He seemed to understand, though all he did was grip the armrests of his seat as he held her gaze.

With tumbling emotions, she forced herself toward the surface. Negotiations had failed. All that was left was to convince Atty to side with her not to kill Firian.

The girls came into her room moments later. Vayci's glance at the candle prickled with guilt, but Kiria didn't need to explain why she had woken up so early and lit the candle herself.

She felt in a daze as they washed and dressed her in a cream-colored two-piece dress. Tingling covered her body. When she opened her eyes, she checked her hands. They glowed with Beauty. Everything that had been out of place now radiated in its perfection.

Fully ready, she went to Atty's room. At the door, she stopped. Was he in there with his new bride? She cleared her throat and cast a questioning look to the nearest guard, who shifted his shoulders back, the blue fabric shifting with them.

"I want to see Atael," she said.

The guard acknowledged her and nodded, opening the door.

She passed into the room. Small, feminine touches edged the corners where they hadn't before. Atty had always been stolid, more about substance than style, and he had not owned many beautiful things. It wasn't that the look of his room had changed drastically, but she noticed hints everywhere that someone else had moved in. Small things, like the way a pillow had been arranged, or a piece of lacy fabric sticking out from a drawer, or embroidered slippers by the bed.

Haved wasn't there. As much as Kiria liked her, she was glad. Part of her felt that she would never be able to have the same friendship with Atty that she once did after seeing the wedding.

His dewy eyes full of joy had said that nothing would be the same again. It wouldn't, but at least they could still talk without Haved present sometimes.

Atty sat on the edge of the bed, putting on his boots. "Kiria, good morning!" he said in a clear voice.

"Good morning. Haved is still wonderful, I assume."

He nodded almost shyly. "Yes, that was the best decision I ever made."

Kiria never would have chosen to marry for an alliance, sight unseen. She inevitably would have ended up with someone far less desirable than Haved Ganesha. "I'm so glad."

Atty finished tugging on one boot and sat up. "She's everything I ever wanted."

"Well, I'm sure she's not perfect..."

"She made me this this morning." He twisted backward and picked up something tiny from the bedspread. It was cream-colored like her dress. She came closer. It looked like a tree made of paper. Atty's palm dwarfed it. The little tree was twice the height of his thumbnail. He gave a private smile as he stared at it.

"Was there a note on it?" Kiria asked.

"No." The dopey smile didn't leave his face, but he put the folded tree to the side. It flopped sideways, immediately lost in the covers.

"You should take her to the docks," she said, prompted suddenly by a memory. "She said she wanted to meet the Navigators."

"She did?" He bent down to grab his other boot.

"Yeah, I told her that we had some here, and she got excited to meet them. She loves the stars."

"I know." The way he said it made her ache a little with the love he had for her. How could those two have known each other for such a short time? Atty wanted to know Haved, and to love her the best he could. Maybe pure intention was enough to make up for time.

"You're coming back to the Main tomorrow, I hear," she said, sitting beside him.

"Yeah." The angle of his shoulders bent slightly heavier with the answer.

"Have you heard what we've been talking about?"

"I haven't asked, and no one's told me." His words didn't have the injured, accusatory undertone they sometimes did. He just didn't care about politics at the moment.

"The Tanyu are... causing problems," she began.

His eyes darted to hers, and he bit the inside of his cheek. He didn't say Firian's name, though. A moment passed.

She continued. "They took over Archer's Point. It's just outside our borders. Very close. Officially, that's the third town that's sworn allegiance to the Academy. A couple others are set to follow. So Cúron's getting nervous."

"The Academy's conquering all these places?"

"Right."

Atty sat up again. The mattress bounced a little with the motion. "What do you think about that?" He didn't add any more to the question, but much was implied. Kiria was the face of the alliance, after all. The touchpoint for the war effort. The one who knew Firian best.

"He has taken over those towns, but I'm not sure why," she said. Firian *could* be building an empire. Everyone had the potential for corruption. "But Cúron's going to suggest that we remove the current leader—"

"Firian Kess." Apparently Atty was done using vague pronouns in place of the name.

She nodded. "He wants to remove him. And I don't think we have enough information to break our alliance like that. I want us to be true to our word. They did help us win the war. Both wars. He called off the other one too." She liked the pronouns herself. They felt safer.

Atty hunched a little as he leaned toward her. "Does Cúron want to kill him?"

Her heart jumped at the words, although the idea had been swirling in her mind for hours already. An almost physical longing to know if Firian was eavesdropping tugged at her. "Yes."

Atty's thick eyebrows twitched together as he understood. "You need my vote."

"Yes."

"If he's taking over towns, doesn't that make him a threat to the Kingdom?" He asked the question without malice, not like Jori would have asked it. Atty hated to think about killing anything.

"Not necessarily. That's the thing. Not *necessarily*. We don't have enough information." It struck her that this conversation, which felt fairly normal, could hold Firian's life in the balance. Firian's wide blue eyes when he had seen his mother for the first time in years flashed over her memory. The tinge of betrayal and longing that made him seem like a child in that moment. His comforting arms around Kiria after the news that her father had been killed. He had stroked her hair.

"We can't order him killed," she said, voice thick.

Atty looked straight in her eyes. She looked back, hoping her face didn't betray too many of her thoughts.

The side door opened. Haved emerged from the sunken washroom, wearing only a robe. Her long dark hair, wound into twists, hung wet over her shoulders. She regarded Kiria politely. Haved didn't often smile, but she observed and there was intensity and kindness in the observation.

Kiria stood. "Please don't make any drastic decision before we know everything," she said, turning back at Atty. Hopefully,

hopefully he understood what she said. His familiar puppy eyes had returned.

Kiria turned to leave, tempted to run from this potentially intimate moment between her friends, but she couldn't go without his acknowledgement. This vote was too important. "Atty. Atty," she prompted.

He finally looked back at her, calm but a little annoyed.

"I need you. I need you to vote with me."

But his thoughts clearly weren't on the next day's session.

She ran her thumbnail over her fingers, irritated. "Say you'll vote with me."

Atty held out a hand to Haved. "I need to think about it," he said, not looking at her anymore.

"It's important," she pressed. When he didn't answer, she swallowed the dread beginning to settle heavy in her throat. "I'll see you tomorrow."

37

KIRIA

Kiria's heart beat a shallow rhythm in her throat.

Firian's life. Should they replace him or let him live?

The three Keepers sat on their thrones. Advisors, military officials, and several others had been invited to this special session to decide Firian's fate.

Cúron, as usual, was the first to give his side. Firian had become a threat because of his apparent ambition. He had taken over Archer's Point. He had killed its Lord Ruler and left his head in the town square. He couldn't continue to be associated with Brithnem if he was building his own empire in the north.

She'd heard all this before. The news about the severed head had come a little later, and it made her sick to think about. She had mulled these things over and over in a nauseating loop. But she held firm to her decision that they should end the alliance, and probably stop him, but not take his life. It wasn't selfish. It wasn't just that she knew him. She felt he didn't deserve to die.

Cúron finished his argument.

Kiria stood up. "Keepers, advisors, distinguished guests," she began, feeling winded, "what the First Keeper says is true. Master Kess might be a threat. But that's the part we need to consider. As a fundamentally wise and peaceful society, we cannot strike without an imminent threat and due cause." She tried to catch Atty's eye, hold his gaze, but he seemed almost distracted, looking all around the room. Her entire back felt tense. Would he vote with her or with Cúron? "Master Kess might be a threat to us, but there is no evidence that he intends to continue. When I questioned him after our last meeting, he indicated that his violent actions at Archer's Point were intended to quell the need for any more conquest. I'm not excusing his behavior, only pointing out that it would go against our principles to murder him now."

Cúron hummed in consideration of her words. Her heart skipped. Had Cúron *ever* changed his mind after it had been made up?

"At most," she concluded, "we could dissolve our alliance." Saying that felt like a defeat. The alliance had been her idea and everyone throughout the Western Kingdom knew it. She tried to swallow the rock in her throat.

Cúron spoke without rising from his seat. "Wouldn't that anger the Tanyu as much as replacing their leader?"

"No," she replied, still standing. "I don't think so. But we do have to count the cost as well. Kingdom lives will be lost if we follow your plan. The Tanyu would know we were there before we reached the Academy. Sending one or two assassins wouldn't be enough, unless you're willing to sacrifice them and not guarantee success." The military leaders didn't stir, but hopefully they considered her words.

With a sweeping look, Cúron brought the knot of people seated at the foot of the dais into their discussion. "The question is about the safety of the Kingdom above all. We all make sacrifices."

He said it as though she didn't know. They had all made massive sacrifices for the Western Kingdom, and would continue to make them throughout their lives. He didn't need to inform her of the difficulty of ruling.

"It's a castle full of trained warriors who won't hesitate to defend their leader. Archer's Point proved their loyalty," she persisted. "We'd have to send an army and make the Tanyu our enemy again."

She accidentally caught Chetana's eye. Her advisor looked back steadily. Without changing her expression at all, she reminded Kiria of the *katah* she had with Firian. They didn't have to send an army. Kiria could kill him in the Unreal.

Kiria's eyebrows twitched downward as she dismissed the thought and turned away from Chetana. Where in the Scroll could it demand something so heartless?

Cúron passed a hand over his gray beard. "General Lincome, given what we know about the Academy, how many soldiers would it take to accomplish this mission?"

The general, a square man with pale birthmarks dotting his skin, stood respectfully. He wore armor similar to what the guards wore, all metal, leather, and blue cloth. "My Keeper." He gave a small bow. "I can foresee no less than three hundred if we attack the castle itself."

They were already planning the logistics of an attack? Again, Kiria fought to lock eyes with Atty on her left, but he wouldn't look at her. She felt sick.

"He has been traveling often lately," Cúron said, as though alone in a meeting with the general.

Kiria spoke up. "We haven't decided whether or not to replace him. Until then, all this planning is unnecessary and morbid." She paused and felt her mind. She didn't go into the Unreal—closing her eyes would have been a giveaway—but she wanted to see if she could feel Firian waiting. The signature warmth was gone.

Cúron nodded for the general to sit, and then turned almost cheerfully to her. "Then shall we vote?"

A hollow feeling carved into her chest. Firian wouldn't have a future with her, but he could still have a future.

Atty had said nothing. There were essentially two sides to this issue, and Cúron and Kiria had expressed those sides already.

To keep or remove Firian. That was all.

Kiria gazed around the Main. The soaring ceilings, many-paneled windows, grand statues, gilt lanterns... Something about its grandeur didn't match the occasion.

Firian was probably in the office she had seen in the Unreal, all gray stone. That room felt closer to the reality of what they were discussing. They were all so detached from the violence they calmly discussed in this room.

The mosaic in the floor drew her gaze. Through the chairs of advisors and generals scattered over it, she could see Maril clearly, holding lavender and a dagger. The image brought prayers to her lips.

Cúron voted first. Yes, they should remove Firian.

Kiria, dry-mouthed, voted next. No.

Atty came third.

Her heart pounded. He had never told her what he intended to do. Maybe *he* didn't know what he intended to do. He stood. She couldn't breathe. A yes from him would mean Firian's death. She wordlessly pleaded with him as much as she could without drawing the attention of the others in the room. He flicked a glance her way, but she couldn't read his expression.

"No."

Breath escaped her and she deflated against her throne. Others must have noticed her relief, but she didn't care. Brithnem wouldn't send people to kill Firian. He could live. Firian would live. Now that the danger was past, she realized how afraid she'd been for him. A surprising amount of emotion gathered in her throat.

Parohim, Cúron's advisor, voted yes, of course.

Chetana stood and voted yes.

Chetana stood and voted yes.

Kiria nearly rose to her feet. Advisors always voted with their Keepers. Always. Even Daelon's forehead creased in bewildered surprise at his mother's pronouncement. This had never happened before. How could Chetana defy her? The lump in her throat turned to anger. Chetana, tall and regal, had an air of independence, but she had never wielded that power against the Ariocs. She loved them. She'd said so.

Before Kiria could think of the right reaction, Reynard stood next. At least he would do the right thing.

"Yes," he said, not looking at Atty.

Her blood was fire. She counted votes in her head: she and Atty counted as two. Cúron, Parohim, Chetana, and Reynard counted as two and a half.

They had won.

Against the will of two Keepers, Brithnem would murder Firian.

THE REST of the session passed in an angry blur. Kiria could barely focus enough to nod or respond when her time came. As soon as it was over, she jumped to her feet and practically ran out of the Main.

How could this happen? How could Chetana vote against her? How could her mother, when she was Keeper, have allowed the Amir a vote at all?

The questions raged inside her like the sea. Somehow, she made it into the hallway. When she realized that she was heading back to her quarters, she spun on her heel and stormed instead toward Cúron's room. His guards didn't have time to bow before she opened the door and went in.

Varinna, Cúron's wife, spun around at her entrance, startled. A tall serving girl with pale skin, even pale eyebrows, stopped lacing up the back of her complicated dress. A small bottle tipped back and forth on the vanity table in front of them. The surprise didn't fade as Varinna's eyes flicked over Kiria's face. "Lady Kiria," she said, a question in the tentative way she said her name.

Kiria knew she looked irate. She took a calming breath. None of this was Varinna's fault. "I need to talk to Cúron."

Waving the girl away from the dress, Varinna adjusted herself in the seat, squaring herself at Kiria. Apparently, she had gathered her wits enough to look disapproving. Her disapproval was smooth-edged with diplomacy, even at its most severe. Kiria had grown up around stares like that, and she was too angry to care now.

"He should be back from the Main any moment," Varinna said with the slightest edge to her tone.

"I'll wait for him here." Kiria made no move to sit. The hot blood coursing through her veins wouldn't let her relax.

"Is everything all right?"

"I have an urgent matter to discuss with him," she hedged. No, everything was not all right.

Varinna gestured toward the servant, who began tugging at the lacing again.

After taking three breaths, Kiria wondered how long the man could talk and cajole with others in the Main before coming back here. After all, he had just sentenced a man to death. How could he be in good spirits?

Finally, the door opened.

"Cúron!" Kiria snapped, surprising herself with the volume

of her voice. She shrank back into herself. "Lord Cúron. How could you let this happen?"

His brow furrowed into deep ridges as he stepped over the carpets of his room. Kiria realized she couldn't remember the last time she had been here. She must have been a child.

"How could I let what happen?" he asked wearily, reaching for a clasp at his throat.

"How could you let the Amir shout down the Keepers? How could you order Firian's death when two of us voted against it?"

He handed his royal robe to a waiting manservant. "They didn't 'shout us down,' Kiria. It was a fair vote."

"Without the majority of Keepers?"

"It was unusual, but not unfair. We agreed that they could have half a vote. Your mother agreed to the notion."

The news prompted a humorless laugh. "She wasn't even going to sessions then."

"She trusted my judgment." He gave Kiria a pointed look.

"I don't," she replied. Her words came recklessly. "In this, I don't." She stood a little taller and stared back at him.

Something black flashed across his expression. "What is this all about, Kiria? You don't like that the Amir can vote? That was already decided on. Sometimes being a Keeper means living with decisions that you don't agree with."

"I know." She hated the heat she felt rising in the corners of her eyes. This was not a time to cry. "But you used the Amir to override us. You're used to being right, but you aren't right this time. You can't kill Firian because he took over a town that isn't even part of the Western Kingdom!" All the frustration that had built over months of small political moves, small condescensions, boiled out.

"I'm sorry you feel that way," Cúron responded in a familial way, like an uncle, which, far enough back in the family line, he was. "I'm surprised you seem to care about him after all the Tanyu did to Brithnem, and what he did to you."

"Of course I care. I don't want to kill an innocent man."

"Innocent," he scoffed, looking away from her.

He was right. *Innocent* went too far. She slowed down her words, trying not to sound quite as desperate as she felt. "You can't let this stand."

When Cúron turned back to her, both he and Varinna gave her stern looks that left no more room for discussion. "The decision is made," he declared in his deep, regal voice. "All you can do is abide by it. Remember that to warn the Tanyu would put our soldiers in additional danger. It would be tantamount to treason."

Her face went cold. To warn Firian of the assassination would be treason against her people? She knew it, but to hear it put so bluntly... She searched the room, as though it held answers about how it had come to this. Cúron's words felt like a puzzle box she couldn't assemble. Firian didn't deserve to die, but if she told him the Kingdom's plans, he would move the entire Academy against the soldiers they sent. Either Firian would be killed, or a company of the best troops in Brithnem. She couldn't breathe.

Cúron's face softened. "I know you love the Kingdom. With the Tanyu acting as erratically as they are, our citizens are restless again. Some are going with almost no sleep. The least we can do as their Keepers is ensure that someone responsible has the Headship of the Academy."

Her mouth felt dry as she tried to force breath in her lungs. She could hardly speak. "Don't send them," she managed. "We'll tell the people... tell them not to be afraid."

"It's done, Kiria."

His statement brought images unbidden to her imagination: Firian lying dead in a pool of his own blood, his head tipped sideways by itself... Her hand flew to her stomach as she felt suddenly sick. It wasn't only the violence that bothered her.

She knew Firian.

She... loved him. To whatever degree, there was part of her that loved him, despite his mess and the shadows lurking in him. The truth struck her like a knife. The timing of this realization could not have been worse. Now there was nothing she could do to save him, either from the Kingdom or from himself.

She shook her head at Cúron. How could this be happening? *Tantamount to treason...*

Only one thing would have kept her from warning Firian, and it was betraying the Western Kingdom. As long as she lived, she would never do that.

38

KIRIA

AT BREAKFAST THE NEXT DAY, Kiria didn't touch her food. She couldn't eat if she wanted to. Even the sweet scent of the laird flowers along the center of the table stuck in the back of her throat.

It was the same group that had eaten merrily together before her coronation tour—Keepers, family, advisors, a few others—but this time was different. Cúron didn't look at her, busy instead with his wife, Atty, and the Amir.

Chetana didn't avoid her gaze, but any time their eyes met, an electric current of challenge ran between them. Kiria felt it in her bones. The challenge wasn't loud or harsh, but constant and undeniable. Chetana could vote as she saw fit, it said. *But you cost him his life!* Kiria wanted to scream. They hadn't spoken since the vote. Kiria felt too hideously bitter. Today, though, she needed to call an audience with her advisor.

In two short weeks, the troops would reach the Academy. The thought of warning Firian popped up, unbidden, all the time. When she was at meals or sessions, talking to friends, falling asleep. But she hadn't. More lives would be lost that way, and besides, he could take care of himself.

He should be stopped, but not murdered.

Her hands trembled under the table. They felt dirty, coated in blood. Others chattered around her. She didn't hear what they said.

When she lifted her eyes, Jori looked back at her from across the table. His trademark cavalier attitude had been replaced by honest concern. She nodded a little so he would know she was okay.

Jori and Chetana. Those were the only two who knew about her continued connection with Firian in the Unreal. She'd called it off, but she knew she could summon him and he'd appear in an instant, never far away.

I'll feel his death.

The thought struck like a kick to the chest. She was going to be sick. When she was in Charäkhnem, she'd known his panic during the assassination attempt. Surely, she'd feel this too. She'd know before anyone told her because she would panic, lose her breath... Would she black out?

She looked back at Jori and revised her response. She slowly shook her head. *No, I'm not all right.* She pointed to her food. *Want it?*

He reached for the plate she handed him.

"You're not eating your breakfast?" her mother asked beside her.

"I'm not hungry this morning. I might be getting sick," Kiria replied.

The meal finished quickly. As everyone rose to leave, she found Chetana. "I need to talk to you," she said in a stern undertone.

Chetana's expression didn't change. She'd expected this conversation. "When would you like to talk, My Keeper?"

"Now." Kiria was tempted to stay behind, but the smell of flowers and breakfast turned her stomach. She needed fresh air.

"In your quarters." That way they could walk across the gardens before reaching the Amiran Academy. There was also a hint of symbolism or justice that the conversation happen outside the palace.

"Very well," Chetana replied, and they left the room.

Kiria's girls followed her into the gardens, but she told them to wait outside the room while she talked to Chetana alone. Because she was an advisor, she lived in the Amiran Academy itself, in one of the private rooms, near Daelon's. The curved side closer to the palace held the personal rooms, the side facing away was for education, and the large domed room upstairs was for religious study and prayer.

Amiran bedchambers were tiny and ascetic. Chetana's barely fit the two of them comfortably. Handwritten notes and passages from the Scroll lay in a neat pile on the desk next to two candles that Chetana lit so they wouldn't be in darkness.

Tanyu and Amir were more alike in some ways than they liked to admit. Neither group cared about worldly comfort. It was easy to see how they came from the same root, although they focused on such different things now.

Chetana waited for Kiria to speak first. She loomed over her, especially with her curly hair, and some of Kiria's fury cooled a little. She sucked her lip for a moment before asking the question that had been plaguing her thoughts day and night since that session. "Why did you vote against me?" She revised. "Was there anything in the Scroll that meant I was doing the wrong thing?" *And if so, why didn't you tell me?*

"*God uproots the tyrant,*" Chetana said evenly.

"*And blesses the one with mercy,*" Kiria finished, glad she had played that Scroll game so often with Daelon during their lessons. He would give half a sentence and she had to provide the rest. She became very good at it.

Chetana's expression didn't change. "My Keeper, the Tanyu

have to be stopped. This greed... I know what this greed can do. They pledged loyalty to the Kingdom but they will not keep their promise."

"Your duty is to God and then to me, and what I think is right to do for the Kingdom. I chose mercy. You should have too." She swallowed, but her throat didn't move the right way. "A man will be dead because of you."

"More than one, I think, and not because of me." Chetana leveled her gaze at Kiria. In the candlelight, she looked other-worldly. "You know what I say is true, but you care too much for him to order his death."

Kiria opened her mouth to protest, but nothing came out. Darkness pressed in, thick and physical around them. "You're supposed to be peaceful," she said. "Wise. God-fearing."

"I hope I am those things now."

Now? What did that mean?

Chetana went on. "I admire your mercy, and I knew you could be as stubborn as the First Keeper."

Kiria almost reprimanded her for being so blunt, but it felt good to be blunt, real. "You're saying that, but you sided with him."

"He sided with us."

Kiria paused. Some of Cúron's decisions clicked into place. It was his idea to give the Amir a vote; he had funded more copies of the Sacred Scroll, sent for research from Charäkhnem, vocally supported expanding their education to include the poorer areas of Brithnem. Most of them were great ideas, so Kiria had missed the pattern. He had wanted the Amir on his side all along. They gave him all the power. She and Atty were tagalongs in his plan. Dull anger simmered inside her.

Chetana was no fool. She had to have seen it happening and allowed it. Did Daelon see it too? Kiria didn't think so. He would have told her.

"There were other ways to get rid of him," Chetana said softly.

Kiria stood silently. A cool draught from the door breezed through the tiny room. She refused to understand Chetana's meaning.

"The *katah*." Light flickered on her septum ring. "But I knew you wouldn't take action. And that's all right. It is much to ask."

She would have Kiria kill Firian herself. The suggestion was repulsive. How could she betray his trust so cruelly?

Kiria's chest ached. She already had betrayed him by not warning him about the coming troops. The conflict inside her made her want to scream.

"My only regret," Chetana went on, "is putting you in danger, My Keeper. But you still have time to extricate yourself from his hold. I know the strength of a *katah*. You are just as strong."

"Chetana," Kiria said, breath coming harder, "your violence and disregard for me demonstrate you are unfit to be my advisor."

Chetana's dark arms flexed, but she showed no other sign of emotion. "I understood that you might feel this way, My Keeper."

Kiria fought to keep her voice from shaking. She reached backward and laid her hand on the cool door handle. "I want someone who will respect me and who will do the will of God. You've followed your own prejudices and it will hurt innocent people."

Chetana lifted her chin a fraction.

"Daelon will be my new advisor. He has greater respect for the Scroll than anyone I've ever met."

Despite everything, a gleam of pride for her son flashed in Chetana's dark eyes.

"And he cares for me. He wouldn't do anything to hurt me unless he knew that God would will it so."

"The same is true of me," Chetana said. "I will always love and serve your family, My Keeper."

Kiria set her mouth in a line, unconvinced. Until a few days ago, she would have believed anything her advisor said. Chetana was mysterious and strong, but had always been loyal.

Light streamed in as Kiria opened the door and walked out.

39

FIRIAN

FIRIAN PURSED his mouth as he looked at the dead rabbit.

Its gray-furred back arched in a U, its black eyes still wide. Around it, the pine needles had been shuffled in its death throes.

A fox or raven would come to take it away. What bothered him was that he kept finding these animals, killed but not yet eaten.

The breeze ruffled the rabbit's fur backward, showing more fluff. A healthy rabbit, broken in its prime. Maybe its neck was squeezed like his was underwater. The creature's stiff limbs made him a little sick. No one had threatened Firian since Archer's Point, but the echo of betrayal still wouldn't leave him. It played relentlessly in his head, waking and sleeping. Sometimes even in the Unreal.

It had to be a person killing these animals. He wouldn't have minded if the rabbits and squirrels were eaten too, but they all lay at the edge of the forest, left to rot.

Some Tanyu had anger, but they all had restraint as well. He couldn't think of anyone who would kill like this for no reason. Even Jovan, prone to violence, needed an excuse.

It must be Torithians. Who else could it be?

Firian turned away from the rabbit and headed to the barracks. He needed to talk to the new instructor anyway, make sure he was pushing the troops until they were ready to jump, to dive, to obey the slightest command. No more killing without cause.

His boots crunched the dead pine needles as he strode toward Old Danior's sweet shop.

Speed kept him from thinking about Kiria. Not completely, but it helped.

Belik hadn't said anything more about Chetana, but the bitterness in his voice told him they must have had a *katah* too.

An old *katah* still rankled, seared a person's insides like the aftershock of a burn, even after the initial sting went away. At least that's how someone had described it to him years ago. He couldn't remember who it was.

Belik had always seemed above such things. Even his regard for Firian felt like an exception to a life without attachment.

Firian still felt the sting. It stabbed him now, touched him constantly. Keeping busy just helped him to push it to the background, an irritating ache, demanding attention. It would rush back in any quiet moment. The Unreal pulled him toward her and he had to wrench his mind in other directions.

If he was going to get her back, she needed some time. It had only been eleven days—eleven and a half days—since she had pulled away from him, said goodbye, severed their connection. He would get it back. He just had to be more patient than he felt.

Firian stepped between the shops to the barracks. Already the carpenters had started building rock walls in front of the wooden ones as he had requested. It could have been Firian's imagination, but they seemed to work faster after he burned Hill House. Either way, grim satisfaction made him nod as he looked at their work.

The new instructor, Master Nedi, came quickly out of the main entrance to the compound. He walked, but gave the sensation of running. Exceptionally tall with long limbs and big hands, he had the look of a man cobbled together from several other people. He kept his brown hair short above his small eyes and big nose. Despite the awkwardness of his appearance, he still moved like a Tanyu, silent and sure. His size and formidable voice, helpful on Torith, now made him the right candidate for instructing drills.

"Master Kess," he said, approaching him.

"Master Nedi, how's my army?"

"Torithians are days away from weapons," he replied. His deep voice sounded as though it resonated through a gravelly cave. Even his voice at an ordinary volume gave the impression of being much louder than it was.

"Good," Firian said, getting louder himself. The people from Raewhith and Imlin must be practicing with weapons already. "Before you give them any, talk to them for me."

Master Nedi's pause asked why.

"Someone's been killing animals. Until that stops, none of them get weapons. My army does not kill without a reason." The Lord Ruler's face appeared in his mind. *He was a sacrifice for order. There was a reason.*

"As you would have it, Master Kess."

"Push them hard."

"As you would have it."

Warmth trickled onto Firian's neck. Or maybe it was just the Unreal. Kiria.

He nodded curtly to Master Nedi and turned to go. If Kiria was thinking about him... if she wanted to *meet* him...

He ducked between some shops, looked to see that no one was close by, and closed his eyes. This demanded his full attention. Immediately he saw her. He sucked in a breath. Beautiful, like a cool drink after a run. Her shining hair was in braids. His eyes slipped down to the jeweled slippers adorning her feet. His chest ached with the desire for her to look at him, but she was talking to someone else. The Third Keeper's brother, Jori. They sat on the edge of her bed in the middle of a heated conversation.

She hadn't come to the Unreal to meet him. A sour wave of disappointment mingled with his curiosity. Why did he think she had called him?

"I can't," she was saying, her gorgeous face contorted in pain. She held her hands open in her lap. "I won't." Her chest heaved with a heavy breath.

Should he make himself known? Should he comfort her?

Jori looked her over sympathetically. He was sitting too close to her. Firian stayed out of sight in case Kiria checked the Unreal.

"I know I can't... do anything now," she said bitterly. "The troops are already gone." A tear washed down her face. Another chased it, and another. She leaned into Jori's shoulder, and he wrapped his arm around hers. Quiet sobs shook her.

Firian's mouth went dry and his hands numb.

"You did what you could," Jori said, rubbing her fine skin. "It could be the best thing. Never know."

"I can't risk them," she said, her voice muffled against him. It was as though he hadn't said anything. "And I didn't... want to risk him either. But they're almost there."

Firian frowned, feeling sweat coat the back of his neck. *Him?*

"Nothing you can do now, love."

"I replaced Chetana," she said, straightening. Her face looked like justice. "She had no right to vote against me, not for something this important. Life or death, Jori!"

Firian wasn't breathing. Whose life was she talking about?

Jori tapped her a few times on the shoulder and let go. "I hate it for you, but you can't—"

"You know I won't!" she snapped. Her hands shook. As though holding in a curse, she bit her bottom lip. "He didn't have to die," she said quietly.

"He didn't have to take over all those cities either," Jori replied.

Cold washed over him. All that planning, all those precautions, all the fear he had battled in the past months, and now this. It was dread come to life.

Firian fought his way to the surface of the Unreal, floundering for the first time in years.

His mind was full, too packed to fit another thought. He might be sick.

They're coming for me.

40

FIRIAN

Firian rolled in sweat-covered blankets. He hadn't slept for two days. Gray light leaked in through the small, high window in his bedroom. Morning again.

Every time he lay down, his mind churned. On the edge of sleep, his heart raced. A dream might start and he'd jerk awake, afraid he was Lost in the Unreal. His muscles ached from tension.

Thirteen and a half days.

Kiria had shown only disappointment in him back in Archer's Point, not fear for his life. She hadn't known what was coming. She wasn't cunning or evil enough to hide something like this so well.

Assuming they didn't send their whole army, it would take about fourteen days to travel between Brithnem and the Academy. At worst, he had one day left. At best, twelve.

His chest constricted and he kicked violently against the blanket wrapped around his leg. Blood raced through his arms, his hands, his fingers, but it didn't feel like strength. It felt artificial, as though he could stand like a dangerous warrior, large against the backdrop of the Academy, glaring lightning, but then the slightest thing would make him fall.

Nausea welled up in him and he sat up, cradling his head in his hands.

He'd told Belik and Bard and all the others to get ready for an attack. Bard also knew that Kiria had voted against killing him, but he'd acted aloof ever since the victory at Archer's Point. It was like Sias Jairon all over again. Bard would be civil if he had to, but he didn't seek out games of Indisfate with Firian anymore. A silent protest.

Belik didn't care about Kiria's innocence in the plot when Firian told him. "It doesn't matter for our plans, does it?" he had snarled. They tripled the border patrol, taught the new soldiers maneuvers, and set one of Gerand's best *katah* students to reach out for the leaders' minds. They were ready.

But how much of that would matter if Brithnem sent the full force of their army, now detached from any other conflict?

They wouldn't. They wouldn't do that. It didn't make sense. Belik had to tell him this a few times. They were only after one man, the one who posed a threat.

In the half-light, he bared his teeth. He could be a threat if they wanted one.

So why was he worried? He'd trained his whole life for this moment. Naturally, conflict would come. He had known that the moment he opened the borders of Tánuil. He just hadn't thought it would come from *her*.

Why didn't she fight for him?

He played the conversation over and over. Kiria had voted against sending the army. But she also hadn't warned him. She voted the way she did because it would save soldiers, and because it was right. She didn't love him, or want him, or save him now.

Her image burned behind his eyes. He wanted to look at

every detail of her: the woven gold belt around her waist, the line where her shoulder joined her neck, her gaze both sympathetic and commanding... He scrubbed his eyes with his fists until he saw bursts of light.

Firian couldn't live like this. He jumped out of bed, pulled on some clothes, and rushed out of the Head's suite of rooms. His heart knocked against his ribs as though he'd been running or holding his breath. He needed something to make his thoughts shut up. A plan. Anything.

When the soldiers come, we'll defeat them. I'll frighten any army from coming close, any nation from breaking an alliance with the Tanyu. And then I'll get Kiria back. I've done it before. I'll do it again.

Firian almost knocked someone over as he sped around a corner. It wasn't his guard.

"Oh, hey!" Bard cried as he moved out of the way.

"What are you doing here?" The jolt of adrenaline made the words cruel.

Bard's eyebrows got closer together for a moment. His black eyes, rimmed with lack of sleep himself, looked hurt and even reproachful. "I came to tell you that the *katah* isn't working. Gerand sent me to tell you. I don't think they brought anybody with the Talent."

So Kiria couldn't call them off. It would be harder for the Tanyu to sense them coming too.

Bard mused, "I've never heard of an army with nobody who touches the Unreal *at all*." He looked up at Firian. "Anything yet?"

"No." He wanted to tell him to go back to sleep. Bard loved sleep. But he couldn't. When they were attacked, Bard had to be awake or risk getting killed.

Firian shook his head rid himself of these thoughts. The soldiers weren't after Bard, and they wouldn't get inside the

Academy. But still, for some reason, he *needed* Bard to be awake when the attack happened.

Bard tipped his chin and lowered his voice. No one was there to hear. Firian had the odd feeling that everyone else had left, that it was just the two of them in the massive Academy, left to fend for themselves. "The patrollers will let us know, yeah?" he said. "How much time will we have then?"

"Not much." Firian caught himself picking the skin around his Master ring and stopped.

Bard's uneasiness seemed to have more to do with the idea of taking lives than it did with the possibility of losing. An Academy full of Tanyu wouldn't lose.

They wouldn't lose. They weren't weak. Still, this felt far more frightening than going to Torith or getting Lost in the Unreal when Belik had gone to get him out. This gnawed at him in ways he could hardly explain to himself. These soldiers, when he pictured them, didn't look like the metal-plated palace guards or the soldiers he had fought alongside on the island. They looked like mountain ghosts he used to battle in his childhood imagination—impossibly strong, supernaturally driven, unbeatable. They could walk through walls and kill at a touch.

"You never told me what you wanted me to do," Bard said.

Hadn't he? Firian flipped through his memory. He'd spoken to almost every group, from the people of Raewhith, to the *katah* Masters, to the veterans of the War Zone and even the Watchman. Bard wasn't good in a fight; he was too compassionate. *Katah* wasn't working. Intelligence might suit him, but Firian had border patrollers and Belik for that. "Just stay with me," he said finally. "I'll be heading operations and... you'll stay with me. In case I need you for something."

Bard regarded him oddly, his face dark in the shadowed hallway. "You sure?" His piercing gaze asked questions that his mouth didn't. *Aren't you going out to fight? What do you really want me to do? Are you afraid?*

"Yeah, I'm sure."

Firian splashed his face with cold water from the basin in the washroom. He only closed his eyes the moment he threw the water, then opened them again.

Coming to this room required an act of will. He'd avoided it since that day in the tub. Before others were awake, he would go to the washroom on the second floor, down the hall from Bard's room, where he had once beaten Tiev. No one had hurt him there.

Jovan's ghost wasn't watching him, but the bones at the top of Firian's spine prickled as though it was. He often felt watched, but there were different kinds of watching.

Kiria had watched him, her eyes like a caress in his mind. There was the time patrollers had interrogated him to test his loyalty to the Academy—they had watched him too. Someone besides Belik had watched him when he was Lost in the Unreal. He still wasn't sure who that was.

Lately, though, the sensation had been like a haunting. As though the watcher were a predator and Firian prey. It was something unholy that made his guts writhe like a scaly creature. At least he'd managed a few hours of sleep last night. It wasn't much, but it was something.

The door behind him opened quietly. He whipped around, slicking off his face as he did.

A border patroller. He had a thick mustache and unevenly chopped short hair. Malto, was that his name?

"Master Kess," he said.

But before he could continue, Firian knew.

They're here.

"Get everyone in position!" Firian cried.

Malto didn't need another command. He hurried to carry out the plan Firian and Belik had ordered.

Firian practically ran out of the poisonous washroom. He felt each wet drop run from his hair down his chin, gather, and drip off.

Crown and swords. He ripped open the door to his office. Heartbeats pounded against his ribs and throat. The Head's crown was in his room next to the bed. He gripped it in his fist. For a moment it felt like a weapon. It could become one if he needed it to be.

Swords next. In a box at the end of the bed was a long sword and a mid-sized curved knife. He'd worn the looped sheaths every day since he'd overheard Kiria's conversation. He already had his boots on, with their compartment for a small, everyday knife. Three weapons. That was more than enough. He could use the crown, the walls, the sun, his legs, anything to fight if he had to.

His mind, if it came to that.

No one would touch him.

When he came out of his bedroom to the office, Bard was already there, all rumpled, breathing as though he had just run. A crease in his face showed how recently he had been asleep. "I'm here!"

Firian was breathing hard too. He couldn't settle down. He had to move, though Bard's presence did calm him a little. It meant that all the Tanyu were being alerted to the threat. Plenty of people to defend the Academy.

But he had never been the kind of person to stand by while others had a chance at glory. He itched to run out, to fight. *Damn these weapons.* He wanted to *feel* the struggle. His blood was high, his power was back, and he knew he would win.

Belik stumped in quickly behind Bard. "They're here," he growled without further greeting. "Tree line. Master Nedi has the Torithians in front, as we discussed. Other soldiers behind. Tanyuin volunteers surrounding."

The words sounded like music, every syllable in its place. Firian had come up with this plan, and it was time. Seeing Belik with his heightened energy caused a profound, almost unearthly calm to come over Firian. "Perfect."

He set his crown on his head. Now he was ready.

41

KIRIA

IT WAS STARTING. Kiria could tell. It had been exactly fourteen days. The jarring sensation came that she had anticipated and dreaded. It wasn't the panic she had felt in Charäkhnem, though. It barely registered. If she hadn't been waiting for it, she might not have noticed. But now it took her out of her reverie.

She stood in the upper room of the Amiran Academy, looking up at the ribbed blue ceiling edged with gold, praying. She didn't exactly know how to pray. There were the prayers the Amir led during special occasions. She knew portions of the Scroll. The passage that Chetana referenced echoed over and over again in her mind. *God uproots the tyrant and blesses the one with mercy.* She wanted... what? She wanted the horrible ordeal to be over. She wanted it all to be a mistake, for the Kingdom soldiers never to find the Academy, for Firian to show them all mercy, for the small force of elite guards not to kill him, for there to be no bloodshed. But there would be.

She held her breath inside her ribs. Daelon sat beside her, studying the Scroll and making notes. He was so focused that it took her a while to catch his eye. When he noticed her holding his gaze, his mouth set in a resolute line. Almost imperceptibly, he nodded at her, in a gesture of solidarity. They were in this together. Daelon was more peaceful than his mother. Blood on either side would wound him, cause him to lift up prayers.

Kiria knelt beside him. He quickly stood and offered his chair. But right now she didn't feel like a Keeper. She felt like a woman who needed help. Sitting back on her heels, she whispered, "Daelon, how do you pray?"

A grim smile tugged on one side of his lips, crinkling his cheek. He helped her to her feet. There were a couple other Amir sitting quietly in corners of the holy place. He glanced at them quickly and then whispered back. "You know the prayers I taught you, My Keeper?"

She nodded. She remembered them, but she needed new prayers now.

He had to lean closer for her to hear. "Always begin with reverence." Daelon lived his whole life with reverence, so it didn't surprise her that this was his first piece of advice. "Acknowledge God's will above your own. He knows better than we do."

She prompted him to go on.

"That's all. Then speak as you would to a ruler." He gestured vaguely to himself and then to her.

Speak as though I'm Daelon speaking to me. "That's simple."

"Truth is often simple. It's just difficult."

His words hung in the air like heavy clouds, resonating inside her. She never should have kissed Firian. Cúron never should have ordered his death. Simple, but difficult.

She cast her mind north again. It was as though thinking of him and the Kingdom soldiers could protect them all. Her duty lay with all of them, with the simple but difficult truth that none of them deserved to die today.

Reverence came first, then submission. But when it came to

the part when she could offer her request, she had no words
at all.

———

KIRIA ALMOST ASKED if there was any news, but there couldn't be.
The army hadn't taken a Watchman with them, or anyone else
who could convey information that quickly.

She knew someone with the Talent who could give her the
answer to that question. But as soon as she asked him, he would
know they were coming. Moments flashed by when she wanted
to give him the chance to defend himself. But it was too
late now.

Prayers had helped—they were all she could do—but she
still felt sick. At odd times her stomach would drop with the
reminder that she would feel Firian's death. The knowledge
made her not want to speak to anyone or appear in public
spaces. If her response to his panic had been so violent, how
would she react if he died? Would she scream? Collapse?

She couldn't risk it, so she stayed in her room. Cúron probably thought she was sulking. Maybe others did too. There were
many, after all, who hated her because of her sympathy for the
Tanyu. Those people would rejoice to see Firian's head on a
stick. She swallowed something bitter.

She'd find a way to make this better. Her throat caught. *How
can any of it be better?* Hot tears filled her eyes and spilled down
her cheeks. She let the Beauty seep away, tingling back into her
old skin, plain and real. Her hands balled in her lap reminded
her of him. She always checked her hands to make sure they
were plain in the Unreal. For all his selfishness, he thought her
plain face was beautiful.

Sobs came hard and thick. She gulped air convulsively. Snot
ran onto her chin. Pounding the blanket on her bed as hard as

she could, she cursed him and mourned him at the same time. She understood him. In some ways, she *was* him. His darkness crept through her chest as well.

She sniffed horribly, rubbing away the tears from her eyes. More took their place so she left them.

"My god, are you all right?"

She looked up in time to see Jori set a bottle down on a table as he rushed over to her. She didn't answer.

He sat beside her and took her by both shoulders, peering into her eyes. "Are you sick?" He ran a hand over her forehead and through her hair. His touch soothed her enough to calm down.

"No." She hiccupped the word.

Understanding dawned. He bit his tongue lightly in a grimace. "Is it time, then?"

She nodded.

He hugged her sideways. "You'll make it through," he said. "There's life on the other side." Because he didn't usually talk about difficult things, even the trite words made it sound like he was trying. "Come on." He switched his manner abruptly. "Haved invited us to the garden. It's a good day for it."

"It's early," she said, eyeing the bottle.

"Ah, you have to spice up a picnic," he said, a mischievous grin spreading across his face.

She wanted a distraction, but his flippancy grated against her worry. "I can't."

He ignored her, looking off to a different point in the room. "You know, Haved is too good for Atty. She's really wonderful."

Kiria didn't agree with the first part, but she did agree with the second. "She is," she said.

"So how about a picnic?"

"Jori..."

His eyes darkened a little, the gray turning stormy. He pulled his legs onto the bed, suddenly looking more at home than she did. "You know I want you there, love, but if you have to wait and see then I'll struggle on alone."

"That's very good of you," she said, and sniffed again.

He spiraled out his legs and jumped off the bed. In an elegant twirl, he grabbed the bottle once more. "I hope you get what you're waiting for." The tinge of a challenge in his voice made her go cold.

Maybe she would go to the picnic. Maybe...

Even as she thought it, she knew she couldn't. Tomorrow. Once it was all over, whatever *it* was, she could go out.

Jori made for her again, as though he thought of something new, or else couldn't leave on such terms. "You know I hate to see you suffer." He patted her leg. "I'll send up a fruit tart. Never too early."

She gulped away more tears. "Thank you." She suspected that it would taste like nothing at the moment, but fruit tarts were her favorite, and Jori knew it.

He winked and went out, leaving her alone to await Firian's death.

42

FIRIAN

TANYU RUSHED by like a flock of ravens, tucking weapons into boots and sleeves. The deadly flashes reminded Firian of sneaking out to the inn to see a Charäkhni traveler do slight-of-hand. Their silent feet beat out the rhythm of Firian's blood, charged and ready.

Bard followed him out into the fountain courtyard with its huge chandelier and terraced upper floor. The sprinting warriors disappeared down side passages so they could emerge unseen on their way to the battle.

Belik couldn't match Firian's pace, so he had stayed behind in the Head's office, ordering the counterattack from there. The fact that someone else commandeered the space would have bothered Firian on a normal day, but he was so eager to get out and see the Kingdom troops that he barely spared it a second thought. He couldn't have sat there through it all. Besides, if Firian appeared on the battlefield, and they still couldn't get to him, it would make the victory more delicious.

Firian and Bard passed alone through the massive double doors. Tánuil looked empty, except for the Sentries bustling from house to house, sounding the alarm for citizens to stay in their houses.

It was early, but no one slept. There was a wakefulness in the air as everyone waited for the fighting to move closer. Each muted scream and clash of ringing metal caused a thrill along Firian's bones. He felt Bard tense beside him.

The sense of blood and danger filled Firian's nose and made the hair rise on his arms. That same haunted feeling crept over him again, but it was different this time. Weakness didn't threaten his mind. His senses sharpened and muscles tensed. He felt big and visible in his black coat, as though he were a famed mountain ghost himself. Something to fear. And he was.

In the gray of the morning, standing on the earthen bridge to the Academy, Firian could just make out figures moving along the tree line. Brown patroller outfits against blue. Black figures knew enough to stay hidden until it was time.

Between the Kingdom soldiers and the border patrollers, it seemed like a fair fight. Firian watched almost disinterestedly. *Is this it?*

"Let's get inside," Bard said in a low voice. He must have felt how visible they were too.

It was the smart thing to do, but it sounded boring, if not cowardly. Firian hesitated.

Bard hit his arm. "They'll see you."

"I know." Curiosity kept him outside a moment longer, as though he were watching a simulation in Strategy. What would the Kingdom forces do next? This couldn't be their entire plan.

Belik's words from the day before came back to him. "It's likely that they'll bring a secondary force, divert your attention, and then attack."

A secondary force. He swept the panorama before him with his eyes, but saw no one else.

"Firian!" Bard whispered.

Restless, he followed Bard back into the Academy. Walking fast, he strode back to his office for more news. They passed a couple of Tanyu—Rian, Tesni, Ardal—who had been instructed to remain in the Academy. There weren't many guarding the interior.

The guard opened the Head's door for them without a word. Belik sat behind the desk, bent over papers as though he belonged there. Something inside Firian squirmed at the image.

"News?" Firian asked. Really, what he wanted was a fight. Man to man. To get this over with. The lack of action frayed his nerves.

"The army approached from the south, the most direct route." Belik's mouth twisted disapprovingly. "Border patrollers are handling it now. Tanyu will pick off any stragglers."

"And the secondary force?"

Belik cleaned his glasses and put them back on. "We haven't observed one, but it's probably there."

Firian ticked off entrances in his mind, as he had the past few nights when he couldn't sleep: main doors, kitchen deliveries, Jovan's back hallway...

"We have guards at every entrance," Belik said, meeting Firian's gaze.

"What about the windows?" Bard asked.

"Most of them aren't on the first level."

"Get people on it," Firian said. *Every window can be a door.* "I want every window watched."

The guard outside overheard and sprinted to carry out his command.

"Should I check?" Bard asked.

"The guard's doing it," Firian answered.

Belik's eyes flicked between the two of them in a question he didn't ask. "The soldiers won't get in," he said instead.

"Fir, have you... talked to them?" Bard asked seriously. "Found out what they really want?"

"Me!" Firian retorted. Bard knew that already. What was he playing at?

"I mean, can you call off the fighting and try to negotiate something?"

"They're past negotiation," Belik muttered, looking back at his papers.

Firian opened and closed his hands. He didn't want strategy or maps or planning or talk right now. He wanted action. The Kingdom might not expect him to go out into the open and join the fray. *So what if I'm the person they're fighting to protect? Everyone fights to protect themselves.* Maybe they thought he'd stay here in this cramped room instead.

The thought made him claustrophobic. "I'm going out."

"Don't be a fool," Belik said quickly.

Bard nodded in rare agreement.

"I can't just stay here," Firian said, turning toward the door.

"You *will*."

Firian glared at Belik. The Master was wise, had practiced strategy for longer than Firian had been alive, but he was not Firian's father nor superior. Belik had no authority over him.

Without a word, Firian swept out of the room with Bard trailing after him. If there was a second force out for his life, he'd find them.

Only a few steps out of the office, Bard spoke up. "Fir, I think this is too obvious. We're underestimating them."

Firian slowed to walk beside him. "What do you mean?"

"They're coming from the south. That's too obvious. It's not the best place to attack from anyway, you know?"

It wasn't, but Belik hadn't seemed surprised. Bard looked uncharacteristically serious as they continued through the hall, inspecting each of the exterior doors and windows. Remembering Kiria's arrow wound, Firian scanned every corner high and low as they moved.

Bard's eyes darted to and fro. It was the same look he had while playing Indisfate. His mouth fell open. "The Sentries!"

Firian checked for the horrible current Sentries created to block the Unreal, but there wasn't a hint of it. "What about them?"

"You made the Sentries Watchmen."

Firian tried to put the pieces together, getting impatient now. "Yes. So?"

"They must have communicated with the army."

"The Sentries are loyal to me." Even as he said it, he felt a prickle of shame. What if he was wrong?

"Yeah, yeah," Bard said quickly. "They are."

"And these soldiers don't have the Talent. You told me."

"Yeah. But the Sentries didn't know about the plan to attack beforehand, when the Kingdom could have asked about the Academy." Bard reached out and touched Firian's shoulder, spinning him around to face him. "The Sentries... their underground tunnel. It leads into the Academy. It has to, or else what was that fire for? Isn't there a—"

But Firian was already running. There was another entrance, if it could be called that. A narrow passage led from the Sentries' prison to the furnace and tribute stores beneath the main level. Bard followed close behind. Firian could count on one hand the number of times he'd been to the vault, even as Head.

The staircase led down from the hallway that held Firian's office and the cursed washroom. How had he not thought of this before?

As they passed his rooms again, he cracked open the door. "Get out," he told Belik. "Go to Jovan's room." There was a guard already stationed down that hallway, as well as an exit if he needed to run. Though he'd never seen it, Firian doubted Belik could fight half as well as the others with his bad leg.

He heard the soft, stumping footsteps leaving in the other direction as he and Bard approached the tiny staircase. Kingdom soldiers put themselves at a disadvantage here too. Without the element of surprise, they trapped themselves. And there was always a guard for the tribute. Maybe Bard was wrong.

The unmistakable sound of metal against metal filtered up the stairs, followed by a keening groan. He cut a glance at Bard, then at the hall leading back to the courtyard, where most of the reserve Tanyuin forces waited. *Get the others,* he instructed wordlessly. Bard understood instantly and sprinted off.

Firian unsheathed the curved knife at his waist and spread his legs, waiting for the first soldier to show himself coming up the stairs. His heart pounded, keeping time in a violent trance. Though his body acted afraid, he didn't feel afraid. Certainty calmed him. They were coming in through the Sentries' entrance.

No one appeared. If the soldiers really had killed the guard, then they'd have had plenty of time to reach the staircase by now. Why weren't they coming up?

He stilled, breathing slowly, feeling every vibration in the floor, listening for every sound.

Movement caught his attention. A strange mix of pride and concern churned in him at the sight of Bard leading a column of Tanyu, most of those that remained in the fortress. Rian took fewer strides with his long limbs, Tesni's braid waved behind her, and Ardal the World Events Master had a short and stocky frame that made him almost invisible as he moved through the rest.

Firian pointed down the stairs.

Ardal nodded curtly, going first. Tesni went next, grim as death. Others followed carefully but without hesitation. Bard shifted on his feet, staying beside Firian as he had promised. Furtive sounds of fighting came through the space.

Fire burned in Firian's veins. Unable to hold himself back any longer, he plunged down the steps.

Only a few torches lit the space. It felt hot and suffocating, not as bad as the Sentries' dungeon, but the sensation was too close to be comfortable. Most of the treasure stores lay behind locked doors, so the large chamber's floor was usually unobstructed. Figures moved in the gloom. Flames reflected against metal armor and blades. It was as though half the Tanyu had disappeared, melted into black shadows.

Perched on the last step, Firian scanned the fight. Three Kingdom soldiers lay on the ground and no Tanyu. About twenty opponents. The Tanyu were making quick work of the small force, lashing out like vipers, cracking necks, stabbing eyes and armpits and anywhere else the armor was weak.

The appearance of Firian on the stairs galvanized the Kingdom soldiers when they saw him. They doubled their efforts, fighting more savagely than before.

"Hey!" Rian yelled. A Kingdom soldier holding him in a chokehold. Flinging himself backward, Rian crushed his attacker into the stone wall behind him. A torch rattled in its holder. When the soldier kept fighting, Rian smashed him again.

Sounds on the stairs made Firian turn. The darkened stairwell filled with faces and weapons. "Block them!" Firian ordered, jumping down.

Tanyu whirled at the coming forces.

More soldiers came, not just from one side, he realized, but from both. More troops crawled through the Sentry opening at the same moment soldiers flowed in down the stairs.

They must have already snuck into the Academy before they figured out the plan. Firian's blood ran cold, then hot.

They were surrounded. Firian stood in the center of fighting and blood, trapped in this underground room. Rage coursed through him. He had let this happen. The ploy was so obvious. He never should have ordered so many of the reserve Tanyu to the same place. Only Belik, new recruits too young to fight, and a few guards weren't in the fray. Unless Bard had set aside some Tanyu for other purposes, everyone else was here.

There were too many Kingdom soldiers coming through both entrances to block them completely. They crawled like bugs out of holes. The small space became stiflingly full of bodies.

As he called in the Unreal to the nearest guards to come help, a soldier muscled past Rian, who still battled, and rushed at Firian sword first.

Firian whipped out his curved knife and met the blade on its way to him, forcing it around and down. Bringing it sharply up again, he sheared the sword hand off. The man screamed, a terrible sound. Firian silenced it. Dark blood slicked the floor.

The Tanyu could outlast them. He knew it in his bones. Guards were coming to deal with any soldiers in plain sight in the hallway. It was a short staircase, so they just needed to empty it. He jumped toward two men coming at him, almost glad. The walls, the floor, the blind tunnel, the tightly packed bodies, the knives... All weapons. All pieces in a game.

The Tanyu drove the Kingdom soldiers back in both directions, black against silver and blue, vicious, relentless, forward, barreling the men backward into their companions. A flash of eye whites. Airless pressure filled the room as they pushed them back, getting heavier as more bodies were added. Boots crushed over the slippery obstacles of dead soldiers.

Were Tanyu dead too? Firian couldn't look around but he thought he saw a pile of black clothes from the corner of his eye.

He didn't take out his sword. It was too long for such close-quarters fighting. The curved knife felt right.

Jumping up using the neck of a man's armor for leverage, he kicked off the wall to get above the fray. As he landed, he flung his knife in a wide arc that sliced through two man leaping down the steps. They fell with the others, choking and reaching futilely for his wounds.

Firian took a breath and realized that he didn't see any more people coming down the steps toward them. Craning his neck to see up, he spotted the dark figure of a Tanyu further up the stairs. A drop of sweat fell from his neck as he turned it. They'd cleared the stairs.

Now the Tanyu had one side of the room, and the Kingdom the other. An eerie quiet settled over them all, save for the sputtering torches and the panting of fighters. The rank, coppery smell of blood assaulted him through the heat. Firian shot a glance to the side. He saw five Tanyu with him: Bard, Rian, Tesni, Ardal, and Makai. Bard was shaking. He had a small knife in his hand.

Were the others alive?

It would matter later. Not now.

He scanned the room. No one else was coming in through the tight opening to the Sentries' furnace. Six against at least forty.

His mind whirred, cycling through strategies. Could they leave them here and set the room on fire? Was it too late to send Tanyu to the Sentry entrance in the woods? He pictured himself coursing forward at impossible speeds, impaling them all cleanly in one motion. But this wasn't the Unreal.

A Kingdom soldier stepped forward. One hand held a sword and the other was raised in a gesture of truce. "We only want Master Kess!" the man announced.

A bland, false quiet fell. Hearts beat in chests. Hands tensed around sword hilts.

Firian snarled, scanning the room full of people again. So many, all poised to kill. No one had sheathed their weapon. Their stances said clearly that they wanted to kill all the Tanyu. Firian peeled back his lips in a grimacing, defiant smile.

The Tanyu wouldn't give him up. Fear and loyalty prevented them. Nobody answered the man. Firian ran his thumb along the side of the knife blade.

The speaker stepped closer, one hand still raised, a moving figure among statues. His face was smeared with dirt and sweat, his expression diplomatic.

Firian tensed as the man took another small movement forward, approaching him as he would a cornered cat. The hairs on the back of Firian's neck stood up. Two of the men behind the spokesman edged forward too, their boots sloshing against shallow pools of blood.

Why was everyone pausing? Why weren't they protecting him? They said the purpose of this assault was to kill him, only him. The man tightened his grip on his sword. Close enough now to strike...

"We just want—"

Firian swung hard, slashing the man across the chest and shearing off his hand. Blood spurted across Firian's chest and face. He spat as the room erupted into chaos.

Kingdom soldiers charged. Rian screamed and rushed headlong toward them.

Two Kingdom soldiers ran forward, already too close when they emerged from the storm of battling bodies. They filled Firian's vision.

Bard jumped forward, blocking him.

Something in Firian snapped. "Get behind me!" he roared, shoving Bard sideways. "Get behind me!"

He risked closing his eyes. The soldiers could slice his flesh at any moment. Quickly, down, down...

He reached out, saw them all. So many... Could he do it?

He let go of the urgency, his imminent death, his fear for others, everything but the beating hearts and brains in front of him. With measured breaths, he leveraged all his strength, all the burning power of the Unreal sucked inward like it had done with Tiev years ago, a pillar of light and intensity, enough to destroy, to shred, to blast to skeletons...

Then, with all the life he had, he burst like a firestorm over them all, breaking as he went.

He was death itself.

In the Second Level, he watched them fall, all of them, ruined from the inside. They broke one by one like huge black branches overcome by a crushing tidal wave. The roar of it—was it a real sound?—thundered in his ears.

Firian had barely opened his eyes when the ground rose sideways to crash into the side of his head. As he fell in a mangled heap, the wave of darkness took him too.

43

FIRIAN

THE FIRST THING Firian knew after losing consciousness was walking slowly down a hallway. Everything ached. His body was a bruise. At first it felt like dreaming, a nightmare, but the details were too real, crawling over him like insects.

The stiffness and sheen of his pant leg crusted with dried blood. The scuffling of feet as more Tanyu behind him took away bodies. The sweat that beaded in his eyebrow and dripped into his eye. The pulsing headache that made him acutely, terrifyingly aware of each blood vessel in his skull.

How did I get here?

Stone walls passed by in a blur. Hands stronger than his own gripped his elbows on both sides, guiding him forward.

His head weighed almost too much to turn. The effort made him squint. On one side, Master Ardal, with blood plastering his hair down near his ear. He cast a grim eye toward Firian. Looking to the side made him dizzy, but he needed to know who held his right arm too.

Bard.

Blinking sweat out of his eyes, Firian blew out a shaky

breath. Bard was alive. He was too tired to smile, almost too tired to stand. Were they all safe now?

Images of the soldiers falling around him set emotions bubbling like a cauldron. How many had he killed? How could he not know them all? An urgent, childish urge to count, to look into their faces and ask their names, almost sent him running down into the storerooms.

Were the Tanyu all right? He had an odd feeling that he had murdered everyone, including himself, and he almost started crying. His eyes felt like hot stones. Tears probably couldn't come from them. Still, he wouldn't have had the strength to stop if another memory hadn't taken its place.

Perfect, fiery power shooting like liquor through his veins. He had stared at an army and taken it down. He had known he could kill them all. He'd wanted to drink that liquor until he burst, but it left him sick.

Heavy exhaustion threatened to crush him. He just had to lie down. The Academy was safe. Bard, Belik...

Still covered in blood, Firian wearily pushed open the door to his office. His fingers trembled against the handle as though someone were shaking him. His muscles strained against the weight of the door. Ardal pushed it open with him and then let him go in alone.

No, not alone. Bard guided him inside. He knew he was leaning on Bard enough to strain him, but at least it was no one else.

In the empty office, Bard let go of his arm. Firian righted and steadied himself, his head pulsing, legs shaky.

Despite the exhaustion and pain, he sensed something dark lingering between them. Bard's black eyes narrowed and his chest heaved as he stood in the middle of the room, more than it should from the strain of helping him. A crackling in the air told Firian that he was there to advise, to criticize something he did.

"Not now," he slurred, moving toward the room where comfort, or at least unconsciousness, awaited him. He could wash the blood off in the morning.

"Fir. It has to be now." Steel wove through Bard's tone. His words were soft, but there was a strength, an urgency, that Firian had never heard from him before.

Firian turned, unreasonably angry. He summoned his energy. "What can't wait?" he asked, separating each murderous word. The pit of his stomach constricted with the knowledge of those he had just killed. He breathed in deeply through his nose and let the air out through gritted teeth.

Even from the opposite side of the room, Firian saw that Bard swallowed, his Adam's apple bobbing. His hands were fists at his sides. "You.... How could you?"

"Did what I had to." He had seen it all. Why did he ask?

"No. No..." Bard shook his head. He looked taller, somehow. "You... didn't have to do any of that."

"They were attacking us!" Firian's face grew hotter. He caught the door jamb to his bedroom to steady himself.

"They stopped! Maybe they would have talked, I don't know. You didn't have to kill them all. And Rian...!"

Rian. So he had killed a Tanyu. Furious shame almost made him vomit. He couldn't stand here another minute.

"And it's not just this. It's the Sentries, and Master Jairon, and Archer's Point." He was breathing hard, but he caught himself. He shuddered back into stillness. "You were like family to me!" Tears welled in Bard's eyes.

Firian caught the past tense. He gripped the doorpost harder.

"Like a brother, Fir." Bard's voice caught and he lowered it. "I want to stand by you. But I can't."

Firian brought his voice low too. "What are you saying?"

"You can't keep doing this. You can't."

"What—?"

"You're a monster, Firian."

His breath stopped. *A monster.* The word stuck, covering him, oozing into his lungs. Bard would turn on him too? His best friend? But he saved him. He'd done this *for him.*

Flashes of the attack came back to him. Faces smashed against the floor. An arm flung at a weird angle over a torch bracket. His own arm twisted underneath him where he fell. Blood pooling on the ground and dripping from stairs. Wild, bleeding eyes left open. He weighed as much as a boulder, couldn't sit upright. His body hurt wherever people touched it to raise him. Foggy layers of horror.

Firian's face felt like wax and his heart beat faintly under thick layers of his body muting the sound.

Bard, stronger now, looked into his eyes with resolve. Tears trailed down both sides of his face.

"Get out," Firian whispered.

Bard breathed shakily, even his fists trembling. "You have to—"

"Get. Out." Firian felt a black abyss under him as he said it.

After a beat, Bard nodded. "Yeah, I know." As though dragging a weight, he turned toward the door. Firian watched him step off the carpet, reach for the door handle, open the door. Time moved sluggishly, pounding in time to the pain in his skull.

Bard looked back once. His forehead creased with anger or disappointment. "I wanted to stay."

Firian didn't reply as Bard disappeared and shut the door behind him.

44

KIRIA

KIRIA STARED AT HER LYRA, but no music came to her. The pain had subsided, but it still racked her whole body with a dull ache.

For hours she'd sat, waiting, knowing that any second...

The stabbing knowledge of Firian's pain had struck more quickly than she expected. She'd tensed, bracing herself for the pain to pitch higher and higher. Maybe she should have called for a doctor.

If only she'd understood the depth of Firian's ambition sooner. She knew what he was, of course, but what if there were something she could have done to prevent this? The thought echoed loudly as it would in a hollow room, again and again. No one could blame her for her grief. She'd chosen the Kingdom above Firian. Even above herself.

"Petra Madola," a guard announced.

Kiria, tired from the ache, looked up to see him opening the door for the military strategist. The tall woman walked forward swiftly and bowed to her. She was clad all in armor as though she were a guard herself.

"My Keeper," she greeted. "I bring news from the Watchman."

Kiria knew what it would be. The only question now was who they put in place of Firian.

"The removal of the Tanyuin Head has been unsuccessful."

Kiria sat up, confused, shocked. "What?"

Petra inclined her head. "All our troops were killed."

"No... they couldn't have been."

"I'm afraid so, My Keeper. We're holding another session today to debate our response."

Kiria put her fist over her mouth. How could this be happening? If Firian was alive, then what pain had she felt? *All* of their soldiers? "How did the Watchman get the news?"

"The young man with the supplies apparently ran to the nearest unoccupied city."

She couldn't think. It didn't make sense. She hadn't known what to hope for, but it wasn't this.

"I will see you in the Main at midday, if My Keeper can attend," said Petra.

"I'll be there," Kiria replied, her mind still spinning.

"My Keeper, Atael Calthwaite," said the guard at her door.

Petra bowed and exited as Atty entered. He wore a simple buttoned tunic, not like his royal robes. His hair was mussed. When he reached the bed where Kiria sat, he turned and indicated that the guards should shut the door. They did.

"Did you hear?" she asked.

"I did." His brows furrowed deep. He didn't look at her. "Just now."

Something was wrong besides the defeat at the Academy. Something that had to do with her.

He paced a couple times. She waited, unsure of what else to do. The blackness of Firian's pain still flowed unevenly through her mind. It wasn't as acute now. He was alive. Just like last time. The loss of soldiers left her little space to be glad.

"Did you tell him? Did he know?" Atty said quickly, his

words slurring a little.

"What do you mean?"

He looked into her eyes. The fear and aggression there took her aback. "Did you warn that Tanyu we were coming?"

She went cold. "Who told you that?"

"Just answer the question, please. I hope you didn't."

Jori told her secret. The knowledge left her a little more broken than before. "No, I didn't," she said clearly.

"Are you still... Were you ever seeing him? Secretly?" Coming from him, the idea sounded ludicrous.

"Not now," she said. "How did you know?"

He pursed his lips. "Haved told me."

"Haved?" The surprise brought her to her feet. She had never told Haved her secret. The only people who knew—she *thought*—were Jori and Chetana, and Firian himself. "What did she say?"

"She heard you and Jori talking about it." He looked away for a moment at his brother's name, as though he felt betrayed or left out.

"I didn't warn him," Kiria repeated.

"You've been in your room all day. Nobody's seen you."

Kiria's fingers started to go numb. Atty didn't believe her. Her breath felt shallow, barely filling her chest. Ever since he became a Keeper, she'd sensed him drifting away from her, but it was just his responsibilities, his busyness, his insecurities that drove him to Cúron. She understood all that, and adjusted. Now, though, he didn't believe her.

She couldn't explain why she wanted to be alone. It wouldn't make sense to someone without the Talent that she still had a connection to Firian even though she didn't go to the Unreal to see him anymore.

"I'm telling the truth," she said. "I'm not lying to you."

"But you didn't tell me about you and the Tanyu before."

"It was…" She sighed in frustration. "You didn't need to know at the time. I didn't tell anybody. Please don't tell anyone else, Atty."

He leaned against the wall by the headboard and crossed his arms, regarding her as he would a stranger.

"I'm still me," she said, guilt settling behind her ribs. She touched his arm, willing him to understand. "And I *didn't* tell him we were coming. I don't know how we lost."

Atty still stood impassive. "Why didn't you come out this morning?"

She could lie. She could say she was sick. "I was waiting for him to die," she said quietly.

Atty pulled away from the wall and drew his eyebrows together. His forehead wrinkled with confusion. "What? What do you mean?"

"I could tell." Her voice was a whisper now. Embarrassment and sadness wouldn't allow her to speak any other way. "I don't see him in the Unreal, the space in our minds, anymore, but I'm able to feel when he gets seriously hurt. Did… did Haved tell you about Charäkhnem? When I panicked?" She knew the answer before she finished the question.

He nodded.

"He was almost killed right then. I didn't know what was happening until later. It was *his* panic."

Atty drew a knuckle over his stubble, digesting her words. "So you can read his mind?"

"Not exactly."

"Can he read your mind?"

She paused. "Sometimes. I think so. Only sometimes."

His gaze pinned her where she stood. "He knew we were coming." His voice grew stronger now, accusatory. If he hadn't been pointing this intensity at her, she would have been proud of how Keeper-like he was.

Was he right? Could Firian have read her mind? She hadn't sensed him there since Atty's wedding, and she could usually tell when he waited in the Unreal. She hadn't told him, but what Atty suggested wasn't impossible. She felt sick.

"I didn't tell him." She could barely get the words out. The protest sounded feeble now.

"I know you wanted to wait until we had more information before attacking. I did too. But these were our people. They're dead now."

"I know!" Her chin trembled with anger and sadness. If Atty felt betrayed, now so did she.

"You said you can tell if he gets hurt," Atty said after a pause. "Did he get hurt?"

It felt like a test. "Yes."

"Will you tell them about your connection to him at the session?"

She took a few breaths. Atty was prodding an open wound. Maybe he didn't know how much he was hurting her.

She didn't answer. She didn't know.

"Kiria," Atty sighed, suddenly younger again. "It's the right thing to do."

He knew that mattered to her. Despite her indiscretions, she wanted to do what was right. She wanted to be good, but she failed over and over again. No wonder Cúron tried to get more done on his own. He had experience, and Kiria kept making the wrong choices for herself, for Brithnem...

"If you don't tell them, I'll have to do it," he said. He lifted his chin as though convincing himself to follow through.

"Please don't." Her heart was in her throat. If everyone knew about her connection with Firian, they might not trust her again. Not after so many had died.

"I have to." He started backing toward the door.

"Please."

He stopped, almost drooping with exasperation and disappointment. That tired look he'd had before Haved crept back in gray shadows over his face. "Kiria, why did you do this at all?"

The question felt painful coming from him, happy in his love for Haved. She couldn't explain. Not to him. She stood silent.

He tipped his mouth, not saying anything either. Instead, he left.

***

Kiria's mouth felt dry as Atty took his place on the throne to her left. Today's agenda was to figure out what to do about the Academy now that their attempt to unseat Firian had been unsuccessful. There was no reason for him to tell her secret, that she'd had a secret relationship with Firian. That was all over now. Though it hurt terribly, she hadn't warned Firian about the soldiers. She had chosen the Kingdom over him. To drag her secret out now would damage her reputation for years, if not for her entire reign. If Cúron found out about it, it wouldn't be from her.

The atmosphere was solemn. So many good soldiers. All dead. Their memory filled the room as though their corpses were present.

Parohim opened the session with a prayer for the dead. Daelon followed with a passage from the Scroll. Reynard completed the Amiran contribution by another prayer for guidance.

After that, Cúron, as usual, began. "As you all know," he said, addressing the small crowd, "our campaign against the Tanyuin Head has failed."

In her peripheral vision, Kiria saw Atty chewing his cheek.

"News has reached us that even the one who survived to give

us the message passed away a short while later." He bowed his head in silent remembrance.

A fresh wound of sadness sliced into her, as she pictured the young face that she might have seen in the garden, training with the guards.

"What remains is to react," he continued. "With all our soldiers killed, it is clear that the Tanyu are no longer our allies." He didn't acknowledge Kiria, but most of the people at the foot of the dais did. "They are clearly against us. We know where the Academy lies, and we know, although they have more soldiers at their disposal than they did, that their forces are still small compared to ours."

Kiria felt empty, the wood of the throne hard under her arms, biting into bone.

"But a smaller force can still succeed if they have better information," Atty said, bold yet hesitant.

She looked at him. *Please don't. Don't do this.* He returned her look like an apology.

"Very true," said Cúron. Kiria breathed again when his gaze didn't cut to hers.

She scanned the little crowd. Chetana briefly met her eyes. The touch was enough to let Kiria know her thoughts. Chetana probably suspected the same thing Atty did, that she had told Firian everything. Did no one trust her?

"Considering the destruction of our last force, we will have to create an entirely new plan, and send greater forces, if we want a guarantee of success."

Kiria nodded, trying to look engaged. Trying to look as though she weren't petrified that Atty would shatter any confidence the Kingdom still had in her.

Parohim spoke up from below. "Is there any evidence that the Tanyuin Academy plans to attack us here in Brithnem?"

A murmur from the crowd. They had wondered the same

thing. Would more people die in their sleep, as they had last winter?

Petra Madola answered, "No direct evidence at the moment, but given their reputation as mercenaries, I doubt that they'll let this statement go unanswered for long. We only just smoothed over the last war with them."

"Lady Kiria could find out for us." Atty again.

She couldn't swallow, though she tried. Everyone watched her expectantly. Some of them knew she had the Talent, at least. "I can see what I can find out," she said.

"You could ask the Tanyuin Head," Atty pressed.

A marked interest angled in her direction. She froze. Some of them knew about her spying during the first war, knew she had the Talent and had communicated with Firian, or at least watched him. "Yes." She cleared her throat. "I watched him for information during the war. I could do the same thing again."

"But he watched you as well," Cúron said. "Would the same thing happen again?"

When I couldn't come to any of the sessions? She hoped not. "I don't... think so."

Cúron turned back to his audience. "But the question remains, what will we do? The Tanyu might strike now or later, but it seems very likely that they will strike. We cannot give them that opportunity."

"Kiria." It was barely a whisper. Atty.

She didn't respond.

Petra said something about numbers and maneuvers or something like that, but Kiria wasn't paying attention. Her own thoughts and blood beat in her ears too loudly.

"Excuse me," Atty said, standing. "I'm not sure that Lady Kiria should be at this session."

Her arm shook against the hard armrest. She dug her short fingernails into the wood to ground herself.

Atty looked at Cúron before he continued, as a son would a father. "She could alert the Tanyuin Head about our plans."

"I'm sure she wouldn't—" Cúron began indulgently.

"I think that's how the Academy knew about our plans today." He lisped the *s*'s, the only clear evidence of how uncomfortable he was sharing this information about her. He, like her, chose the Kingdom over companionship. He thought he was doing the right thing. She was a traitor and he was their savior. He might as well have stabbed her. She could barely breathe around the lump in her throat, much less speak. If Firian learned about their approach from her, it wasn't intentional.

A hush fell like a smothering blanket on everyone in the Main.

Finally, she said, "I would never tell them." She hated the weakness and hesitation in her voice. The sound made the whole picture real, as if remaining silent could have frozen the moment and prevented it from moving into reality. Tears sprang into her eyes.

Atty continued, sounding choked up as well. "It's the only explanation for how things went."

She mouthed his name, pleading.

Atty tore his eyes away from hers. "She was in her room all morning, and the Tanyu were clearly ready for us. This was no surprise attack."

Warm tears fell freely down her face now. She stood beside him. "I didn't tell them!"

He turned back to her, his eyes tired and mournful. "But you care about the Tanyuin Head. You didn't want him killed."

"No, but I would never betray the Kingdom."

"He knew we were coming." The softness in his voice almost broke her.

Their soldiers were all dead, and it was her fault.

She couldn't answer for a moment. Steely anger rose up in

her slowly, starting from her fingers and feet. "How could you accuse me of treason? Because that's what you're suggesting. I said that I would never betray the Kingdom. I vowed it. Do you not believe me?"

"He knows your thoughts. You meet him in the Unreal. You love him."

Again, he stunned her to silence. She wasn't sure which accusation to deny, if she could deny any with certainty. Every second that passed sealed the destruction of her reputation. As surely as if it were a piece of fabric burning, she felt each strand frayed end eaten away like smoke.

"Is this true?" Cúron asked.

She had almost forgotten he was there. She and Atty might as well have been alone. Her stomach turned over itself.

"I don't meet him now, and I didn't warn him about our attack," she said with all the strength she could muster. "I swear." She held up a hand and cast her eyes up to the Scroll passage etched on the ceiling.

After an awkward pause, Cúron said, "We'll adjourn the rest of this meeting until tomorrow."

Now that her secret was out, they didn't want to continue with her in the room. Somehow it was worse that they knew after the relationship was over, when she could feel the full brunt of her mistake.

She cared about Firian, still did, but she had known his ambition was bigger than any feelings he had for her. She knew he was dangerous. That was one of the reasons she liked him. She wasn't proud of it, or herself, but at least she could own up to the truth.

She looked at Atty one more time before stepping off the platform. He looked back with love in his eyes. She loved him too, but he had broken their friendship. It could never be as it was before. He had ruined her.

45

___

FIRIAN

"Sit up," said a voice above him, brusque but not unkind.

Firian angled his arms so he could push himself up without opening his eyes. The blanket and pillow were damp with sweat. At the movement, his head swam. The room tilted when he pried open his eyes.

"That's it. Have this."

Firian took the cup of water Belik offered him. He brought it to his clammy lips. The cold liquid made him shiver. Had water always been so tasteless? It was as though his senses were heightened and dulled at the same time. He was always *feeling*—the weave of the blanket, the ache of his bones, the piercing light in his eyes—but some of his senses had left him completely. Time, for example. He had no idea how long he'd lain there. It had to have been more than a couple days.

At least Belik was taking care of things in his absence. Firian hated being useless, but he had no choice now.

After a few sips of water, the room stopped spinning so much. He rested his back against the headboard as he looked at Belik. The Master's presence scared away the monsters in his mind, so a weak wave of thankfulness came over him.

Belik's mouth flattened in a smile as he regarded Firian through his glasses. "The doctor says you'll live," he said.

Firian didn't reply.

"That was quite a performance. I'm surprised you'll pull through. But you were always strong." His tone was fatherly.

Firian let the words wash over him like a balm.

You're a monster, Firian.

Those words had repeated, echoing through his skull through all the long nights of his illness. *A monster, a monster, a monster...* Bard could be fearful, but he was rarely wrong, especially about him. But Belik knew him too. He was one on a very short list of people who understood him, at least better than others. And Belik thought he was strong, not a gory monster.

He wished he could hate Bard, curse him for those words, but he couldn't. When Firian thought of that day, he felt shame, not hatred. Shame and sadness were worse than hatred, but he couldn't make himself feel any differently.

"Of course the Kingdom isn't happy about it." Belik breathed a mocking laugh through his nose. "There was a riot yesterday. Nothing serious, just a few broken windows and enough to scare the princess and her friends."

"Riot?" In his feverish state, Firian couldn't piece together why there would be rioting in Brithnem.

Belik brightened at his response. Firian wondered again how long he'd been lying in bed, feverish, clinging to life. "The alliance," Belik said. "The princess. Something about how she's pro-Tanyu."

Keeper, not princess. He kept back the retort to save his energy. Instead, he shook his head. She wasn't on the side of the Tanyu, not since their last meeting.

Belik raised an eyebrow, reading Firian's face.

"Some people want Merian back in power," Belik continued. "Fine by me. She never did a gory thing."

Firian held the cup tighter. He couldn't help thinking that Kiria would agree with what Bard had said before he left for Enderin.

"Either way," Belik continued, "it doesn't take a genius to figure out war's coming again."

Dropping his eyes, Firian felt the uncomfortably slimy sensation of wet sheets on his legs. Nausea welled up in his throat, went back down.

Belik jabbed his arm lightly with a blunt finger. "You did what you had to do. Few casualties." He meant Tanyu. "But Brithnem isn't happy. They'll come again, now." He paused and pulled on his earlobe thoughtfully. "And I can't ask you to do this again. It isn't practical."

And I'd probably die.

"When you're up, we need to talk about a counter-strike. It's the only way to get the upper hand here. Offense, not defense."

What would Bard say to this? Normally, Firian had two voices, even though so much input often annoyed him. Attack Brithnem? Is that what Belik was suggesting? It was much larger than anything they had overtaken before. They had more soldiers. They had Kiria...

At the thought of her, his whole body ached again. He was losing everyone. Her presence was like medicine. If she held him like she had done before, he would heal. His need almost over-whelmed him.

For a second he forgot what Belik was talking about.

War. That was it.

He looked dully back at his mentor. Time had little relevance right now. Surely he could sleep and think and no time would pass. Or he could reach out to Kiria and avoid war altogether. Slowly he brought the cup to his lips again and nodded.

"You know your little friend left," Belik said.

"Don't go after him," Firian rasped. Hopefully no one had

been sent to track him down already. In his delirium, the possibility hadn't crossed his mind.

"I know. You two had a connection or something. Where did he go?" Belik's casual tone revealed more interest than it hid.

Home. Firian didn't say the word. Belik hadn't promised to leave Bard alone. Even if he had, his promises twisted too often into lies. Bard didn't deserve to have Belik go after him for disloyalty. Disloyalty wasn't the right term anyhow. How could Bard ever be disloyal?

"You don't know?"

But Firian was done talking.

Belik hummed and stood, favoring his good leg. "I'll be back tomorrow," he said. "You look like shit." Then he smiled and walked out.

46

KIRIA

Kiria laid her palm on the new glass pane. She stood by a potted *sachion* tree, half hidden from anyone who might walk through the wide palace hallway. The glass was cool against her hand. It looked clearer than the other smudgy panes, crisscrossed with black metal.

How could she lead a nation if the people didn't trust her?

Atty had done what he thought was right. It's what his father Aylmor would have done. Atty thought she was a threat to security, and he had always cared about safety, even more than she did. Kiria, at least when she was younger, took risks that made him shudder.

Firian was one risk she never should have taken. How else could the Tanyu have known that they were coming and had time to prepare? She was the weak link. Her face felt hot and she laid her forehead against the glass.

Days before, the window had been shattered by protesters. Rioters were a better name. People of Brithnem had reminded her of the crazed mob at King's Heights, shouting her name, throwing any hard object they could find. Finally, guards had to put them down, disperse the crowd. The memory still seared.

They hadn't screamed for anyone else. Only her. She was the enemy.

Looking through the window, she saw the green lawn sloping down through manicured hedges to the main streets into the city. Almost out of sight, her favorite statue peeked above the stone buildings. *People need to remember their heroes...* Her own voice came back to her like something out of a dream. Then she remembered when she had said those words, or something like them.

"You keep talking about doing good. What will you do when you're the Keeper?"

She had told him. A good beginning, he had called it.

"You only live one time. You get one shot. Is that what you're going to do with it? Or do you have the courage to do what isn't safe?"

It certainly seemed like she'd wasted her time as a Keeper ever since ending the two wars. Here she was on the brink of a new one, and this time it was her fault. She breathed in the clean scent of the tree beside her. She couldn't do this.

Where was Daelon? He was her new advisor and now was a very good time for advice.

She pushed off from the window and turned. To her surprise, he already stood behind her. His long robe settled in a way that suggested he had just approached. Daelon wasn't one to spy on her.

"My Keeper," he said, and bowed. "You weren't in your room." His face was neutral, his posture characteristically stiff. Her request that he take over for his mother didn't seem to fluster him. Chetana had accepted it as a necessary consequence for her actions. Maddeningly, she seemed to think her vote was worth being dismissed.

"They want my mother reinstated." She didn't realize those would be her first words to him.

"They don't know what they want," Daelon said kindly. He

walked closer beside her. "It's easier to see out now." He peered through the window.

She sighed. The pane didn't match. It would snag her gaze every time she walked this way.

"Lovely view." He side-eyed her. "*Those who keep their eyes above—*"

"*—will never want for wisdom,*" she finished. Despite herself, she smiled. She'd always loved the Scroll game. She'd been good at it, and they hadn't played for so long. "Is that what I'm missing, Daelon? Do I need perspective? Or prayer?"

He considered, weaving his fingers together behind his back as he continued to look through the glass. "It's always difficult for those who have compassion big enough for both sides of a conflict." He turned to her, smiling sadly.

"What should I do?"

"Continue to love the Kingdom. It may take years, or even a lifetime, but they'll see it. You don't serve the Kingdom for praise."

"No, of course not," she said quickly, realizing the words weren't as true as she wished they were. "It's not wrong to want to be loved, though, is it?"

"Even Keepers are still human," he replied.

"That doesn't do me a lot of good."

He cast his eyes to the ceiling with an expression that reminded her how young he was. "I remember a little girl," he said, "who caught fireflies one night. I think she got more than the boys."

Kiria shook her head. Atty had gotten the most.

"All right," he amended. "As I recall, she came to me afterward, angry because she was afraid the boys would squish their fireflies to see if the insides glowed. I told her to go to bed, but then I heard the next day that all the boys' fireflies had disappeared in the middle of the night. It was a great mystery, until you were late to my lesson. Didn't your mother find you playing the anthem of Brithnem to those poor fireflies? Your skills on the lyra were... not as polished back then. Perhaps they felt more patriotic after you freed them into the garden."

She laughed, a little embarrassed at the memory.

They started to walk slowly back down the corridor together, abandoned but for the guards. "I know you, My Keeper. You wouldn't betray Brithnem. My mother doesn't think so either."

Kiria's chest tightened. Chetana thought she was wrong, but not a traitor. Her own mother, Merian, had looked horrified as soon as she found out the truth about Kiria's connection with Firian. Since then, even their relationship had been strained. "Thank you, Daelon."

"The best leaders continue to serve even when they are maligned. *'Does a man want power?'"*

"Greatness is found in service and majesty in love." She'd always pictured that service done for an adoring public. Or, if not adoring, then at least not hostile. "I know, but it's harder in real life."

"My mother has told me that joys are better in real life too." He cast a glance at her as if to ask if he were bringing up Chetana too often.

Chetana, at least, knew the lure of the Unreal, so she could compare them. Kiria missed the Unreal. She couldn't share it with anyone besides Firian, and now she couldn't even do that. Its freedom was intoxicating, exhilarating. The air flowing past her dress as they walked reminded her of flying around the field. Her feet moved heavier at the memory. She hadn't experienced many joys lately.

Daelon stopped walking. "Not everyone hates you. There are many who still believe your word. I'm one of them."

At that, she hugged him tight, squeezing her eyes shut and pressing her face against his shoulder. He smelled like soap and candle wax. For a moment he held his arms out, unresponsive, but then he patted her back gently. "It'll be all right." He nodded against her hair. "You'll be all right."

An unmistakable dark shape materialized behind her eyelids, growing in her mind. She felt as though she were being dragged into the Unreal after it. It was hard to tell if Firian forced her down, or if she made the decision herself. She swam toward the surface, but found she couldn't quite reach it. Like a drowning woman, she could see the way out but darkness pressed in all around her and she gave into it. Just for a moment.

"Kiria." Firian stood in front of her, close. He said her name in a fragile way that made her think he wasn't feeling as strong as he looked. She didn't either. Damn it—despite everything, part of her still loved him. "I don't want war with you," he said. So, he wasn't going to pretend everything was normal. He must have known he only had seconds to speak.

"Then you've fooled us all," she sneered, surprised by the bitterness that nearly blinded her.

He opened his mouth.

She didn't want to hear him. "There's nothing I can do, or would do, for you. War's coming." The thought turned her bitterness into black sap, heavy and exhausted. War, again. She pulled on the edges of the darkness with her mind. The arena turned into Shifra turned into the hallway where she stood now. The power of the Unreal rippled under her skin. The control distracted her from the misery trying to cling to her.

Firian looked at her as if he knew what she was doing. The hallway turned into bridges over treetops and islands with waterfalls and far off deserts. He'd always loved the Unreal too. "It doesn't need to. I don't want to hurt your people. I just want you."

She scoffed, backing away. Her feet sank in the sand of the dune. She almost stumbled backward. "You killed everyone, and I'm being blamed for it."

"You? Why?" He didn't deny it.

She leveled a look at him.

Understanding lit his face.

It occurred to her that if he overheard her thoughts in order to prepare for the assassination, then he would know that she chose not to warn him. He already knew her choice, so why did he persist? Why did he want her this much? "Leave me alone," she said. "Don't drag me back here again."

"Or you'll kill me?" His face was hard to read. Sadness, amusement, and anger all barely surfaced one after the other in the blinding light of the desert sun.

She didn't answer. Which meant yes. She'd have no choice.

He raised white-scarred knuckles toward her face. She flinched away from his touch. He extended a finger in time to touch her jaw, but she shoved his hand away.

"I did what I had to do," he said in the same tone he'd used to describe killing the last Tanyuin Head, Sias Jairon. The only difference was a stronger note of sadness. "I don't want to hurt more people."

The repetition grated against her skull. It was meaningless, like a child's nursery rhyme. He'd proved himself more than willing to hurt her people. She was right not to keep him by her side.

"What you say doesn't matter anymore," she said, her strength spent.

A long silence stretched thin.

"I'll come for you," he finally murmured.

A threat? A promise? A declaration of love? His tone almost suggested that he said it to himself, not to her.

Open your eyes! She practically shouted the words out loud as she struggled to get out of the Unreal.

Then—victory!—she emerged and lay in the darkened corridor with Daelon again. He was fanning her face.

"I called for the doctor," he said steadily, though his eyes were tinged with the wild fear she had seen in them that day Torithians attacked her. "You fainted, My Keeper."

"I didn't faint. I'm fine."

"He'll check you out."

"I'm fine."

Daelon stopped fanning. "Were you...?" He hesitated, apparently not wanting to finish his question. Still he waited for a response.

"I haven't seen him in weeks. He forced me to stay and talk to him. I told him nothing. We're nothing." The confession came out quickly and angrily. Somehow the truth would get out anyway. It was best to rip it off like wax. He helped her carefully to her feet.

Running footsteps sounded through the hall. Two men jogged toward where Kiria and Daelon stood—probably the doctor and an assistant.

"She'll be all right," Daelon assured them, raising a hand. Then he looked at Kiria, speaking so only she could hear. "You'll be all right."

47

FIRIAN

FIRIAN TOOK A TENTATIVE STEP. He could walk today, but he hated the weakness in his limbs. His sinews trembled a little when he put weight on them. Still, he preferred to focus on that than anything else.

Forty-two people.

And Bard gone.

Kiria wouldn't see him.

Rian was dead.

And he had killed forty-two people.

He jumped up and down, testing his legs. The effort burned his calves in too short a time, but he kept going anyway. The headache started to return, and still he kept jumping. It wouldn't take long to get back in shape. He'd devote all his time to it.

No, not all his time. He had to get Kiria back. He would come for her, just like he promised. Despite the pain and accusation he'd seen in her eyes the day before, there was care and desire too. She wanted everything to be all right between them. And she was good, maybe even forgiving. He jumped faster.

A cramp in his calf made him double over, cursing. Stars spotted his vision, along with all the images he tried to block out. Gripping the sheets on the side of his bed with one hand to steady himself, he replaced the horrible images with her. Her hair, her eyes, her heart-shaped chin...

"Feeling better?" Belik stood over him, favoring his good leg.

Firian stood, letting out a breath. "Yes."

"So maybe we can finish that conversation, hm?" Belik didn't wait for an answer, but went out into the office.

Firian followed. The room smelled dusty and abandoned. A large scrap of green fabric caught his eye. It was the new addition from Archer's Point, part of their flag. It lay next to the green of Raewhith and the yellow of Imlin.

Belik settled into his usual chair across from Firian's. Firian eased into his seat, rubbing his hands along the armrests.

"I've been directing things in your absence," Belik started. "A few of the troops were hurt in the fight, but not many. All the burials are complete. I've been preparing for our counter-strike."

"I never authorized a counter-strike." The past days, maybe weeks, were a blur. Had he said something in a moment of delirium?

"It's the only way to move forward," Belik said, not minding him. "If we allow this to stand, it means the end of your reign."

Firian regarded him darkly.

Kindly, confidentially, Belik leaned toward him. "I know you can take on an army by yourself, but clearly you can't do it over and over again. You're a human, not a god." He paused. "You know I could help you. Having someone else with your abilities means we could be twice as powerful. Think of that!"

Firian ran the three flags through his fingers, feeling the rough fabric, checking his fingertips for dyes. He didn't answer.

Belik continued with some derision in his voice. "A strike against Brithnem would be tricky, but they're not as secure as they claim to be. The outer edge farmland and the docks are the most vulnerable."

"What do you want to do, scare them?" Firian wanted revenge as much as anyone, but even he hadn't considered taking over Brithnem in the name of the Academy. It was an impossible target.

Belik shrugged one massive shoulder. "You've seen how easy it is to control a city." His eyes fell on the copy of the Scroll lying on the desk. Its pages were warped and yellowed, its stiff cover propped up with Brett's note. "Brithnem is particularly religious. In three, four steps, it could be ours."

Belik's meaning was slow to connect in Firian's mind. "If that's true, then why didn't we do that during the last war?"

"You know why," he retorted. "Sias was a coward. He never knew what was good for the Academy. Tanyu deserve better." He gestured with a meaty hand. "They got better."

Firian pressed his lips together. Belik rarely stooped to flattery.

Take over the capital? That still sounded too outrageous to be true. His gaze darted around the room as he tried to process the idea. If he controlled Brithnem, he could rule with Kiria. The Academy *and* the Western Kingdom. The concept was so enormous that it confused him, but that might have been the lingering weakness from killing all those people. The idea felt unreal. A tantalizing thought experiment. A lesson in strategy. "What are the steps?" he asked carefully. He realized he was gripping the green and brown flag of Raewhith in a tight fist.

Belik blinked knowingly behind his glasses. Though Firian hadn't told him about the state of his relationship with Kiria, he felt sure Belik already knew. "You look tired. We could talk about this another time."

"No. It's all right." Firian released the flag, trying to seem nonchalant.

"I'm not sure you're well enough yet." There was a hint of challenge in his tone.

Firian lowered his eyebrows. "I'm fine. Tell me the steps."

"Does it bother you that your girl is there?"

"Tell me the gory steps," he growled.

Belik ran a thumb through a blackened score in the tabletop. "Threats alone might do it. Offer to burn the outer edge."

"Dreams," Firian offered. Just like they had done before. The thought was distasteful, but he knew that had to be part of Belik's strategy.

The Master nodded. "The palace next, from the sea. There would be no need to fight more than a few guards at the palace. Once the Keepers knew we were serious, we'd have them swear loyalty on the book." He looked again at the Scroll.

That was far too simple. He was leaving steps out. Even taking over Archer's Point had required killing the current leader, burning Hill House. Well, he hadn't strictly needed to burn it.

A vein at Firian's temple started to pound again. He shook his head. "No, that's... that's not enough." Simmering anger bubbled up inside him. Belik was always hiding something, always keeping something back from him.

"I admit it would be easier if you'd let me carry some of your weight for you."

Firian eyed him, considering. Killing was the only ability he'd ever had that was all his own. Belik hadn't taught him that. A sick kind of pride made him protective.

But Belik was right too. If they did get into another battle, or if the Academy was attacked again, it would be helpful to have someone else who could take the brunt of the fighting too. Obliterating Brithnem's forces had almost killed him. Had they brought a back-up force, he would have been useless to defend everyone. Bard would have been on his own. The thought made him bite the inside of his lip hard. Coppery blood leaked onto his tongue.

"It's directional," Firian admitted. "You have to be facing them in the Second Level."

Belik sat motionless, but his eyes were alive with anticipation.

Firian hesitated. Any measure of control he had over Belik came down to two things: the crown and this one skill. "That's it," he lied.

Belik's cheek twitched. "I taught you the Second Level," he said tightly, but didn't press him further. He stood. "Just say the word and we can be mobile within the week."

Within the week. Firian felt lightheaded. He wanted Brithnem like he wanted to fly: it was a stupid dream, no more than that. Yet here was someone claiming to have the magic words. He couldn't let himself believe it, or he would make a fool of himself.

Despite all his rational thoughts, his heart thumped hard against his ribs like a chased animal. "I'll tell you when," he said. He'd meant to say something else, not *when,* but the sentence poured out of him naturally. Desire for the Kingdom began to pulse through him, growing stronger despite all the reasons he knew it couldn't work, it wasn't smart, it didn't make sense...

You're a monster, Firian. The words came again. He wished he could claw them out.

Maybe Bard was right. Kiria had seen it too.

Maybe he was a monster.

The door clicked closed as Belik left. Again, the memories came, thick and fast—the faces of all the people he'd killed, Kiria's terror when he'd held her hostage, Hill House going up in flames, Master Jairon kicking against him as he smothered him in his bed. Sickness pressed against his throat.

They were right.

A blank moment of self-awareness stilled him. The sickness subsided. No anger rose up. Instead, he felt oddly calm. Darkness throbbed in his veins, his thoughts, terrible and powerful. Maybe this is where he'd been heading all along. He'd never meant to be a villain. He had just wanted to matter, to be the best, to get what he wanted and help other people with his power. Certain people, at least. He'd sacrificed his life for those things. The thing was, he still wanted to matter, to be the best, to get what he wanted. Now he just had to do it alone. His breaths were shallow as he considered it.

All right, then. I'll be a villain.

48

KIRIA

Jori, from across the table, took Kiria's glass and filled it with sparkling wine. He winked at the servant standing behind her who no doubt felt snubbed or ashamed at shirking that duty. Kiria didn't protest when he handed it back.

The atmosphere at dinner was tense. Kiria's mother had invited Chetana, although she wasn't normally invited to such intimate gatherings anymore. Daelon sat beside his mother, his eyes often on Kiria.

Atty was the opposite. He could barely look at her. It had been well over a week but the tension hadn't softened.

She took a sip of wine and spoonful of the hearty soup in front of her. It smelled like creamy onions and beef with the slight tang of fish sauce.

No one talked about the inevitable conflict with the Tanyu. It was heavy on everyone's minds, so she suspected they kept silent because of her. Well, not silent. Atty talked to Haved, Cúron to Parohim, her mother to Chetana. Jori slyly exchanged money with the servant standing behind him. Jori's latest passion was going to footraces on the beach and betting on the outcome.

When he learned the competitors' names, he asked everyone he could for information. Servants knew the most, he told her. He had competed in a couple of the races himself, but had placed very poorly. At least he would say so. She had gone down to see one of the races. Jori, shedding his embroidered vest for the occasion and running with his arms pumping more wildly than the rest, had finished in the middle of the pack. She was even a little impressed, but he had gone back to betting rather than running.

A guard entered the dining room, wearing full armor, including his helmet. He wasn't one of the two who normally guarded the door. The chatter hushed then died. "Please pardon the intrusion, My Keepers," said the guard. "We apprehended a Tanyuin man outside."

"What's his intention?" Cúron demanded.

"He wants to meet with you."

Cúron's eyes flashed to Kiria. "I don't think it's necessary for all of us to meet with him."

"With respect," interrupted the guard, "he says he wants to talk to you, My Keeper."

He, and then everyone else, looked at Kiria.

Her heart stopped for a beat. She set down her spoon. Was Firian here?

The reactions around the table ranged from accusation to protective kindness. Some of them must have sensed her fearful uncertainty, because several of the harder looks transformed into something more curious than angry.

It might not be Firian. It could be someone coming with a formal declaration of war, as though the events of the attack hadn't been clear enough on both sides. She straightened.

"We'll meet him now. In the Main," she said. No need to wait.

Chairs scraped back and everybody rose. Cúron whispered

something to Parohim, and Atty nodded to Reynard, his advisor. There was a tacit agreement that anyone in the room could come as they received the Tanyu. Kiria almost hoped they would all join her. When they observed her interaction with whoever it was, they would see she loved the Kingdom and wasn't itching to sell it to any handsome Tanyu.

In the end, there were a few who elected to stay behind, but most of them came, even Jori, who could rarely contain his curiosity. Normally the sessions in the Main bored him, but this wasn't a session. This was a Tanyu. Kiria wasn't surprised that he joined the small group as they trekked from the dim dining room through the sumptuous hall to the Main.

The three Keepers settled on their thrones. Kiria glanced down at her hands on the armrests. Beautiful. If it was Firian... It crossed her mind to change back to being plain. No, she would stay as she was.

"Let him come in," she called to the guard at the entrance.

Small against the massive wooden doors of the Main, three figures entered—a Tanyu flanked by two armored guards on either side. She knew in an instant it wasn't Firian.

Why had she thought it was? She would sense his presence getting closer if he came to Brithnem. And there were enough people who would recognize him that they would have used his name.

This young man held his head lower, keeping his eyes on the ground before him. His black hair was wilder, his skin darker than Firian's. A light beard covered his jaw. The guards had bound his hands behind his back. Unlike Firian, he didn't wear a long black coat. Presumably he had one, but the past few days had been hot. The knees of his dark pants were light with dirt, and his boots left crumbs of dried mud on the pristine marble floor. When they got closer, she saw the young man wasn't as tall as Firian, still strong but not as broad in the shoulders.

He looked more and more familiar.

The guard on the right grabbed the boy's arm roughly and flung him forward, at the mercy of the Keeper.

Immediately he knelt on one knee, his head still bowed. "My Keeper, Kiria..." His faltering voice echoed around the Main's empty expanse. The accent was lilting, foreign. Maybe Endrian.

"What is your name?" Cúron demanded.

The young man cleared his throat. "My name is Bard— Bardhon Tanery—and I..." He looked up and his eyes widened when they settled on Kiria. Awe glowed in his face. "I want to help you. With the war." He spoke as though he had almost forgotten what he wanted to say.

Kiria remembered where she had seen him. "Bard?"

He nodded vigorously. He didn't smile—he seemed too nervous—but his eyebrows rose hopefully.

She had heard of him. But what was he doing here? Was this a trap? She knit her brows. "How would you help?"

"I...um..." His dark gaze, almost completely black, moved briefly around the enormous room and then to each of the figures standing around her—Cúron, Atty, the guards, Chetana, Jori—before returning to her. He moved with some of the grace of a Tanyu, but he didn't have their trademark arrogance. In fact, his face turned ashen, and he dropped his eyes. His hesitation became pointed.

"This is ridiculous," Cúron muttered. The light in Chetana's eyes showed that she agreed with him. Cúron flicked his sleeves as he always did before he called the end of a meeting.

"Wait!" Kiria held out a hand to stay them. "He came to see *me*. I want to hear him out." She probably shouldn't have called more attention to the fact that this Tanyu was appealing to her rather than the other Keepers, but at that moment, she didn't care.

Bard looked up gratefully and a grin seeped sideways across

his mouth—a little glimpse of joy. It was a wide smile that split his face even though he didn't show teeth. He rolled his shoulders. One of the guards looked sharply down at him when he moved.

She nodded at him to continue.

"I just want things to be right again... between us and... I think you know."

He was talking about Firian. Neither of them wanted to use his name in case the mention of him snapped his tenuous thread of credibility. She nodded again.

"I've, uh, I've got a lot of information about the Academy and I think they need to be stopped. No bloodshed," he added quickly.

A muscle in Cúron's cheek moved with skepticism. Kiria wanted to be skeptical too, but found it difficult. It was odd, but she wanted to trust this strange Tanyu. His eyes were sincere rather than cunning. *He's a Tanyu. You can't trust them, especially under the circumstances.* Brithnem and the Tanyuin Academy were moments away from declaring war on each other. This could be a trick to gain information. If so, it was a clumsy one.

"Stand up," she ordered.

Bard hopped easily to his feet, his hands still bound behind him. The two guards moved in.

She regarded him. He had a nervous energy that showed in many small ways: how he blinked and looked around, moved his mouth, resettled his shoulders, shifted his weight... His very hair seemed mobile, full of static. Dirt smudged his cheek, and the faint smell of body odor wafted from him. He'd traveled far. How was he still so antsy? She'd made that trip before. It was a long and tiring one.

"You'll give us information about the Academy?" she asked.

"Yeah. Yes. Just don't kill him."

He sounded like her own thoughts the past few days. That

someone else felt the same way—or said he did—made warmth blossom in her chest. Could they really end this conflict with minimal damage to both sides? The idea tantalized her. Even if it meant publicly associating with another Tanyu, she would follow this lead. Serving the Kingdom wasn't about her own image, after all; it was about serving the Kingdom.

Kiria looked for a sympathetic face in the small crowd at the foot of the steps—Jori, who watched Bard with unabashed interest. "I think we should hear what he has to say," she said. "He knows a lot about the Tanyu—how the Academy's run. We could use him." She ran her thumb over her other fingers to steady herself. "He can stay in my wing until we find out all he has to tell us." She turned to the guards, avoiding everyone else's gaze. "You two stay with him. You can release his hands."

Silently, the guards obeyed.

Bard's arms fell to his sides and he flexed his fingers with grateful vigor. "Thanks... thanks! Thank you so much. I'll help you. I promise."

As soon as the guards led Bard out of the Main, Atty turned to Kiria. "You think we can trust him?" His expression was openly skeptical.

"I'm not sure, but if he is telling the truth, then we should listen to him."

"Do you know that young man?" Cúron asked, his tone accusatory.

"We've never met," she said. She had seen him before, though. Firian had shown her his image when they first started practicing in the Unreal, and his name had come up a few times in their travels. But she left all that out.

"None of us should meet with him alone," Cúron said, his

meaning clear. Atty nodded. "His appearance is too suspicious. He must have left the Academy immediately after the massacre of our soldiers."

"What information do you think he would have to give?" Daelon asked softly.

"I'm not sure," she replied, feeling the growing weight of all eyes on her. She hadn't engineered this meeting. She wasn't in charge of it. But she always stood at the epicenter of all the Tanyuin movement around Brithnem, and there was no way to move out of the eye of the storm. "Like I said, he'll know more about the inner workings of the Academy than we do. Something there could help us." Kiria longed to find out what Bard knew, but didn't want everyone staring at her while she talked to him. Nothing could look more suspicious than meeting with him alone, though.

"Is it safe to let him stay in the palace?" Atty asked.

"I'll set extra guards outside his room," she said, a little exasperated. Bard didn't strike her as dangerous, but she'd been wrong before.

Cúron stood, shaking his sleeves in that peculiar way. Kiria and Atty stood as well. "He can't be allowed to wander the halls," he said, with an air of finality. "Meals will be brought to him, until we can figure out what to do with him."

As the group began to disperse, Kiria called to Daelon. "Would you come with me to make sure that the Tanyu is settled into his room?"

His eyebrows rose just a fraction at the request. "Of course, My Keeper. Is there anyone else you would like to bring?" The question was a suggestion. Daelon understood her reputation well.

She thought for a moment. "The Calthwaites." Jori would take the edge off the conversation, and Atty could see that she wasn't betraying them by wanting to hear Bard out.

A fragment of bitterness lodged in her throat for a second as she turned to Atty. "Would you like to come with me to check on the Tanyu?" Her tone might have come off as haughty to compensate for sounding too indulgent toward Tanyu before.

His eyes darted over her face. If he read anything there, he didn't say it.

"Daelon's coming too," she said, in case his hesitation had to do with caution. "And Jori, if he'll come."

"Ha, he'll come," Atty said humorlessly.

Most of the crowd had disappeared through the doors on their way back to supper.

"Will you, too?" she asked.

"After dinner."

"Right. After dinner."

"Okay. I just won't stay long." There was always Haved to get back to.

Kiria, perhaps strangely, didn't feel bitterness toward Haved for eavesdropping on her conversation with Jori back in Charäkhnem. She'd had a good reason to worry about Kiria then. How could she have known the damage that her gossip would cause? No, it was Atty, her childhood friend, who had hurt her the most. Their relationship could never go back to its innocent beginnings, but it seemed right to reach out and try to repair the breach, at least. They would have to rule together for the rest of their lives.

The meal passed swiftly. Opinions passed freely. Most didn't like or trust the new guest at the palace. His appearance was too coincidental, his offer too outrageous, his focus on Kiria too reminiscent of recent events.

Across the table from her, Atty leaned over to his brother and said something in his ear. Jori's face lit up in surprise and he looked at Kiria, who nodded. A mischievous look crossed his face. With Daelon, Atty, and Jori in the room, she could count on balance, or at least something like it.

After dinner, she rose and went out with her serving girls. Daelon followed with the Calthwaites. There were several guest rooms in every wing of the palace, most situated near each other, so she knew approximately where Bard was staying. The small group didn't speak on the way there, although the air buzzed with questions and, from Jori, snarky comments left unsaid.

Five guards outside one room reminded her suddenly of Firian's last visit.

"We are here to see the Tanyu," she announced to the guards, who immediately let them all in.

The room was very like the one where Firian had stayed. A fireplace crackled, and the sumptuous carpet ended in stairs leading down to a private washroom.

At the announcement of the visitors' names, Bard bounced off the large, four-poster bed where he had been lying on top of the blankets. His eyes grew as round as plates when he saw them enter and his wild black hair stuck out in every direction, smooth with the dampness of a recent bath. Judging from the messiness of the sheets, he had been pretending to swim the backstroke.

His mouth moved with greetings and responses he didn't say aloud. Instead, he tightened his robe, Brithnem blue and purple. His Academy clothes lay balled in a corner on the far side of the bed.

Kiria avoided looking over at Jori, who no doubt was trying to catch her attention with a private joke. She held up her hand toward Bard in a peaceful gesture. "Hello, Bard. We're just here to see how you like your quarters."

His chest rose and fell, his nervousness palpable but fading.

"Very much. Thank you." He craned his neck to peer around the room as though to demonstrate how much he liked it all.

"Can I have the servants get you anything?" she asked. Bard was essentially under house arrest, so it seemed like a kind gesture.

The word "servants" seemed to catch him off guard. His eyes darted around the room with the alertness of a Tanyu, though with none of their predator instinct. "Could you—" He stopped, his cheeks turning darker. "Do you have cinnamon bread?"

Beside her, Jori beamed. "We can have that sent right up," he answered looking back and winking at Candrae, who left silently to fulfil the order. "Are you from Enderin?"

Now it was Bard's turn to grin. His wide smile split his face. "Yeah, yeah! I saw... I saw some Endrian stuff here. The trees in the hall."

"*Sachion* trees," Atty offered. His small contribution made Kiria glad. Atty wasn't withdrawing. He might even be open to peaceful talks with Bard after all. She wanted to squeeze his arm encouragingly, but refrained.

"Yeah," Bard said again. "They're wonderful. I've never seen them inside." In a moment, he seemed to remember whose presence he was in, and fell silent, shoulders stiffening.

Daelon stepped forward, formal as always, but he spoke warmly. "Enderin has been our strong ally for a long time."

Bard nodded rapidly. "I know. My brother... he fought in the Torithian War. Jac is his name. Jac Tanery." He said it as though he expected one of them to remember him.

"Jac Tanery," Kiria repeated, hoping Jac had made it out of that conflict alive. She'd never heard of him.

"Yeah, he joined the army a couple years ago."

"Why didn't you go back to Enderin instead of coming here?" Jori asked. His tone was curious rather than insulting, but, without knowing him well, it was hard to tell the difference.

"I wanted to," he began. "But I knew what would happen if I didn't do anything, so I thought..." He swallowed and left the thought unsaid.

Kiria didn't know that any Tanyu had emotions this transparent. Their training seemed to harden them all, or at least every other one she'd seen.

After a moment, he continued. "Someone needed to... make this right. Or stop it before..." It looked like he wanted to say more. His black eyes flitted to hers, dropped again.

"Well, we certainly want an end to this conflict as well," Daelon said kindly, breaking the silence. "If you can help us, then you are very welcome to the palace."

Bard gave a watery smile as the door behind them opened. Candrae was back with the toast. Her blonde head weaved by Kiria as she brought it to Bard, who could only nod happily at her, too overwhelmed to speak. The scent of cinnamon filtered through the room.

"We'll leave you for now," Kiria said, sensing he was out of words. He needed to rest after his long trip. "We look forward to hearing your ideas."

He took a crunchy bite of toast. His shoulders instantly relaxed at the taste. "Okay." His voice dropped to a whisper. "What... what should I call you?"

Atty looked at Kiria strangely, trying to interpret the question.

"My Keeper," Daelon replied, bringing his hand respectfully to his stomach in a bow that didn't materialize.

Bard bowed low from the waist. "My Keeper," he repeated, balancing the toast in one hand.

Jori glanced at his brother with a raised eyebrow when Bard bowed deeply to him next.

"We'll let you sleep. Welcome to Mon Párinath," Daelon said.

Everyone filed out the door, leaving Bard alone with his meager meal.

Jori bounded over to Kiria. "I think I like him," he said. "He's nothing like that other one."

On both counts, Kiria had to agree.

49

—————

KIRIA

BARD HAD BEEN at the palace for a few days, and still neither Cúron, Atty, nor the generals made a serious attempt to find out what he knew. It became clearer and clearer that they had no intention of taking his help. He was allowed to stay in the palace to appease Kiria, to make her feel like she was doing something toward the war effort, and nothing else.

She had brought up the suggestion to talk to him several more times, but no one responded. Suddenly meals and meetings and nameless appointments dominated everyone's schedule. So Bard was left alone.

Frustration built up in her as she sat at her vanity. Cúron, Atty, and Chetana wanted Firian dead. They weren't even open to other options. Justice demanded that she at least find out if there *was* another alternative.

Candrae leaned toward her in the mirror as she arranged Kiria's hair. "Is My Keeper well today?" she asked quietly.

Kiria forced her face into a neutral expression. She was too easy to read. A Keeper couldn't afford for everyone to know her thoughts. "Very well, yes." The rebellious streak that characterized her childhood rose up, furtive and exciting. "We have a meeting this morning."

"With whom?"

"Master Tanery. You and Vayci are coming with me." She'd noticed Bard's red-stoned ring when they'd met, so she assumed the title matched Firian's.

"The Tanyu?" Vayci's voice was small on the other side of the room where she trimmed the candles. Kiria saw her turn away, as though her question had been impertinent.

"Yes, the Tanyu. He might have information that will help us, and no one is asking him about it."

She glanced at the white-yellow light streaming in through the window. It was still early. Cúron would certainly be awake but might not see her in the hallway yet. The sooner they could meet with Bard, the better. Fewer prying eyes.

"It can be simple, Candrae," she said, touching the hair just above her ear.

Candrae finished rapidly, twisting her hair back from her temples and pinning it in a simple bun at the nape of her neck. The simplicity matched the purple-gray dress she wore, plain and therefore underscoring her Ability.

Vayci finished preparing the candles and fireplace and joined the two of them as they left the chamber. Bard's guest room wasn't far from her own.

She'd sworn to serve and protect the Western Kingdom. That's what she was doing, she reminded herself. Words and warnings swirled through her mind.

Do you have the courage to do what isn't safe?

"Tell Bardhon Tanery that I am here to see him," she told the nearest guard, heart thumping.

"Of course, My Keeper."

After her announcement, she and the serving girls went into the room. Dishes cluttered the open surfaces and corners of the floor. On the bed a boardgame and its pieces had been meticulously set up, though unplayed. The room smelled like cinnamon and old vegetables.

Bard had shaved his beard, which made him look younger. He was probably her own age, though, no more than twenty. "My Keeper," he said, bowing low and keeping his eyes on the floor.

She held back a smile. He held his hand exactly as Daelon had the other night.

"It looks like you're getting comfortable here."

His tan skin colored a little. "If you need me to clean up…"

"No," she laughed. "It doesn't matter." Between the ages of eleven and fourteen, Jori's room had looked ten times worse. The servants played betting games to determine who would clean it. She caught them at it once. "I've come to hear what you have to say about the Academy."

He looked up, then away again, unable to hold her gaze. He clasped and unclasped his hands as he stood before her.

"Please sit down." She waved toward the bench at the foot of the bed. It opened as a trunk for extra blankets and had a pillowed top embroidered with the same *laird* flower as the flag.

Obediently, he sat. She settled beside him.

Bard's nervous energy didn't wane. He twitched as though he wanted to hug his knees to his chest, but forced himself to stay still. Candrae and Vayci hovered by the door.

"Has anyone come to speak to you?"

He shook his head.

She pursed her lips in frustration at the confirmation. "I want to know what you came here to say. Can you tell us about the attack?"

He sucked in a long breath through his nose, lifting his chin as he did so. When he let it out again, he looked more composed. "Thank you." His eyes widened in fear. "My Keeper," he amended.

"Kiria when we're not out with the others."

He nodded, relieved—he seemed to do that a lot—but didn't revise her title.

"So you want to help us," she prompted.

"Yeah, yes," he said, catching hold of the opening she gave him. He balled his hands into fists in his lap. "I'm glad you came. I thought you, more than anybody, would know what I meant. I just didn't know..." He crooked his jaw, his gaze darting to the floor.

"If this makes you that uncomfortable, I can change." The Tanyu already knew her other appearance, so changing back wouldn't compromise security. "It's an Ability," she went on, "Original Beauty, but I can always go back if I want to."

"Beauty," he said, "is not a grand enough word." He blushed at his own boldness.

She smiled. Closing her eyes until the tingling sensation covered her, she became plain again. "There," she said, feeling deflated. "Now we can talk."

Recognition flashed across his face as he looked at her now. Had he seen her image as she had seen his, in Firian's mind?

"How well do you know Firian?" she asked, all pretense gone.

"Better than anybody, or most people. We were roommates." He seemed genuinely more at ease now that she wasn't using her Ability. "What about you?"

The returned question surprised her. She wasn't sure how to answer. "I'm sure you know we traveled together," she said carefully. "I'm not sure what Firian told you."

"Not a lot, but he was different when he got back. He thinks about you all the time."

A flush of regretful pleasure filled her cheeks. It was strange hearing about this from a stranger. His confirmation made her loss more real. "We got to know each other fairly well during the trip," she said.

"And you must have the Talent, or else he wouldn't think about you so much."

This nervous Tanyu understood more than he let on. "Yes," she admitted.

He watched his hands as he spread them over his knees. Bard was wearing brown and blue, she realized. Firian wore black even in the Unreal, but Bard was someone else underneath the Tanyuin training. "I don't know you, really, but I figured you might be the one to talk to about... stopping him. Because you probably care about him. Do you, at all?"

"I don't want to kill him. So you are talking to the right person."

His mouth quirked. "He's... he's done some terrible things. I know that. I know he has. I was there. But I thought we could make it right, you know?"

"When did you leave?" she asked softly, guessing the answer.

He gulped and for a while he was silent. When he finally answered, his voice was quiet, almost a whisper. "He's gotten more afraid, lately. Which makes sense. There are people out to get him. But it's made him different." He paused again, unwilling to go on. He flexed his bare feet up and down.

She felt the weight of the silence. If Bard left when she thought he did—after the Kingdom's attack—then explaining all that could feel like he was betraying his friend to the enemy.

"You said he needs to be stopped," she prompted.

"He does." The words came out flat and sad.

"Why do you say that?" The Kingdom had their reasons, but Bard's might be different.

"He's... I think he's panicking. But it's made him..." He trailed off again, tipping his head toward the ceiling as though he could find answers there.

"Power hungry?" she offered. "He was always like that."

"Yeah," Bard agreed. They smiled at each other, the instant bond of people who had the same intimate knowledge that they'd never shared before.

She needed to ask what Bard knew about the attack, but he didn't seem ready. "I think we're on the same side, Bard."

By the door, Vayci shifted her weight. Bard's sharp eyes noted the motion.

"But," she continued, "he killed our soldiers."

"You attacked us," he said very quietly.

"After Firian took over Archer's Point."

Neither of them seemed to like this exchange at all. She felt her dinner roiling in her stomach, and Bard looked queasy too.

He scratched the back of his head, almost as though he were clearing his thoughts. His black hair spiked even more. "I told him not to," he said.

Kiria resisted the urge to squeeze his hand, to thank him if what he said was true. Firian needed more voices like his. "I found out too late," she said. She squared her shoulders at him. "What made you leave?"

His brows lowered and jaw clenched. After a while, he said, "I tried to stay, but... It was a lot of things. The day your people came, I couldn't..."

"Couldn't what?"

When he finally looked up at her, his eyes shone glossy with tears. Her eyebrows shot up in surprise. "Did I do the right thing?" he asked.

The question reverberated inside her too. *Yes. You got away. We need to stop him. We're in the right and he's in the wrong.* But all the words rang false. Right and wrong, good and bad, didn't describe Kiria versus Firian. Both terms described her, and both described him. The difference was the choices they made, the side they took day after day. "I don't know," she said finally.

"It's just, you know, he's... he's like my brother. And I thought, if I need to stop him, I had to come here. That maybe you would understand."

"I think I do." She gave a sad smile.

Bard turned to face her, and their gaze connected in understanding, as deep as coming home to family. The strength of that understanding startled her.

He warmed up to the conversation as though he had held it inside him, just waiting for somebody to listen. "I want him to change," he said. "To go back to how he was, or more. He could be better."

She wanted the same thing, but that was looking more and more impossible. How could they stop him without killing him? Did they imprison him? Exile him? Replace him with someone else? Or would he listen to two people who cared about him, and give up this ridiculous quest for control?

"What do the other Keepers think?" Bard asked.

The change in direction was noteworthy enough that she felt they had strayed too close to something Bard didn't want to talk about. A secret about Firian? She burned to know what it was, but she'd have to earn Bard's trust first.

"Well," she said, "you can see that no one else will talk to you. Understandably, they don't like Tanyu at the moment."

He nodded again.

"Hopefully they'll try to get to know you."

"Like you're doing," he said.

"Mm hm."

"Do you trust me yet?"

About to say no, she stopped herself. She did trust him for some reason. He seemed completely ingenuous, with none of

Firian's calculated responses. It probably wasn't a good idea to let him know, in case she was wrong.

"That's okay," Bard said after she paused.

"I want to," she said, and smiled. "But first you have to tell me what you know about Firian and the Academy."

He chewed his bottom lip, considering. His shoulders twitched as he thought for a long time. The secret wanted to come out. Kiria waited, perfectly still. "You don't want to kill him either?" he confirmed.

"Not if I can help it."

"He... Firian, he..." Bard cracked his neck, stalling. "He can kill, um... I don't know how, but he can kill people just by looking at them."

Heat flooded her body, disbelief, fear. "Just by *looking* at them?"

"It's something with the Unreal, obviously, but I've never heard of it. I don't know how it works."

Her gut sank. Firian was even more of a threat than the other Keepers realized. How could she justify a plan that would keep him alive now? Their only hope was negotiating until he was on their side, with terms phrased like an ultimatum. Break this agreement and it would mean instant death. But if he could kill someone with his mind, then who could they send to carry out an execution? Her head swam.

"We'll figure out something," she said, just above a whisper. But she didn't know whether even a Keeper and a Tanyu could figure out a way to save Firian from himself.

50

FIRIAN

EVER SINCE FIRIAN agreed that they should capture Brithnem, Belik seemed charged with tireless energy. "Tanyu originally *were* the army for the Western Kingdom," the Master explained as he led Firian out of the barracks. The stone walls, far sturdier than the wooden ones, had been completed while Firian battled the fever. Bright morning light washed them white. "Bad leadership led us away from that position. It's always been something we deserve, that we could do."

"I know." A clump of gray fur caught Firian's eye. Another dead rabbit. He frowned.

Men and women scurried out of their way as they strode out into the light of the field beyond. It was harder now to tell who used to be a Torithian pirate. Most had grown out their hair. A couple still insisted on shaving their heads, but many of them didn't bother to continue.

"Didn't we want to expand to other nations besides the Western Kingdom, though?" Firian asked. He'd heard their history before. "We could do more that way."

"Make more money too," Belik growled contemptuously. "The Amir hated us for it. That and a lot of other things. Can you think of an Amiran hero, anyone who turned a battle or saved somebody? No? That's because they're all Tanyu. Corso, Naedra, Anewa... Of course we wanted to expand beyond the Western Kingdom, but we deserve to rule there more than anywhere else. Amir are jealous, and pissed that we don't waste our time memorizing the Scroll. Have you heard of Original Plan, Firian?"

"Yes." This wasn't the first time Belik brought it up. They were a radical group that hated Tanyu. They used the word "Original"—like Kiria's Original Beauty or Firian's Original Talent—to suggest that they had some extra ability, like understanding the will of God. There had been a fierce conflict in the Unreal between the Tanyu and Original Plan before Firian was recruited.

Belik cursed the Amir in an undertone. "They were a gory scourge when I was your age. And now they practically rule the place."

They took the dirt path through the shops that led back to the Academy, dark in the near distance. Firian's legs had tired from a hike that would have been nothing to him mere days ago. He forced his breathing even.

His decision to assert control in the Western Kingdom was about respect for the Tanyu, not revenge against the Amir. Belik was harping too much on the past. Firian didn't need these explanations. "I don't think they ordered the attack on the Academy."

"The vote, Firian. Use your head!"

Firian ground his teeth, biting back a reaction. Maybe Belik was right. He had assumed that the male rulers had banded together, as they often did, in spite of Kiria's protests. She must have protested on his behalf. The thought made him wish he'd seen it. Now his breathing had little to do with their swift walking pace.

Belik limped quickly between the standing carts that choked the road. A two-week trip required provisions for three. With a small army on the move, the trip wouldn't go as quickly as it would when Firian was alone. Firian edged through, glad it was warm enough not to wear a jacket that might catch on the wheels.

Belik started explaining the waves of transportation and logistics the army would implement, but Firian was barely listening now. They had already talked about the big ideas—the outer edge, the demands, the almost peaceful transition, the banishment of the Amir. It was all quite simple. They hardly needed an army at all. The existing leaders would pay homage and tribute to the Academy, obeying their demands but continuing to function in their current roles, subservient to Firian's will.

He planned to solidify the plan through Kiria, but he kept that part to himself. Belik might see that as weakness, after all his warnings about her having power over him.

As the dirt road sloped upward to the main entrance to the Academy, Shiro came out through the main doors. His stare flashed first with fear, then hatred. Firian returned his gaze long enough to show he wasn't intimidated. Shiro was Rian's good friend. Was. Firian found himself picking at the skin around his ring again. He stilled his hands and paced into the castle with Belik.

He allowed his mind to drift down into the Unreal. Where was Kiria? She wasn't hard to find. Her imaginative mind glowed like a new color. She came into focus, beautiful and windblown, walking. Firian stayed hidden. Her surroundings were slower to appear—they mattered less. In fact, they didn't matter at all, except to flesh out the picture. Sand, water, sky. She was on the beach, her expression serene.

She had extra guards around her. That made sense, since she

had been attacked near the beach when she'd been struck by a Torithian arrow. Had Firian really learned about that in World Events less than a year ago?

There was someone else too. It took Firian a moment to tear his attention away from Kiria to realize that he knew this person. It was just so radically out of context that his mind couldn't make the connection at first. He was so constantly on his mind that Firian could barely distinguish his presence from his own thoughts sometimes.

Bard.

Bard was there with Kiria. What was he doing in Brithnem? A confusing storm of emotions raged through him. Bard talked about his family back in Enderin all the time. Why didn't he go there? Firian thought he remembered Bard telling him where he was going. But Firian had barely been conscious at the time. His memory could be playing tricks.

The two of them walked side by side, not close. Bard didn't wear Academy black, but something else. Something breezy but fine, as though he'd gotten it at the palace. Was he staying there?

Firian struggled to understand. He felt wrong, almost dizzy.

Bard was in Brithnem. With Kiria. Jealousy flashed through him. Kiria was Beautiful for him. Clearly they weren't in an official meeting. He studied their hands, their body language. All innocent.

What was he thinking? Bard would never go after Kiria in a romantic capacity. He had to have gone for a different reason.

You're a monster, Firian.

Had he... defected? Turned his back on everything the Academy stood for? Turned his back on *him?* It didn't seem like Bard to help the Kingdom kill him, but what other explanation could there be? Rage and betrayal ripped through him like a wound.

Just before the surface of reality, he screamed with fury. The corners of his eyes were wet with the sheer force of his anger. They'd left him—*left him*—and now they were conspiring against him. He was shaking.

"...ready tomorrow." Belik's voice seeped back to his thoughts.

"What?" he snapped. His vision blurred.

"We'll be ready to move tomorrow."

It felt like someone was grabbing his throat, choking him. Bard was in Brithnem, and the Academy's forces would move tomorrow. The possibility that the Keepers wouldn't agree to their demands broke through for the first time—a thought he hadn't allowed before. What if this conquest wasn't bloodless? He could save Kiria. She was valuable enough to bargain with. But Bard?

He couldn't swallow, couldn't breathe.

Belik came into focus near him. He stood close, as though shielding him from prying eyes in the hallway. Which hallway? Which way had they come? "Firian." He frowned at him, looking genuinely concerned. "Get yourself together. Do you need to lie down?"

Firian bared his teeth.

Belik raised his chin knowingly, brought it down in a nod. "We'll push back the departure one day. You need to rest." He was again alive with control as he turned away from him, shouting at various people to delay their preparations.

One day. That wouldn't nearly be enough time to come to terms with what he saw.

51

KIRIA

Four guards seemed excessive.

Kiria and Bard walked along the beach behind Mon Pári-nath. Despite the grim soldiers around them, Bard's grin hadn't left him since they reached the sand. Shoes dangling from his right hand, he looked out at the ocean as though he couldn't get enough of the sight. His toes dug into the wet sand with every step.

His happiness was contagious. Kiria found herself letting go of her spiking worries too as she gazed out to the hazy white line where the sky met the calm sea on the horizon. At that moment, Bard's horrifying information about Firian didn't matter. At that moment, she could forget.

This was a false peace—no, just a temporary one—but she relished it.

Bard turned to her, a breeze shuffling his wild hair. "This is great," he said. "Why are you being so nice to me?"

"You've been helpful," she said easily. She didn't feel that she'd been that nice to him. After all, he'd been relegated to his room alone for days except for when she asked for information. This was the first time he had been allowed to go outside since he arrived. If he was from Enderin, it made sense that he missed the sea. The Academy was landlocked. She'd missed the soothing splash of waves when she traveled over the mountains —the sun glaring almost too bright on the water, the smell of salty air, fresh seafood...

Bard pried his eyes away from her. Since they were outside, she had worn her Beauty. After a few conversations, though, Bard seemed much more comfortable with her than he had been. His uncertain words and nervous tics had settled into greater confidence. He gave information piecemeal, as though trying to figure out what could help and what could hurt his former friends. The idea of doing the wrong thing haunted both of them, simmering just below the surface. That nagging doubt that they were betraying people they cared about. So they treaded carefully.

"I used to swim all the time," Bard said, looking over the water. Despite living near the ocean, Kiria rarely swam. "I'd have competitions with my brothers and sisters. Jac." He turned around to see if she remembered the name from the other day. "I was pretty good. But I haven't done it in ages." He moved his jaw as though he were chewing on something.

"I think it'd be all right if you wanted to swim," Kiria said, glancing at the nearest guard for confirmation. He remained stone faced, which she took as a yes.

Bard smiled wide. "You sure?"

"Go ahead."

Kiria settled herself on a boulder nearby as Bard carefully folded his shirt and shoes in a pile and leapt headfirst into the water, not bothering to wade out first. Twenty breaths later, he reappeared, breaking the surface gleefully and shaking his hair like Jori did after it rained. Then he went back down. He made it look easy, as though he were a sea creature himself, full of joy.

"What are you doing down here?" When she spun, she

saw Atty, hand in hand with Haved, walking down the steps in the grassy embankment toward the sand. He carried a satchel in his free hand, perhaps food for a picnic. Two of the guards parted to let them through to the beach.

Though Kiria didn't come down to the shore as often as she'd like to, Atty frequently did. He enjoyed being alone in nature. Or alone with Haved. She suspected his new favorite was both.

Haved saw Bard first. "Oh, look," she said. "Is that the Tanyu in the water?"

Bard was far out now, but his hair gave him away.

"Yes," she replied, an edge of defiance in her voice. "We were talking."

Atty made a noncommittal noise.

"He keeps giving helpful intelligence."

"And you believe what he says?" Atty asked.

The question stung. "He said that the Head has a new ability that could change our odds in the war."

"Positively?" Haved asked. The word was delicate in her Charäkhni accent.

"No."

The two of them didn't come close to the rock where she sat, their distance mirroring the distance she saw in Atty's eyes. But he had to hear this.

"Atty, come here." She waved him forward. "This is serious. He said that he can kill people... with his mind." It sounded almost silly when she said it.

"Isn't that what the Academy is for?" Atty asked, a little irritated.

"No, this is different. He can just look at someone—they don't have to have the Talent—and they'll die."

"He just looks at them?" Haved knit her brows.

"I don't exactly understand how it works, but Bard told me about a Torithian—"

"I think he's messing with your mind, making you afraid," Atty said, shifting the bag in his hand, clearly ready to leave. "You shouldn't listen to them."

She stood and faced the couple. "He's given us good information. The layout of the Academy."

A splash sounded in the distance, and a laugh.

Atty was unmoved. "Why do you trust them? Why do you side with them?" His voice was strong, no slurring at all. "You're becoming friends with this Tanyu. Do you meet him in the Unreal too? That didn't work out last time. It's like you're trying to join the Academy."

She blushed angrily. "I'm trying to do the right thing, Atty," she said, glaring. "And you were the one who wanted to join the Academy when we were little. Don't pretend you don't remember. I'm just trying to make sure that we have all the facts before we rush in and kill people. There's nothing wrong with that."

"There is when our people get killed instead," he said softly.

Her mouth worked. "You know I didn't mean for that to happen."

Atty gazed back at her, as though he were embarrassed on her behalf.

Kiria's mouth went dry, but she couldn't think of anything else to say. Miserable, she sat on the rock again.

Haved put her hand on Atty's broad shoulder and leaned close to him. "I think I see a place over there," she said, apparently unruffled by her husband's tense conversation. Haved had the kind of calm that Kiria aspired to.

As they headed across the beach, Kiria looked back to the ocean, where Bard still splashed in the waves like a ten-year-old. How could he find joy in this moment when, to her, everything seemed so dark?

She hadn't even thought about meeting Bard in the Unreal. As a Tanyu, he had the Talent, but she hadn't considered it. Firian and the others who came to the palace held it like a precious secret. Bard's ability must be an aspect of his personality that he didn't cultivate to the exclusion of everything else. She glanced at his neatly folded shirt, golden tan this time, lighter than his skin.

Even surrounded by guards, she felt alone. Without the comfort of friendship, she kept all the accusations and pressures inside her, packed close, insulating her from the world until she felt that she was looking in from outside. Bard was a new friend because she needed one.

The warm breeze blew across her face. She breathed it in. She'd never been good at choosing romantic relationships. There was Tanis the guard-in-training, Anton the soldier, and Firian the Tanyu. Why couldn't she find someone kind, who loved her as she was? Instead she was apparently drawn to arrogance.

Loud splashing announced that Bard was trudging happily back to the shore. The sun glistened on his dark tan shoulders. His smile was blissfully happy. When he arrived on the beach, he looked a little out of breath, judging from his back's rising and falling. Other than that, he was surprisingly still. He didn't seem so ghostly or antsy anymore. This was a glimpse into who he was away from the Academy, from Brithnem, from all those things that had tried to define him. It was clear the Tanyu had only done that poorly. It was strange that the two of them shared so much without actually knowing each other. They both cared for a dangerous, broken young man enough to put their reputations on the line for him.

Part of her wanted to ask Bard more about Firian's new killing ability, but a sense of peacefulness fell over her. The sea stymied any more serious talk. The rhythm of the waves was like the rhythm of her blood. She sat silently for a good while. Nearby, Bard did too. The sun warmed her feet around her leather sandals as they looked out at the Kheltor Ocean.

The sky changed slowly as they watched it. Bard was the first to move. He threw on his shirt and walked back toward Kiria. She felt the guards tense around her.

He nodded before he spoke, that odd, quick nod he always did. "This has been the best. The best."

"I'm glad you liked it."

"Would it be okay to do this again? Or... it doesn't have to be tomorrow or anything, but I really loved this."

"Sure." She had loved it too. A moment of peace, away from Firian, away from judgment, away from all of it.

His eyebrows darted downward. "Don't you have other things to do?" He asked the question as though it had just occurred to him that a Keeper shouldn't be able to give him any time at all.

"I always do. But I'm the only person who will talk to you, so it's probably a good idea to get all the information I can out of you." She gave him a teasing, sad look.

He caught a glimpse of Atty and Haved, who were enjoying their meal almost out of sight along the shoreline. "They don't believe me, do they?"

She stood. "No, but they will eventually."

"You believe me, though?"

"I do."

He nodded, more slowly this time, and they started to walk back up the steps to the palace. It rose above them majestic, wreathed in gardens. The domed Amiran Academy sprouted up on the left. Kiria wondered if Daelon was inside reading.

"I think I saw you brought Indisfate all the way from the Academy?" she asked Bard. "That didn't look like a palace set."

He beamed. "Yeah! I play all the time. Used to." His face darkened. "Before the war, especially."

"Were you there?"

It was clear what she meant. *Were you there when all the Kingdom soldiers were massacred?*

He sucked his teeth. The sun shone on a black freckle directly on top of one of his ears. "Yeah. It was awful." He scratched the back of his head. A few droplets sprayed in her direction. "Oh, I'm sorry!" he cried, holding out his hands. He accidentally touched her arm and he yanked the hand away as if she burned him.

She waved away his apology. "I'm fine." The lawn grass gave way to paved walkways. "Did you see him?"

"I'm with him all the time." He bit his lip, amending. Not anymore. He looked down at the bright path in front of his feet.

She waited in anticipatory silence.

He twisted his fingers together before continuing. "They came into the Academy," he said in an undertone. "I guess you have to know what happened. They came in, and Firian—" He paused, glanced at the guards, then at Kiria, who nodded encouragingly. "I was with Firian. He asked me to be there, so I was."

Kiria tried to picture Firian asking Bard to be by his side in a fight. Was Bard a better fighter than he let on? He did have surprising skills, like his adeptness as a swimmer.

"They came in from both sides. We all knew they were there to kill him, so... we had to defend him, you know? We all had our jobs. But then we got trapped downstairs. I was afraid..." He closed his eyes to steady himself. "I was afraid that there were too many. None of them had the Talent." It was almost as though he was talking to himself now, getting out the images he'd held with him. "There were so many in that tight space. I thought it might be over, that there was nothing I could do. Firian was fighting, and the rest of us." He seemed to remember Kiria was there, maybe thinking of the map he had provided her the day before. "There were even more coming in on both sides."

She felt a confusing swell of pride at the idea of her army doing their job so well, overwhelming even the Tanyuin Academy. Of course, if this were true, then how were they defeated? She pictured rows of blue and silver soldiers in a large room made of the same stone as the Tanyuin Head's office, where she'd stood in the Unreal. A little ashamed of the memory, she knit her brows.

"I thought that was it, that we were going to die. Or maybe barely win. We had some good warriors with us." Bard skimmed one hand over the top of a hedge, still not meeting her eyes. "I tried to help, but Firian wanted to take them all at once. I didn't think he could."

She found she was hardly breathing. Firian took on her troops *single-handedly*?

"And then"—Bard squeezed his eyes shut, his voice hitching —"he just closed his eyes and the whole room felt tight, like my heart wouldn't work right. And... everyone just died. They just died. There was screaming."

A lump rose in her throat.

Bard's hands traced parts of his own face in a haunted way, as though he remembered something about the way they died that he couldn't say aloud. His words thrilled into heavy quiet. Birds chirped in the trees. Their footsteps sounded loud over gravel.

Was that the moment she had thought Firian died, when he killed all those men? Had the process hurt him somehow? But Bard had subsided into a profound melancholy, and she doubted he would say anything more.

They made it all the way to the palace before either of them spoke again. She hated to leave on this dark note. Bard was something positive in her life right now, even though her friend-liness with him made others suspicious. Let them think what they wanted. "You'll have to show me how you play Indisfate sometime," she said as the guards began to conduct him back to his room.

"Whenever you want." He resettled his shoulders, back and forth, considerably lightened. But the worry didn't leave his eyes.

52

FIRIAN

Firian cracked his knuckles. When he squeezed his fingers together, small raised scars snaked across them. Only the slightest noises sounded behind him in the dusky pines. Anything louder and he would go back and remind his warriors what was at stake. If Brithnem knew they were coming, the Kingdom could plan for their arrival. If they planned for their arrival, more of the Tanyuin army would die. He let out a slow breath as he gazed out over the shredded clouds.

Under normal circumstances, Tanyu only made camp after dark, but the Torithians were having trouble continuing after the sun had gone down. After eight agonizing days of walking, he had finally conceded that tonight only, they could make camp early. A child could have gone faster than this new army. Firian's pulse raced when he thought of it. He went three times as quickly on his own. But he couldn't execute a full counter-attack by himself. He could fantasize, but it wasn't realistic.

A shadow rose next to him. Firian knew him by his presence as much as his shape. "Belik."

The Master settled on a rock near him. "We could have gone until the moon was up," he grumbled.

"I know. Gory Torithians." Honestly, he knew Belik struggled with the march too, despite getting one of the only horses, but he never liked to admit it pained him.

Belik shifted, looking over the rocky landscape. "Secrecy is the most important thing," he said, as though it were an admission. "Speed is secondary."

Firian pursed his mouth. Belik was right, but this delay bothered him. He couldn't have said why speed seemed so important. Maybe it was his pent-up energy, all that he had lost over those feverish days. Or he could be rushing toward what felt inevitable —his confrontation with Kiria and Bard—though he didn't know what he would say when he got there.

They didn't talk for a while. Soft sounds of camp filtered up behind them. A clank, a curse, a footstep. None of the voices were Tanyu. They knew better.

"I always worked in strategy," Belik mused. "It's been a long time since I've done something like this."

Firian drew his brows together. Belik was almost never forthcoming. So, he stayed silent, waiting for more.

"You could go mad around so many people," Belik growled.

Firian smiled at the small rush of warmth in his chest. He felt exactly the same way.

"You take after me, I think."

The mountains rose in front of them, stony with patches of green, growing black in the deep shadows. A chilly breeze blew past.

Belik angled toward him. "You're done with that girl, aren't you?"

"Yeah." It was mostly true. There was no need to tell him how often he still thought of her, how she dominated his thoughts of Brithnem, even now. How the only future he envisioned was one where he earned her adoration, and she told him it would be all right, and her arms weaved around him, and he pressed her to his body...

"Good. No distractions."

He realized he hadn't told Belik about Bard. He doubted he would tell anyone. No clear ideas filled his head at the thought. It was wordless pain.

"This will fix our problems," Belik said, stooping down to pick up a knobby pine twig. He ran a thick thumb over its rough bark. "We've deserved this a long time, and I could wait a long time." He caught Firian with a piercing look. Above his eyes, the clouds reflected in his glasses. "You were a godsend. You idiot," he said almost affectionately.

Firian scraped his heel against pine needles and mulch, digging a hollow that he covered back up. He didn't want Belik to be his only ally, but he was glad he had one. Belik was a powerful ally to have.

"Almost there," Belik continued. "Soon years of injustice will be... improved." He stood and clapped Firian on the shoulder. "Almost there." With that, he stumped back to the camp.

Almost there. He breathed. Almost to Kiria. The takeover moved his blood, but Kiria was the real goal. Firian could force people to give him what he wanted. He'd taken the Academy; he could take Brithnem too. But Kiria was different. He couldn't take her. He had to coax her, seduce her, make her see all he could offer.

Hadn't he tried all that? His words didn't seem to impress her. It was when he was out of his element, stumbling, vulnerable, that her eyes softened.

How could he get her to look at him like she did before? Was that before she realized how monstrous he was? How hungry? Need burned inside him, not only for power, but for the shadow of goodness that followed her and filled the shadowy places within him.

Maybe if he acted gentle and inviting ... What if he caught her when she was happy and generous, like that time in Shifra? The memory, once sweet and heady, tasted like ash.

She couldn't be fully his until she looked into his eyes and loved him. Then he would burn and she would burn and nothing else would matter.

He cursed, almost laughing. He couldn't lie to himself anymore and say she didn't have power over him. She did, it was true, but she wouldn't use it against him.

The clouds had disappeared into the dark blue of evening. She would be going to bed. Maybe she'd even be sleeping. Tonight, when he was sure she was asleep, he'd steal into her thoughts, kindly, and start to win her back.

53

KIRIA

KIRIA RECOGNIZED THE FAMILIAR WARMTH. Where was he? She turned around but everything had the haze of a dream. Knowing that her dreams met the Unreal, she solidified her surroundings so she could see shapes and lines clearly.

She stood on the Salt Flats. The empty stretch of land mirrored the sky above so it seemed like she was floating or walking on a still lake. Firian was a distant black line shimmering on the horizon, growing larger as he walked toward her. His coat swayed behind him. He wore more confidence than she had seen in their past few encounters. It was as if he expected her to welcome him.

Bard's words from the day before rushed back to her. *And... everyone just died.* Something Firian did made all her troops fall dead.

She was nervous, but something—probably something naïve within her—was sure he wouldn't kill her. As Chetana had predicted, his actions had hurt her, but now he probably wanted her to forgive him and take him back.

He was close enough to talk now. *Why am I not moving? Why don't I just wake up?* But she had the detached curiosity of a dream, yearning to know what would happen next, and that was all. It was as though she watched herself. She hoped that she wouldn't say or do the wrong thing, as she would wish observing another person in an important meeting.

When she looked down, the Salt Flats had morphed, just slightly, into actual blue sky. The change didn't surprise her as it should have. Firian stopped walking. His feet angled downward a little to show that he was hanging in the air too. One side of his mouth lifted, teasing, and he floated backward as she had done in the field. She followed him, swinging her legs in the expanse.

Firian increased his speed, flying through misty clouds. Tendrils of white clung to him and dispersed. She reached out to touch them but they dissolved, a spray of cool mist, before her fingertips reached them. Firian didn't seem to be going anywhere, just flying, enjoying the sky. The bright light made his eyes burn blue.

He halted. She couldn't stop before she collided against his firm chest. Unfazed, he scooped her in his arms and held her there. As though sinking into mud, he sank backward. The mirror of the Flats had returned. Or something that looked like it. Now it was a shallow pool of water that reached in all directions like glass. He leaned back into it. Warm water lapped at her feet, her ankles, her calves. She wanted to sleep in the comfort of the water and Firian's arms. She lay on his chest, feeling his heart beat beneath her. His warm breath played on her cheek and ear.

Maybe if they didn't speak but just held each other, it would all be all right. The moment felt like a memory, one that had to be told carefully, leaving out details that would ruin it.

Firian kissed her hairline. His touch had two effects. It made her want to stay, and it made her more conscious, which made her want to leave.

For a second, she lay very still. Then something in her hardened against him, slowly growing more upset.

As she started to wake up, finding her way to the back of her eyelids, she shuddered at the dream. Firian had actually been there. She was sure of that. He had engineered the dream as a nonthreatening way to get her to warm to him. Hopefully that was all he meant to do. With the semi-consciousness of a dream, she hadn't been thinking clearly, couldn't tell him off as she would have if she had been awake.

She opened her eyes in darkness. Dim shapes of the bedposts and draped fabric ghosted her vision. Slim moonlight came in through the window of her bedroom. All was sleeping beneath its bluish glow.

Bard's story came back to her again. Firian had killed all those people. She smacked her lips as if she had eaten something bitter. This back and forth was tiring. She didn't want to love him.

How could she guard herself against his advances? Was there more she could do before she slept to resist him? Or could she fight? As soon as the thought came to her, she shoved it aside. If Firian was an expert in anything, it was fighting in the Unreal. She would stand no chance. But surely she could improve in closing her mind against him. Tanyu had to have their methods.

She rolled over beneath the covers. The stalk of the candle on the bed table stood cold and dark. Her mind roiled.

After a few minutes, she sat up, folding the soft blankets over her crossed legs. There was one more person she could ask. Did Bard keep the same hours as Firian? Bard confessed to being Firian's roommate for a time, so it was possible.

She closed her eyes again and tried to remember what Firian had taught her about creating a space to meet, reaching out with her mind... It became easy to do with him, but she had never attempted it with anyone else. The palace hallway materialized around her, a setting she had created multiple times. Would she recognize Bard's mind when she came to it?

Yes, there it was! It was like meeting a familiar smell—not easy to describe, but unmistakable nonetheless. "Bard?" she whispered.

He flickered into view, his eyes puckered with sleepiness. Drawing the back of one hand across them, he frowned in confusion as he looked at her.

She realized she was plain again. She'd never intentionally used her Original Beauty in the Unreal. She wasn't going to start now.

"My Keeper?" he said uncertainly, more questions forming in his expression.

"Could you show me how to get someone out of my dreams?" She ignored how vulnerable the request sounded.

Bard blinked a few times and scratched his head. Studying his fingernails, he said, "Fir? Is it Firian?"

Fear? At first she was going to protest that she wasn't afraid, and then she realized that "Fir" was a nickname. The idea would have amused her if she weren't so troubled. "Yes."

"*Katah*?" he asked through a grimace.

"Yes."

"That's hard, yeah." His fatigue made him act more familiar toward her than he ever had.

"Did I wake you up?"

He shook his head widely, like a shaggy dog shaking water out of its fur. "No, I was, um... I've been trying to stay awake through the night."

"Why?"

He licked his lips, finding the words. "I left the Academy, so, I figure they might try to kill me. Dreams, you know? But I take naps during the day. Hopefully they can't find me then." She could tell he was trying to keep his lilting words casual, but true fear edged his tone. He gave a huge yawn, an honest one.

Watching him made her yawn too. His plan didn't sound foolproof.

He squinted as though the hallway were bright with light, but every time she had imagined it, she'd seen it at night, dark with shadows.

"So there's no way to prevent him from getting in my mind?"

"Sentries would do it," he said.

Dimly, she remembered what Sentries were. "We don't really have any."

"Then I don't know."

"Would he really try to kill you?" she asked after a pause. The idea made her shudder. Bard seemed so innocent, and he had been Firian's friend.

Bard's jaw worked. "I didn't think so, but then he killed Rian..."

"Who's Rian?"

"A Tanyu. He was there. At the attack. Just in the way, I guess. He didn't get behind him." Bard began floating absently above the floor. "He wouldn't kill me, though."

"Then who would? Why are you afraid?"

He looked at her as though he'd never asked himself the question, but, now that he did, he knew the answer. "It's Master Belik, I guess." He clamped his lips together and bit down on them. "Yeah, he'd do something like that. Say I was a traitor to the Academy or something. He'd do it."

The name lingered between them. Master Belik. She'd heard that name before. Wasn't he the one Firian left in charge of the Academy while he was fighting in Torith? This was the first time Bard had mentioned him. If he could kill Bard without Firian's approval, then he must have massive influence at the Academy. She tucked the information away.

Though the hallway was dark, the only light coming from the sconces along the walls, the colors seemed more vibrant in the Unreal. She'd missed this. To find someone non-threatening to meet felt suddenly liberating. She floated too.

His face split in a grin when he saw her do it. "Hey, look at that!"

She smiled.

"What else can you do?" he asked. Without waiting for a response, he shrank away to nothing and a streak of blue light shot across the hallway.

She gaped. "How did you…?"

Bard reappeared, holding a small ball of blue light in his hand. It licked up like fire but held its shape, reflecting the light oddly and casting wavy shadows. She realized it was made not of fire, but water. "This is one of the first things they teach. You know, once you have the basics."

"No, he didn't show me that." Had Firian been withholding things from her, or was she just not advanced enough?

"Here, hold out your hand." His blue light vanished and he held his empty palm face up. It looked almost black in the night-time corridor.

She did as he said.

"Then you picture it. Believe it's there."

She stared at her hand, the lines on her palm. She waved her fingers as though that would help the light appear.

He screwed up his face in confusion when nothing happened for her. He tested it in his own hand, the ball of light appearing and disappearing quickly once, twice. His face looked unearthly, underlit with blue. "Okay," he said, having an idea. "Okay. It can't just be the way it looks. You have to think about how it feels, or if it weighs anything. Focus on it like it's a real thing. Act like it's a real thing. That's when you stop thinking so hard. It'll work then."

She followed his instructions the best she could. A feeble blue glow grew between her globed fingers. She stared at it, mesmerized, then up to Bard, who was smiling. When her attention shifted, the light went out like a dying ember.

"That's all right," he said. "That was good! You're not a Tanyu or anything." He cut himself off, embarrassed. "I mean—"

"I know. That's fine," she said, stretching her fingers. "I'll practice that."

"There's a game with it, once you get it down."

"A game?" She was intrigued.

"Yeah, I used to play with some friends. Not Firian, usually. He was too serious most of the time. Other people."

That didn't surprise her. Firian was always serious. His focus, as he liked to say, made him the best. But it probably cost him some fun at the Academy. She'd not considered that people might have fun there, but Tanyu were people, just like everybody else. Bard certainly broke the stereotype.

"I do know how to play Indisfate, though," she said.

"I thought you wanted me to show you." He alighted on the rug.

"Show me how you play. Not teach me."

He scrunched his face in an impish expression, bothered and almost impressed. The board appeared between them, all its pieces in place. Bard changed the background subtly to a place she didn't recognize. It was a cliff of tufted grass that sloped down to the sea. The grass waved in the breeze, but she didn't feel cold. The air smelled like horses.

"I did that with Firian too," she continued.

Bard laughed. "I bet he hated that!"

"Yeah, I beat him."

He doubled over with high-pitched, barking laughter. When he straightened, he pressed the heels of his hands to his eyes. "Oh, that's wicked. I beat him too." Peeling his palms away, still gleeful, he looked at her. Mischief glinted in his eyes. "Okay, let's have a game."

———

BARD WON the first game of Indisfate. Kiria won the second.

She and Bard had both beaten Firian at this game before. Maybe strategy wasn't his strong suit. Maybe it was sheer force, in the Real and Unreal. If she could outthink him somehow...

The later it grew, the clearer their situation became. Firian—and Belik, from the sound of it—wouldn't suffer an insult like the Kingdom's attack on the Academy without retaliating.

She blew a breath through her nose as Bard magically put the pieces back again. The Vipers and Men and Falcons all moved, very slightly. At first it seemed a trick of the light, as though a new shadow had fallen across the intricate figures, but then she saw that they actually ruffled their feathers or stretched their bows or snaked out forked tongues. An unconscious smile crossed Bard's face as he looked at them. She hated to ruin his calm.

"Bard," she said quietly.

He raised his eyes to her.

"Has Firian used his... ability... any other time?"

A tiny horse walked across the game board. "A prisoner escaped, one of the pirates. That was the first time." He corrected himself. "The first time I saw it. But he knew what to do, so I'm pretty sure he'd done it before. Maybe on the island."

Her stomach clenched. "Is that it?" *Isn't that enough?* She picked up the Man gingerly and set him down. She couldn't will the pieces to their positions yet.

"That's all I know. I think he probably did it one other time, but I'm not sure."

"When?" She wasn't sure she wanted to know.

"Um..." He hesitated as if he wasn't sure how much she already knew. Bard understood that the connection between her and Firian was strong. "There was a... another Master who wanted to control everything. Yeah, so he almost killed him. A big guy. He was huge, so I don't know how Fir could have gotten out of it unless he just..." His voice faded away again. The Viper coiled around and around in a circle.

"It works on a lot of people, then," she said. The words were empty, but maybe they would jog some idea that could solve the problem.

"Yeah." His piece moved on its own to the correct spot.

Kiria recognized the same pattern he had used before to win the game. "What do you think he'll do now?" It was a question she'd avoided asking, but she couldn't put it off anymore. She needed to be a strong Keeper for her people. The Western Kingdom was far more important than one man, no matter who it was. She couldn't let anything get in the way of Brithnem's safety. Mercy had to have a limit.

Bard twitched one shoulder upward, shrugging. "What do you mean?" he muttered. Apparently, he didn't want to think about it either.

"Will he stay there or come here?"

"I left right after, so I didn't hear."

He paused, but she refused to play her turn.

"But you have a guess. You know him better than I do."

He gave his signature rapid nod. "He'll do something soon. He was sick for a while."

"When?" This surprised her. He hadn't seemed sick in the dream. But everything could be different in the Unreal. She could make herself plain when she was using her Beauty in the real world. Firian was so advanced, he could probably make himself look like anything he wanted.

"Right after the attack," said Bard.

She raised an incredulous eyebrow. "Didn't you leave?"

"Sometimes I know what he's doing anyway. Or I check, just check up on him." He waved at the board.

"Do you know what he's doing now?" she demanded, annoyed that he hadn't mentioned this before.

"Not right now." He seemed oddly hesitant as he drew figure eights on the floor in front of his crossed legs. Lines tightened around his mouth and eyes. He cleared his throat.

"Could you look?" Firian had the ability to spy on her, but she could never get the hang of doing it the other way around. He always knew she was there. But if Bard could watch him, that could be exactly what they needed.

Bard looked up at her meaningfully, chin tilted down. What if they both found what they dreaded? Even if Bard found Firian making a speech at the Academy about how he wouldn't attack Brithnem, they still couldn't trust him not to turn on them. He had that killing ability, so no matter what he said or did, he was a threat.

Was there anything Firian would trade, or someone he would listen to, in exchange for peace? Besides Master Belik, who seemed to hold some sway, the only options she knew were paying Indisfate on this cliffside. She searched her memory. Was there really no one else? Then she remembered Firian's sister, and their emotional reunion. She might be another one to add to the very short list.

"One of us should talk to him."

"Yeah, I know," he said, as though he had been waiting for her to say that, but hoping she wouldn't.

She moved her game piece. The Falcon flapped in her gentle grip. "We don't have a choice. This is bigger than us."

Bard's nostrils flared with the force of his intaken breath. Then he nodded again, more slowly this time. "Sorry I didn't do it sooner," he said quietly.

"I don't blame you."

He gave her a wan smile.

"But we have to do it now. We'll both talk to him." She couldn't watch Firian the same way, but she could get his attention. She was sure of that much.

A Horse ran off the board. Bard cupped his hand to lead it back where it belonged.

"Not at the same time, obviously," she continued. "Do you think he knows you're here?"

"I don't think so. I think I would know." The Horse settled in place.

"Separately, then."

Nothing definitive changed about Bard's breathing, but she suddenly noticed it. It seemed more careful. He was nervous.

"We have to," she said.

"We have to," he echoed.

When they looked at each other, they had a grim understanding. They would do it for the Kingdom. They would do everything they could, but Firian would choose his own fate. She prayed he chose the right one.

FIRIAN

FIRIAN TRIED to ignore the blisters on his feet. Surely they were bleeding into his boots by now. When they stopped, he would try to find running water and bind them. If anything, the pain reminded him of where he was going and anchored him to his surroundings. He'd grown too soft.

He jumped lightly up a cluster of boulders on the side of the path where his army trudged. Below him, heads bobbed as they moved by.

Higher than some of the smaller trees, he knew he was conspicuous, should anyone else be traveling in these mountains, and he didn't care. Belik would tell him he could just use his extra ability. The thought made his blood curdle, so he pushed it away.

Even at their worm's pace, they would arrive in less than two weeks. Brithnem. What had Kiria said? It meant Beautiful City, or something like that. It had been beautiful, he supposed, but he hadn't focused on that when he was there. Beneath its appearance was power, the kind of power he'd felt in his test with Tiev, when all the light and wind and intensity spiraled like a tornado.

He turned at the sound of a familiar voice. But it wasn't a voice. It was the Unreal. Someone was waiting for him. Quickly, he dove in.

Bard stood in their room back at the Academy. For a mad second, Firian wondered if Bard really had gone back, only to find most of the town and fortress emptied. He looked around the little room for the tell, the change. The bunk bed with its dirty sheets, the dresser, the candle, and even the faint scent of cinnamon and sweat were all the same. Bard scrubbed the back of his head, sending his spiky hair flying. Then he spotted Bard's wooden figure of Corso, the Tanyuin hero, on the window ledge.

"I told you to get out," Firian said, relief and anger battling for dominance.

"I did." The same edge of defiance that he'd had during their last interaction punctuated his response. "I wanted to see how you were, mate. You weren't... feeling good when I left."

An unexpected swell of emotion caught Firian by the throat. He swallowed it roughly down, waiting to see if Bard would admit where he had gone. Maybe he was going to tell him what he was doing at the palace.

"Is there a reason you came?" Firian prompted.

Bard's black eyes grew visibly nervous. "To see how you were," he repeated. "And to see what you're up to. I was thinking, Jac's in the army, you know, and I just... wondered about the Kingdom. I was hoping you wouldn't... after everything that happened..."

Firian fixed him with a glare. So that was it. Bard was trying to learn how he would retaliate because of the recent attack. He had officially gone to the other side. The side that had sent soldiers to ravage the Academy. That had tried to kill him. Firian felt his fingers tremble with rage.

Bard was the one friend he never thought would betray him. He'd doubted Kiria and Belik and all the rest, but never Bard.

That he would ask for information to give the enemy... Firian could barely see, his vision spotted black and red.

Bard seemed to realize Firian's intention the moment before he struck. He crouched to avoid a sheet of flame shot from Firian's hands. "Wait! I only—"

But the landscape shifted away from their small room at the Academy. The fire flared to nothing as the Pillars of Awel materialized, at least the way Firian had always pictured them. Impossibly tall stone pillars overlooking the ocean, with a four-posted room cut out of the top for spying ships.

Firian stood at the top of one of the pillars, Bard at the top of one nearby. Firian threw a dagger at him. It evaporated in the air, as he expected. He didn't mean to kill Bard, but to send a clear message: *Leave me alone. Take your gory questions and never come back.*

"Firian!" Bard wrapped one arm around the nearest post, as though he anticipated what Firian would do next.

The world tilted hard, tipping the two of them to the right. Firian almost tripped at the force of his own illusion, but he stepped carefully from the stone floor to the wall to the ceiling as everything turned around.

Bard hung onto a thin stone pillar holding up the roof, as though he thought the world would keep turning. From upside down, he stared at Firian, but didn't move to fight.

Firian hopped to the lip of the roof, the drop from that ledge now impossibly far, into the dim sky and out of sight. Above him, the dark ocean churned, its spray falling like light rain. He liked this. He just needed to give Bard a lesson.

The ocean released. As water fell with a roar, Firian jumped. The adrenaline of falling subsided into something like calm as the sky lightened around him.

He slowed and landed on the roof of Mon Párinath. Long blue and purple flags snapped around him. Toward the sea, the

Amiran Academy looked a perfect circle from up here. On the other side of the palace, a green lawn reached down to the city streets. Just like he remembered. It was close enough to the real thing. The only addition he made was adding grass in wide swaths along the flat rooftop, with walkways of stone along the sides.

Bard appeared in one corner of the roof, popping into existence like a bubble. He eyed Firian but didn't cower. Firian was proud of Bard's courage. What guarantee did he have that Firian wouldn't hurt him?

When Bard merely set his jaw, Firian summoned more fire. It burst from his hands in two thick orange streaks.

Bard stumbled back, struck. Firian's heart turned over. Recovering his balance, Bard conjured a shield of water. It was an elementary move, almost comforting. The water spread out as though as though it splashed onto a circular pane of glass, though nothing was there. Beads of it sprayed up and clung to Bard's face. That, or he was starting to sweat. As Firian's fire disappeared into the water shield, he realized that Bard hadn't gotten wet from the falling ocean. He must have disappeared in time to avoid it.

Firian's veins, raised and glowing red, felt like the firestream. Why didn't Bard fight back? Firian snapped away the fire. He'd try something new. One by one, he replicated himself until six Firians stood on the palace roof.

Bard's water shield evaporated. Without that barrier, Firian could see blood dribbling from one corner of his mouth. Not much. He would be fine. Bard's eyes widened as he looked from form to form, all identical, all staring back at him. "Firian!" he shouted. "Stop! I don't want to hurt you!"

Firian's mouths curved in a bitter smile. At last he got a reaction.

Bard's chest heaved as he looked around at the copies of

Firian. His face betrayed his belief that any one of them could strike if he wasn't paying attention. "Firian, where are you now?" His voice had grown hard-edged. He didn't mean which copy was the true Firian. That wasn't the right question. He meant in real life. Was he on the way to the capital?

"Where are you?" The words sounded eerie coming out of so many mouths.

They both knew the answer, but he waited for a few heartbeats, freshly aware of where they stood. If Bard were honest about going to Brithnem, at least Firian would know Bard hadn't changed as much as he feared. Firian clasped his hands behind his back as his Masters used to do, waiting patiently for the correct response.

For a second, he thought of warning Bard to get out of the city, but that would just alert him to their plans. So he stayed silent.

Quiet surged around them, as though there had been white noise during the rest of their confrontation. Now it was truly still, even breaths muted.

The implication was clear: *You betrayed me.*

And you're a monster, Firian.

They stared at each other, neither one backing down, though the longer they looked (Bard had chosen the center Firian to stare at), the more the silence gained the color of memory, and Bard's eyes rimmed red, and Firian started to fear that his own eyes looked the same from rage. Firian found himself wishing he could erase the past couple weeks completely, maybe the past couple months of his reign, and start over. At the beginning, he said he would do this right. That was why he had killed the previous Head. Yet here he was, having lost everything that mattered.

When no one spoke for a few beats longer, Firian opened his

eyes. Squinting against the bright sunlight on the rock, he cursed.

55

KIRIA

THE CONVERSATION at the session had exhausted her. Charäkhni trade agreement logistics seemed trivial compared to the secret project she and Bard were working on. Two days ago, Bard had tried talking to Firian first. When Kiria went to get information from Bard later that day, he didn't want to talk about it. He almost looked as if he'd been crying. That was so rare among Tanyu that her heart had jolted with fear—they were lost, Bard had told him everything, Firian was going to retaliate and kill them all...

Bard did admit that Firian knew he was in Brithnem, and then he said he couldn't go again. It wasn't new information that had broken his heart, after all.

Enough time had passed that Kiria hoped her visit wouldn't seem suspiciously connected to Bard's. The possibility existed that he would figure it out, but she had to try anyway. The Kingdom needed to know any plans he'd made against them. And the list of people Firian cared about enough to tell grew smaller and smaller.

Reaching her room, she startled to find that someone

already stood there. "Oh!" she cried. "Jori, where did you come from?"

"Here. That's what they tell me."

"I told the guards not to let anyone in tonight."

Obviously chewing on something, Jori gave a lopsided grin. "You underestimate my powers of sweet talking."

"They still wouldn't have—"

"They *might* have, but I got in a different way. Lots of ins and outs in this castle."

Kiria didn't know of another entrance besides... the chimney? She felt instantly foolish for thinking it. There was an emergency escape tunnel as well in all the Keepers' rooms, strictly off limits unless the worst were to happen. "Tunnel?" she asked.

He pointed at her, still chewing, as if she'd won a point.

Now that she looked, the knees of his blue pants looked particularly thread-worn. He'd also buttoned his vest, which he only did for some special occasions and, apparently, when he didn't want the front dragging in the dust as he crawled through a tunnel.

"You should know better than this," she said. He was nineteen and acted like he was nine.

"I doubt that'll happen any time soon," he said lightly. "There's a party just outside the palace wall tonight. Unsavory characters, flowing ale, non-royals. I thought you might be interested."

"You know I can't."

"I don't know that."

"I have things to do."

"Tanyuin things?"

She tried to stop the creeping blush. Her hesitation was enough of an answer. Had she promised never to see Firian again? She felt like she had. Well, this time it wasn't selfish. In fact, she'd have gotten out of it if she could. But the Kingdom needed information, needed her.

Jori's face fell. "I'm sorry Atty's treating you like an idiot, but you do run off to the Tanyu more than you should."

Her mouth fell open. "Excuse me?"

He raised his eyebrows almost into his hairline. "You want to invite the Tanyu too? I'm sure that would go over well."

"You don't know what you're talking about."

"I do, I do," he said, spinning on the balls of his feet to look at something at the side of the room. "You've told me."

But you don't know everything. You don't know that I'm dreading this meeting but I'm doing it anyway for you and the rest of the King-dom. She couldn't say any of that, so instead she said, "Jori. Jori!"

He redirected his languid attention to her.

"Do you trust me?"

He paused to consider the question, looking first at her, then around the bedroom, as though searching for an answer. Maybe he just wanted to make her squirm. If so, it was working. He met her gaze again. "I think," he said deliberately, "that the Tanyu irritate me, but I also think that you are one of the best people I know." In his eyes was a challenge, as though it was up to her to keep it that way. "So yes, I do trust you."

"Thank you," she said, the relief too obvious. "Okay then. I need you to trust me now and leave me alone. I have to do something."

"Will this something take all night?"

"I hope not."

"Then ask for Tanis Restino at the north gate when you're done and they'll point you in the right direction. I'll be there. Possibly drunk. You might want to tone it down a bit before you come." He scanned her with his eyes.

At the mention of Tanis, the first boy she'd ever liked and the first one who had suggested that her Beauty was all that mattered, she knew she wouldn't go to his party. Years had passed, but he still reminded her of bad decisions. Hopefully she was better at reading people now. Thinking of the task ahead, she wasn't so sure.

She nodded at Jori. "All right."

He headed toward the door.

"The guards will hate you," she said.

He turned around and winked. "They love me." When he yanked open the handle and let the heavy door settle into place after him, she heard him say, "Boys, you miss me?"

She shook her head, stifling a grin, and turned her thoughts to the task at hand. She'd played it over in her mind a thousand times. Firian was rarely forthcoming with information. Even on his best days, he preferred to keep an air of mystery about him. Now, with more at stake and less reason to trust her, he would probably stay as tight as a barnacle.

She bristled at the idea of coaxing the plan out of him in more devious ways. The best she could come up with was to appeal to his better side. It was naïve, and quite possibly wouldn't work. She knew that already. The army of Brithnem was at the ready if he refused to side with her, though she didn't want to use them, or even bring them up, if possible.

Somewhere deep inside him was a man who could see the value of peace. It had to be true. For a moment, she had the odd sensation of looking back at herself with pity, as though her failure had already happened.

She took a few deep breaths.

Reverence, submission, prayer. *Let there be peace in the Western Kingdom.*

The words sounded childish. Was peace even possible? With so many moving and vying groups, the possibility felt remote. But she still wanted the same things she had wanted as a child: peace, goodness, wisdom. Maybe it was good that she didn't have strong political instincts, that her vision for Brithnem and the rest of the Kingdom was so simple. Someone had to hold onto that vision.

Now, though, it fell to her to secure it by finagling information out of a dangerous man.

She shook out her hands and rolled her neck. She could do this. She *would* do it. If Firian really was planning a counterattack against the Kingdom, she might be their last hope of finding out.

Weight pooled heavily in her gut as the implication hit her. She had to do all in her power—*all in her power*—to get him to talk.

She blew out a quavering breath as she closed her eyes and wove a setting around her. She'd already chosen it. The hollow where the two of them had stayed the night after the attack in Raewhith. He had comforted her during a panic attack. She had bandaged a long sword wound down his back. She remembered him gazing bleakly at his sword sticking into the dirt, running his thumb along the crossguard. Red blood had soaked his bare back, and then the sash she'd used to clean it off. It was one of the only places where they had both been vulnerable.

The memory, oddly, was a good one. That day marked the first time she'd seen who he could be without his swagger and arrogance. She liked that version of him, the one who saved her from Torithians and spoke kindly to her when she didn't have the strength to keep walking.

As she set the little stream in place, and the rock where Firian had sat, a pang of regret or mourning struck her like a stomachache. She missed this Firian. Maybe she should have chosen a different place to meet.

A dark shape snagged her attention. Firian stood on the lip of the hollow. At the sight of him, she stumbled one foot back.

She hadn't called for him. He looked at her with a confusing expression on his face, at once glad, desiring, and careful.

Dealing with her imaginary scenarios already seemed easier than dealing with the real thing. Regaining her composure, she stood tall, reminding herself to breathe.

What was she thinking? She actually could grow taller here. She rose up until she was about as tall as Firian. Everything looked a little different from his height.

Her skin prickled with nerves as he strode down into the hollow toward her. When he reached her, he scanned the length of her, clearly noting the height change.

Her heart thudded. "I was hoping you'd come," she began, unsure of what else to say.

His eyes lit up with hope and irony. "Were you?"

"Yes..." *Now what?* She couldn't just ask him outright. He'd refuse. All the practice conversations she had invented completely abandoned her, left her alone with him. Her cheeks heated. Then an idea came to her. "Firian, I need to know if I'm in danger."

He frowned and touched her arm just above the elbow. Realizing she had been wringing her hands, she dropped her arms to her sides.

"Why would you think that?" he asked.

"I... know what happened at the Academy," she said, looking up at him. How had she become smaller? It was probably too much to focus on both keeping up the illusion and directing this conversation.

He kept his expression neutral.

"And I was afraid you might do something rash," she continued.

"Did you make the order?" he asked, almost deadpan.

"No!"

A flutter of eyelashes signaled relief on his face.

"No." She amended the word with less emotion. "I didn't."

"Then you wouldn't be in danger." He sidled up to her, even closer, barely a whisper of distance between them.

She held her ground, despite her dry mouth and roiling insides. She turned to the side to speak. Body heat from his chest warmed her left cheek. "Is anybody else? In danger, I mean?"

"There's always someone." A fingertip near her temple sent chills down her body. Firian gently drew stray hairs behind her ear, taking his time. Right now it felt like that she was that someone.

Angry now—at Firian or herself, she didn't know—she tried to clear her cloudy mind. "There doesn't have to be," she said.

"Are you begging for your kingdom?" he asked smoothly, bringing her face up to look into his. "Or do you just want information?" His lip curled on the last word. His steel gaze meant he had guessed the reason for her visit. Dark hair fell into his blue eyes.

Her pulse galloped. "I want you to be the man you could be, without letting this go too far."

He deflated a little, releasing her chin. Kiria stepped back, giving herself room to breathe.

He thought for a moment. "I won't tell you anything. Today," he said. "Maybe tomorrow."

His meaning was clear. She had to return if she wanted him to reveal anything useful. She set her jaw. "*Will* you tell me tomorrow?"

"Let's say I don't." He clasped his hands behind his back. "What would you do?"

He was playing games now. Lives were at stake. He had to end this flirtation and come to some peaceful understanding. "I have an army."

He smiled as though she had just put on her Beauty. "I don't think you'd use it."

"I think I'd have to." Suddenly, it surprised her that he rarely won games of Indisfate. Now, at least, he didn't seem averse to risky strategy.

"Then we'll see tomorrow," he said. He looked at her for a long moment, until his cocky demeanor turned to pain, before he disappeared.

56

FIRIAN

SHE SMELLED like lavender and sweet oranges and musk. Firian tried to breathe it in again as he walked through the darkness, past skinny black tree trunks. It took a few seconds for his heart to stop pounding after he left the encounter with Kiria in the hollow.

She was coming back tomorrow. It didn't matter that he made her do it. She was angry; so was he. She hadn't warned him about the attack against the Academy and now she wanted to know his plans, as Bard had. But now he had leverage to make demands.

Forcing her to meet him tomorrow was the kind of thing Bard would probably think was monstrous. Well, if it was, then it was worth it.

His disparate troops had crested the mountain and now had the arduous task of going down the other side. The pirates kept gasping in the thin air and drinking the extra water reserves. Firian found himself hating them more and more. But the Tanyu didn't give him any trouble. In fact, now that he thought about it, he hadn't worried about a mutiny since before the

Kingdom attacked. Even Tanyu weren't fool enough to fight him now, it seemed.

Belik stumped up beside him. "We need to find a place."

Firian didn't see a spot to make camp, but there was probably a cave not too far away. He and Kiria had stayed in several of them on their trip, and he had taken shelter in one on his way to Brithnem later.

Tomorrow. The word beat like a drum. He would see her again tomorrow. After going for so long without her presence, even their time in the hollow felt delicious. He wanted more.

"You're still seeing her, aren't you?" The question came like something from his own mind, but he caught Belik's eye and knew he'd asked it.

Firian didn't answer. They were far enough away from the others that they wouldn't be overheard, even if he did speak.

He heard tiny sounds of the army behind him. Belik looked at him, but Firian didn't acknowledge him, instead focusing on the long, thin clouds.

"You have to break that *katah* if it kills you," said Belik in an undertone. "Cut her off, set a Sentry—"

"Shut up. I'm handling it."

"You aren't handling it." Belik set his glasses fiercely. "You told me you were done. But I can tell you aren't. You have to free yourself before we reach the city or you'll put everyone here at risk."

Firian glowered at Belik. His connection to Kiria hurt no one but himself.

"That's ten days. Cut it off. Kill her if you have to, but get out of there."

Firian's blood burned with rage. He imagined grabbing Belik by the throat for that comment, but he did nothing.

"Your allegiance is with us," Belik continued, as though he didn't sense his danger for speaking to him this way. "The Tanyu need you. The world looks up to us. Kingdom be damned. But if you're still entertaining that *katah*, she will take us all down. Do you understand me?"

"She's not—"

Belik said it slower this time. "She will control you, and take us all down."

"Damn it! If I want her, why does it matter to you?"

He felt waves of anger radiating from Belik. He grated out, "I thought, at one time, that it didn't matter. It didn't matter what I did. I was above it all. And that was true, mostly." His voice fell until it was uncharacteristically small, rising just above the sound of their own footsteps. "I was the Strategy Master, so sometimes Amiran groups, radical groups, would send women after me. Declare *katah*. I killed them, Firian, to protect the Academy and its reputation."

A chill washed down Firian's spine.

"But..." Belik hesitated, watching the dark ground before them for a while before going on. "There was one who was different. I entertained her for a while. I thought I would kill her later, but she wasn't afraid and she didn't pose like the others. She looked me in the eye. She could have been a Tanyu if she weren't so gory stupid." Firian thought the comment seemed unwarranted, but the statement seemed aimed also at himself. It took Belik a moment to collect himself from a choking bitterness. "So the *katah* took," he said in an angry sigh. "I should have been more careful, but I thought she wanted me too, after a while. We talked about being together. That's always how it goes. They make you believe it. She even came to a place nearby—I never told her where the Academy was, but I was traveling—and we met in the Real. Several times. I thought she'd stay there." He spat. "When she got pregnant, I thought she'd stay there. It was my son. She should have stayed. But she wanted him to be an Amir." He cursed creatively. "My son, an Amir! I told her she had to stay, that my son would never be less than a Tanyu." He took a couple breaths as he finished his story, slow and deliberate. "We could have fought in the Unreal—I would have won—but she broke my leg, left with my son, and destroyed my hope of becoming the Tanyuin Head."

Firian hardly dared to speak. Chetana. It had to be Chetana, Kiria's advisor. The one he had seen on his first day in Belik's room.

"She's still in my gory head!" Belik pounded his skull with a finger as he hissed out the words, more sound than talk. They walked on in silence as the words spiraled out. "So," he said, his voice clear now, dark with meaning, "it doesn't matter if she's nice or tells you everything you and your dick want to hear. You will break off the *katah* before we reach the capital."

Firian swallowed, but it didn't wet his dry throat, not even enough to tell him off. With anyone else, that would work, but not Belik. Belik had been there for too long. He'd seen too many things. And suddenly parts of Firian's memory clicked into place.

Firian saw a large cave opening ahead on the left. Belik saw it too and left to order the army to stop and make camp.

Belik's horrible history with Chetana didn't have any bearing on Firian's situation. Kiria was different. He felt complete when he was with her; every moment excited him. And she was good. Despite everything, she still cared about him.

A whiff of pine floated past on the cool breeze. Nothing would go wrong if he saw Kiria again. He *would* see her again, and he only had to wait until tomorrow.

57

KIRIA

Kiria found Cúron emerging from a meeting with his advisor. They had been drinking strong coffee in the solarium that looked out onto the gardens and the ocean beyond. At the sight of Kiria, Parohim took Cúron's small porcelain cup and set it clattering on a tray with his own.

Kiria started to walk into the solarium before she paused. "Lord Cúron," she said, "I'd like to have a word with you about something important." Hopefully if she didn't look at Parohim, he would realize that he wasn't invited. Bitter-scented steam from the coffee rose from the cups.

Cúron pursed his mouth. The short white hairs around his lips stuck out. "Is it particularly important? I was just going to—"

"Monumentally," Kiria said.

Cúron paused a moment, and then turned to Parohim with a look that said he would fill him in later.

"Thank you," she said, descending the two steps into the solarium. Plants and flowers and trees from the farthest reaches of the known world grew there. Large, pale pink, tubular flowers that drooped over their bases, plants with leaves as long as

Kiria's arm and three times as wide, stalks that brimmed with thorns from the base to the top, its arms sticking out at fantastic angles. From the roof hung fruit and long, trailing vines. Half of the room was sided with thick glass that gave onto first a barrier and then the landscape beyond.

She and Cúron settled into chairs. His sharp eyes took her in when he thought she wasn't looking. When she faced him, he fixed his expression as an indulgent father would. She set her jaw. He had to believe her, but lately that hadn't been in vogue.

"I think he's coming here," Kiria said, without preamble.

"Who's coming here?" he asked, loudly enough to suggest there were more people in the room.

She quickly looked behind her, but they were alone. "Firian."

His bushy eyebrows rose, then lowered. "How do you know?" He asked the question as he used to do when she was a child, soothingly, disbelievingly.

"He plans to take revenge. On you. I don't want that to happen."

"How do you know?" he repeated, obviously knowing the answer but wanting her confession anyway.

She breathed in the thick green scent of the room. The humidity was already starting to coat her skin. She wondered how Cúron could stand to be here wearing his favorite heavy blue robe. "I'm one of the only people who can get information out of him. I knew this was a possibility so I went to talk to him. For the Kingdom."

His blue eyes became cloudy as he looked at her. "For the Kingdom? Kiria, you know he's dangerous."

"I know." *But Keepers should be willing to face danger.*

"You shouldn't have gone. He's done nothing but hurt us, and yet you run to him every chance you get. It's like he's cast a spell on you."

She felt her face getting red. "I didn't *run* to him. I went to see if he would retaliate for our attack on the Academy. I think he will."

"You think? Did he say so?" He sighed, settling his sleeves. "Kiria, I'm worried about you. You keep thinking the Tanyu are good, but they're our enemy. All the advisors see it."

"They're all Amir."

"Which is why they make such good advisors. You trust Daelon, don't you?"

"Absolutely."

"So do I."

Running her thumb along the intricate ridges of the chair's armrest, she looked out the window.

"We have our own ways of getting information," Cúron continued, "so stop putting yourself in danger by talking to those Tanyu." His ideas came out as though they were the only logical option. "How many guards do you have for the one staying in your wing?"

"Four."

"I thought there were more."

"There used to be, but four is enough." She turned back to him.

He cocked his head in blatant skepticism. "See, you're even sympathizing with that one. They're master manipulators. I'm going to add a couple more guards to his room."

"Bard wouldn't hurt us." The very suggestion sounded ludicrous.

He returned an almost pitying look that made her shoulders tense. She was trying to help the Kingdom and she got pity. Deep down, she cared for Cúron. He'd been there for her when she was growing up, but his condescension became more pointed as she got older.

"He wouldn't!" she cried. "Have you met him? He's nothing

like the Tanyu that used to come here, or like Firian. I think Firian might hurt you. You have to get ready."

He regarded her for a long moment.

"You should mobilize the troops." She rolled her eyes. "Don't say it was me. Don't tell them where I got the information, but you have to be ready."

"Have you told Atael?"

"Not yet." The truth would just drive a deeper wedge in their friendship. "Would you do it?"

"Have you told the other Tanyu?"

"Not yet."

"He could tell the Tanyuin Head our plans. You can't tell him what we plan to do."

Remembering Bard's desolate expression after his last encounter with Firian, she doubted he would tell Firian anything. "I won't give him any details," she promised.

"And I'll inform Atael," he said, rising with bustling finality. His head brushed against one of the trailing leaves. "Stay away from the Tanyu, Kiria. Brithnem doesn't need any more unrest. You are with *us*, not them."

She hated that the words echoed some of her own thoughts. She'd never wanted to go against the Kingdom, or betray it. But she still found it oddly difficult to think about the Tanyu in such black and white terms. Life didn't work like that. Everyone in Brithnem wasn't good and everyone at the Academy wasn't bad. Their choices made them what they were.

Her choice was to see Firian again, to risk her reputation to get more facts Brithnem could use to protect itself. The idea rattled her with nerves, but it was the only way forward. It might not be good enough—her efforts rarely were—but it was something.

"I am with you," she agreed.

58

FIRIAN

Firian's heart lurched when Kiria appeared. During the entire day's march, he'd been dipping in and out of the Unreal, testing different settings. It took away the monotony and kept his skills sharp.

The current setting was an indoor pool casting patterns of light on the ceiling. Water could be difficult to reproduce correctly in the Unreal. A shadow would be wrong, or a swell too perfect, and the illusion would be shattered. Kiria did well at the beach for a beginner, but Firian had practiced for years.

Kiria appeared on the opposite side of the pool, her head instantly tipping up to see the dancing webs on the ceiling. She had her hair tied back and wore a simple linen dress that covered her from her collarbone to her ankles. He couldn't even see the tip of her royal tattoo rising over her shoulders. Most of her dresses dipped down in the back to highlight it, but this one didn't. Still, the blue and white and black reflections encircled her, caressed her. He watched them for a while, savoring the quiet moment. Soon enough, they would speak and things would get more complicated.

She seemed entranced by the vision he'd created, gazing

around before her eyes lighted on him. "Is this a place you know?" she asked, remaining still on the opposite side of the space. Her voice echoed around the room.

"No." A smile grew across his features. She was here with him. He didn't move to go around the pool either.

A line formed between her eyebrows. "I'm back. So...?"

She didn't waste any time. They were often alike in that way. Today, though, he preferred to waste time. "Relax," he said, sitting at the edge of the pool. "You seem like you could use it, Kiria."

She didn't sit. "I'm just here to find out what you know so the people I care about don't get hurt."

"I won't hurt you," he said, feeling like he'd repeated himself a dozen times.

"What did you do to Bard? Whatever it was, that hurt me."

"Did it?" he said through clenched teeth. She wasn't going to pretend, then. "Sit."

"I prefer to stand."

"Kiria." Her name came out in exasperation. She was fighting herself, fighting him. Couldn't things go back to the way they were? "I didn't hurt him," he said.

She grabbed her elbow with her other hand. "There's more than one way to hurt somebody."

His jaw flexed as he remembered Chetana. They stayed in awkward silence for a while. She stood, he sat, separated by the dark pool. This conversation was already going badly. "Yes, there is," he agreed, fixing her with a look to remind her that she wasn't innocent either.

"I didn't have a choice."

"There's always a choice." Her words from when he took her hostage for the Academy. *Always a choice.* His life had felt like a series of inevitabilities. What choice could he have made to make Bard stay, to make Kiria love him?

She must have recognized the words because she bit her lip as though biting back a response. The gesture brought memories that made Firian's stomach swoop.

"How did you know?" she asked, meaning the attack.

"I listen."

"I'd listen," she said, now with both arms around herself, "if you'd tell me anything."

I'll tell you everything. He almost said the words, but they were a blatant lie, and she'd know immediately. Other girls he'd been with expected lies, almost demanded them. It was the language of flirtation, but Kiria knew better. She wanted something real, and he didn't know what to give her.

To buy time, he stripped down to his underwear and jumped into the pool. Its cool water enveloped his head and swirled against his skin. Tiny bubbles zigzagged up the hairs on his legs and over his chest. *One, two, three, four...* He held his breath, but it was suddenly gone. Water meant death. To suck in air through his nose or mouth would drown him even as he tried to save himself, water burning thickly in his lungs as he choked.

He thrashed to the surface, gulping. The splash of his head and arms sounded as loud as a scream.

Kiria, sitting on the edge now, looked down at him with concern. Her arms weren't crossed anymore. She even leaned forward toward the water. Her thin veil of pretext was torn.

His shame dissipated quickly. He lapped up the look, holding her gaze.

"Are you okay?"

Still trying to catch his breath, he made the pool shallower. His bare toes gripped the rough floor. "Fine."

"You sure?"

He half-swam, half-walked to her side of the pool. Reaching it, he slicked back his hair. "Yeah, I'm okay."

The moment suddenly reminded him of a few months ago.

I'm glad you're alive. She hadn't liked admitting it then either.

"Why do we do this?" he asked.

The skirt covering her crossed legs moved as she flexed her feet underneath it. "Because you're probably coming for revenge and won't tell me."

"I might tell you tomorrow."

She huffed. "This isn't a game, Firian!" A flush of anger or sadness darkened her cheeks. "If you don't tell me... if you don't leave us alone... we'll have to kill you, and everyone who helps you. I won't be able to stop it, and..." Her voice trailed off. She looked away.

"And what?"

"I don't think I would."

He stepped back. The water swished with the movement. "Does Bard think that too?" Of course he did. Firian was a monster, after all.

"I don't know," she said. Did they talk about him all the time? How well did the two of them know each other?

"I can look out for myself," he found himself saying. He was done with talking. It was getting them nowhere. He didn't intend to tell her where he was or what he was planning. She didn't want to talk about anything else. Blue patterns webbed across her sullen face. Seized by a desire to touch her, it took considerable strength to hold himself back.

Maybe just one more question. It burned inside him. She, like Bard, tried never to lie. She put up a front sometimes, but she couldn't hide how she truly felt. And he didn't know how she would answer.

Those seconds in the water looking up at her felt like adoration, like judgment. "Come in with me," he said, surprised to find his voice a whisper. The sound barely reached the walls, quieter than the drips echoing from somewhere.

She shook her head, but there was a tiny hesitation. He

latched onto it. "It's the Unreal," he said, reaching out a hand toward her, reminding her and himself. Her dress wouldn't even get wet. Not really.

"Firian..."

"Come on." He tried not to sound too desperate, but he wanted her close for this question. He wanted her close even without anything to say. Holding her would calm his heart a little, or at least make it beat from something other than nervousness. His stomach twisted. He had to know the answer, but asking felt like jumping from a height and hoping for water instead of stones at the bottom.

His hand wavered in the air for too long, but he didn't take it away. She regarded it, focused on his dripping palm and fingers. She couldn't understand the power in that look. "Will you tell me what I want to know?" she asked.

"You first. I have a question."

Wary creases formed at the corners of her eyes. She took his hand and with the other held her dress down as she slipped into the pool. The wet fabric clung to her legs. It was thick enough not to outline the shape of her body, but his heart thumped anyway.

He could drown her, he realized, immediately disgusted by the thought. That meant, though, that she trusted him, at least a little. Little was better than nothing.

Her face was still impassive, not inviting him any closer, but he drew her toward him anyway. Despite the water all around them, his mouth felt thick and dry. Surely, he was strong enough to ask a simple question.

He wrapped one arm around her back to speak in her ear. He was right that the dress revealed no bare skin. A shiver passed through his body as a finger gently touched the long scar on his own back. A moment, and it was gone. The touch pushed him over the edge of that high place.

"Kiria," he breathed, "do you think I'm a monster?"

A long silence. Too long. He tightened his grip on the fabric of her dress to steady himself, staying by her ear. If she had the worst to say, he'd rather hear it than see it on her face.

Then she whispered, "You always have a choice."

59

KIRIA

Kiria and Jori sat on the floor of Bard's guest room, playing a game called Slug. It required acting quickly to collect matching objects from the floor. Players took turns, but the turns were often so fast that they almost overlapped. According to the Calthwaite boys, there were times when it was acceptable to skip someone's turn. Every year, the rules multiplied. Kiria had grown up playing the game, but she suspected Jori had invented it himself. The origins of Slug had long since fallen out of memory.

Bard caught on quickly, his dark eyes darting over the small objects strewn in the middle of their little circle. He seemed particularly focused. Maybe he was glad to had something mindless to focus on as well.

Kiria's meetings with Firian frustrated her. He refused to tell her anything substantive, though she'd seen him multiple days in a row. For so many reasons, she no longer wanted to be with him, but her body betrayed her. Her pulse raced and she fantasized about being in his arms, but only in the Unreal. She'd gotten used to it as a secret space, where it didn't matter what she did. But obviously it did matter. The Unreal, despite its name, could be just as real as this moment, now, with Bard and Jori.

Jori lashed out a hand to grab a ring and drop a token. Kiria was collecting stones, so his move didn't help her. Bard seemed to be trying for a collection of small figurines of the royals. Kiria rarely went for that set. It was dumb, she knew, but it felt a little weird. Jori knew that, and used her preferences against her. Try as she might, she had never become a master of Slug. Jori basically controlled the game every time, reminding them all of "rules" they had forgotten, so she might not have stood a chance anyway.

With one hand, Bard grabbed a ring and a figurine of Kiria. With the other, he blindly took a bite of cinnamon toast. He'd ordered tons of the stuff ever since his meeting with Firian almost two weeks ago. Since he didn't eat with the Keepers or the servants, Bard seemed to live on orders of cinnamon toast and oranges.

She refocused her attention on the game in time to see Jori snatching a coin aloft, stretching it toward the ceiling in triumph. "Ha! I won!" He laid out five coins neatly in front of his crossed and booted legs.

Kiria and Bard showed their hauls. She had three stones and two tokens. Bard had four figurines and a ring. The face on Cúron's figure had almost rubbed off completely from years of playing.

"Ah, you were close," Jori told Bard, "but I'm the king of Slug."

Bard gave a broad, close-lipped smile.

"You know what I just realized?" Jori said, pointing to them both. "You have the Talent, you have the Talent, and you also have that Beauty. I'm the only one without an Ability. What are those others? I could have had one of those." He looked down and snapped, trying to spark a memory.

"Knowledge, Harmony, and Language," Kiria said.

"Right, right!" He hesitated. "There are five? What's Harmony? Maybe I have that one."

"Nature can't hurt them."

He smiled. "Well, maybe. I do like rain."

"It's different. You could still get struck by lightning."

"Thank you, darling. Always the optimist." He winked at Bard. "And why is yours called the Talent? Aren't you born with it? I find that supremely unfair."

"It takes practice to do it right," said Bard.

"Is that so?" Jori turned to Kiria, who nodded.

Some of the smaller pieces bounced over the rug as Jori swept them all toward himself with his hand. He produced the badly sewn leather bag where he kept the pieces. When they were younger, he had scraped his name near the bottom in uneven letters. Above it, in larger and slightly more mature handwriting, it read "SLUG."

"Is it getting late for you, my darling?" he asked Kiria.

She peered at the window. It had been black for some time. Out there somewhere, the troops were ready to stand against an Academy attack, according to her orders. Well, according to Cúron's orders. The rumor around the army was that she had warned Firian about the impending assassination and so she had indirectly doomed the soldiers who marched to Tánuil. They weren't quick to trust her now. She had to gain back that trust, drop by drop, over years.

But she didn't have years. Each time she met with Firian, the more certain she became that the Tanyu were marching to the capital. At least all the Keepers could agree that they should prepare for the possible threat.

"Kiria?" Jori prompted, readjusting one of the larger figures so it would fit in the bag.

"Yes, it is getting late." Her eyes felt grainy and rough. Sleep had been hard to find the past few nights. It took Firian about two weeks to travel from the Academy to Brithnem. That time had come and gone, but that meant she didn't need to add extra time for travel. Tanyuin forces could theoretically arrive at any moment, if that really were their plan.

"Thanks for coming by," Bard said, scratching his head with both hands.

"Eh, you're not miserable company," said Jori, standing, with a roguish smile.

Bard hopped to his feet. It almost always looked like he jumped, rather than stood, as though he were weightless.

Jori tightened the strap on the leather bag. "I think it's time we said good night."

A swell of appreciation for the two of them rose in her. They hadn't abandoned her. They weren't the best political allies, but they cared and she loved them for it.

When she gave them each a quick hug, Jori hugged her back but Bard stiffened in surprise. "Good night," she said. "Thanks for the game."

Bard waved awkwardly as she and Jori left the room.

"What was that?" Jori asked, meaning the hug. He looked past her to smile at a guard, who didn't smile back. "Feeling lonely?"

"Something like that," she said.

He lowered his voice. "I think Atty will come around, the idiot."

He said it lightly, but she took it seriously. "I hope so." To lose a friendship that had meant so much to her growing up pained her more than she liked to say. Even Haved would be welcome into their little circle. She had hurt her, but Kiria still didn't think that Haved was fundamentally mean-spirited. Kiria admired the courage it took to marry a stranger for the sake of her own kingdom and then to love rather than resent him for it.

Kiria thought of the little paper tree. Just the other day, she'd seen a corner of delicately folded paper sticking out of Atty's breast pocket.

They reached her room in seconds and Jori said goodbye. Candrae and Vayci helped her wash and get ready for bed. She couldn't have said why her stomach was in knots.

As she put her head down on the soft pillow and closed her eyes, she found out. The Unreal engulfed her as though she had fallen through the mattress into darkness beyond. The force of Firian's call overpowered her.

Something was different this time. There was no setting. There was only Firian, dressed in black. His agitation was palpable. She looked, expecting to see dark circles under his eyes, since his presence gave the impression he hadn't slept, but the Unreal washed away those imperfections.

His blue eyes blazed. "I'm going to tell you everything."

FIRIAN

BLOOD OOZED from a torn piece of skin under Firian's Master ring. He hadn't realized he'd been picking at it again.

The few lookouts in the Gray Forest were easy to find and subdue. Now, if he got closer to where the woods thinned, he could see Brithnem. Yellow lights peeked through the dark like an inverted sky. At the crest of the hill sat the palace. Flags on the battlements waved like ghosts in the thin light. Bard's black eyes when they'd both stood on that roof came back to him. He ignored the memory.

Belik hadn't caught him meeting with Kiria during the rest of their journey. His fury wouldn't change Firian's mind, but he kept the secret anyway.

Before them lay the farms of the outer edge, sprawling to the thick city wall. This was the first step to taking over Brithnem. His lungs contracted as he glared through the trees covered with a mix of unfamiliar pine needles and leaves. Desire and anxiety battled within him. Governing the Academy had gained him enough enemies. But to have a kingdom...

A kingdom.

His breathing grew shallow with longing. It was time to issue the ultimatum: surrender or suffer the outer edge to burn.

The demand would send the army out to meet them. His army was ready, mismatched though they were. They'd trained for anything, including a conflict with the largest military on the continent. Belik suggested that he send the message early in the morning, when everyone had rested. That meant Firian would get no sleep.

A tent had been set up for him near the center of the camp, but he was far from it now. He couldn't keep his eyes off the palace glinting in the distance. To demand loyalty was one thing. To win it was another.

Now that they were here, something felt wrong, as though he'd thrown a bone out of joint. Everything would be fine if Brithnem surrendered, but the odds of that were so small. Belik acted as though it were the most likely scenario, but they both knew better. It would take more than a threat and a book to make the capital bow to him.

If he could find some other way... He shivered, but it wasn't cold. The answer came slowly, inevitably, irresistibly. His pulse pounded. The buzz of his mind came into focus around one idea, an idea that could satisfy him, and satisfy her.

Kiria was the key. As Keeper, she *was* Brithnem. With her power and beauty, influence and honesty, she was everything he wanted. As long as he had her, the rest of the Kingdom could go to hell.

He wiped his bloody finger on his pants. What a victory it would be to steal a Keeper! She'd come willingly. He'd seen it in her eyes. She just needed a strong reason that it was better to come with him than to stay. He could give her that reason. Now.

His heart raced with the strength of the new idea that didn't feel new at all. Kiria always talked about his using power for good. This way he could do that. Lives would be spared. He could call off the rest of this conflict. She'd love him for it.

He licked his dry lips. Why hadn't he seen it before? Kiria for the Kingdom. It was a fair trade.

Plunging into the Unreal with so much force that it felt like some of the night went with him, he searched for her. She appeared quickly, as though he had torn her to this level with him. She looked around disoriented for a moment, glanced at her hands, then at him.

"I'm going to tell you everything," he said.

The force of the words hit him like an aftershock. He knew it was true, but for a heartbeat he didn't know which "everything" he meant.

He pulled out of the Unreal far enough to see both her and the city beyond with double vision. The beautiful lights of the palace and surrounding buildings twinkled behind her. Brithnem and Kiria. The power he yearned for, the person who consumed him. His soul ached.

He paused so long that she considered him as though he were an apparition, as though he might not have said those tantalizing words. Her light brown eyes looked up at him in that heart-shaped face and he melted.

If he demanded the Kingdom first, she might run or fight back or... he wasn't sure. Sometimes she was easy to read, and other times he couldn't anticipate her at all. The choice was clear. He had a choice, and it was Kiria.

"We're outside the city walls," he said.

Her hand flew to her mouth before she forced it back down. Words formed on her lips, something like "I knew it." Angry tears formed on the base of her eyelid.

He hurried on. "The Tanyu are set to take over Brithnem. In the morning we'll burn the outer edge if you don't surrender."

His words sounded horrible, all wrong. "But you, you can stop it."

His heart jumped painfully in his chest. He felt naked.

She glared at him, chest heaving, as though every nerve strained toward hearing what he would say next. Was she hoping for the same thing he was?

"None of that needs to happen," he said, his voice irregular and frantic. He forced himself to calm. "There's an abandoned farmhouse on the edge of the Gray Forest. It's east of the Abrecan Gate. I'll be there until dawn." Tanyu had found it sweeping for scouts. It was a safe place to wait. Belik wouldn't suspect that he was gone during the night. But he couldn't let a whiff of his plan reach the Master. He would tell him once it was successful, then Belik would see Firian's *katah* wasn't like the one he had with Chetana.

"If you come to me, I'll call everything off. But you can't tell anyone. No one. I'll know." His skin burned with adrenaline.

Her lips parted with amazement and her eyes widened until white showed all the way around. "Firian, I..."

It wasn't clear which part she protested. This was the best solution. This would save lives. She just had to have the courage to give into her desires.

"You can't tell anyone," he repeated. Firian refused to be a diplomatic debate. The most disgusting option was for her to yield because government officials and Amiran advisors told her to. He wanted her passion or nothing. He had to choose him. Their combined choices would save Brithnem. "Come to me, secretly, and I'll leave the city alone."

She was shaking, gripping the long sleeves of her gown. "How could you do this?" she gasped.

He recoiled. He hadn't expected her to look at him with such horror. Even now, when he would call off an attack on her city that he had every right to make. "You have until dawn to decide," he said, then he softened. "Kiria, come to me."

She didn't bend. Instead, she disappeared.

He came back into reality, heart hammering. It wasn't a long walk to the farmhouse he'd mentioned, but it felt like he was walking through sludge. The heft of his thoughts weighed him down. She might refuse.

She might refuse.

The ground seemed to tilt beneath him. If she did, then he would give into the monster clawing inside him. This felt like his last chance to do something merciful. Wouldn't she approve of that? And this allowed them to be together, to finally free their bottled passion. They could rule together, make plans, comfort each other. He could teach her to fight in the Unreal and she would be the voice of kindness. They could start a dynasty. Belik would eventually see she wasn't a threat to them.

He looked back toward the trees. Dawn was a long, long way off.

She might refuse. The thought intruded again. She'd denied him before, but despite it all, she still cared about him. He could see it in her eyes, in her answers, in her studied posture. Those tiny assurances had been his lifeline.

What if they weren't? What if they were just the desperate hope of a person too far gone to see the difference?

Why did he make this deal in the first place? If dawn came without her, it would be difficult for him to contain the rage he'd want to unleash against the Kingdom. All his monstrous instincts would have precedence. He knew what he was capable of. He could tear through the city like a hurricane. Part of him wanted to do that now, instead of waiting there, subject to her whim. That exposed feeling came over him again, as though she could overhear all his anxious thoughts, tear him open and mock every weakness.

He weighed the options as he pushed open the heavy barn door. Either she loved him and fought against her feelings because of the politics of the Kingdom, or she didn't love him and now he was demanding to own her in exchange for the safety of her people. In both scenarios, she would come to him that night. Savior or monster—the question wasn't as urgent as whether he would hold Kiria in his arms.

Sadness crept over him. He remembered his eleven-year-old self, so anxious to create a legacy, and regarded himself through those eyes. Would he be proud of the man he'd become, or would he recoil too?

61

KIRIA

KIRIA REELED, sitting bolt upright in bed. She couldn't catch her breath. She would have let out an angry scream if her serving girls wouldn't come running.

How could he? How could he?

His last betrayal—betrayals—had been bad enough, but this was beyond enduring. He dared to threaten her city to blackmail her into being with him? It seemed impossible, even for him. Before, he had been paranoid about threats to his crown— something she didn't agree with, but to some extent understood. She felt similar stresses in her own reign: the desire for control, the inability or unwillingness to give up her own interests... But this!

Time seemed to slow, every movement suddenly comprised of creaking bones and flexing muscles and the wisp of air past her skin. She felt every place her nightdress touched her and every hair falling on her shoulder.

She had not acted carefully around him—not enough, anyway. She'd known that he wanted her and she gave into that part of herself that wanted him.

That part was gone. For a fleeting second, she regretted that their soldiers hadn't completed their mission at the Academy and killed him when they could.

Now she couldn't tell anyone about this. She had to make the choice on her own. To go to him and possibly save the Kingdom from domination, or to refuse and risk hundreds if not thousands of lives in the conflict?

Something wet hit the blanket beneath her with a tiny thud. Furious, she scrubbed away the tears. What if Firian was bluffing? What if the Tanyu weren't poised outside the city at all?

But that wasn't possible. He said he'd be at an abandoned farmhouse. He was certainly there, and there was no reason for him to come alone. So other Tanyu were there too, and their reason had to be retaliation, as he said.

If she didn't go, the Tanyu would demand that Brithnem surrender. None of the Keepers or advisors would agree to that, so they would have to fight back. Firian said that he would set the outer edge on fire. Her blood seethed. They'd have to put out the fires and fight, potentially, hundreds of Tanyuin soldiers.

Would Torithians be there too? The thought struck her like a fresh wound. When Firian had asked the question several nights ago, she should have answered differently. *Yes. Yes, you are.*

She sat numbly on the edge of the bed, only her thoughts and her own body real to her. What if she told someone who could sneak to the farmhouse instead of her and end the conflict that way? Firian would know. He said he'd be watching.

She feverishly flipped through options—a note, a signal, a weapon of her own? Nothing would work.

She turned to the option she'd dreaded. What if she gave herself up to him? What if she snuck through the city and met him at the farmhouse? Even with all his twisted desire and horrible decisions, she couldn't fathom that he would attack Brithnem after he had her. He was telling the truth when he said he'd trade her for the Kingdom. The idea didn't make her feel at all comforted.

And if she was still being naïve, like Cúron thought she was, then she could escape from him again, and the conflict would start as though she'd never gone. That was an idea too terrible to contemplate for long. Firian was a tyrant, but she saw sincerity in his eyes, an almost fearful vulnerability that made his evil more tragic.

Brithnem could be safe if she did this. Probably. Nausea grew in her gut as she considered logistics. Since her mother was still alive, she could step in as the Second Keeper, so the Line wouldn't end with Kiria, at least not right away. She could disguise herself fairly easily to go through the streets and out the main gate. Even if the best were to happen—she went with Firian, who treated her well, and Brithnem was safe—everyone would think she had betrayed them all. Those who knew her background with Firian might think she had chosen a passionate love affair over the good of the Kingdom.

She made it to the sink before she wretched. There was no good outcome here. The best she could hope for was to be viewed as a traitor and pariah who'd left all her friends, her family, her subjects...

Her friends. They'd all be in danger if she didn't go. But none of them would understand why she did it because she couldn't tell a single soul. She wiped her mouth with the back of her hand, still tasting vomit on the back of her teeth. She spit. Jori, Atty, Bard, her mother—the catalogue of people seemed to grow every time it cycled through her thoughts. Servants and guards were added, people who rarely spoke to her. They all seemed to matter so much now.

If she could only talk to Daelon, or someone else who was wiser than she was, to help her make this decision. She wasn't good enough on her own. The certainty of that made her sink to her knees on the hard floor of the washroom and give into sobs. They shook her violently, tears washing in a steady stream down her face.

A sound made her look up. It was Vayci, her face underlit by candlelight. Her dark brows announced deep concern. "My Keeper, you are unwell?" She knelt before her, feeling Kiria's brow and pulse.

Kiria stopped crying long enough to respond. "I got sick," she said, gesturing feebly at the sink.

"Let me help you to bed," Vayci said, crooking her arm for Kiria to take.

Together they stood. Vayci's thin, strong arm steadied Kiria mentally as well as physically. By the time she reached the bed, she had made her decision.

"Thank you," she said. "I think I just need to sleep."

"I'll bring you a cup of water."

Kiria didn't protest as Vayci rushed to fetch her water and returned with Candrae by her side, her blonde hair glowing in the flickering light.

"What happened?" Candrae asked, gently taking Kiria's hand. Kiria couldn't help thinking how dirty that hand was, but Candrae didn't seem to mind at all.

The truth almost spilled out of her, but she bit it back. The overwhelming desire to say *something* filled her until she could barely breathe. "Are you ever afraid that you'll never be good enough?" she said, hiccupping with the sobs that still threatened to overtake her.

Candrae smoothed a strand of hair away from Kiria's wet face as Vayci handed her a cool towel. "I don't think anyone thinks they're good enough, not for the job you do. If they did, then maybe they wouldn't be fit for it."

Kiria sniffed, an unflattering sound.

Candrae let go of Kiria's hand to allow Vayci to press the

water cup into it. Trembling, Kiria brought it up to her lips. With all the shaking, some of the water splashed onto her cheeks and nose and dress, but she managed to drink some of it down.

Vayci chimed in. "We know you love the Kingdom. Those protestors don't know you like we do."

Kiria took another sip. Though they misunderstood, their words felt like medicine. She swallowed thickly before thanking them.

The girls smiled serenely, promising to check on her later that night, and left her to her own thoughts again. Her mind was not so kind, but it was made up.

For Candrae, for Vayci, for all of them, she would sacrifice herself. They'd all see her as a traitor, and she wouldn't have time to explain, but that was the choice she had to make. What had Daelon said? *"You don't serve the Kingdom for praise."*

It was better if they thought she'd betrayed them. The Keepers would be less likely to start a war with the Tanyu—she would be the only casualty.

She tried not to think about what Firian would do with her. She gazed around her comfortable, lonely room by the light of the candle Vayci had left, dwelling on details she hadn't noticed in months, if not years. A corner of her vanity table was discolored from the time she dropped oil on it when she was fifteen. One of the session recorders, a girl named Hada, who was about her own age, told her it would make her eyelids an attractive color. In the heaviest blanket was a tiny snag whose threads formed a shape like a dog's face. She used to trace it with her finger when she was younger to help her fall asleep. She must have been only six or seven.

If time had gone slowly before, he seemed suddenly to speed up. Even on a fast horse, it would take her an hour to get to the outer edge. Longer to find the right farmhouse. Her chest ached with the desire to linger but she had to go.

Hastily, she threw a couple simple outfits and necessities in a bag. She hesitated. Would carrying a bag draw too much attention to herself? She had to pass several rounds of guards. Her plain face would disguise her in the city, but not in the palace, where she sometimes switched back and forth. She sighed as she realized with certainty that she would be Beautiful when she met him. This was official business, Keeper business. She would wear her official face. She was tempted to curse and leave the bag lying on the bed.

Poised precisely between taking and leaving it, she stood frozen in the middle of the room. These things were the least of her worries and they angered her for being so trivial. Spite finally decided for her. She unpacked so as not to rouse suspicion too early, violently jamming her clothes in their trunks.

Breathing deeply, she composed herself before going out for the last time.

62

FIRIAN

FIRIAN COULDN'T REMEMBER A SLOWER night. It was like four nights strung together, shot through with anxiety. Fear and anger and hope chased each other like rabbits through his mind. His shoulders ached from all the tension.

The farmhouse reminded him a little of the abandoned structure where he and Kiria had stayed one of their first nights away from the palace. Only a few rooms composed its simple layout. A structure attached to the outside of the house clearly had saved harvested crops when it was in use.

Firian stayed in the main room because the only external door led into it. Kiria could find him without searching.

His gaze found a messy mouse nest in the corner, strung with hemp and thread and grasses. Maybe the house was abandoned during the Tanyuin War. That timeline would be logical, since the house wasn't completely overgrown. Nature had only started to move in. The layer of dust on the floor was thin. Waving cobwebs glinted on the ceiling when he moved, like a trick of the eye. He'd struck a few lights around the room. It was still dark, but he was used to darkness. It was like the barrier between the Real and the Unreal, so it didn't bother him at all. He did want to see her, though, when she came in. If she came in.

He could sense that she was on her way, but it didn't feel real. She hadn't talked to anybody else. Even if she came, would that mean what he thought it did? His fears were illogical, but they consumed him, nerves inhabiting his body as though it were haunted.

He huffed out a breath. Taking over Brithnem would burn power through his veins, but it wouldn't be voluntary. It would be won with blood, and he'd already had enough blood.

He pushed his hair back from his forehead. Rian, Salaar, Master Jairon, the unnamed Torithians in Raewhith—the everlasting images assaulted him again. He hadn't meant to kill Rian. One second they all lived and thought, and the next they were just a thing. Firian's throat tightened. *There are many ways to kill a man.* Jovan had been right. And then Firian killed him too.

Kiria wouldn't come. He had done too much. His hands curled into fists and his core hardened into a painful knot. He couldn't go back to change anything. Even if he could, would he? He would make most of the same decisions again. He would take over the Academy, he would kill the Amir Salaar, he would defend himself against Jovan. The knowledge calmed him. It wasn't the calm of peace, but the calm of closure.

She might love a monster anyway.

Bard didn't.

He worked his jaw, spinning the Master ring on his finger and reopening the wound there. He watched as a dark drop of blood beaded against it and overflowed down his knuckle.

It would all be all right if she chose him. It would all have been worth it if Kiria Arioc, Keeper of Brithnem, chose him, Firian Kess of the little backwater town of Raewhith.

He cursed. Why dwell on the past? It held pain he had no desire to relive.

To shut up his thoughts, he fell to the floor and did push-ups until his arms burned. Physical pain was always better than other kinds. More helpful too.

The crunch of a soft footstep.

He froze, listening. Had he imagined it? The silence seemed to deepen in response to his intense desire to hear.

The sharp intake of breath. No, he hadn't imagined it. He leapt to his feet, heart thundering. He reached out in the Unreal.

It was her. It was Kiria.

He could barely hear over the blood pulsing in his ears. The door opened slowly, arcing over the dust-free semicircle on the floor. Her presence grew stronger as though the farmhouse were the Unreal and she were materializing into it. He felt her in his mind, but couldn't feel his own hands.

When she slipped into the room, he felt weak, stomach flipping. There were no words. She was light in darkness, soul in a lifeless body, meaning in life. Better than he imagined. The Unreal didn't carry the glorious force of her Beauty. It was like a shadow in comparison. This reminded him why he was alive.

Pain like a sword thrust winded him. He wanted that pain to last forever. She was Beautiful. For him. The air between them tasted like victory. Life when he had eyed certain death. He could breathe again and he was moving, rushing to close the gap between them.

They collided and he held her tight with trembling arms. He pressed his lips to hers with fierce passion. Tasting her warmth, he realized this was the first time they'd kissed in real life. He dug his fingers into her sides as he held her more firmly. Her lips felt different. He tried to memorize the feel of them, the peaks and edges.

She was here, she was here! He pressed himself against her, desperate to get closer. Feeling drunk, he smiled in his kiss, teeth against lips. Everything floated hazily around them, darkening like an Unreal setting until only the two of them remained, enclosed in each other's arms. He licked at the salt in the corner of her mouth.

Then it struck him. She wasn't bending into him. She wasn't even kissing him back. That salt, was it tears? Still holding her, he gave her one more soft kiss before pulling away. It took a moment for her expression to register. Those golden eyes, so full of wisdom and truth, looked back at him through tears. Fear, anger, sadness. The wide eyes and wary expression had been set in determined lines, afraid but immovable.

He dragged his hands around her back and sides as he let her go. She didn't speak aloud, but her rod-straight body and defiant look spoke for her.

She hadn't consulted anyone before coming. He'd checked. This decision was hers and hers alone. She had chosen to come to him. But she didn't love him.

A rock ached in his throat. He felt his world fall, almost as though he were dying. He didn't want to speak, but the question forced itself out. "If you don't love me, why did you come?"

A tear fell from her eye, down her flushed cheek. He should have noticed she was distraught the moment she came in, but he had been too overcome with relief and joy and her Beauty to think of anything else.

She could barely answer, her voice catching. "Because I love them."

Heat drained from Firian's face. She loved *them*, not him. The emptiness inside his ribcage stretched and echoed the words back to him. Time stopped. All the triumph he had felt turned to dust. He wasn't sure if he would tear the room apart or kiss her again.

The charged silence dragged on. Neither he nor Kiria moved.

Slowly, thoughts started to form coherently again out of chaos. She had given herself up, but not because she loved him. She considered it a sacrifice to save the people she actually cared about. He had promised not to conquer Brithnem. But she didn't love him. She didn't love him. Relentless pain beat in every muscle at the knowledge, the news he never wanted to hear.

He could keep her anyway. Her Beauty burned and allured him as nothing ever had. It would fit the deal they'd made. His foot moved toward her. His fingers twitched forward, then fell. Another drop of blood fell from his finger onto the boarded floor. What a monster he'd be then. The temptation made his insides curdle, pulling at him like a clawed creature.

He looked in her eyes. They'd never turned away from him. She still knew him, even the darkest parts. Maybe she feared he would take her for his pleasure. It would be a lie to say the idea didn't eat at him. She knew his other sides too, though. In the pool, she'd said he had a choice.

He wanted Kiria, but if she didn't want him, then at least he could resist the monster in his chest. He could be the man she thought he could be. Maybe she still thought there was hope for him. There had to be.

But that meant he'd have to send her back, to get nothing, to return alone. The notion made him feel weightless, hovering over darkness.

Still she waited.

He couldn't help himself. Furrowing his brows, he kissed her again. "Go back," he rasped, pulling away. He teetered on the edge of taking back the words even as he said them.

A light, followed by confusion, came into her eyes. "What?"

"Get out," he said again, straightening.

"You won't attack Brithnem?"

"No." He threw out words like weapons. They felt more dangerous, more reckless. "I won't. Go." It was the best he could manage, and he regretted it already. He longed for her even though she hadn't gone.

She twisted, eyeing him experimentally as if he would attack.

"Go!" he cried, furious now. If she stayed any longer, he would change his mind. She had to run or his will would dry up.

She turned and ran.

WHEN SOUNDS of Kiria and her horse had faded into the distance, Firian stirred. Hollowness made him move like a corpse.

What did I just do? He could have kept Kiria for his own. He could have experienced that burning Beauty and those understanding eyes, that skin and those lips, for as long as he wanted. Doing good was supposed to feel good too, wasn't it? He didn't know what had made him think so. Bard often seemed so worried, and Kiria looked heartbroken and afraid just now.

His promise felt oddly unbreakable, stronger than the strands of his life. He wouldn't burn the outer edge or threaten to take over the city. Now all that was left was to tell Belik.

His gut sank further. What a travesty this trip had become. But he was still the Tanyuin Head. If he told his armies to return to the Academy, giving the Kingdom nothing but a warning, then they would. Firian felt weak, but he wasn't in a bargaining mood.

Somehow he got himself back to the camp, ignoring the pull, like a snagged thread, of checking on Kiria. She would warn her military, telling them where the Tanyuin forces camped. That was fine. They would be gone before a battle could start.

He ducked into Belik's tent without ceremony. The Master lay under a thin blanket with his meager provisions haloed around his head. His glasses balanced on a waterskin just in front of his nose.

"Belik, wake up," Firian said, softly but clearly, toeing him in the side.

The blankets bucked under the speed of his waking. Belik grabbed his glasses and glared at him, a look that would have crippled Firian's younger self. A red crease lined one side of Belik's face where his pillow had folded under it. "Gore, Firian!" he swore.

"We're calling off the attack." He felt beyond the reach of consequences.

Belik grunted as he trundled to his feet before answering. He stood a little shorter than Firian but he could still look him in the eye. "We are not calling anything off." He frowned, eyebrows ticking downward. "Have you learned something?"

"They just need to know we could have conquered them. We'll release one of those scouts from before. They'll run home. That's enough. We're leaving."

Belik grabbed Firian's shoulder in a meaty fist. "We are not leaving," he said through gritted teeth.

Firian plucked the Master's hand off his shoulder. "We are. Get them ready."

"Damn it, Firian! We've all marched through the gory mountains to do more than send a message! These people tried to kill you. Did you forget?"

"No," Firian said, fury rising.

"Tanyu have deserved this for years and you're just going to throw..." His voice faded as realization made Belik's face go slack. It hardened again and he lowered his head, dangerous intention through every pore. "What have you done?"

"I've made a decision you're going to follow."

"It's the girl. It's Kiria." Belik snarled with rage. "She convinced you to do this. Because you wouldn't be such a *gory idiot* otherwise. What did I say? I said this would happen."

Somehow Belik was closer to Firian than he had been. Firian saw Belik's fisted hands. There was a wildness to him that Firian wasn't used to, an unpredictable violence. Firian tightened his muscles.

"Master Belik," he said calmly. The hollowness was coming in handy now. "You will do as I say. Let our troops know to pack and leave before first light." He stared steadily back at Belik's furious face.

Firian had just made fists too when Belik's demeanor suddenly relaxed, though the change didn't make him seem any less dangerous. "You don't think the Tanyu deserve this?" he asked, almost teacherly.

"I think it's unnecessary to make our point."

"And it would hurt your little girl."

Firian's elbow went back almost before he realized what was happening. He smashed Belik in the jaw, the impact rattling up his arm.

Belik stumbled and fell to the side, catching himself on his hand without making a sound. The Master stood, slowly, and looked Firian in the eye again, as though the violent outburst had never happened. Finally, Belik sighed. A yellow bruise was already blooming under his skin. "Okay," he said. "We'll march back in the morning." His red, watery gaze took in Firian from his hair to his sternum. "Have you been up all night?" He acted as though he knew the answer, and the reason.

Firian didn't respond.

"We have a few hours," Belik said dismissively. "Have a drink.

Get some sleep. It's a long march back." Belik didn't disguise his bitter disgust.

Firian doubted he could sleep, even though his eyes ached at the suggestion. When he found his own tent, a bottle had already been left for him. The strong liquor burned his throat as he shot it down. Chucking the bottle against the wall of the tent, he flung himself down and fell into a dark sleep.

63

———

KIRIA

Kɪʀɪᴀ sʜᴇᴅ her Beauty as soon as she left Firian, but she still felt wildly exposed in the streets of Brithnem as her horse clopped up the quiet roads to the palace.

He let me go. Her thoughts wouldn't settle. Of all the scenarios she had considered, this wasn't one. She was too confused and upset to be relieved. Now she only had one course of action—to tell the other Keepers that Tanyuin forces were camped right outside their door.

She got back as soon as she could, making flimsy, unnecessary excuses for the guards who let her into the palace. The hall rugs felt softer than usual under her feet as she ran back to her room.

Stopping short, she saw Bard arguing with her guards, who circled around him. He waved animated gestures in the air. Though the shortest among them, he clearly held his ground. Something about his composure reminded her he was Tanyu.

When she approached, he turned and his face brightened. The guards saw her too and their postures relaxed enough to show they were relieved to see her.

"What's going on?" she asked. Nobody should have been awake at that hour. Had something happened?

"Are you all right?" asked one of the guards, stepping on Bard's question coming at the same time.

"I'm fine," she said, realizing that her face still had to be puffy from sobbing. The way down to Firian's abandoned farmhouse had been blind and punctuated with smothered screams of frustration.

Bard's quick eyes didn't buy her answer. "I need to talk to you," he said quietly. "They won't let me in your room."

"Let him in," she said wearily, passing through the guards, who opened the way for her. Bard followed behind.

Both her mother and Chetana whirled around when she entered. With a cry, her mother jogged forward, catching Kiria in her arms. "Oh, Kiria! I thought you were gone!"

Kiria glanced at Chetana over her mother's shoulder. The Amir was glaring at Bard, who had entered after her. "I'm fine," Kiria repeated.

"Chetana told me you were missing," her mother said, her red eyes probably mirroring her own.

"Chetana? How did she know?" Kiria realized that her response basically admitted that she had been away. "I just... went for a walk."

"Was it Jori again?" her mother asked, drawing a sleeve across her eyes. "I swear I'll kill that boy..."

"No, no," Kiria said. "I just went for a walk." She gave the excuse more strongly now. Glancing at Chetana, who looked imperious in the dim light, she remembered the crucial news. Speaking more loudly, she said, "I got a message. The Tanyu are here. They're camped right outside the wall. We have to get our soldiers out there."

Her mother's eyes widened in fear and surprise. Chetana,

however, betrayed no surprise at all. "I'll tell the general immediately," her mother said.

"Yes, go," Kiria agreed, not sure she had the strength herself. "As soon as they're ready, they can go. They'll start with the outer edge!" She yelled the last instructions at her mother's back as she disappeared through the door.

Alone with Bard and Chetana, Kiria wasn't sure where to start. Chetana probably wouldn't want to speak freely in the presence of a Tanyu, and the feeling might be mutual. At this point, it didn't matter. Now was not the time for pettiness.

"What did you come here to say?" she asked her former advisor. She probably had arrived first, so she got the first question.

"My Keeper," she hedged.

"Ignore him," Kiria replied, her tone clipped.

Chetana rubbed her lips together thoughtfully, but she obeyed. The rusty accents of her curly hair glowed dark orange in the candlelight. She straightened her back as she spoke. "My Keeper, I came to warn you about the Tanyu, but it sounds like you found out more than I could tell you."

"How did you know about them?" Kiria asked.

"There's one I could tell was nearby, nearer than he'd been in years, and he's dangerous, My Keeper. Very dangerous. If there are more of them, then you were right to summon our military."

"A *katah*?" Kiria asked, putting the pieces together. So this is how she knew so much about it when Kiria hadn't woken up in King's Heights. She had one herself.

"Very old," she said. "Daelon's father."

Kiria's eyelashes fluttered. This was too much to process at once. She turned to Bard beside her instead. His wild hair revealed how distracted he'd been with his news. "What about you?"

"Same thing. Well, not really." He cast a glance at Chetana, but didn't shy away from her withering look. "I knew Firian was close by. I didn't know if you could tell, so I thought you should know. Somebody should know."

She almost asked the same question—*katah?*—but stopped herself. After Bard finished, Chetana's eyes softened just a little from hatred to mere skepticism.

"They're all here," Kiria affirmed.

A glow flared in the corner of her vision, drawing her attention to the window, where unnaturally bright orange light rose and fell in the dark. She gasped and clasped a hand across her mouth. Chetana turned to look too.

"They're burning the farms!" Kiria cried. Firian promised not to. Was it too late to help them? Hopefully her mother's message would mean instant action. But that wouldn't be good enough.

Despite how haggard Kiria felt, she had to warn more people —Cúron and Atty, at least. Her mother was only one person. News had to travel faster than that.

She tore out of the room, telling guards as she passed them. A couple of them sprinted off to spread the news too. Fast, quiet footsteps told her that Chetana and Bard followed her. Maybe her serving girls. She didn't look back to see who it was.

Cúron's bedroom was in the front wing, so it wasn't as far to run. Everything inside her was chaos, but the wide hallways were eerily silent. Darkness dampened the sound. Her own ragged breathing was the loudest noise.

She passed Kader's room. Cúron was just around that corner. She sped past the portraits and trees, skidding to a stop in sight of his door. She felt a bolt of ice stab through her. Sprawled in unearthly shapes, like demons about to rise and crawl on many hands, lay his guards. They slumped where they'd fallen, black against the floor. Her heart beat mercilessly against her ribs.

Chetana rushed past her and knelt by one of the guards, putting two fingers to his throat. She looked up almost instantly. Dead. They were all dead. Chetana rose and pushed open the door to Cúron's room. As though she were in a nightmare, Kiria's feet wouldn't move to join her.

One peek and Chetana rushed back to Kiria. "Go. We need to go!" she hissed, grabbing Kiria by the hand and dragging her back where they'd come.

Tingling covered Kiria's body. It felt like putting on her Beauty, but she knew she was going numb with shock. What had happened to Cúron? Was his wife Varinna all right? Kader?

The castle seemed even quieter this time. A tomb. An abandoned structure with no one left alive. Kiria couldn't hold onto a thought for longer than a second at a time. But they circled back, and back, and back. She caught them with feeble hands each time they flew by. *Outer edge is burning. Cúron is dead. We're under attack. Firian lied. I have to warn everyone. Where's Mother? Where's Atty? Where is everyone?*

Time slicked by like oil, sticking to her and moving erratically. She forced her feet to move, one in front of the other. Chetana was leading her back to her room. Were they going to escape? Would this hellish vision fade into unreality once they reached the safety of her bedroom?

What she saw made her shake. The guards who had remained at their posts were dead outside her door. Shock rose from her core to the back of her eyeballs. It didn't make sense. They hadn't been gone more than a few minutes. Who was doing this?

Chetana pulled her forward, making her step over the guards on the way to her room. She forced down bile as it rose up in her throat. There was less blood on the ground than she had thought would come from so many bodies. But they were dead. They were dead.

Bard and her serving girls picked their way around the bodies after her. Kiria gasped in relief when she realized that Candrae and Vayci had followed her when she'd run out. Otherwise, they might have been dead too.

Chetana went in first. She seemed to know exactly what to do, fiercely alert but otherwise calm. Kiria watched her every movement, ready to do what she said.

In the middle of the room, Chetana stopped and raised her head like an animal, listening. She gestured toward the serving girls. "You, open the hatch."

Vayci and Candrae hurried to the emergency tunnel on the far side of the bed, their legs only a little unsteady. Together they pried open the small square opening, disguised in the wainscoting, easing it back and forth until it gave.

Where's Jori? Kiria's chest hurt. There were too many unknowns. She caught Bard's gaze. It was wild, but beneath the panic was a center of calm or understanding.

"...wasn't here." Faint voices sounded from just outside, too calm to be on their side.

"She's here," answered a gruffer voice.

The second voice made Chetana jump. "Go!" she said, pushing Kiria roughly toward the hole. Candrae and Vayci crawled inside. "Go now!"

"You go," Bard told Chetana in a breathless voice. "Make sure they're okay. I'll... hold them off."

Chetana didn't argue. She nodded once in grim acknowledgment before turning to the escape tunnel.

Kiria looked back at Bard once before wedging her body into the opening. His dark figure rolled his shoulders and his neck as he faced the door and made to open it. Her abdomen hurt from worry. The man on the other side of the door had made Chetana afraid. What could Bard do against someone like that?

He's dying for me, she realized.

"Go! Get in!" Chetana whispered, shoving Kiria all the way into the tunnel. She didn't remember stopping.

Crawling forward into blackness, her knees kept catching on her skirt. She hauled up the front, gripping it in her fist so she could move faster. Chetana wedged the square panel back into place behind her, shutting them in complete darkness.

64

FIRIAN

FIRIAN WOKE GASPING. Reality refused to spiral into focus, but his heart still beat with panic. He hauled himself up on one elbow, panting out breaths as he tried to remember what was a dream and what was really happening.

A soft crackling sound guttered outside. Too slowly, his eyes adjusted and he saw orange shadows crawling like phantoms over his tent. He staggered upright and ran outside. The camp was abandoned. The farms were on fire. He ran to the edge of the fields, scanning the tree line for the person who had acted against his orders. *What was going on?*

The drink. Belik had sent him a drink. There was no way Firian would have slept through a moving army, even one as silent as Tanyu could be, and setting the outer edge ablaze. This sleep was induced, forced on him by whatever was in that bottle. Which meant that Belik had drugged him in order to take control.

His blood surged again with panic, unconnected to his black and red rage. He wasn't panicking. He was thinking it through. He was going to take his army back. He was going to find Belik and kill him.

Then the panic couldn't be his own. With a jolt, he realized he felt Kiria's fear. He dove into the Unreal toward her, simultaneously running toward the city walls. Avoiding swaths of flame and men riding horses and blackened fields of smoldering heat, he leapt across the outer edge as fast as his legs could carry him. He barely stayed upright in his speed.

Where is she?

There! He saw her in the Unreal. She wasn't alone. She was surrounded by others with the Talent. One presence Firian knew almost as well as his own: Bard. Some of the fear was from him.

He forced his divided attention toward Kiria. She was in her room... no... disappearing through a hole. Would she be safe there? Firian felt his way forward in the passage where she was and hit the faint buzz of another mind. He didn't recognize it. It wasn't one of his Tanyu. Chetana, maybe? Odds were that she wasn't going to harm Kiria, but he shouldn't take a chance.

Firian skirted a burning field, charging onto the main road, not caring if he was seen. Oppressive heat pressed in on both sides. Smoke swelled on the air, making it difficult to see if anyone was coming. Shouted orders in the distance meant soldiers were on their way, probably to put out the flames.

The great city wall loomed closer. Guards would never let him in through the gate. He would have to climb the wall.

His attention wrenched back to the room where Bard was. Bard rolled his neck and shoulders, facing the inside of Kiria's door. He walked out and Firian knew instantly why he was so afraid. In the hallway, Belik and Shiro stood there beyond a pile of dead guards.

Belik splayed a hand toward Shiro, who looked ready to pounce like a cat.

Firian increased his speed, ignoring the heat that threatened to blister his shoulders down to his forearms.

"You can't come in," Bard said. His voice was surprisingly even but his brow furrowed as though he were staring at something bright.

Belik's face showed curiosity but also, most of all, frustration. He shifted his weight to the other leg, then limped forward a step. "It's by order of Master Kess."

Firian hissed a curse. So they didn't know he hadn't ordered the attack.

Though the news sent shock flickering over Bard's expression, he stepped forward too and set his palm on Belik's chest, jutting his jaw defiantly. Bard's Adam's apple bobbed a couple times before he spoke again. "You're not going in."

Shiro made to walk past him, but again Belik signaled for him to wait. What was he waiting for? Did he want Shiro to watch him make an example of Bard? Firian didn't know what damage Belik could do. He'd never seen him in a physical fight. Next to himself, Belik was the best fighter in the Unreal, but they weren't in the Unreal now. They were in that palace, on that hill, past that wall.

Firian slammed into the wall, stifling a grunt as he reached high for a handhold. He climbed recklessly, aware that one misstep could send him crashing to the ground, dead if he fell from too great a height. But he still practically jumped from stone to stone, calling on all the strength his fingertips had as they wedged into the mortar. His arms were faster than his legs, which did little more than steady him.

He hauled himself over the top, scraping his abdomen across the metal guardrail. His lungs and muscles burned, and he came out of the Unreal long enough to contemplate the way down. It was too far to jump without breaking bones. He sprinted along the top until he came to an attached stable. It was hard to judge distance in the dark, but it looked close enough that he could jump and roll onto the roof with enough power left to get to the palace.

He hit the stable a heartbeat past his expectation, his teeth clacking together. Painfully, he let himself fall off the peaked roof. He landed on his side on the flagstone street below, but was up before the impact fully registered. The stable would have a horse. There would be no time to saddle it. But it would be faster than his own legs.

The space smelled like hay and mature. Most of the stable doors were already open, and a girl no older than fifteen stood in the shadowy recesses near a wall where large poles were sticking out. She wore a cap over her short hair. As she turned and saw Firian, her hand rested on the only remaining saddle as though she forgot it was there. Were all the horses already gone?

Casting around for a remaining mount, he heard a muffled snort. A horse was left in a stall close to the doorway where he stood. Snatching the lead rope and throwing the gate pin to the ground, he dragged the mare outside. The stable girl came alive as soon as Firian vaulted onto the horse. Her shouted protests followed him as he kicked the skittish horse into motion.

Once he was flying through the streets, another pang of fear sheared through him. He looked back at Bard and Belik. Belik's face had hardened into a murderous stare. Bard met his look with determination, his light brown hands balled into fists.

Then Belik closed his eyes. Why would he do that? It was tactically stupid. Unless he wanted to go into the Unreal. But Belik could do that with his eyes open, as Firian was doing to watch them.

Neither of them could go to the Second Level with their eyes open, though. The thought hit Firian like a punch to the gut. Why would Belik go into the Second Level now?

Dread pooled inside him until he felt full of black poison. No. Belik didn't know how to...

Bard's eyes widened. A cry of surprise escaped him as his spine bent unnaturally backward.

The rabbits. Firian couldn't breathe, kicking his mare with enough force to leave marks.

Soundlessly, Bard's mouth opened wider. Shiro glanced nervously at Belik, who concentrated with his eyes still closed.

Then the screams started. The noise shredded through Firian's whole body. He wanted to scream himself at the horror.

The horse became slick with sweat beneath him.

Bard's screams didn't last long. Falling silent, he arced backward. His head hit the carpet with a sound that was too quiet, too final.

Belik opened his eyes. Shiro looked at him, awestruck, but Belik didn't look back. "Now you can go in," Belik said.

As Shiro stepped past the unmoving forms littering the entrance, Firian snapped back to the present. He had to focus on getting to the palace.

It took too long. There were too many streets. The hooves clattered up and up. Behind him, the glow of the firelight was growing. People were starting to come out and gasp or scream. Guards ran quickly in unison down toward the gate. A few cried out when they saw him but he evaded them, his reflexes sending the horse down side streets before a hand could grab him or a something could knock him to the ground. The automatic movement made him feel precise and dangerous, but detached. His body was accurate, but his roiling mind couldn't focus even on his own peril.

When he reached toward Bard again, he sensed nothing. No word, no thought.

Mouth bone dry, he reached toward Kiria instead. He couldn't let his mind wander too far into possibility. The weight of it could crush him. Belik, Bard, Kiria...

She was there. She was alive. Her shock and sadness and

anger burned like the flames behind him, but there was no fear or pain. For now, at least, it seemed she was all right.

Soldiers sped down the main streets, forcing Firian to keep taking side roads. This ride was taking too long, too long... Shouldn't the sun be rising?

Finally close enough, the shadow of Mon Párinath, awash with red light, blocked out the sea and stars. Firian skidded the horse to a stop and vaulted to the ground in the same movement. His feet scrabbled for purchase on the gravel, the first few steps too slow. Then he was racing.

An armored guard blocked the nearest way in. Firian didn't slow. The guard yelled for backup just as he hurdled forward, aiming the point of his elbow at the guard's face. As a wet crunch sounded in the helmet, the hand reaching for its sword released its grip on the hilt. With no time to finish him off, Firian shoved him up against the wall and left him crumpled behind him, wrenching open the door and flinging himself inside.

The cool dark of the corridor felt ghostly as he ran and ran. Extra soldiers must have emptied to put out the flames. Kiria probably told someone the Tanyu had camped just beyond the outer edge. They'd go to meet them head-on, unaware of the enemy already within their gates.

One more guard peeled away from a door where he was stationed to block his way, rising before Firian's narrowing vision. This one already had his sword unsheathed. "Where are you going?"

Firian didn't answer. The man's eyes grew larger when he saw who it was: Firian Kess, all in black, the Tanyuin Head.

The man swung his sword. Firian rushed into his arms and wrapped the man's sword arm in front of them, prying at the fingers. When the man wouldn't let go, Firian jammed a heel into his instep.

Armored boots. He jammed harder. Again.

Finally, the guard cried out and loosened his hold just enough for Firian to send the sword sailing to the ground. It skidded across the carpet and hit a pedestal, which tilted crazily from the impact. Its fall sent a vase of flowers crashing. Water spilled out on the floor.

Firian made for the sword but a hand yanked him back. Furious, he launched himself backward, aiming to headbutt the guard, but the man moved in time to avoid him. Firian stumbled and fell. The man kicked him in the side on his way to the sword.

Flexing his foot, Firian locked his ankle around the man's foot and sent him sprawling to the ground. The wet carpet squished as the man fell, wheezing as the wind was knocked out of him. Good. A few more seconds before he called for help. Leaping up, Firian left the sword and the man and continued running.

He only fully realized where he was going when he arrived. Bodies were arranged in front of Kiria's room just as he had seen them in the Unreal. Belik and Shiro were gone. A moment of confusion threaded through him. He expected himself to pursue Belik in revenge. The thought passed as he fell to his knees before Bard's prostrate form. Too much time had passed since he'd crumpled to the ground. *Be alive, be alive, be alive.*

It was a slim hope. Bard's spine was still bent backward, not as violently as the rabbits' had been, but enough to make Firian's skin crawl with the comparison. Bard's fingers curled in on themselves, his teeth showing in a grimace. A dribble of blood leaked from one tightly shut eye.

"Bard." Firian grabbed Bard's arm tightly, feeling for a pulse. The arm was limp but it felt warm. Something hardened painfully in Firian's chest as he pressed his thumb into Bard's wrist. Nothing. He pressed harder, as though Bard were a lever that would give if he pushed hard enough.

Firian willed his own frantic heartbeat to slow, so he could distinguish Bard's pulse from his own. He still couldn't feel anything. He cursed under his breath and brought his fingers to Bard's neck instead. A beat. Firian's heart skipped. Had he imagined it? He put the back of his other hand against Bard's mouth and nose. Another beat.

Firian's breaths came fast. He must not have been breathing before. He shook Bard lightly, gripping his forearm again. Now he could feel a faint heartbeat in Bard's wrist and the crook of his elbow. Raised veins pulsed in Firian's arm—he could see them—and Bard had just a whisper of life. Firian held on as though he were the one giving Bard the strength to keep living.

Muted running down the hall meant that more guards were coming.

A small movement focused all Firian's attention on Bard's right hand. Weakly, the fingers closed around Firian's arm.

"I'm sorry." Firian's own words surprised him as they came out. "I'm sorry." Firian couldn't manage anything else. His face felt red and bloated as he looked down at his friend.

Bard opened his blood-stained eyes enough to see. Taking a real breath, he squeezed Firian's arm, the pads of his fingers barely but unmistakably tightening. The meaning was clear.

Everything grew hazy. Firian couldn't see.

Footsteps and clinking metal grew closer.

Firian swallowed, blinked, and hauled Bard upright. It was obvious that Bard wouldn't be able to hold onto consciousness, much less walk. He felt heavy as a corpse. Bracing himself, Firian manipulated Bard's body until he lay across his shoulders. A faint, wheezing breath gasped at his ear. If Bard was alive, he should stay that way.

Galvanized into action, Firian took off away from the sound of the approaching guards.

Belik. Belik did this.

Rage gave him strength. Belik had tried to kill Bard and Kiria. He was a traitor. There was no excuse he could give that could persuade Firian to show him mercy.

Blood roared in his ears. Bard hardly slowed him down, though the hands that held Bard's wrists and ankles trembled.

Firian knew his next steps with diamond-cut clarity: save Bard's life, and then kill Belik where he stood.

65

KIRIA

THE CRAWL through the tunnel seemed interminable. Without light or enough space to stand, the journey felt as dreamlike as a nightmare. Everything Kiria had witnessed didn't seem real, but it had to be, or else she wouldn't be making her way to the safe house.

Her knees rubbed raw, and she was sure that her hands and shins and dress were covered in filth. With darkness covering her, she had let hot tears fall, careful not to be loud.

Who's left?

Chetana's reaction at Cúron's room left little doubt about his fate. He, and probably Varinna too, was dead.

She had escaped. Maybe Atty and Haved had too. Maybe they were crawling through a similar tunnel, running for their lives. Maybe they would all meet at the safe house together.

Nobody spoke. Kiria wanted to ask if the safe house really was safe against the Tanyu, but she couldn't make herself breach the silence. So they all just went forward on hands and knees, on and on. Serving girls, Kiria, Chetana.

Her hand splashed in a puddle. The air in the tunnel was

stifling with disuse. Maybe the sun was starting to rise now. This night was as long as several long days.

Jori had used this tunnel recently. It couldn't be much farther. *Jori.* Was he alive?

Exhausted, she couldn't consider the questions as deeply as she should. She didn't have the strength. Her head felt sore and hopelessness threatened her with the inevitability of sleep.

She took another shallow breath, crawled forward another step, and refused to give into despair.

Whoever was in front, Candrae or Vayci, stopped suddenly. Kiria's face rammed into the fabric of someone's dress. She sat back on her haunches like a dog, waiting.

Ahead of her, lines of white light cracked open, forming a perfect square. Blinding light pierced the space and she squinted. Her serving girls crawled through the opening.

Kiria followed them, and Chetana came out last. All four of them stood gazing at their new surroundings. It was a nicer space than Kiria had envisioned from the tortuous crawl through the tunnel. There were tapestries on the wall alongside lanterns and provisions. A hall led away from this small storage room to the rooms beyond. It felt as though they were underground. Maybe they were. The only window was a small slit near the ceiling. The wall around it radiated murky firelight.

Kiria tore herself away from the group and pushed a chair against the wall. Ignoring the dirt and protests, she leapt up and tried to peer through. Only on her tiptoes could she see.

The palace was burning.

Horror seized her throat. "The palace..." she breathed in a gasp. Her mother was in there. Everyone was in there.

Firian lied, Firian lied. Relentless and violent, the thought joined the tumult in Kiria's brain. *Did anyone else make it out alive?*

Legs suddenly watery, she sank down into the chair she'd

been standing on. Vayci offered her water. She thought she said yes. Her shaking fingers closed around a cup. The liquid did little to wet her gummy mouth and dry throat.

She looked at Candrae and Vayci, both standing at attention. There was something hollow and fearful in their faces. Their friends, their family, were in the palace too. Kiria gripped the cup harder.

Plans started swirling through her mind. Guards had to be here, right? They were probably just outside. "Chetana, tell the guards we're here." The Amir hurried to obey.

Kiria took stock of the situation as best she could. They were at war. The First Keeper was dead. She was alive. She didn't know about Atty. Her train of thought hitched into vague but intense pain at the thought. The three Keeper Lines needed to be saved. They had to find a safe place to go. They should control communication and supplies...

She became lightheaded and realized how quickly she was breathing. Vayci seemed to notice it too, because she knelt beside her and gently took her hand. Kiria squeezed back, taking another small sip of water.

She took a deep breath and stood, resolve hardening inside her. Letting go of Vayci's hand, she turned again to the window that flickered orange with fire shadows. The air started to smell thick like distant smoke.

The Tanyu—maybe Firian himself—had killed Cúron and taken over the palace, her home. She would not let this attack go unanswered. There was still at least one Keeper left alive.

And she would get back her throne.

ACKNOWLEDGMENTS

This one goes out to Jamie, my dear friend who died of cancer eight years ago. She read an early version of *Firian Rising* when it wasn't half as good as it turned out to be in the end. It was still called *The Tanyuin Mind* then. Good thing I didn't keep that title!

When Jamie knew she was going to die, she called up several of her best friends and told us to dress in ball gowns. We all wore tiaras—she included!—and gave out roses at the mall. She gave us instructions for what to do as we handed them out. "Give them to every woman and little girl, and tell them that they are loved and valuable." So that's what we did.

Every year, on Jamie's birthday and on the anniversary of her death, I try to do something kind for someone else. I hope that, if you've stuck around to read this, you give a rose to a stranger too, or a gift card, or a free coffee. If you do, I'd love to hear about it. Let's hide bubbles on playgrounds and change on parking meters.

Let's remind people that they are loved and valuable, in honor of Jamie.

I also want to thank my incredible beta readers: Summer, Levi,

Natalie, Carolyn, my mom, Caitlyn, Quinn, Kristina, Bekah, and Alyssa.

This story wouldn't be as awesome without my writing group: Amanda, Ed, and Debbie.

I wouldn't know how to take over a town without Nate, have this awesome cover without Damonza, have a beautiful map without exoniensis on Fivrr, or feel so supported without my wonderful parents.

And to my readers, thank you all! I hope this story was everything you wished for. Don't forget to review the book, and let me know what you thought. I love hearing from you!

ALSO BY CARLY STEVENS

Firian Rising

ABOUT THE AUTHOR

Carly Stevens lives and works as an English teacher in Colorado. She plans to keep writing adventure-filled fantasy novels about courage and hope.

To find out more about upcoming projects, check out her website: https://carly-stevens.com
Her author newsletter is the best place to get an exclusive, behind-the-scenes look at Firian's world. You might even win free books for signing up!

www.ingramcontent.com/pod-product-compliance
Lightning Source LLC
Chambersburg PA
CBHW031605180726
48284CB00005B/1407